MOONFELL
WITCHES
BOOK
TWO

AMBER MOON

SECRETS, INK, AND FIRELIGHT

TJ GREEN

Amber Moon: Secrets, Ink, and Firelight

Mountolive Publishing

Copyright © 2025 TJ Green

All rights reserved

ISBN eBook: 978-1-991313-28-7

ISBN Paperback: 978-1-991313-29-4

ISBN Hardback: 978-1-991313-30-0

Cover design by Fiona Jayde Media

Editing by Missed Period Editing

Contents

One

Moonfell 2025

With only two days to go until Beltane, Birdie Cornelius, the High Priestess of Moonfell, wasn't sure whether to be excited or exasperated.

The second of the cross-quarter days, Beltane—or May Day, as the non-pagans called it—was a popular celebration on the seasonal calendar, one associated with love and fertility. In her youth, she had quite enjoyed rowdy celebrations with several libations around the fire; now, she was wondering whether she might strangle her younger sister, Horty, and offer her to the gods.

"I am not celebrating sky clad, Horty! I'm sixty, not sixteen. And you're even older."

"I see you like to rub that in again." Horty snorted, still sensitive about the fact that Birdie had regained years when she had not. "And since when does age have anything to do with getting naked?"

Birdie sighed. "I am not rubbing it in. I am merely saying that the years when I would merrily cavort around the fire naked have gone. Actually, I only think I did it once anyway, and that was with Cosworth. As a rule, our family does not get naked for celebrations."

"Well, I did."

"Because you were flirting outrageously with the gardener's son. If poor Harold had known what you two were getting up to, or our father..."

"Well, they didn't, and we had fun. Plus, I was sixteen, and he wasn't much older." She giggled, looking like a mischievous teen again. "He was such a dish." Then she suddenly sobered. "Where does time go, Birdie?"

"Don't." Birdie softened at her sister's regret. Horty was now a stout, robust woman, nothing like the slender thing she had been in her youth. "Get naked if you want to. I shall avert my eyes as you recapture your youth."

They were in the small sitting room on the ground floor that faced west, a room they called the snug and which they didn't often use. However, after Morgana declared she was changing her bedroom and moving to the second floor, Birdie decided they should use a variety of the rooms in their cavernous house a lot more. She was getting set in her ways, and she didn't like it. *Maybe Horty was right*. Perhaps she should shed her clothes like a second skin and reinvent herself.

This room was as vigorously decorated as the rest of the house, in shades of soft rose and bold magenta, with deep green accents. A garden room, designed to enjoy afternoon sunshine and twilight hours. Its double doors led out to a small patio, although the doors were firmly shut now, and the fire was lit in the grate. The afternoon had grown chilly, and they were enjoying tea while planning the Beltane celebrations. *Although, perhaps it was almost G&T time,* Birdie reflected as she noted it was almost four o'clock.

Horty refilled her cup with tea. "No, you're quite right. I have no wish to get naked in front of my nephews and nieces, and age is no insulation against the chill—not like it used to be." She gave Birdie a sly glance. "Fancy you remembering the gardener's son, Henry. He had such pretty eyes."

"Oh, it was his eyes you liked?"

"Amongst other things. Anyway, this is not helping our Beltane plans. We're having a fire, obviously."

"Yes, I was thinking by the south moon gate. It seems appropriate, as it symbolises fire."

Horty smirked. "No bees?"

"No. Very funny!" Their Ostara plans had gone awry after Birdie had invoked an old ritual with the bees to welcome Giacomo and Lamorak to the house. They had inadvertently caused Hades, her familiar, to disappear, and invited an elemental Earth spirit into the garden. "I would like something far less dramatic. No old rituals. Just something positive to welcome the warmer weather."

"I'd have thought you'd have it all planned by now," Horty said, lifting her eyebrow. "It's most unlike you."

"We've all been sidetracked by our shifter friends, and the Hall of the Wey Wolf." Horty had only arrived a couple of hours earlier, and they'd barely caught up with the news. "We had to find missing shifters who were possessed by ancient wolf-shifter spirits."

She updated her sister with the details. The previous few days had been filled with checking up on the affected shifters, and being kept up to date with the investigation into the ancient Anglo-Saxon hall found beneath Finsbury Park.

Horty sat up with a jerk, almost sloshing her tea. "You kept *that* quiet!"

"It's hardly something to casually drop over the phone. I decided telling you in person would be more fun. If I'm honest," Birdie dropped her voice, "after the initial euphoria of beating the shaman and absorbing some of Nahum's Nephilim power, I had a bit of a slump. I've been taking it easy in the garden." She caught her sister's concerned expression. "I'm fine now. Don't worry. It's like any big spell—you need time to recover. Morgana and Odette were the same. They found it all quite sad, too. All those trapped souls. Odette was particularly affected by the shaman's power. It was all-pervasive, and you know how sensitive she is." Birdie was still worried about Odette, if she was honest. She seemed more subdued than normal.

"Then Beltane is just what we need. A little fire magic to refill the well. That should be our theme."

Birdie smiled. "That is an excellent idea."

"It's a shame that Lam and Como won't be here. They would love Beltane."

"I think they would have loved the Hall of the Wey Wolf, too, but it can't be helped. They have their studies. Not long now." Horty looked disappointed, no doubt missing her grandson, Giacomo, who lived in Italy with his parents. "Cheer up, Horty. You'll see him much more once he moves in."

"I know, but Yule was lovely, and I missed Ostara. Oh, well. There's still the big Litha party to look forward to. You are still doing that, right?"

"Of course. Plans are afoot. It will be fabulous." *With a house full of family, it will also be exhausting.* "I think I might invite some of the Storm Moon Pack."

"To Litha or Beltane?"

She shrugged, not sure if Horty would like the idea. "Maybe both. I like them. They're fun, and I'd think they'd enjoy it. We could always do our rituals first and invite them later. That might work."

Horty eyes widened with intrigue. "I like that idea! I haven't met them yet. I definitely won't be sky clad if they're here."

"They will be if they shift. I've honestly not seen so much naked flesh in years." She watched Horty over the rim of her cup. "Such firm muscles, too."

"Tease! Where are Odette and Morgana?"

"Morgana is putting the finishing touches to her new bedroom suite on the second floor, and I think Odette is painting."

"Morgana is moving?" Horty looked gratifyingly shocked.

"Yes. I was quite put out, like a silly old lady. It's fine, of course. She can go where she wants. I know what she means, too. The second floor does have an ambience all its own, and the rooms look lovely."

"Which is why we are in here." Horty nodded as she glanced around the space. "It's always been one of my favourites. Change is good, and there are too many wonderful rooms in this house that are under-used."

"Actually, we found some very interesting things in the India room on the second floor. Do you remember it? The red room?"

"Yes, it smelled of incense and musk and had lots of exotic things in there."

"Most of which should really be in a museum. They are all wonderful."

"Nonsense. It's our history."

"True. We found magical instruments made for travel, and one of them was a Wayfinder to search for shifters. Honestly, the entire room is fascinating, but we've barely been in there since. It needs organising." She looked at her expectantly, hoping Horty would take the hint. She loved organising things. "I especially want to know who our fabulous explorer ancestor was. I mean, I know we had a few, but I'm sure it's just one man who was responsible for the India stuff. Eighteenth century, I think."

Horty narrowed her eyes and downed her tea. "I knew you'd end up getting me to do something while I'm here, but I can't resist a challenge. No time like the present. And let's take a bloody G&T with us."

Two floors above, Morgana sat on the floor in the middle of the India room and inhaled sandalwood, dusky rose, and secrets.

She laughed at her sudden fancy. *Secrets*. Stories, not secrets.

Lots of stories.

Morgana had just finished moving into her new suite of rooms on the second floor, but too restless to settle after all the cleaning and furniture rearranging, she was instead drawn back to the India room, which seemed to have lodged in her brain and was currently occupying most of her thoughts. The collection of jewellery, art, weapons, and travel-related ephemera seemed to have bewitched her—and not just her, either. Odette and Birdie were similarly affected. It was as if by exploring the room only a week or so earlier, they had released an enchantment.

The rich red walls and polished wood, a mixture of ebony and something golden, drew her in and ignited her imagination. She could be sitting in a Mughal palace, not Moonfell's Gothic mansion. Peacocks should be strolling the grounds, not foxes and badgers. She closed her eyes briefly, seeing red earth and dust, vibrant *saris*, colourful *bazaars*, and marble halls with fretted windows to protect the women's quarters. A fan lay on her lap, a concoction of feathers and inlaid pearl, and she fanned herself, fancying she caught a whiff of jasmine.

The contents of the ebony box they had opened the week before were scattered around her, but she picked the Wayfinder up, the one they had used to find the Hall of the Wey Wolf, and ran her finger over the fine engravings. *Who was this ancestor who had hunted shifters?* So far, they hadn't found any paperwork in here other than maps, but surely whoever had curated this collection would have kept everything together. *Or had they been so wedded to the library that any other paperwork had been placed there?* Well, now that her bedroom project was finished, she could delve into it more fully. Another bit of research to add to her interest in Moonfell's origins, and the significance of the grounds. Her gaze landed on a small inlaid box on the bottom shelf of a display cabinet. They had been so sidetracked by the many other objects in this room, it remained unopened.

She uncrossed her legs and scooted to the cabinet just as voices carried down the hall. *Horty and Birdie.* She would recognise Horty's strident tones anywhere. Her voice carried down the corridor as if she had a megaphone. Knowing that her moment of peace was about to vanish, she steeled herself and turned to the door as her stout great-aunt bustled in, Birdie on her heels.

"Morgana! What are you doing down there?" Horty asked, hands on her hips.

"Rummaging. How are you, Horty?" She lifted her cheek to be kissed as Horty enveloped her in a gardenia-scented hug. As always, she looked smart in her tweeds and cashmere, quite unlike the witches who lived in Moonfell, who erred distinctly towards more informal clothing.

"All the better for being here. Blimey, what a mess! Do you never shut cabinets?" Her gimlet eyes darted everywhere. "Birdie has been telling me about your latest adventure. Shifters and Wayfinders. How intriguing!" She mooched around the room, peering at shelves and into cupboards. "I spent time in here as a child, until I became obsessed with the library. Oh, and then the tower room, of course. So many places here to develop obsessions about. Look at these miniature portraits," she said, picking up one of them. "They are beautiful."

"I thought," Birdie said, casting an almost apologetic eye at Morgana, "that Horty could help identify the name of our ancestor who is responsible for all this."

"It's one of my aims, actually, and it might not be just one," Morgana said, pulling out the small casket inlaid with ebony and pearl. "I spotted this that we haven't opened yet."

Horty had already moved on, her head in the lower cupboard of a large cabinet across the room, and her voice came back muffled. "There are more boxes here."

While Birdie hurried to help her sister, Morgana eased open the metal catch and opened the box. It was lined with dark blue silk that looked slightly brittle, but was otherwise intact. Within it were layers of tissue paper. Expecting to find more jewellery, Morgana carefully prised back the layers and instead sat back with shock at the pack of letters within them. She worked them free, desperate to see their contents, but not wanting to damage them. The paper was thick and creamy, and very good quality, and a dark red ribbon bound them together.

"I've found letters, and they're scented, too." Morgana inhaled, her senses once again assailed with the past. "Attar of Roses, I think."

Shocked that Birdie and Horty weren't rushing over, she looked up to see them wrestling with a large wooden box. Their heads together, they muttered and swore, and Morgana subdued a smile. She could only imagine what trouble they had caused as young girls. "Would you like some help?"

"No, we're fine," Birdie said belligerently, as if determined not be beaten by the box. "You carry on. Letters, you say?"

"Yes. From a woman, I think. They smell of roses."

Morgana cleared a space on the floor next to her to ensure she kept the letters in order, and opened the one on top, careful not to tear the paper. Again, like the silk, it felt brittle, but she smoothed it open on her lap, noting the looping cursive handwriting. The date caught her eye first. *May 1792.* It was addressed to Meli. *Dearest Meli.*

A love letter? A friend or relative? Male or female?

"It's addressed to Meli. Any idea who that is?"

"None at all."

Morgana scanned the contents, flicking to the signature at the end of the two-page letter. *Your beloved, Fitz.* The writing was flowery, but scanning the contents, the letters seemed upbeat and described the impressive décor of the Residency. *Residency?* She had barely glanced at the address, but she studied it now. *The British Residency at Rajgarh.*

Morgana's imagination soared again. "What about Fitz? Have you heard of him? He sent the letters from the Rajgarh Residency. I'm quite excited. Did one of our witch ancestors live in a residency? That would be amazing. Maybe," she added, thinking of all the exploring equipment, "Fitz is our ancestor who's responsible for all this."

"Perhaps," Birdie said. "Maybe they're addressed to a family member?"

Horty struggled into a chair, wheezing after the effort of dragging the box out. "I genuinely have never heard of Rajgarh, but I'm already intrigued. Fitz must be Fitzroy, or maybe Fitzgerald? Meli is unusual. Melinda, perhaps?"

"I spy trouble!" Odette said, standing at the doorway and watching them with interest. She was dressed in her painting shirt that was long over her old jeans, her feet were bare, and her face was smudged with red paint. As usual, no one had heard her catlike approach. "You three look like children on Christmas morning. Hi, Horty." She kissed her great-aunt's cheek. "I thought you two were planning Beltane. Is this a little side-project?"

"Perhaps," Birdie said, delving into the large wooden box placed between her and Horty. "We have found what looks like journals." She lifted a slender volume bound in leather.

"This one is, too." Horty flourished another. "And there's a name in the flyleaf. *Fitzroy Westerly*."

"The name in the letters!" Morgana directed Odette's attention to the letters in her lap. "I found these in a pretty box. I was expecting to find jewellery."

"Another type of treasure entirely, then," Odette said, sitting cross-legged on the floor next to her, and lifting an envelope from the pile. She stroked the surface as she asked, "So, who is Fitzroy?"

"Potentially, he's our ancestor who's responsible for all these things." Morgana's gaze swept the collection again. "I'll know more once I've read the letters. I'll take them to bed with me tonight. They're to a Meli. No idea yet if that's a man or a woman. A woman, I suspect. It's addressed to *dearest* Meli."

Odette smiled, a dreamy look to her eye and she lifted the thick creamy paper and inhaled. "Jasmine—and cigar smoke, I think. How intriguing! I'll have them once you're done, then, if that's okay?"

"Of course. They're ours, not mine." Although Morgana admitted to feeling a slight ownership of them.

"Hold on." Birdie flicked through another journal. "There is another name on the front of this one. *Edmund Swift*. There are sketches in here, too. Well," she sat back, eyes wide as she emitted a palpable air of excitement. "This is quite a conundrum. Three names, journals, letters, and more maps in here, too. I think this calls for another G&T!"

Two

Rajgarh 1792

Fitzroy Westerly, newly arrived in the state of Rajgarh in Bihar in the north of India, stood atop the low hills overlooking the city of the same name that sprawled below them on either side of the River Ganga, and sighed.

"It's a warren, Ed. We'll have trouble hunting down there."

"Nonsense. It's nothing worse than any place we have been to before." He passed Fitzroy their spyglass. "Of course, it all depends on what we've been summoned here to do. We might just be here to make up the numbers for dinner. We should stay as long as we can get away with, and avail ourselves of the luxuries of the Residency. We don't often get invited to such places."

Fitz snorted. "Invited or commanded?"

Ed smiled, the skin around his eyes crinkling, made more obvious by the layers of dust they had accumulated during their travels. "It was a polite command, at least."

"I think you'll find we'll be spied upon and questioned endlessly. If they don't know what we do and then find out, it could make life rather uncomfortable."

"We can handle it. Frankly, after weeks of travel, I'm desperate for a comfortable bed and daily baths. Surely you are, too. There's a limit to how much basic accommodation I can cope with."

Edmund was 34, the same age as Fitz, and they had been friends since childhood. Both had avoided marriage—fortunately, being second sons had allowed for that—and they had travelled to seek their fortunes. *Perhaps not fortunes.* They had those in spades. *Excitement.* Both had travelled for years, first across Europe, before eventually making their way to India. There they had stayed, bewitched by the country, and entertained by their unusual pastime that had become their job.

The East India Company, the English trading establishment, held land in Bihar, Bengal, and the southeast coast, but Fitz and Ed didn't just stick to those areas. They had travelled through Rajputana and the Maratha Confederacy with an Indian called Vikram Singh, who had become a good friend. Most foreigners travelled with a team of men for protection, but Ed and Fitz weren't ordinary people, and with Ed's ear for languages, they picked up Persian, the official Court language, and Hindustani reasonably quickly. They also knew a smattering of Bengali and Marathi, too.

Edmund was slight of build and quick of mind, with a thatch of thick, reddish-blond hair that he swept back from his face. He also sketched, made admirable maps, and was an excellent shot. Useful in their line of work. Fitz was dark-haired and heavier set, but both were now very brown after years spent in India.

Fitz sighed, aware his clothes were dusty, and he was covered in sweat. "No one at home would recognise us. Moonfell is like a dream."

"My place, too. I don't think I miss it, though. Not yet. You?"

"No. I'm enjoying the freedom of this place. The hunt. Moonfell, however quirky, is not this."

Moonfell was Fitz's ancestral home, which meant he was a witch and magic was in his blood. Ed was not a witch, but he was familiar with the occult and paranormal world. Both knew that there were many dangerous paranormal creatures that preyed on the unwary, and in India it was no different. That was their job. They hunted and either killed or banished them, depending on what its nature required. Sometimes it made them money, but it always gave them satisfaction and kept boredom at bay. It was also fair to say that the paranormal creatures in India were quite different from the ones that were in England and Europe, which added to the challenge. Well, some of them, at least.

Vikram was from Rajputana and was of a similar age to their own. He was currently ahead of them, and was also very familiar with the supernatural world. They had joined forces a few years earlier when he needed help with a supernatural entity that had attacked his family, and since then, they had travelled together. Vikram, like Fitz and Ed, came from a moneyed background. His father was a Court Scholar who collected texts on mystical phenomena, exposing Vikram to the supernatural from childhood. Skilled in sword-fighting, archery, wrestling, and an experienced horseman, he was an excellent addition to their team. Sometimes the urge to explore dictated their path, and other times requests for help influenced where they travelled. Often, it was a happy combination of each.

Fitz swept the spyglass across the city again, noting the Royal Palace, a collection of dramatic structures all ringed with a high wall, and several other impressive buildings along the River Ganga, one of which he suspected would be the Residency, and a busy port. It was already mid-afternoon, and suddenly the prospect of a cool bath and a drink in the shade appealed.

"You're right. I'm saddle sore and tired. Let's go. With luck, we'll be in time for cocktails." Fitz raised his voice. "Vikram, are you ready?"

Their friend turned quickly, handling his horse with ease as he returned to their side. Vikram had thick dark hair and a trim beard, and like many Indians, had a slim build. "I'm ready. It's an easy road into the town."

"And you're sure you have somewhere to stay?" Edmund asked. Vikram would not stay at the Residency with them.

"I have an old friend here who has already offered me a room." He smiled. "It will be good to spend time with him, and no doubt he will know if there are any issues we should be aware of here."

"Politically, or otherwise?" Fitz asked.

"Both. The Company has a small port here, and many connections. It may be that there is trouble, which is why we have been summoned."

"If it's political trouble, the Resident will have little joy with us," Edmund complained, reiterating an earlier argument. "We keep out of all of it."

"Which is why I suspect there are other issues," Vikram said with a knowing smile. "I doubt it will be a restful visit."

The Residency was a long, white building with broad verandas that wrapped around the house on both floors. It was set in a shady garden with an extensive collection of outbuildings, an oasis after the dust and heat of the narrow streets that comprised most of the city.

They were met at the entrance to the Residency by a smartly dressed Indian butler whose eye twitched at the sight of their dishevelled state, but that was as much reaction as he gave. Their horses were taken to the stables, and after being informed that the Residency staff were currently busy, which was a relief to Fitz and Ed, they were quickly ushered along pristine, silent corridors to two excellent rooms placed closely together on the first floor. Baths were run, their bags unpacked, and dirty clothes whisked away by a small army of servants, until finally they were left in peace.

When Fitz emerged from the bathroom an hour later, smelling far sweeter than when he went in, his evening wear that had been crumpled after being wrapped in his saddle bags was laid out for him without a single crease. The *dhobis* who were responsible for the washing would have been busy steaming it and brushing it down while he washed away the dust and dirt of his travel. Carrying such clothes was the last thing Fitz wanted to do, but knew that as a wealthy Englishman, he had to look the part when occasion required it.

He helped himself to the gin and tonic placed on a small table and paced to the window. His room was at the back of the Residency and looked over the grounds that ran to the River Ganga, one of the longest rivers in India, and the site for various ports belonging to the East India Company. Rajgarh only had a small port compared to Patna in the east and Benares to the west, but it was still important strategically. The Company was always looking to expand and increase its trading partners. It was just like one of the ravenous beasts that they hunted.

From this view, Fitz could see the variety of outbuildings and servants' quarters, as well as the large stable block. The grounds were immaculate, no doubt kept that way by the *Malis*, the Indian gardeners who maintained the grounds. They were one of the cogs of the huge array of domestic staff who helped the smooth running of the Residency.

It was only now that Fitz realised how tired he was after seemingly endless days of travel. They had been on the road for weeks, chasing down various paranormal creatures as they travelled across Bengal, until they had been summoned to Rajgarh ten days earlier. They had stayed in clean accommodations, but none of them were like this, and since receiving the telegram that invited them here, they hadn't stopped to rest properly. He was still curious as to how the Resident had known where to find them, and assumed it was because they had been in another Company-controlled area in the interior of Bengal where they had associated with a few English Company members.

His gaze travelled around the spacious room, noting the polished teak floor, large windows with shutters to keep out the heat of the day, the heavy, dark wooden furniture, and pale plastered walls with Indian decorative touches. Certainly, no expense had been spared. Fitz felt for magic or any hint of the paranormal, wondering if there was a problem in the house, but so far everything felt very normal. He wasn't sure whether to be relieved or not.

The bed beckoned, but it was now close to 5.30pm and the butler had warned them that dinner would be served promptly at 6.00pm. Drinks would be provided beforehand, and hearing the gentle knock at the door, he realised it was the servant sent to collect them until they were familiar with the layout of the house. Not always comfortable with social gatherings, Fitz plastered on a semi-forced smile and exited the room. Ed emerged at the same time further along the corridor, also wearing formal evening dress, and with a look in his eye that suggested the night would be long. Ed, however, was much better at socialising than Fitz.

The servant escorted them down the sweeping staircase, and more alert than he'd been earlier, Fitz noted the teak wooden flooring on the ground floor too, as well as white plastered walls, a mix of Indian and English art, huge portraits in oil, and decorative Indian touches around the doors and arched entrances to some rooms. The fact that there was quite a lot of Indian furnishings suggested that the Resident ran a cosmopolitan household. Not all were so accepting of Indian style. Fitz was relieved. He loved Indian influences, and already he was feeling more at home.

The servant paused at a pair of double doors, knocked, and then swept inside, introducing Fitz and Ed to the room. They stood on the threshold of a large, airy room with a series of doors that opened onto the terrace to catch the evening breeze. Beyond was a broad veranda decorated with cane chairs and tables, and a stunning view of the river at the bottom of the lawn. He barely took it in, attention instead on the group of people turning towards them, their conversation faltering.

"There you are!" A tall Englishman with a regal bearing approached them, hand outstretched. "Perfect timing," he said, shaking their hands perfunctorily. "I am Henry Cavendish, the Resident of Rajgarh. So sorry we couldn't meet when you arrived. I was caught in a meeting with Roger, my secretary."

"Fitzroy Westerly, and my good friend, Edmund Swift. Thank you for the invitation. We came as quickly as we could."

"Much appreciated, too." Henry Cavendish was, Fitz estimated, in his mid-forties. His mahogany brown hair was swept back, and he had a trim beard and moustache. His suit was immaculate, and he exuded confidence and utter self-conviction. "But we won't talk of work yet. Introductions, drinks, and then dinner. I trust you found the drinks we sent up to your room?"

"The gin and tonic?" Ed asked. "Yes, it was wonderful after our dusty journey. Thank you."

"I'm glad you are able to manage drinks with us now. Sherry?"

Of course there was sherry. The English were obsessed with it. A servant stepped in front of them carrying a tray, and they each took a glass of sherry as Henry started the introductions. "My wife, Elizabeth, and her sister, Miss Alicia Markham." Both women were much younger than Henry. Late twenties, perhaps. Elizabeth was blonde and blue-eyed, while Alicia had honey blonde hair and deep brown eyes. Both were dressed in silk gowns with tight bodices and both smiled, but where Elizabeth looked simpering, Alicia had fire and intelligence in her eyes.

"Please," she said, with a gentle nod, "Call me Alicia. Miss Markham is so formal, and we are such a small group here."

In bewildering speed, they were then introduced to the Assistant Resident, a short, stocky man called Anthony Davies, and a very thin man called Roger Arbuthnot who was the Secretary of the Residency.

"Just the five of us tonight," Henry said. "Our doctor, Montague Robinson, couldn't make it, nor Captain Jonathon Townsend. You will of course meet them soon. Tomorrow, hopefully. Now, you must tell us about your journey. Has your guide found suitable accommodation? He could have stayed here."

"No, Vikram has friends in Rajgarh," Ed explained. "He is looking forward to seeing them, so it's all worked out well. As for our journey, it was long and tiring as we were far from the river and had to travel over land. Nothing we are unused to. I must admit that we are intrigued, however," he said, glancing at Fitz, "as to how we can help?"

Henry waved airily. "We will discuss it after dinner, with port. Now, Edmund, I confess that I know of your uncle, Benjamin. When he said you were close to here, it was natural to contact you with our current situation."

Fitz's mood fell, knowing that it was Benjamin Swift who knew of their whereabouts. He was a member of the East India Company, and although Ed had little to do with him, he kept an unnervingly close eye on their activities. A disapproving one. He thought that *dabbling in the occult*, as he called it, was an unseemly occupation, and therefore Fitz was even more surprised he seemed the source of their invitation.

"You know my uncle?" Ed tried to contain his shock.

Henry drew Ed aside, and for the next few minutes while they talked, Fitz tried to contain his curiosity as he chatted to the other guests. Anthony, the Assistant Resident, was an ebullient man in his late forties who was clearly very fond of his own opinion and was already suspicious of Fitz. "So, you travel, you say?"

"Yes." Fitz nodded politely, not sure how much Anthony might know of the paranormal. Hopefully he wouldn't know that Fitz was a witch. The name suggested danger and dark magic to many. "We're exploring India with our friend Vikram. We see no reason to stop yet."

"And yet," Roger said, fixing him with a piercing stare, "you aren't involved with the Company?"

"No, we have no reason to be. I have no problem with it, of course," he added hastily, aware that travelling with an Indian who was more friend than servant might make him look anti-East India Company. They were trading extensively and striking deals with Indian royalty, and already some Indians regarded their advances warily. "We're fortunate to have our own resources, and as second sons, our respective family estates are managed by our older brothers." Fitz's own older brother was the High Priest of Moonfell, with different objectives to running Moonfell than most, but he certainly wouldn't mention that.

"And no doubt," Roger continued, sharp eyes seeming to see right through Fitz, "you have several interests?"

"Many. I love India's history, its wild country and wildlife. There is plenty to keep us both occupied. It's wonderful, however, to be in such splendid surroundings. It isn't always the case when we travel."

Fitz was already desperate for air. The parlour felt claustrophobic, and he still had no idea why they were there. No doubt, with the ladies present, no one would discuss any troubling issues. In so-ciety, women were considered fragile creatures that must be pro-tected at all costs. Although, that certainly wasn't his experience. His female sisters, aunts, and cousins were all formidable witches who were fully involved with everything.

Fitz glanced longingly at the open doors to the terrace. "Any objections if I have a quick look at the grounds?" he asked Roger. "Just to stretch my legs. I have been riding all day. Just a stroll along the veranda, perhaps."

"Not at all." Roger seemed severe, but pleasant enough. "I'm afraid my leg is a little stiff, though. I had a fall off my horse a couple of days ago. Minor, of course."

"I'm so sorry to hear that."

"It will be fine, thank you."

"Let me show you," Alicia intervened, leaving her sister's side. "It's very pleasant out there at this time of day, and the views," she said, walking Fitz to the open doors, "are wonderful." Once out on the veranda, she lowered her voice. "We should sit out here, but my sister doesn't like the bugs."

Fitz suppressed a smile. "I see. They can be very large in India."

"Except the servants ensure that there are no bugs at all." She gave him a wry smile, quite forward considering they had barely met, but her informality was refreshing. Raising her voice again, she said, "Let me show you the best spot to sit for a breeze. I can show you more of the house, too."

Alicia led him along the veranda, pointing out the billiard room, the library, and the dining room, asking questions about where he and Ed had been travelling, until he asked, "You are here keeping your sister company for a while?" *And probably seeking a husband,* but he didn't say that aloud.

"She's not long had her third child. She needed help, and I wanted to be here rather than England. The children, of course, are with their *ayah* in the nursery. Two sons and one daughter, so Henry is happy he has heirs."

The *ayah* would be their Indian nanny, a common staple of English households with children. "Of course. Are you enjoying it here?"

"I love it. Waking to the sound of peacocks is liberating, although they do make a dreadful racket." Fitz could see three spreading their magnificent tail feathers as they walked across the lawn. However, Alicia waited until they reached the end of the veranda before saying any more. "Let me show you the bowling green. Lawn bowls is very popular here." She stepped on to the grass, and when they were away from the house, she still lowered her voice to almost a whisper. "You have no idea why you're here, do you?"

Trying to keep his voice casual, he said, "No. Do you?"

"I'm not supposed to know, but I do, and I want to help you."

"Help me? I don't even know what I'm doing yet."

Her eyes darted around her, even though she smiled as if she hadn't a care in the world, no doubt to keep appearances up in case anyone was watching from the house. "There are problems in the port. That is common knowledge. But they are odd, *unnatural* problems that women are deemed too fragile to know." She didn't look at him, instead pointing out a heron on the river.

Uneasy, he asked, "Really? Thefts with shipments?"

"No. Unnatural, as in something *not normal*. Not of this world." She looked at him directly, her dark eyes suddenly serious. "I am aware of what you do, as are Anthony and Roger, of course."

"Is that so?" He looked at her with renewed interest. "What do you know of unnatural things?"

"Spirits, Gods, unusual creatures, demons... Should I go on? The women talk, you know. Whispers reach us of all sorts of things if you gain the trust of your servants. And your reputation precedes you. Amongst the Indian population, at least."

"Henry knows of this?"

"Yes, which is why you're here. He's desperate. But he doesn't know that *I* know. I have discussed it with my sister as well, who is not as foolish as she looks. It's a guise that many women are forced to adopt." She laughed suddenly as she turned back to the house, and Fitz saw that Roger was calling them in. "Just smile."

Fitz laughed at her instruction, a show for Roger, surprised at the speed at which he had been drawn into subterfuge. But he was worried about her earlier statement. "You want to help? I don't think so. I have no idea what we might face, but we are trained, and you are not."

Her eyes flashed with amusement at that. "You have no idea what I am capable of, Mr Westerly."

Three

Moonfell 2025

Odette left Birdie and Horty in the India room, still searching through the boxes for more journals, while Morgana headed down to the main kitchen to cook dinner for all of them.

She was tempted to stay with her grandmother and great-aunt, but decided she would rather return to her studio in what they called the new wing, to work on her latest project. *Well, one of them.* She always had a few paintings in the works, and at the moment, one in particular haunted her days.

The new wing was actually far from new, but was recent in Moonfell terms. It was a relatively small addition that had been added in the 19th century, and jutted out to the northwest at the far end of the main building, creating one wall of a courtyard on the ground floor, and it also bordered the kitchen garden. It had been built to house the ever-increasing number of relatives that stayed at Moonfell in the 1800s. Their ancestors had large families, and they all stayed at Moonfell for several years. The place must have felt horribly busy. But by the early 1900s, those numbers had dwindled dramatically. Odette half wondered if the house itself was sick of them, and encouraged them to stay away.

The rooms were large and spacious, with squared-off sash windows and marble or wooden fireplace surrounds, but lacked the quirkiness of the original building, and consequently it was the least used wing of the house. For the current inhabitants, at least. It also had a very dramatic and large ballroom, very much required in the 19th century for the residents who maintained wealthy connections, and of course, the design played down the witchy side of their family considerably. The ballroom remained largely empty and was utilised only on rare occasions now. The entire wing's lack of use, however, suited Odette, because it was where she had her studio.

The wing connected to the main house on each floor by means of huge double doors at the far end of a passageway. Odette's studio was on the second floor, and comprised of two interconnected rooms with lots of windows. There was no attic above the new wing, and consequently there were several skylights—meaning that her studio was filled with sunshine and moonlight, and she even had access to a small, flat roof using a narrow staircase at the end of the hall. It was gloriously quiet, and in general Odette remained uninterrupted there. Should she choose to play loud music, if the mood struck, she wouldn't disturb anyone at all.

Her studio space was filled with canvases in a wide range of sizes, many of which were waiting to be used, several unfinished pieces, and some that were finished and ready to be collected by the galleries that displayed her work. It smelled satisfyingly of white spirits, incense, candle wax, and magic, because this was one of the places where Odette's magic was strongest. She weaved between the stack of canvases and low tables with interesting arrangements, an array of wooden models, and all sorts of interesting ephemera that inspired her, and stood before a large painting in subdued acrylics. It had a hazy quality, but it was clearly the west moon gate, officially called The Waning Moon Gate, which was made of huge, undulating bronze strips. Like the other gates, it seemed rooted in the very fabric of the garden itself.

Odette dragged a large Moroccan floor cushion over, the colours much faded and the fabric slightly moth-eaten, then lifted the painting off the easel, propped it against the wall, and sat on the cushion to gaze into its depths. She wasn't entirely sure why she had been drawn to paint it, but a few days earlier she had woken out of a deep sleep knowing that it would be her next subject. She had chosen a large canvas and the image filled it, but as yet, it was incomplete. She had still to finish the bands of sinuous metal that either flashed with reflected light or were dull with cloud cover, and the view through the gate was blank. Normally, if she had been facing the bulk of the garden and the house, she would have seen the pond through the archway. Staring through from the east, she would catch a glimpse of the summerhouse, and the trees and shrubs that comprised the boundary. As yet, she hadn't discerned what she should paint within it.

Yet, there was something about the gate that bothered her. The bands of metal didn't seem quite right. She thought it was twilight, a ground mist rising as the earth chilled, but maybe not. Much was uncertain. *And why this gate? Why now?* She stared into the archway, letting her mind drift as her gaze lost focus. *Water. Definitely water.* She reached absently for her brushes and palette, and started to paint the flat, muddy brown surface, smiling as it began to reveal itself.

The edge of a lawn. A stone jetty. And a peacock.

Morgana retired early after dinner, keen to read the letters she had found, and to enjoy her new suite of rooms.

Horty and Birdie were still planning and plotting their Beltane celebrations, although the discovery of Fitz and Ed's journals was distracting them. She had left them in front of the fire in the kitchen, deep in conversation as they decided how to split their time most effectively. Odette hadn't hung around after dinner, either, and had been noticeably distracted throughout the meal. That wasn't unusual. She was having an intense period of painting, and her thoughts were often with her creations. With Beltane approaching, energy was rising, and it affected all of them in different ways. Not that she had said what she was working on. Morgana had learned over the years to respect her privacy on the matter.

Morgana stood with her hands on her hips as she studied her new bedroom and nodded in satisfaction. *Perfect.* She had opted for paisley wallpaper, and the rich blues and striking magentas made her new space, which included a seating area around the fireplace, restful, welcoming, and exotic. The colours were echoed across her ensuite bathroom and dressing room, keeping the dramatic themes of Moon-fell while making this portion all hers. She'd found a wonderfully ornate bedframe and furniture, and had spent days moving things and rearranging the rooms. Mrs Bell, their cleaner, was fortunately very understanding, saying it was time for a spring clean, and she and her daughter, Emily, had swept through the upper floor like a whirlwind. Doors and windows were thrown open, rooms were aired, and spring sunshine illuminated treasures and paintings that Morgana had almost forgotten. Her private kitchen could be accessed through a connecting door, and although small, it was fully furnished with a fridge, sink, cooker and hob top, and a range of cupboards. A table sat under the window, the perfect place for intimate dinners with Monroe, the wolf-shifter she was dating from the Storm Moon Pack.

Feeling calmer and more centred than she had done in months, she lit candles that were placed in the huge floor lanterns with a word of magic, and a stick of incense so that the heady scent of patchouli filled the room. With a word of command, the fire roared to life in the fireplace, and she settled into the comfortable chair, exchanging a glass of wine for Fitz's letters that she'd placed on the side table. Her anticipation had been building all afternoon, and after checking the dates and arranging them chronologically, she started reading the first letter.

Dear Meli,

I'm so sorry that I haven't written for a while. Ed, Vikram, and I have been particularly busy. Vik has found us ample work through his contacts, especially in The Maratha Confederacy. We stayed in a variety of accommodations, many basic, but some were small palaces, or the houses of rich merchants and scholars. It is a world away from Moonfell and London society.

I fear the land is changing, though, with the advent of the East India Company. They are expanding and seeking new trading partners. We keep out of that business and stick to exploring and hunting. I will send some of Ed's papers out the next chance we get. Please keep them for us. I think you will enjoy looking through what we have found. Hopefully you received the last package we sent.

Today, however, we are staying somewhere quite different. A couple of weeks ago we were invited to the British Residency in Rajgarh, a small town in Bihar that is now British territory. We finally arrived today, and I met a most interesting woman who I think you would greatly admire. Her name is Alicia Markham, and she is the sister of the Resident's wife. My meeting with her is what prompted me to write to you, actually. She is as feisty and independent as you. I thought she was here to find a husband, as that is normally the reason unmarried women come here, under the guise of course of being with sisters, mothers, or aunts, or acting as paid companions, governesses, or unpaid nannies to nephews and nieces. However, after only a brief conversation, I think she is after something quite different. Freedom. Now you know why I thought of you.

It seems she knows of what we hunt—and wants to hunt, too. She is not a witch, of that I'm sure. I said no, of course, and then I thought of you, and what you asked me four years ago when we last returned home. You were cross with me, I know, but I was right. You could not have come here, and I could not have looked after you properly. Staying at Moonfell and learning your craft was the best thing to do. You are free at Moonfell in ways you would not be here. There are so many rules! I trust you are learning lots, and that Peri and Dita are helping you. Perhaps you even visit Arti sometimes? Or maybe you have married, after all. In which case, congratulations. If I'm honest, I hope you haven't, and that you are crafting your independent life right now. If anyone knows how the need to be independent feels, it is I—and my companions, of course. I think, however, that many Moonfell residents are rebellious. It's in our blood.

Morgana paused, already feeling a kinship with Fitz and Meli. *Meli, Arti, Peri, and Dita.* Nicknames, most likely. *Siblings? Some type of family member, surely.* Morgana, foolishly, had not picked up a pen and paper to make notes, but she drew their names in the air so that they floated in front of her with a searing orange light, and then added, *1792. Check Moonfell grimoires.* And then she added Alicia Markham's name, too, before continuing to read.

If anyone from home sent us letters here, we have not received them. We travel far too much. Consequently, I know nothing of Moonfell, but trust that all is well, or no doubt a telegram would have found us somehow. I should stress that we are also well, despite our dangerous work. It's exhilarating, and very interesting. Although today we heard that Henry Cavendish, the Resident, knows Ed's Uncle Benjamin. I can't call him Ben. It seems far too informal for such an officious man. Of course, you don't know him, but I have met him several times. He tolerates me, which makes me want to hex him for his superior attitude. I haven't, of course. Moonfell, despite its size and our influence, is not influential enough for him. It seems he is in Bengal, the neighbouring state, and wants to see Ed, and unnervingly knew that we were in a small Bengal town, too. That is where we received our invitation to the Rajgarh Residency. Ed is not pleased about it, but hopefully we will get news from home. Depending on his uncle's travel plans, we may even send some things back to England with him—and on to you, of course.

However, none of that is the most important news, which is why we were summoned here. Alicia hinted at it, but after dinner, over port, from which the women were banned, as usual, Henry told us there was an unnatural presence at Rajgarh Port. The natives will not go there after dark, and many are now afraid to go in the daytime, too. Tomorrow we will see for ourselves, as we have arranged a visit. Ed wanted to go tonight, but after so many weeks of travel, I insisted we should rest. And besides, Vik will hopefully find out more from his contacts before we go. We will meet tomorrow to compare notes. He stays in the town with old friends, and will have much better intelligence than us.

So, dear sister, I will leave it there for now. However, I find this is an interesting way to document our current dilemma, and hopefully you will enjoy it. So, if I can, I will write again tomorrow. Perhaps I shall send these letters in one bundle, or several.

Take care, your loving Fitz.

Morgana added another name to the ones floating in front of her. *Vik.* And Fitz was Meli's brother. The question was, should she pick up another letter, or try and find who these people were first to add context? But the weight of the letters in her lap commanded her attention, and carefully folding the first one away, she picked up the next.

Horty always loved being back in Moonfell. She always felt younger, somehow. *Obviously not as young as Birdie,* she thought sniffily, as she studied her sister's profile while she bent over the journals they had discovered, *but young enough.* It brought out her childish inquisitiveness again.

Currently more interested in the cartographical equipment and the magical hunting tools than the journals, she rummaged through the box they had brought downstairs and started placing the instruments out on the coffee table.

"Someone," she mused aloud, "must have made these."

"Obviously!"

Horty scowled at Birdie. "I meant someone with *magic*."

"Perhaps they bought them from other magical practitioners, or spelled them afterwards," Birdie said, flicking through a notebook.

Horty shrugged. "Perhaps. I must admit to knowing very little about cartography, but these look like fairly sophisticated items."

"I have found a name in the flyleaf of this book," Birdie said. "Edmund Swift again. It has all manner of sketches in it. Quite good ones. A few landscapes, portraits of Indian men, and several sketches of instruments." She adjusted the book, turning it around as she squinted at the page, and then she looked across at Horty. "Maybe you're right. This is quite technical. Perhaps he designed one."

Horty picked up the Wayfinder used to search for shifters. "Surely he couldn't have just bought this from anywhere. It must have been made to their specifications. In which case, he'd have been an educated man."

"And Fitzroy's friend, obviously. But why are his journals here and not with his own family?"

"Not everyone treasures their histories as we do," Horty pointed out. Restless, she placed the Wayfinder on the table and continued to search the large box. "If Edmund wasn't a witch, and we are yet to know that, then maybe Fitz bewitched the items? I feel like such a twit. I have no idea how these things work. I mean, what is this, for instance?"

She stood up so as better to wrest another wooden box out of the larger one. "Ooh! A lantern?"

Birdie pushed her reading glasses up on her head. "It's quite chunky. Why put a lantern in a box of exploring equipment?"

"You can't explore in the dark!"

The wooden lantern wasn't exactly lantern-like, though. There were no glass panels, and it had a door in the back, and a hole in the front, and when she opened it up, there was something inside. She pulled out a bundle of cloth and unwrapped it, finding what looked like a camera lens, and some kind of slide contraption. Horty prided herself on her clever, inquisitive mind, and with a bit of fiddling and examination, nose to the box, she said, "I think it's some sort of camera."

"From the eighteenth century?"

"It looks like it." She peered into the large box she had taken it out of, and found another box at the bottom containing a set of slides with painted images. "By the Goddess! It's a projector."

"Don't be ridiculous!"

"It is. What else could it be?" Horty fumbled and fiddled with the box until she had put the lens in place, her heart pounding with excitement.

Birdie abandoned the journals and scooted to her side. "Well. How very intriguing. Who would have thought we would have such a thing?"

"And you know what else? It feels magical. It's making my fingers tingle." She slid a slide into place, eyes inches from the mechanism, to make sure she was doing it properly. "I think it's a landscape. We need a candle or torch or something to shine through it."

"Witch-light," Birdie said impatiently, placing one in the box, while simultaneously dimming the kitchen lights with a click of her fingers. In moments, an image appeared on the wall, grainy and indistinct.

Horty could barely breathe she was so excited. Especially when within moments, the image floated off the wall and hovered in front of them, turning slowly and becoming more distinct as it rotated. "Good grief! It's a garden, and it's so exotic."

"Lotus flowers. And look at the archways in the distance. It's Indian," Birdie said, clutching Horty's arm. "I can smell the dust and the perfume."

"I can feel the heat," Horty said, extending her hands as if before a fire. Both sisters were standing now, mesmerised by the image. "I knew it was magical, but I didn't expect *this*."

"Put another slide in!" Birdie urged.

Horty picked another from the pack, sliding it into place carefully, hoping the image would bloom as it had before. She needn't have worried. This time, the image swelled even quicker, showing another aspect of a garden, one with a shady pool and an elaborate fountain surrounded by lemon trees. Suddenly, the water sprinkled across the paths and the scent of lemon manifested.

Horty stumbled back in shock. "That's clever magic."

Birdie pulled her back even further. "It's getting bigger! Don't touch it. Who knows what might happen."

Horty tore her eyes away from the hologrammatic image. "Move the furniture, quickly!"

They pushed the sofa back and dragged the coffee table away with all the precious instruments and journals, including the lantern, until the area in front of the fire was completely empty. It was lucky they did, because the image continued to swell in size. It was now almost large enough to step into.

"I wonder," Birdie said, a note of panic to her voice, "if my witch-light has done this, or made it worse. Perhaps a regular candle might not have triggered it. I think I should stop it. Extinguish my light."

"But what if there's a message in there?"

"What if it sucks us back in time?" she countered.

"It's just an image!" Horty knew that wasn't true, but she was mesmerised and didn't want it to stop. "Can we contain it, somehow?"

"Salt circle and protection. If that doesn't work, I will definitely extinguish the light."

They scrambled to act, Horty rushing to grab the salt from the cupboard, while Birdie readied a spell. Horty poured a thick line of salt onto the floor, keeping a good distance from the bubble of the image. Birdie cast her protection spell, and the ring of salt ignited with a flash of blue. The witches were ready to retreat until the spell worked, fixing the image in place. But the fountain still erupted with water, and the faint scent of jasmine carried to them.

"Time for more slides, I think," Horty said.

Four

Rajgarh 1792

Some things don't change, Ed reflected as he eased back in his chair after dinner with a glass of port and unbuttoned his jacket.

The English abroad strictly maintained their societal standards, so the women, just Alicia and Elizabeth, had retired to the drawing room, and the men had remained at the table for port and cigars. The doors were still wide open to let in the cool breeze, and the *punkah-wallahs* were seated outside the room, operating huge cloth fans to reduce the heat. It was late April, and the weather was already hot. In a few weeks' time it would be even hotter, and Ed, Fitz, and Vikram would find somewhere to settle for a few months until the heat dissipated. As yet, they hadn't decided where, and it varied every year.

Now that the women had left the room, the earlier air of chatter and polite conversation vanished, and Henry, Anthony, and Roger looked grim.

"Thank you for coming," Henry said, eyes darting between him and Fitz. "I realise that I have not been entirely forthcoming, but there are things I did not wish to commit to paper."

"We understand," Ed said, nodding politely. "Although, surely Residency communications are trustworthy?"

"Of course, but even so, we wanted to take precautions. Rajgarh is a small part of the East India Company's business, but nevertheless it is important strategically, and the port is always busy, and not just with our business, either—although, we are restricting that. In fact, we wonder if that could be part of the problem." He paused as if reluctant to say more, and Ed wished he'd just get on with it. However, he did not wish to insult the Resident by rushing him.

It was Roger who prompted him instead. "Henry, please, we need help. Do you want me to—"

"No." Henry cut him off, and then stared at Ed and Fitz. "I am not a superstitious man, but I cannot ignore the reports that are coming from the staff who work at the port. However, first I need to know if what I have heard about you two is correct, and that I can rely on you to be discreet."

"In our line of work, we are always discreet," Fitz said, amused. "However, you need to be specific about the type of work you think we do." Neither Ed nor Fitz cared that people knew, but it certainly wasn't normal dinner party conversation. They always declared themselves travellers and explorers if anyone asked.

Henry shuffled in his seat. "I gather that you are monster hunters. It seems incredible, but I have several reliable sources who say that is so."

Ed nodded, keen to get information. "Yes, we hunt monsters. Although, the supernatural creatures we come across are not all monstrous. Some are lost. Some are manipulated against their will. Some are murderous, scavenging creatures who only desire blood or souls.

It's an unusual line of work, but we like it. I presume my uncle told you of our business."

Henry nodded, eyes narrowing suspiciously. "Yes, and a couple of Indian merchants in the town who suggested we contact you. It sounds an unseemly business."

Fitz laughed, not caring for a conventional response. "It is an unseemly business, but we are very good at it, and it suits our natures and abilities. You would be surprised how often our services are required."

Roger fidgeted with his napkin. "How very worrying."

"It pays well, too," Ed added, just to make sure Henry understood what was required to hire them. "We risk our lives fighting such creatures."

Henry waved his hand dismissively. "If you can get rid of our problem, I will make sure you are well paid."

"Thank you," Fitz said. "Having established we are what you need, please tell us what the issue is."

"As I said, we have had odd reports coming from the docks. I was inclined to think it was just the Indians who had become excitable," Henry said, "but then our English staff also reported seeing an unusual creature at night. Something large. Inhuman."

"Can you describe it?" Fitz asked, leaning forward eagerly.

"Describe it?" Henry looked appalled. "It's something unnatural! Isn't that enough?"

"No. There are many supernatural creatures, and it's important to find out what it is before deciding on a way to banish it," Ed said, needing specifics.

Henry spluttered, face flushing. "I don't know. It had a lot of limbs, apparently. Claws. It moved so quickly, though, that I gather it was hard to be sure. I certainly haven't seen it. None of us have." He indicated the men at the table. "Only the port staff and the locals from the surrounding streets."

Ed was beginning to dislike Henry. For a start, he seemed to be dismissive of Indian opinion, which wasn't unusual, but it still annoyed him. Secondly, he hadn't thought to investigate it properly himself.

"I went to the docks last night," Anthony said, chiming in. "Well, at twilight actually, with the *sepoys* and Jon—that's Captain Townsend—but saw nothing. It doesn't appear every night. Not yet, at least." The *sepoys* were the Indian soldiers who generally outnumbered the amount of British soldiers in a regiment.

"But you must have questioned those who saw it," Ed persisted. "Surely someone, particularly the Indians, could have described it well?" In general, the Indian population were very well-versed in their own myths and legends, even if the Europeans weren't.

"A few coolies were killed almost three weeks ago," Anthony explained, using the Indian slang term for the dock labourers. "A late shipment arrived at the docks and had to be secured in the warehouse. Everything had been unloaded, checked, and put in storage, so only a small group of men remained. One of the Customs Officers was in his office a short distance away, and he saw a creature attack them. He said it howled and seemed to change shape, but that could just have been the darkness confusing him. The lights in certain areas of the docks are poor. He didn't stick around, not surprisingly. He ran for help, but by the time he returned with a few locals, the men were dead. Their bodies were found in the water later, and the creature had vanished." He sighed heavily. "We all thought there had been a fight and he was mistaken, until the same thing happened again a couple of weeks ago. A week after the first attack."

Anthony went on to describe another couple of incidences where more men had died. It seemed they had hoped that it would stop on its own, but instead it was happening more often. The small vessels that used Rajgarh had threatened to stop coming. Staff were threatening to walk away. Some already had. Textiles, rice, and indigo from the surrounding area were stored in the warehouses and needed to be shipped. Ed grimaced. No wonder they had called them in. No matter the loss of life; trade was threatened.

Fitz pressed for more details. "Has anyone else seen the creature?"

"It strikes at night," Henry said, seeming to have recovered his composure, "and only last week was seen in the narrow streets around the dock itself. A hulking creature, with flaming eyes and claws. One of the witnesses gave it a name, but it escapes me..."

"Rakshasa," Roger said. "I have made further enquiries amongst the staff. They did not wish to speak of it. We risk losing staff here, too. They say we are cursed."

Ed groaned. "That's a type of demon. It shapeshifts, and can even become invisible. Has it appeared since then?"

Henry shook his head. "Not for almost a week now, but other men have gone missing, though no bodies have been found. Our regiment searched the docks last week, but found nothing. However, since then, they stand guard around it every night. That's where Jon is now. He insists on staying with his men."

"Have they any protection?" Fitz asked.

"Just guns." Henry sipped his port. "Perhaps that is enough to have scared it off. It may be that your services are not needed after all. I half wonder if someone is dressing up, just to scare us and ruin trade. That it's all an illusion."

Fitz huffed with disbelief. "An illusion that kills, and therefore no less dangerous. But that is highly unlikely."

Ed shared Fitz's scepticism and exchanged a concerned glance with him. "No, guns will not drive it off if it is a Rakshasa. We will need to investigate it first, to make sure, then devise a way to get rid of it." And it was more complicated than that. They needed to find out *why* it was there. Hopefully, Vikram would learn more.

"I take it that your wife and her sister don't know of this?" Fitz asked.

"They know we have trouble at the docks, but not its nature, and they must not find out," Henry insisted.

"So how have you explained our presence here to them?" Ed asked, wondering what role they should play.

"I have said you have contacts that could help us discern who is behind the issues, and have otherwise left it vague."

Ed laughed. "Then we shall try and be equally vague, eh, Fitz?"

Fitz just shook his head, clearly perplexed.

Henry continued. "The trouble is, rumours are spreading now, and I'm worried about hysteria in the local population. More men could die. We might lose ships, shipments, or even the warehouses could be damaged. We cannot afford that to happen. And what if the creature starts attacking beyond the docks? Or attacking houses along the river?" His gaze drifted to the lawn and river beyond before fixing on Ed and Fitz again. "The important thing is, can you deal with it?"

Ed didn't even need to confer with Fitz. "Of course, but we will need to be here for several days to investigate it, find out exactly what we're dealing with, and then set traps. And we need to interview people. I trust you are happy for us to do that?"

"Yes. And your price?"

Fitz named their fee, knowing full well the Company could afford it. They sometimes tailored their prices depending on who employed them, and sometimes they even worked for free. "That does not include expenses. We may need to buy supplies."

Henry didn't even blink. "Agreed, I just want it over as quickly as you can get it done, and with as little life lost or Company property damaged as possible."

Ed was eager to start work, the hunt as usual gripping him. "Can we go to the docks tonight?"

Fitz shook his head. "We've been travelling for days, Ed. I think we should sleep tonight and see what Vikram has found out first. Forewarned is forearmed. Then we can see the docks in the day so that we fully understand the layout, and we can talk to the staff down there."

"I have asked Jon to send word to us," Anthony said, "should it appear tonight. If it does, we can get there quickly. We're only ten minutes from the docks."

Ed nodded reluctantly. Fitz was right, and Anthony's arrangements were sound. "Fine. Tomorrow, then."

"You can meet with me after breakfast," Anthony suggested. "I can give you background on the staff and the work we do here, and then I'll accompany you to the docks."

"Good suggestion." Henry stood. "And now I think we should join the women and try to forget this nasty business for a few hours."

As soon as Fitz entered the drawing room with the other men, Alicia caught his eye, a quizzical look in her own. It was only for the briefest of moments, but it was there.

As yet, Fitz hadn't been able to talk to Ed about his earlier conversation with Alicia, but after hearing about the attacks in the port, he was determined to put a stop to Alicia's involvement. It was a ridiculous notion. He had no aversion in general to women being involved in anything. In fact, in his own family, they were all headstrong and independent. But his family were witches, and all had powerful magic to protect themselves. Alicia had no such advantages, and there was no doubt that this creature, whether a Rakshasa or not, was very dangerous.

Already he was running through the various other creatures it could be, sifting through those they had encountered in the past. Vetalas had been one of their most difficult challenges. They were spirits that reanimated corpses, and they had come across a group of them years ago that had required all their cunning to defeat. Ed had been seduced by an Apsara that had managed to fool them for a short while. Only recently, they'd had to fight an enormous poisonous scorpion in the desert that had been plaguing a small village. It didn't sound like any of those. They were the more memorable of their fights. He and Ed had also faced a multitude of ghosts and restless spirits, and several varieties of shifter creatures that were rapidly becoming their staple work. They hadn't faced a Rakshasa, though, if that's what it was. He was inclined to believe it was, if the locals had said so.

For a while, he and Ed entertained their hosts with stories of their travels, leaving out monster hunting, of course, and then Henry, Anthony, Ed, and Elizabeth settled into a game of Whist, Roger retired to bed citing a difficult day, and Alicia invited Fitz to a game of Piquet. They sat at a small table close to the window, just far enough from the other group so as not be heard.

"I love this game," Alicia confessed as she shuffled the cards. "Such a challenge, don't you think?"

"It certainly exercises one's memory." He gestured to the table they sat at. "A dedicated table, no less. It must be popular here."

"Roger and I often play. So does the doctor, Monty. He's very good. Henry and Beth love Whist. They make a formidable team. Ed and Anthony will have a battle on their hands."

"I suspect that I will, too," Fitz said, noting Alicia's deft hands as she dealt the cards. "Henry seems to run a fairly relaxed household here.

I note the amount of Indian décor. And yet," he ventured, "he seems not to want to take their word for the events at the docks."

Alicia's eyes sparkled. "He does listen to them. It's one of the reasons that you're here. He just doesn't like to advertise it too much. Our *khidmatgar*, Akash, is the soul of discretion, but offers invaluable advice. Much like myself." She used the Indian term for butler.

"Miss Markham…"

"Alicia," she insisted. "Formalities make me feel so old."

"Alicia, I must stress that you should not be involved in this situation. Henry thinks that neither you nor your sister know anything of the true nature of this matter."

"The supernatural element?" She smirked. "As I said earlier, we both do, and my sister needs to know that her children will be safe. I would like you to keep us apprised of your progress—and share details, of course."

Fitz glanced across to the Whist table, noting they were already fully absorbed in the game, and Elizabeth's attention was on her hand of cards. Clearly, she was not as simpering as she had first seemed. "What exactly is it that you think you can do? Especially when no one knows that you know. You appreciate I will share this information with Ed and Vikram?"

"I was thinking I could help defend here, should the need arise. I am an excellent shot. Our country estate at home afforded me many opportunities to practice. You will find that I'm adept at doing things in secret."

Fitz kept his eyes on his hand. "Perhaps information gathering will be your strength. To do more will risk your standing in society here. And Henry's position. I can't see that Captain Townsend would be happy if you were involved, and potentially we might be working with him and his regiment, although I'd rather not."

Her finger tapped the table aggressively. "Just information gather-ing? Really? Well, I shall see about that."

She then proceeded to beat him quite ruthlessly, leaving Fitz in no doubt that she would not be easily sidelined.

Five

Moonfell 2025

Odette had forgotten she was painting.

She was so absorbed in the image that was appearing from her brush that she felt as if she had fallen into the painting. Well, sort of. When she had returned to it after the meal, she wasn't entirely sure how to continue, because she had no idea of what she would paint next, but she decided she would have to trust in the process, as she always did. So far, there was an elegant lawn with a strutting peacock, the wide, somnolent river at the end, and to the side, a few long, low buildings, but there was more to come. Something under the trees, in the shade. Ensuring she had a full array of paints and brushes next to her, she placed the painting back on the easel and began.

It happened in moments, and she slipped back into her trancelike state, the brush an extension of her being as her insight manifested.

A long dress, a tight bodice, and hair swept up. The scent of jasmine she had detected earlier from the letter filled the air, as did the singular scent of cigar smoke. And that's when she saw him. A man with dark hair and tanned skin talking earnestly with the woman. There was a note of intrigue to the way they stood. *Or was it romantic?* Odette could feel tension between them, and although the sky was bright blue, a shadow seemed to hang over the scene. Whispers surrounded her, and the water made a pleasing sound as it splashed against the small jetty. It was hypnotic, until the loud screech of the peacock jolted her out of it, and the long toll of a bell echoed through Moonfell.

Odette jerked backwards, the paintbrush falling from her fingers as she looked around in shock. The room was in darkness, except for a pool of light around where she sat, a lamp illuminating the painting. *What time was it? And the bell?* That must be Birdie summoning them to the kitchen, the noise resounding within her like a GPS location.

Reluctantly deciding the painting could wait, she dropped her brushes into water and headed down the stairs, the house filled with a sense of expectation. They were on the cusp of something. Beltane, perhaps? Or maybe the India room had triggered something, much like the bees had at Ostara.

Hopefully without such devastating consequences.

She met Morgana in the corridor, already dressed for bed in pyjamas and a silk kimono. "What now?" she asked her cousin.

Morgana rolled her eyes. "I felt a flash of magic and wondered if it was Beltane planning. That really wouldn't warrant a summoning though, would it?"

Odette shook her head and pushed the kitchen door open, pausing on the threshold as she saw a mirage of a garden at the dining end. "Oh! What have you two done?"

Horty, flushed with excitement, and maybe gin, said, "We did a thing!"

"I can see that. How?"

"We found a thing!" Birdie added, almost gleefully.

Morgana huffed. "A *thing*? Can you two elucidate, please? There's a bloody great hologram in the kitchen!"

"It's a projection," Horty explained as she tapped a box in front of her. "From this."

But Odette was far less concerned about what caused it. She was more interested in the image, and she stepped closer. "I've just been painting that garden. I think it's the same, anyway, although seen from a different angle. I drew those." She pointed at the long, low buildings arranged within a cluster of foliage. "There's a river at the end of the garden, and I saw two people under the tree. But I couldn't see that!" She pointed to the corner of a large building surrounded by a deep veranda on two levels.

"I think," Morgana said cautiously, "that it's the Rajgarh Residency. Fitz referred to it. I'll tell you more later. It's very much what they looked like, because I checked. Where did you find it? How does it work?"

Horty directed their attention to the coffee table that had been hastily dragged back, rucking the rug up in the process. It was stacked with journals, paper, and other ephemera, as well as the bulky box that looked like a lantern. "I found this, and although it looks like a lantern, it's actually a primitive projector. I also found hand-painted slides, and we haven't seen half of them yet."

Excitement stirring, Odette asked, "Are there any of the inside of the house?"

"Not that we've found yet," Birdie said, as transfixed by the image as the others. "We found images of what we think were an Indian palace's gardens, though."

It was then that Odette looked down and saw the salt circle. "What happened that you needed a circle of protection?"

"Oh, that?" Horty said, a flash of worry in her eyes. "It kept grow-ing, so we thought we should contain it. It's worked—for now, at least."

Odette crouched to examine the lantern. "Intriguing," she said, noting the witch-light glowing within it and the stack of glass slides. She picked one up, holding it up to the lamp light. "It's painted with such precision. Such skill. I feel a tingle of magic, too."

Morgana joined her, examining another slide. "And yet the image it projects is so realistic. This is almost like something you could have done, Odette. Do you think another ancestor had your skills?"

She shrugged. "I presume so. Or perhaps they just cast a spell on the slides. Is there any paperwork telling us anything about them?"

"Not that we've found yet," Birdie confessed, "but we haven't gone through everything. Could you discern any emotion from the paint-ing you're doing?"

Odette cast her mind back to the feeling of falling into the image. "Yes, definitely. A sense of intrigue and mystery. Secrets. I heard the river and the peacocks, and I scented jasmine." She closed her eyes, feeling its pull again, and that's when it struck her. Her eyes flew open again. "The frame of my painting is the west moon gate, except it looks slightly different. A little plainer than it is now."

Horty gasped. "You saw a moon gate, too? That must be signifi-cant."

"I know, but I was too busy painting to give it much thought. What if..."

But Horty was already ahead of her. "We project this onto the moon gate!"

"Yes. It's big, so we could let the image expand...if it works again."

"Of course it will," Birdie said with a huff. "Why wouldn't it?"

"Any manner of reasons," Morgana said curtly. "Maybe a spell made it activate once, but it won't do so again. We don't know what's going on. This could be purely for fun, or there could be a message in these images."

Odette could feel the tension building between the two of them again. Birdie was a tad sensitive to Morgana's suggestions lately, and Morgana always responded with forced patience, as if she was talking to a wayward child. Before things could escalate, Odette said, "You used a witch-light. Did you try a normal one first? I'm just wondering if you needed magic to trigger it."

Birdie dragged her gaze from Morgana to Odette. "No, we went straight for the witch-light, but you said yourself, the slides feel magical."

"And we are still," Horty added, "going through that box. Forget that for now, though. Let's go to the moon gate."

Odette dragged a cushion to the floor and knelt on it to better see into the box on the coffee table. "Humour me a moment. Let's see what else is in here." She knew what Horty could be like when she was gripped by an idea. "Morgana, please tell us about the letters while I search."

"I've only read two so far." She sank onto the sofa. "Fitz was writing to his sister, Meli. He referred to other family members, so I will start looking into them tomorrow. Essentially, he told her that they had been summoned to the Residency to catch something supernatural that was attacking the port. He referred to a woman who wanted to help, but of course, it would have been frowned upon at the time. I also had the sense that there are probably other letters to Meli somewhere, as Fitz was resuming his previous correspondence. The woman he refers to reminded him of his sister." Morgana sighed, fingers playing with the tie on her kimono. "I felt his excitement, but also that he worried about Meli. His life sounded so exciting, though, and it seems she wanted to travel with him, but he said no, and reiterated how right that was. I think he was reaching out to make amends. He must have made the slides, too, or asked someone to," she said, idly picking one up. "A way of helping her see what he was doing, and where he was." She nodded as she spoke. "Yes, that sounds likely. She was younger than him. The second letter talked about his first visit to the port and what they saw there. It was all to do with the East India Company, of course. They were just starting to expand then."

"Where's Rajgarh?" Birdie asked.

"Bihar, in the north of India, and it's set on the Ganges. I gather the river was a very important part of the Company's structure at the time, although Rajgarh was a smaller port compared to the others."

Odette felt the twitch in her fingers again as she searched the box. The urge to paint as impressions filled her head. "I need to check the map. Oh! What's this?" The box still contained many journals and rolled documents that she had placed on the table, but underneath them all, she found a tissue-wrapped object. She extracted it and unwrapped it carefully, finding small, silver bells on a chain. She shook them, and the tinkling sound was like another spell. As if she had awoken Tinkerbell. The sound carried out of the room with a shimmer of magic and seemed to ripple through the mirage of the Residency.

Birdie folded her arms across her chest, eyes narrowed with worry. "I'm not sure if that was a good thing or not. I felt it go straight through me."

"Me too," Horty agreed.

Odette could still feel the tingle in her fingers. "Who do you think these belonged to? I mean, Fitz must have sent them."

"Or Edmund," Morgana reminded her.

"Oh, yes," Birdie leapt in. "We think he was our inventor, but we can tell you about that later. Are we going to the moon gate now?"

Odette exchanged an amused glance with Morgana, knowing that Birdie and Horty would probably do it anyway. "I think we must."

Birdie felt the change in Moonfell as they walked through the dark garden. The noise of the tiny bells seemed to linger in the air, even though she knew they had long stopped ringing.

If she paused to listen, the soft tinkling vanished, but when she walked again, she heard it anew, as if someone was following her with bells around their wrists and ankles. She shook her head, certain she was being fanciful. Still, she searched the shadows knowing her coven heard it too, just from the way they cast each other inquisitive glances, even though they didn't mention it.

Mist was rising off the large pond and sinuously twisting around the lower part of the Waning Moon Gate, becoming part of the bronze strips to make it seem as if the gate was rooting itself more firmly into the ground. Morgana set up the small garden table they had bought with them, and Horty—surprisingly adept with the antique contraption—set it up again.

"Which slide?" Odette asked, shining her torch on the selection.

Birdie, half her attention on the garden, said, "You choose." The garden was busy at this time of night, and the hedges and bushes twitched with the small, scurrying creatures that made the night their home. "I wish Lam were here. I'd like to know what he could hear the creatures saying. Is he practising?"

"It's hard because he's revising," Morgana said, a note of regret in her tone. "Plus, I don't like to bother him when I know he's busy. I also know he's eager to be back here, though. So is Como. I messaged him." She smiled at Birdie. "They're excited."

"Good. So am I." She studied the bronze gate, her attention returning to Odette's earlier comment. "How did the gate look different in your image?"

"It was simpler. Just the big bronze metals, I think." She made her selection and gave Horty the slide. "Set it up, but don't light it yet, please." She strode to the gate, fingers sliding over the design. "Yes, I think these narrower pieces that are woven within it were missing."

"As if they were added later?" Birdie asked, tapping her lip with her finger.

"Exactly."

"Interesting. I've always assumed the entire thing was built at the same time. All right. Step back everyone. Let's keep behind the lantern."

"Birdie," Morgana asked, eyeing the lantern and tightening her lips, "should we cast a circle again?"

"I'd rather not. What if we're missing out on something by restricting it?"

"Our garden is very receptive to magic. Look what happened with the bees! What if we trigger something else? We let loose a creature the last time." *Or you did*, her accusing stare seemed to say as she looked at Birdie. *That damn séance.*

Horty hefted a bag of salt. "We came prepared."

From the set of her shoulders, Birdie knew Morgana wasn't happy, though Morgana was always cautious. But if she was right, Birdie couldn't bear it. "Fine, but let's make it larger."

Ten minutes and lots of salt later, the circle was in place, well beyond the area of the gate, running almost to the edge of the pond. They lined up with the boundary behind them, so that the lantern was projecting through the gate towards the water. Horty nodded, and Birdie floated a witch-light into the mechanism again. This time, a stunning Indian-style garden bloomed within the gate. Paths wound through the lush planting towards a pavilion that was surrounded by water, its reflection mirroring its elegant lines. Birdie's breath caught in her chest, and a compulsion to step forward to follow the path caught her by surprise.

As the image hit the gate, the metals fizzed with light like an array of stars. The sound of tinkling bells manifested as the image soared out of the gate and travelled across the ground, swelling in size once again. It sailed straight over the ring of salt until it floated on the pond in its own radiant light. Sunlight danced on the waters, a patch of cloudless blue sky above, and the pavilion and the garden floated on the past lake that was also the present pond, as if it had found its rightful place.

"Shit!" Morgana's eyes widened with worry. "The gate must have strengthened the image."

"Perhaps," Birdie said, too enchanted to be worried, "but it's stunning, and I can't feel anything malevolent."

Her coven was already walking to the pond's edge to see it better.

"But how?" Morgana asked, perplexed. "I mean the gate must be tied to these slides. Or maybe just this one..."

"Why?" Odette asked.

"It's a gift from Fitz," Horty said, very sure of herself. "For his sister who he had to leave behind. He wanted her to be part of the story. He was hunting, you say, Morgana?"

"Yes. In the second letter he said a creature was attacking the port, killing men and threatening the company's business. I need to read them all, but I'm too tired tonight." She turned to Birdie, face etched with worry. "I sense there is more to this story than just the hunt."

Birdie's antagonism towards her granddaughter drifted away and she squeezed her arm. "I feel it too, so we will find out everything. But for now, let's check another couple of slides to see if the effect is the same, and then bed. We'll start afresh tomorrow."

Six

Rajgarh 1792

It was mid-morning by the time Ed arrived at Rajgarh Docks with Fitz, and the size of it shocked him.

It sprawled along the river, the sheer number of buildings, people, and the noise they generated all more than he anticipated.

He turned to Anthony, the Assistant Resident, who had accompanied them. They had spent an hour with him earlier as he explained their processes and the issues at stake. "I thought this was a smaller port?"

Anthony smiled with a trace of smugness. "It is, but we are growing. Surely you have seen Patna and Benares? They are far bigger. More goods are coming from the interior, and we have grown to accommodate them, just as I mentioned earlier."

They had entered from the road, through a large gate wedged between a variety of buildings. Some were big warehouses, some looked like offices, but one was clearly the Customs House. Wooden jetties stretched along the river to either side, as well as the *ghats* at the far end, a mix of wooden and earth embankments leading down to the river, all choked with a multitude of staff. Small ships and boats were lined up, both mid-river and in the port, and a steady stream of goods were being hauled on and off the boats, supervised by Indians and English men.

"I thought business was being damaged by the creature?" Fitz asked.

"It's busy here now, because it's daylight. By late afternoon, unloading is suspended, and it's causing delays. Merchants are reluctant to store goods here now, too. I mentioned it, remember?"

Ed nodded, trying to recollect everything they had discussed that morning. Anthony had reeled off many names and positions, and outlined their routines and the other businesses involved, and he knew he wouldn't remember it all. At least now he understood why reports of the attacks had been so unclear. The boats, buildings, and distances would not make spotting the attacks easy. He hoped Vikram had more information, and he checked his pocket watch, wondering if he had arrived. He had sent word the previous evening with a servant, saying he would meet them in the Port Officers' building.

Anthony pointed to one of the warehouses close to the river. "That is where the first attack took place, and there," he pointed again to a smaller building set further back, "was another. I can walk you around later."

Anthony led them along the docks towards a white building, and Ed studied the best places where he could set up their equipment. That was Ed's strength. He was a man of science and exploration, and enjoyed designing tools, not remembering the structure of how the docks worked. His bags contained several items that he had designed himself, and that Fitz had spelled. He planned to set a couple up soon, but the rest could wait for that evening. He just hoped they could work alone, as they often did. He did not appreciate an audience.

Keeping his voice low as they trailed behind Anthony, he said to Fitz, "Now that we're here, I see how hard this will be. The size alone will make it difficult." He shivered, despite the heat, hoping it wasn't a portent of things to come. Something dark hung over these docks.

"We've tackled bigger places. The Maharaja of Rajipan, for example."

"Yes, but his gardens were enclosed, and he was not a sceptic. In fact, he was most receptive to our presence. Here is very different."

For all of Anthony's helpfulness, the man had adopted an air of polite suspicion, and even doubt. He was a man of influence in the British Residence, and Fitz and Ed, despite their family wealth and education, were distinctly *different*. Men like Anthony didn't like different. For a start, they travelled independently and were friends with an Indian. The son of a Court Scholar with his own money and connections. Anthony seemed to disapprove when he had asked them about their companion earlier.

Anthony led them past a collection of temporary shelters for trade goods, and some open yards full of wood. The smell of burning cow dung and the river assailed them at every point. That was a smell that Ed actually enjoyed. The authentic part of India, along with perfumes and spices that carried from the markets, and the sacks ready for shipment. He wasn't sure he ever wanted to return to England, although he did want to present his instruments to The Royal Society, the membership of which he owed to his uncle.

"The main offices are here," Anthony said as they reached a building in white with a broad veranda. "This is where you'll find the Harbour Master and other port officials—all Company men, of course. The Customs Officers, English and Indian, are housed in that building." He pointed across the space to a building closer to the docks.

"Some of which are the Indian officials from the old Mughal system," Fitz said, clarifying what they had been told earlier.

"Yes. Hopefully," he said entering the open door of the Port Officers' building, "we will find your interpreter here."

Fitz rolled his eyes behind Anthony's back, impatient with the word he had chosen to describe their friend.

Vikram was seated in the reception area, resplendent in his *achkan*, a knee-length jacket in fine cotton, and tight-fitting trousers called *churidar*. He had opted for a modest turban, and looked wealthy enough to momentarily silence Anthony, although he recovered quickly while Fitz made the introductions. He was with a similarly attired older gentleman who Anthony appeared to know well.

Anthony gave a curt nod. "I had no idea that Mr Westerly and Mr Swift's companion was a friend of yours, Mr Sharma."

Vikram's friend smiled and spoke with excellent English. "Vikram's father and I were scholars in an old Mughal court in the state of Rajputana. That was some years ago, and we have remained in touch after I left to continue my family's trade interests. I am honoured to host Singh Sahib at my home. Especially when I learned he was to help with our problem. It is a pleasure to meet your associates," he added to Fitz and Ed. "Harishchandra Sharma, at your pleasure."

"And you also, Sharma Sahib," Fitz said, shaking his outstretched hand. He introduced Anthony formally. "Mr Davis, this is my colleague, Vikram Singh."

"Mr Singh." If anything, Anthony looked even more uncomfortable as his eyes darted around the reception area. "Let us discuss our issue with the Harbour Master in his office."

After climbing the stairs and progressing down corridors of white plastered walls and wooden floors, they reached an office overlooking the docks. The door was open, and a man sat behind an enormous desk, his face flushed, and a stack of paperwork before him as a skinny, nervous man stood close by, whom Edmund presumed was his secretary.

Again, a round of introductions were made. The Harbour Master, a man called Neville Lambton, looked harassed and worried, and while tea was brought, they were urged to sit at the small sitting area provided. Ed ignored it, sick of the formalities already. He had spotted an opportunity and wasn't about to waste it.

"May I study the port from your window?" he asked Neville directly. "It offers an excellent view, and I have some instruments I would like to use while I can." He hefted his leather bag, full of his precious equipment.

Flustered, Neville just nodded, and Fitz smoothly took the offered seat with Anthony and Harishchandra, so much better at sourcing information than Ed. They often worked like this.

"I will assist you," Vikram added, hurrying to his side. It was unusual to see him in such finery. Normally, he looked as dusty and casual as he and Fitz. "We can listen and work, correct, Edmund?"

"Of course." The windows were sufficiently far enough away that they could talk with lowered voices and not disturb the others. As Ed extracted his first instrument, he asked, "Did you find out anything useful last night?"

"That tensions are rising between the British and the Indian community. The Company is making it harder and harder for Indian merchants to access the port and ship their own trade. They charge more and offer them a smaller area. It is the same along the Ganga, but we have heard such stories before."

"What does Sharma Sahib think of the situation?"

"He is frustrated, but knows not to show it."

Ed nodded, frustrated for him. "And the creature? Does your friend know what it could be, or who might be responsible?"

Vik shook his head. "Not yet, but thinks it is far from random. He believes that an Indian is behind it all because they have manipulated a supernatural creature that is also Indian in origin. Although, to have killed the coolies is unusual."

"Not if you were trying to cast suspicion on the English instead," Ed pointed out.

"True. This will be difficult to unravel, my friend, and will no doubt increase tension. Harish-ji," he said, referring to his friend affectionately, "is worried, but very grateful we are here. He is a good man and a good friend. He will invite you to his home later."

"Something I shall look forward to." Ed hefted his Temperometer from his bag, a bulky object made of brass, wood, and specially treated glass that he had designed to specifically look for changes in the veils between worlds, such as seams or rifts that would escape normal human detection. Anomalies that might indicate how this creature—or any creature—could attack and not be traced. He set it up on a sturdy wooden tripod. "How come these attacks haven't caused people to flee this place?"

"The usual. Where would they go? But some of the locals are using common charms and talismans for protection, even though they do not know what exactly against yet. You know."

Fitz nodded, understanding what he meant. He and Ed had noted the Evil Eye drawn on doors to counter harm, and red threads around the wrists of the locals, as well as the tiny mirrors sown onto garments to reflect negative energy. Those were common everywhere. "And the gaps between attacks? Has he a theory for that?"

"Only conjecture. Something to discuss tonight, perhaps."

Ed nodded, distracted now that his equipment was ready. He lowered his eye to the scope, focussing first on the dock area by one of the huge warehouses where the first attacks happened. Despite studying the area for some time, he found nothing of interest. It wasn't until he studied another section, close to the *ghats*, that he saw the tell-tale shimmer in air quality that denoted a change in energy. Magical energy.

"There," he said, pointing out the spot to Vikram. He adjusted his angle, sweeping around the dock slowly, finally noting another shimmer at the end of one of the narrow wooden jetties, but this one was razor thin, and for a moment, he wondered if he'd imagined it. "And another."

He quickly pulled a notebook from his bag and started to sketch the dock. He would add more details later, but for now he wanted to fix certain places in his memory.

"I'll use the Lumina Lantern," Vikram said, extracting it from the bag. "This will help us compare later."

The lantern was one of Ed's most prized inventions. Using Fitz's magic, Vikram's occult knowledge, and his own skills, they had transformed the basic magic lantern into something more useful. A way of capturing places onto glass and then projecting them later.

Ed nodded. "Get as much as you can, especially when you reach the areas I have just spotted. Did you come here last night?"

"I wanted to, but the *sepoys* were everywhere. Hirash-ji said we should liaise with you first, so they know to expect us."

"Tonight, then." Ed was eager to get the hunt underway, and they could go after they dined with Sharma Sahib.

"I also heard your uncle was aware of the issue." Vikram kept his eyes on the Lumina Lantern. "He is on his way. Did you know?"

Ed sighed, eyes sliding to the group around the coffee table who remained deep in conversation. "Henry, the Resident, mentioned it last night. I'd rather not see him, but I may not have a choice."

It was through his uncle's influence that he was elected a Fellow of the Royal Society, but he was less than impressed with Ed's choice of lifestyle. What had once been a good relationship was becoming tense. Something else to worry about.

Ed decided to focus on their immediate issue for now. The rest could wait.

Seven

Moonfell 2025

It was dawn when Morgana awoke, and through the break in the curtains—she never drew them completely—a clear, blue sky promised a warm Saturday.

Heat was building, and Beltane's energy was rising. Even just lying in bed, she was attuned to the energy of Moonfell and the coming celebration. Today that energy would increase when Merlin, her brother, arrived with her two nieces, Ellen and Marion, feeding their magic into Moonfell's. Two teenagers with endless energy and enthusiasm—and turbulent magic, although hopefully Merlin was helping them control it by now. She could do without tantrums and moodiness and unpredictable spells, especially with the unusual events of the night before. Merlin's wife would not come. Ariana was a lovely woman, but found Moonfell too unnerving to stay in for long, as did many of their extended family, which she understood. It was not for everyone.

Perhaps she would introduce Merlin and her nieces to Monroe. She hoped they would like him, but how could they not?

In fact, she thought, collecting her muddled thoughts, *Monroe should be around today.* Some of their friends from the Storm Moon security team liked to exercise their wolf in their gardens. It gave her an unexpected thrill to see them slinking through the undergrowth and rolling in patches of sunshine. They could share their latest discoveries with them and get another perspective on the situation.

She rolled over to look at the pack of letters next to her bed, itching to read them, but she had things to do first, such as baking a welcome cake for her nieces. Plus, she also wanted to find out more about Fitz's family before she continued reading, hoping it would give her greater context, and that would mean either reading the journals they had discovered or visiting their library. Or possibly both. As for the intriguing magical lantern...well, that needed more investigation, too. But they couldn't forget their Beltane plans, either.

Filled with enthusiasm for the coming day, she dressed quickly, aided and abetted by Abbot and Costello, her cats who were skulking around the room waiting for breakfast. They had been indignant when she had moved rooms, but like all cats had quickly adjusted when they found that their food would be served in her new, small kitchen. Patting their silky heads, she made coffee and stepped onto the narrow stone balcony that ran alongside her rooms.

Morgana could see the pond from here, the smooth waters unblemished although the aquatic plants lining the edge rustled with wildlife, but it seemed to her that the images they had projected onto it the previous night lingered. The colonial mansion that she presumed was the Rajgarh Residency, and the stunning gardens of a Mughal palace that must have been in the area. They haunted her. *What had happened there that they could resonate so deeply? That they should warrant such an elaborate way of preserving memories?*

Feeling spellbound, she headed downstairs, leaving the letters by her bed for later. But heading downstairs meant passing the India room, and without even intending to, Morgana found herself pausing on the threshold, and it was then that she heard the silver bells again. She turned quickly, sure she had seen a flicker of movement in her peripheral vision. The tinkling sound, gentle and teasing, receded down the corridor, and she scented patchouli. *Intriguing.*

Ignoring her need for breakfast, she headed to the still room next to the kitchen on the ground floor, searching the many jars of dried herbs until she spotted the one she wanted. *Mugwort. Perhaps yarrow, too.* She wasn't as adept at seeing the unseen as Odette, but perhaps later that morning she could try a tisane. Plus, it was Beltane, and as at Samhain, the veils were thinning, which might help her, too. She could try in the summerhouse, or on the banks of the pond with another projected image over the water.

The tinkle of bells sounded close by again, and returning to the kitchen, she saw the pages of a journal flicker where it lay open on the table. It was Edmund Swift's, full of technical drawings of wonderful instruments and jotted notes. Edmund was as much a part of this as Fitz. *Was he a family member, too?* Morgana was not prone to flights of fancy. She was pragmatic, calm, and serious, and yet this was already getting under her skin. Triggered, she realised, by the events only a couple of weeks earlier when she had seen the spirits of long dead wolf-shifters that had saddened her so much, the feeling had lingered for days. Thank the Gods her brother and nieces were arriving later. She needed a distraction.

Resolving to remain logical, she made toast and another pot of coffee, and settled in to investigate Edmund and Fitz's journals, noting that as well as technical drawings and scribbled notes, there were sketches of places and faces, as well as some distinctly paranormal beings. Scowling faces with long, sharp teeth, or overly large eyes, scales, clawed fingers, rearing snakes, and what seemed to be spirits. Names were jotted next to them. *Vitala in Udaipur. Naga in Dehradun. Kinnara in Amritsar. Apsara in Dudwah. Tiger-shifter in Jaipur.*

Morgana laughed with delight. *Wow. Some of the creatures and where they hunted them.* Another couple of images immediately caught her eye. Portraits of Vikram and Fitz. Both caught laughing, and although the drawings were in pencil, she could see the flash of sunlight in Vikram's hair. He was handsome and dark-haired, with large, expressive eyes, and Fitz, broad-shouldered and stocky, was standing in front of a makeshift camp. *Their ancestor.* Could she discern a likeness? Upon closer inspection, he actually reminded her of Como.

There were sketches of others whose names she didn't recognise, too, and then one who was stern of eye, with thick jowls and a mutton chop beard. *Uncle B. 1792 Rajgarh.*

Edmund's Uncle Benjamin, surely? Excited at the mention of the date, she flicked through the pages surrounding it, finding sketches of a busy dock from various angles, and Indian women washing clothes on a series of stepped embankments by a river, with the scribbled name wedged in a corner. *The Ghats, Rajgarh.*

Morgana placed her coffee cup down with a clatter. This was the same time that Fitz sent letters to Meli. *But who was Edmund, other than Fitz's friend? How could she even start to trace him?* With a flurry of excitement, she riffled through other journals, by now recognising Ed's writing and sketches. It was next to one of his detailed drawings of a type of scope that she saw a comment. *Presented to the Royal Society 1788. Mixed Reception. Too soon for the Lumina.*

The Royal Society. She knew that name. It was a prestigious group of scientists that was still active today. If Ed had been a member, it meant he had money and was well respected. That would be the starting point to discovering more about him. Vikram would be another matter entirely. Grabbing a notepad from the drawer, she jotted down names and years, and then the names mentioned in Fitz's letter that were exasperatingly vague. *Meli, Arti, Peri and Dita.*

Suddenly decisive, Morgana stood up. *Time to visit the library.*

Horty felt like Mary Poppins as she stood in the middle of the library, casting spells to look for Fitzroy Westerly.

She hummed the tune of "Bibbidi-Bobbodi-Boo," magic fizzing at her fingertips. Except, that song wasn't from Mary Poppins. She paused as finding spells whizzed around like fireflies, her slipper-clad foot tapping the wooden floor. *Cinderella. That was it. The fairy godmother.*

She had barely slept a wink all night because she had been so excited, sure it was a mix of their discovery and Beltane magic. The veils were thinning, and the past was stepping closer. *Except,* she noted, her excitement ebbing as her dancing fireflies whirled aimlessly, *there weren't any books that mentioned Fitzroy Westerly.*

If only Birdie would organise the place better.

Deciding she was being too specific, Horty raised her voice commandingly. *"Books of mine, books divine, full of knowledge spread through time, unlock your past, reveal to me, the books containing Westerlys."* That did the trick. Her fizzing balls of golden light bounced over the relevant books, and she summoned them using air. *"Out, out, to the table, a neat pile as much as able."*

Books shot off the shelves like bullets, and she heard a *thud* from above and the splintering of glass. *Bugger.* Birdie would be furious, but she could fix it before she found out. Fixing spells were one of her specialities.

"*Tardus!*" she commanded, using Latin to slow the books' flight. And then, just in case of more disaster, she yelled, "*Finis!*"

The rapid flight of the books slowed to gentle bobbing, and half a dozen books floated to one of the tables in the middle of the room, landing as softly as feathers. A shower of glass descended with one of them, making her wince.

"Horty! Are you breaking things?" Morgana's clipped tone made her jump, and Horty spun around to face the door. Morgana stood with her hands on her hips, eyes stern, but lips twitching with amusement. "What have you done?"

"Shush! Come in and shut the door. I've had a small accident."

Morgana's gaze drifted upward to the mezzanine level where some of their precious, more expensive books were stored. "Good grief! If you've damaged …"

"It's just glass."

"It's what crashed through it that worries me." She crossed the room quickly to check on the books on the table. "You were doing your Mary Poppins impression again, weren't you?"

"I do not do Mary Poppins!"

Morgana smirked. "Birdie told us how you used to whirl things round as a child and try to turn books into birds."

Horty groaned, wishing some things had remained a secret. "At least I didn't dance on the chimney pots. Although, I wish I had. It always looked like so much fun in the film, and we have so many!" She'd keep quiet about wanting to be Cinderella's godmother.

"Did you try with Anton and Jemima? The birds, I mean?"

"Once. A book exploded into feathers, and we never repaired it. *Famous Five Get Into Trouble.*"

"How very appropriate. It sounds like fun."

Horty sniggered. "It was. I take it you couldn't sleep after last night's shenanigans?"

"I slept very well, but I never sleep in. Not in the spring and summer. The light wakes me. That and Abbot jumping on my chest. But I know what you mean. It's all very intriguing." Morgana reached for one of the books on the table. "Do these belong to Fitz?"

"The Westerlys in general. I haven't even opened them yet." There were a variety of leather and linen-bound books on the table; others had covers of stiff card that looked distinctly homemade, some with gold lettering, some with painted designs. Cocking her head, Horty listened for any noise, but the library had fallen silent. "I don't think there are any more, but I ended the spell after the glass incident."

"You check the books," Morgana said, heading to the spiral staircase that led to the mezzanine. "I'll check up there. I've found a link for Ed, by the way."

"Have you? How?"

"He referred to the Royal Society in his journals." Morgana's voice faded as she ascended the stairs. "I'm going to investigate. Somehow."

"Good idea." Horty studied the books, and choosing an intriguingly hand-painted one, carefully opened it and gasped when she saw that it was full of tarot card images. A very ornate script inside the front cover said, *A Guide to the Tarot by Melusine Westerly*. "I have a name!" she yelled upstairs. "Melusine. It's a very early guide to the tarot."

Morgana hung her head over the banister, hair falling around her face. "That explains the broken glass, then. It's come from the tarot collection. We're very bloody lucky they didn't come sailing out, too. But, ooh! Meli?"

Horty nodded. "Melusine is Meli. Yes, that makes sense. Well, it does unless anything better presents itself." Melusine was no great artist, but nevertheless, the book was illustrated well enough, and she had written descriptions of the cards. "Actually, I don't think these are tarot. They're simpler. Oracles, perhaps. No..." She shook her head, perplexed as she carefully turned the pages, sitting on a chair so she wasn't bending over so acutely. The tarot would have been in its earliest incarnation as divination cards then. They would have been more simplistic.

Leaving the book aside for further examination later, she tried a thicker, leatherbound volume and found the name Peregrine Westerly inside. *Peri.*

This was it. They were actually getting somewhere.

Eight

Rajgarh 1792

Rajgarh 1792

Fitz was immensely relieved to be dining with Harishchandra Sharma that evening, rather than in the Residence.

Spending hours with Anthony that day being endlessly questioned as they investigated the docks had been exhausting. They had tried to shake him off, but he was dogged, as if he thought they were about to unveil the monster within their midst and terrify everyone. At one point, the Harbour Master had tagged along, and that was even worse. In the end, Fitz put his foot down and sent them away.

It didn't help that Vikram was far more educated and well connected than Anthony had presumed, which seemed to annoy the Assistant Resident immensely. Plus, Ed was brooding about his uncle, who was becoming more and more bullish about Ed's supernatural hunting activities.

Fitz and Ed were childhood friends who met at the local grammar school and together went to Oxford. Their families had similar levels of wealth, although for very different reasons. Moonfell money came from a mixture of witchcraft offered to private clients and their actual business as respected apothecaries. Plus, some members of Fitz's family were artists of varying disciplines, whose work was highly sought after. Ed's family were merchants and bankers. Following Ed's success at Oxford University, when it was clear that Ed had an appetite and skill for science, his uncle had introduced him to the Royal Society, where Ed had quickly become a well-respected member. While Ed and Fitz had studied at Oxford together, Fitz favoured literature over science, and had a keen interest in the occult and botany, not unusual for his family. Ed knew all about Fitz's magic and his family's skills, and the more he had learned, the further he had been drawn into the occult. He had discovered that with his design skills and Fitz's magic, they could make clever instruments that were adept at uncovering the paranormal for those who weren't witches. It was an exciting pastime that had enhanced their travels and led to their current circumstances.

However, Ed found he had to become choosier about what he shared with the Royal Society. They weren't all open-minded, and Ed's uncle's connections made it even harder. Benjamin Swift had invested in the East India Company, and Ed's family were moneyed and influential, so Ed trooping around India investigating the paranormal was considered distinctly ungentlemanly.

But not here in Vikram's friend's *haveli*. It was airy, cool, and beautifully decorated with Indian motifs that soothed Fitz's soul. Carved wooden screens called *jharokhas* covered the windows and deep divans offered comfortable seating. Before they left the Residency, Alicia had tried to question him about their investigation, but Fitz had made his excuses, not wanting to involve her in the dangerous hunt. Besides, they had only vague plans as yet, and wanted to flesh them out that evening.

Vikram obviously knew Harishchandra's house well, and after a servant had let them in, Vikram led them through a series of rooms to a spacious inner courtyard with a magnificent pavilion situated in the centre of a shallow pool that was surrounded by lemon trees.

"We are eating out here for privacy as well as comfort," he explained as they sat down on low divans arranged around a table inlaid with silver. He poured some rose sherbet out for them all to cool off with. "As you can see, there is nowhere for prying ears to hide."

"Sharma Sahib will join us, though?" Fitz asked, admiring the garden as he settled in his seat.

"Of course. He is very keen to assist us."

"Any objection," Ed asked, pulling a notebook from his bag that he always carried with him, "if I sketch?"

Vik smiled. "I'd be surprised if you didn't. Harish-ji will be honoured."

Ed laughed. "Not when he sees my infantile attempts."

"They are far from that, as you well know," Fitz said.

"Ah! Here he comes now." Vik nodded to a doorway in the far wall that exited another area of the house. "He has been in the *zenana* visiting his wife and the other women of the household."

"Are they overlooking us?" Fitz asked, glancing up at the screened windows. Like all Indian households, the women had their own private quarters here.

"No, they overlook another courtyard beyond that building that is just for the women. Harish has two daughters, and his mother lives here, too. No doubt, though, they would love to see you." He raised his drink, amused.

"Does he have sons?" Fitz asked, wondering if they would join them.

"Three, but the youngest is travelling on business, and the elder two remain at the office for now."

Harishchandra joined them, wearing more informal clothes than he had earlier that day. Just a tunic and *dhoti* now, the baggy loose trousers, much as Vikram wore. Fitz wished he was wearing the same. He had adopted such clothes often, depending on where they were travelling. After greeting them warmly, Harishchandra indicated the puris and chutneys. "Please, eat what you need. These simple snacks are just until the main meal arrives." He beamed. "I thought we should ease into the evening."

For the next few minutes, they chatted about nothing of importance as they all relaxed, until Harish leaned forward, eyes bright as his jovial demeanour faded. "Now, what did you find out today when you searched the harbour?"

"Evidence of the thinning of the boundaries between worlds," Fitz said, cautious not to overstate their success. "But this is just the first stage. I'm sure Vikram has told you how we work?"

Harish nodded. "He has, all of it. I'm impressed with your instruments, and what you have achieved. Not just today, of course. Vikram keeps me well informed of your work." He shot him a look of annoyance. "Not as often as I would like, however."

Vikram laughed. "I am far too busy to be sending constant updates."

"I know, but I confess that I worry. It's a dangerous business. Has Vikram told you of my theory of these attacks?"

"That you believe someone is behind it all?" Fitz said. "Yes, but that is an unexpected suggestion. Creatures attack randomly, and often favour certain areas over others. We have experienced this many times." He looked to his team for support.

Harish shook his head. "Not here, I fear. I think someone is directing it, because it is too convenient just to target the port. Yes, it has been seen in the streets around it, but I think that is for show. It is an attack on the Company, and we in Rajgarh cannot afford that to happen. They will strengthen the garrison and impose sanctions." He stared at Fitz and Ed. "Has there been suggestion that the Resident would take such action?"

"No, not to us," Fitz said, shaking his head vigorously. "If they did suggest it, I would argue against it. That is even more reason for us to work quickly. But say you are right, surely an Indian must be behind it purely for the fact that we are facing an Indian supernatural threat. Though considering your concerns of sanctions that is illogical, unless they aim to drive the English away."

"Everyone knows that will never happen," Vikram said.

Harish nodded in agreement. "Exactly, which is why I think it is an Englishman keen to exert more control by using such a threat."

"You mean to make it look like an Indian is behind it?" Fitz groaned. "What a nightmare."

This was a big, hot, political mess, just the type of incident that Fitz and his team were keen to avoid. Now they were in the thick of it.

"Just think about it," Harish said. "It is worth considering." His gaze fell on Ed's large leather bag. "I wish I had been able to study your instruments earlier today."

"You are welcome to see them," Ed said, lifting his head from his sketch. "I have brought some with us, but while they guide us where to look, we need to search all of the docks tonight, when it's quiet, to see if we can find evidence of how the breach between worlds has occurred."

"The magic I felt," Fitz added, uncertain of how to describe it, "was unusual. Obviously, magic is different all over the world, and witches are different, too. For example, my magic is grounded in the elements, but I am more attuned to the spirit and earth than the other elements. After years spent here, though, I am used to the Indian supernatural world...but even so, it was odd." *Perhaps that fact supported Harish's suggestion.*

Ed put his notebook down and extracted the Lumina Projector from his bag to show Harish, leaving Fitz to consider his earlier impressions. He had listened to the descriptions of the attacks, and the repeated fears of what they would do to trade—had done, in fact—but earlier that day he had insisted on speaking to the Customs Officer who saw the first attack. Even with Vikram interpreting, the description was unclear. Plus, there was no breach of worlds in the far area of the dock where the first attack had happened. He couldn't detect even the slightest ripple of the Otherworld, and Ed had been unable to see anything using the Temperometer. However, when Fitz had reached the end of the jetty, the place of the second attack, he felt a shift, as if a portal had opened and hadn't been closed properly. It was detected by a subtle change of pressure and the tingle of something Otherworldly. He had closed portals before, but something about this puzzled him. The other, smaller attacks were spread across the dock area. And of course, there was the matter of the rift by the *ghats*, and so far, there were no reports of an attack there.

"Vik," he said suddenly, looking over at his friend, "most of the creatures we've banished or killed had not come through a portal at all. They skulk in the shadows of the natural world where they hide in plain sight. Could this suggestion of a portal be subterfuge, to send us astray?"

Vikram shrugged, eyes narrowed. "Anything is possible. I have questioned the servants here hoping they would have heard something, but they are afraid, and do not even wish to discuss it for fear they will curse the house. Even here, in the wealthy quarters of Rajgarh."

Harish lived a short distance from the river and the port, the *haveli* set close to the vibrant marketplace. "There have been no sightings or attacks here, though, correct?"

"None," Harish agreed, breaking off his conversation with Ed. "But perhaps you should use your instruments in this area, too. Even if someone is behind it, a monster must be summoned from somewhere. At first, I thought it might have come in a shipment somehow, either on the river, or from the interior..."

Ed blinked in shock. "I hadn't considered that! What a good idea. But for an Englishman to be behind it, they would have to have both excellent knowledge of India and skill in the occult. Surely, that must limit our suspects."

They all looked to Harish, knowing he would know everyone in the area. However, he spread his hands wide. "I only know the public faces they present." He passed his hand over his face. "What is beneath could be very different. You are in the Residency now, so you are in the perfect place to investigate. The Resident will have excellent connections in the community. As for the English staff at the docks, there are many. I certainly do not know them all. Could one be a secret summoner of the supernatural?" He shrugged. "Perhaps."

"We haven't even met everyone in the Residency yet," Fitz informed him. "We haven't seen Captain Townsend or the doctor, and we certainly haven't encountered all of the Indian staff, and there will be lots of those."

"I suggest that you find an ally among them and question that person," Vik suggested.

"I think there are more English officials in the grounds, too," Harish said. "There are many buildings on the site."

Fitz frowned at Ed. "I don't recall Anthony mentioning any, but we should check. I am certainly no expert on Residency staff. As for other English merchants, are there any?"

"Certainly, but they are all part of the East India Company."

Fitz sighed. "I think we should suggest a large dinner so that we can meet everyone. There are too many moving parts to this that I do not like. I'll feel better once we have seen the port tonight. We'll meet the captain, too. He has been advised to expect us. Not you, though, I'm afraid, Sharma Sahib," he said, addressing him respectfully.

Harish waved it off, unoffended. "I have other things to look into." He picked up a small silver bell and rang it several times. "Now, we need to eat, for tonight we shall hunt."

Nine

Moonfell 2025

At just after nine in the morning, Birdie was on her way to the Waning Moon Gate, keen to check the effects of the events of the night before, when she heard vehicles on the drive.

Rounding the side of the house, she spotted Maverick's car. The wolf-shifters had arrived, no doubt drawn by the blue skies and warm temperatures, and pleased they were taking the opportunity to run in the garden, she hurried to meet them. She arrived just as Maverick, Arlo, and Monroe exited the car. Maverick was the pack's alpha, and Arlo the pack second. Monroe was dating Morgana.

"Birdie!" Maverick waved as he spotted her. "I didn't phone, so I hope you don't mind. We needed to unleash our wolves." He swept his dark blond hair back, revealing his clean-shaven, square jaw, and a broad smile.

"Of course I don't mind. It's an open invitation. We've had some excitement here, actually. You might even be able to help."

Monroe, broad-shouldered with skin as dark as a ripe Victoria plum, frowned, no doubt worried about Morgana. "Nothing bad, I hope?"

"No, far from it. It's extremely intriguing. Are you going to see Morgana?"

"After my run, if she's free."

"She'll be free for you," Birdie said, smiling. "Why don't you follow me round to the garden, and I can tell you all about it."

They all bristled with energy and vitality, and she couldn't help but be invigorated by their presence. All of the shifters were fit and muscular, self-assured and confident, and as they fell into step around her, they displayed their patience, too. They all towered over her, but they matched their long strides to hers, peppering her with questions.

"No weird bloody creatures, I hope?" Arlo asked, scowling.

"Not yet." She grinned at him. "My sister is here for Beltane, by the way, and we have more family arriving later—just so you know. Horty is a force of nature. And, before I forget, you are invited to our Beltane celebrations tomorrow night—all of the security team, that is—if you want to come, of course. No offense if not."

"I'm not turning down a party," Monroe said, "especially here! I doubt anyone will."

She patted his muscular arm. "You're very flattering."

"Hunter told us of a strange experience he had once at Beltane," Maverick said. "It scared the crap out of him, apparently. Not planning on that here, are you?"

She blinked in surprise. "Hunter? Scared?"

"Unexpected, isn't it, from the cocky Cumbrian? He said strange things were afoot that night. Lots of wild magic."

"Well," she said, hurrying them to the Waning Moon Gate as they eyed her with curiosity, "we are certainly not planning on *that*, but we had our own unusual experience last night. A flashback to the past. I suppose we have you to thank for it, actually."

"Us?" Arlo asked in surprise.

"Well, it's because of your pack and the missing shifters that we went looking for Wayfinders and delved into the India room. It gripped us, and we've found more interesting things."

The huge, bronze gate was close now, and the metals glimmered in the sun. Narrowing her eyes, she was sure she could see a magical aura still on them. She ran through what they'd found, and the images they'd projected onto the pond, and for a moment, the shifters stood in silence, gazing through the moon gate to the water as if they might see them again. Meanwhile, Birdie extended her hand, hovering her fingers over the smooth, curved metal bands, trying to feel magic.

"Well?" Maverick asked. "Can you feel a change?"

"It feels charged," she admitted. "As if it captured magical energy."

Monroe cocked his head. "I thought they had magical energy anyway."

"Not exactly. It's hard to explain." Birdie considered how best to describe the strange conundrum of the moon gates. "As you know, they're aligned to the four main compass points and have moon phases and other elemental magic linked to them, but we still don't know how they came to be built, or who by. We do know they're older than the house and linked to the bees. However, they do not feel independently magical, if that makes sense. They are magical because of what we imbue them with."

"You think," Arlo said, as he started to strip his clothing, ready to shift. "After all, Odette sees events through them, so that must mean they have some type of magic. Anything to be worried about in the garden?" He obviously couldn't wait to shift to his wolf.

"No. Nothing I can feel, anyway. Nothing significant." She paused, opening herself to the large garden that was thick with Moonfell magic. "All is as it should be. Go, have fun. We'll chat later."

"Thanks, looking forward to it. You know," Arlo lifted his nose and inhaled, "I think it's Beltane energy. I just *have to* shift."

In seconds, he loped off in his wolf and Monroe quickly followed, but Maverick stood bare-chested, looking at her with concern. "You're worried."

"Well, yes, but no. Oh, I don't know…" Birdie trailed off, as always perplexed by the moon gates and annoyed she hadn't fathomed out anything significant about them. She leaned against the cool bronze ribbons again, feeling the flutter of energy like a thready pulse. "For as long as we have been at Moonfell, these have always been here. Constant structures that weather everything. It's like they're rooted in the land, just like the orchard. I sometimes feel as if they connect underground. The spells we cast certainly connect them in other ways."

Maverick stepped inside the gate, face cast in shadow, and reached overhead to touch the curves. "I often see if my wolf feels any difference with them, but I never can. I can't now, either. The metal lit up, you say?"

"Yes, it glowed, as if with starlight, and the projected images, which were most definitely magical, ended up on the water, despite our salt circle. This gate seemed to enhance the effects of the slides. We chose it, as I mentioned, because of Odette's painting."

He nodded. "Which was framed by this gate."

"Exactly. She painted what we think was the Rajgarh Residency garden, and we believe some of the slides are images of it, too. She recognised portions of it, although I am yet to see her painting. I haven't had time." She sighed, head aching at all the threads they had yet to weave together. *The letters, the journals, and the instruments, certainly.* "Morgana is intent on finding out more about the moon gates, and it is probably a good idea, but part of me likes the enigma of them."

"I would imagine that whatever you find will only add to their enigma."

"True." Birdie sighed, feeling the weight of her years. "What I'm more interested in right now, though, are the magical slides. They might just be to share or record events, much like we use photos now, but part of me thinks there's a message in them. It will all unfold eventually, I'm sure. Please don't hang back on my account. Head out for the run."

Maverick studied her a moment longer. "All right, but we'll talk later. I'd like to meet Horty."

"Not half as much as she'd like to meet you!"

Maverick laughed, shifted, and vanished into the undergrowth. In the silence that followed, she felt the gate pulsing gently, and heard the tinkling of silver bells. She spun around, but spotted nothing. It was then she remembered that Odette had mentioned that the extra metals hadn't been in her painting, and she reached out to touch the slender silver and copper bands that fitted among the bronze ribbons so cleverly. *Was there a hint of rose gold, too?* Her fingers traced their contours, and she ran through their elemental correspondences.

Silver was easy. It was strongly associated with the moon, intuition, and psychic abilities, and was also associated with feminine energy. Copper was also associated with feminine energy, but healing too, as well as being linked to Venus. Bronze made up the majority of the gate, and that was distinctly masculine energy and associated with strength and durability. It was connected, on occasions, to the sun and Mars, and was also used for protection. *Were copper and silver added to balance its energies? But if so, when? And why?*

She huffed with annoyance. They could have been added years before the events in India, or years after. Actually, it must be after, or

Odette would have painted them—which meant it was surely irrelevant to this issue. Getting crankier by the minute, Birdie huffed again and decided to find the rest of the family.

Odette discovered Morgana, Horty, and Birdie in the midst of a sea of paperwork in the library, all looking excited, exasperated, or annoyed at turns. The scent of sandalwood hung in the air, and the cluster of candles invited confidences and secrets.

Birdie looked up, a flash of excitement in her eyes. "Any more insights?"

"I have painted a lovely garden full of intrigue." She sat at the table, still feeling half a world away. "*Lots* of intrigue. If the painting is about Fitz, and I'm sure it is, then this is no ordinary hunt."

"Really?"

"I sense layers of subterfuge and lurking danger. The garden may be lovely, but darkness hangs over it."

Morgana had been making notes, but now she looked across at her. "Can you identify the layers? I mean, where the danger is from? Other people, perhaps?"

"Not yet. I thought I would sit beneath the gate."

"I was considering that, too, but I think I'm better off leaving that to you. I'm going to go to the Royal Society to look for Edmund Swift. I've made an appointment for Monday. It's closed tomorrow, and you have to book ahead. Today I'm going to gather as much information about him as possible. We've also found out more this morning." She updated Odette with their latest discoveries. "We now know that Meli is Melusine, Peri is Peregrine, and Arti is Artemisia."

Odette smiled. "What interesting names."

"All family members," Horty added, a flush to her cheeks. "And all Westerlys. The fourth, Dita, is short for Perdita, Peri's wife."

Odette stored the information away, wondering if it helped her with her painting. "And Fitz fits in where?"

"Second oldest son. Peregrine is his older brother and High Priest at that time, and we think Meli is a half-sister. But," Horty warned, "we don't know details yet. The library revealed Peregrine's grimoire, and he listed his siblings and his wife in the front, as usual. Artemesia, Fitz's other slightly younger sister, is frustratingly vague. Meli is definitely the youngest of the four."

Odette nodded, pulling one of the journals towards her. "Well, you—*we*—have only just started investigating. Shouldn't we be preparing for Beltane, though? Isn't Merlin coming today?"

Morgana groaned. "Bollocks! I was going to bake a cake." She checked her watch. "It's nearly lunchtime, too. I am so sidetracked with these letters. It's like they have bewitched me. I really wanted to read more of them, too."

"Merlin will forgive you if there's no cake," Odette said, trying to calm Morgana down. "I'm sure he'll be as interested in this as you are." Her cousin Merlin's magical strengths were with water, so considering their current pond issue, he could be very helpful. "As for the girls, I'm sure the shifters and the promise of Beltane will entertain them. Let's rope them into Beltane prep! They can build the fire and make the decorations." She tried to be practical, desperate to clear her head of the fog from India in 1792. "They can gather hawthorn and collect the sacred woods for the fire. It will be perfect training for them, actually."

"Good thinking," Birdie said, nodding, her attention still on the paperwork on the table. "It will keep them out of trouble, too. I can supervise. By the way, Maverick, Monroe, and Arlo are here."

Refusing to rise at the mention of Arlo, because she knew her family was sure there was a frisson of *something* between them that Odette had no intention of thinking about, Odette said, "I know. I saw them from the window. Are you catching up with Monroe later, Morgana?"

Morgana nodded. "I'm going to see if he wants to visit the Royal Society with me."

"What exactly are you hoping to find there?" Odette asked, idly examining the tarot card illustrations in Melusine's book.

"How long Ed was a member. What discoveries might be attributed to him. Where he went. Known associates. Whatever I can. And about his uncle, Benjamin, who sort of sounds like a big deal as well as a hindrance."

"Oh!" Odette sat up suddenly as an idea struck her. "The Royal Society is for scientific exploration and discovery, right?"

"Many things. Lots of very famous scientists were members. Newton, Darwin, Stephen Hawking..."

"Is that something Harlan and Olivia may know about? Or is it worth asking them about Ed's occult instruments? They may be able to give us some insight as to whether there are any more on the market. Black or otherwise. Antique or modern."

Morgana nodded. "I'm not sure they'd know much about the society, but asking about the instruments is a good idea. I'll call Olivia. I wanted to check on her pregnancy, anyway. And now, I must make cake."

"How can I help?" Odette said, trying to root herself in the here and now before she left. "I feel we need a list of things to tackle. My head feels all over the place."

"Well," Birdie said, thoughtfully, "we really need to understand the family's structure at the time. Just to give it context. I'm curious about

Melusine, but maybe we start with Peregrine seeing as he was the High Priest of Moonfell.”

Odette stood, suddenly sure where she should go next. “Then I’m heading to the attic to find his portrait. Plus, what about Meli’s tarot deck?” She tapped the journal. “We have several packs. Have we found one that looks like her illustrations?”

Morgana gave Horty a shifty glance. “We haven’t checked, actually. We were sidetracked.”

Odette was sure there was a story there, but she ignored it for now. “In that case, I will also find the deck and take it and her tarot book to the attic with me. I might get a feel for Meli through them.”

Ten

Rajgarh 1792

E d shook hands with the gruff Captain Jonathon Townsend, feeling his disapproval and suspicion as he assessed him from his head to his toes. He eyed Fitz and Vikram with equal disdain, lips settling into a thin line.

"You're here to do what exactly?" Townsend was tall and imposing with a fleshy, middle-aged face.

"Survey the area." Ed hefted his heavy bag full of equipment. "We have instruments we need to use, but you can continue to guard the port. We won't interfere. As you know, the Resident has requested that we do this."

"It's most irregular," he complained.

Fitz was far too impatient to be polite. "So is a supernatural creature killing innocent men in this port. Have you seen anything unusual tonight, or last night during your patrols?"

"I think you would know, don't you?" Townsend smiled superciliously. "I would have roused the Resident."

Fitz's fingers were twitching, and Ed intervened before Fitz could hex him. "Not just the creature, but any suspicious activity, such as someone trying to access the port?"

"I am aware what entails suspicious behaviour. No, we saw no one approach, either by land or water."

Ed inwardly sighed. *It was going to be like that, then*. They had arrived at the docks only a few minutes earlier after a pleasant evening with Harishchandra. They had returned to the Residency only to change their clothes into something more suitable for hunting, and had succeeded in slipping in and out without seeing any of the English staff or Alicia. They had timed their arrival to be late, very keen to avoid Anthony, too. It was close to midnight now, and the docks were quiet, lit only with the dimmest of lanterns. Even from where they stood just inside the gates, Ed felt that the air was charged with expectation.

"That's good, then," Ed said, feeling like it was anything but. "If we need you, we'll shout."

Townsend drew himself even more upright than he already was. "I have been instructed to accompany you."

"There's no need," Fitz said smoothly, and Ed, used to his magic, felt the flash of glamour that rolled off him. "You are quite happy to leave us to investigate alone." Townsend blinked as confusion suddenly marred his features. Fitz continued, "You trust us to do our job very well, without needing any supervision. We will call you if we find anything significant."

Townsend nodded, face slack. "Yes, absolutely. You carry on."

"Excellent." Fitz turned his back and proceeded confidently into the docks. "We may be some time."

Ed and Vikram hurried after him, and Ed felt Townsend's stare between his shoulder blades, glad once they turned the corner out of sight.

"I hadn't expected him to be so aggressive," Vikram said, stealthy as always as he progressed to the jetty that had the rift at the end of it.

"He has a point to prove, perhaps," Fitz suggested. "Maybe he resents the fact that Henry didn't trust him to solve the problem."

"Or maybe," Ed said, "we are ruining his party. Right now, I suspect everyone."

Fitz shook his head. "I don't think Townsend has anything to do with this. He doesn't have the slightest whiff of magic about him. Plus, the *sepoys* were watching, and no doubt he has a reputation to uphold."

The steady lap of water against the numerous jetties was the only noise other than their voices to disturb the silence. The *sepoys* were spread around the docks, both outside and inside the perimeter, and Ed had a rough idea where they were stationed—but like his team, they kept to the shadows.

Ed hurriedly set up the Temperometer again, leaving Fitz using his magic to detect any sign of supernatural threat. Meanwhile, Vikram readied his weapons. Fitz had imbued magic into daggers and a short, curved sword called a *tulwar*, as Vikram was well trained in combat. He was quick on his feet, and also fought using a mixture of wrestling techniques. In addition, he had brought along a spear he wielded with deadly accuracy. Its tip was clad in spelled metals, and the wood inscribed with magical symbols, similar in design to the staffs that Fitz and Ed carried.

Ed was not as comfortable using weapons, but had no choice considering their line of work, and also carried a dagger. Fitz used his staff to enhance his magic, but for Ed it offered protection against attack, and also contained a few basic spells to counter any supernatural threats. Fitz had taught him a few simple incantations in case of emergency, but generally all magic was left to Fitz.

Once again, the Temperometer picked up the disturbance they had seen earlier that day at the end of the jetty. At night, its strange, spectral light was even more apparent as a flickering bluish-white glimmer that appeared like the aftermath of a lightning strike. They were surrounded by sailing vessels of all sizes, and many were anchored mid-river, but no one was aboard the landbound vessels, and they were all sealed up tight. When he lifted his head, Fitz was pacing nearby, hands raised and lips moving silently as he worked magic. Vikram, meanwhile, was undertaking a cursory search of the closest vessels.

"Fitz, I can see it clearly now," Ed called over to him. "It looks like a rift filled with lightning."

"I feel it," he called over his shoulder. "It doesn't feel Otherworldly, and yet the energy it contains is unmistakable."

An idea took shape. "Could it be a rift in this world?"

Vikram jumped down next to him, jolting the wooden boards beneath them. "A way for the creature to step from one place to another unseen?"

"Perhaps." Seized by another idea, Ed turned his scope to the other area he had identified earlier, and saw the same shimmering, lightning-like energy. "The other rift is the same colour." He fell silent, scanning the scope across the docks, but too many objects were in his way to see properly. "I need to get higher. The office, perhaps."

"Or up there," Vikram said, pointing to a large vessel a couple of docks down. "The deck is high. You should get a good view."

Within a few minutes, Ed had relocated and set up his scope again, and this time had a much better view of the area. But what he saw was unnerving. Unusual symbols had been painted on some of the buildings, invisible to the naked eye, but only too obvious using the scope at night. "Vik." He elbowed his colleague who had accompanied him. "Look. Sigils of some kind." While Vik saw them for himself, Ed searched for Fitz and found him at the end of the jetty.

"By the Gods!" Vikram murmured next to him. "Yantras, but they have been subverted. Mixed with other symbols."

Ed had come across yantras before. They were geometric designs, associated with energies and deities, depending how they were used. "I agree, perhaps *mandalas*?"

"Yes, I would say so." Vik lowered the scope. "Magical energy. It must be. But they are high on the building, too. They must have used ladders to daub them."

"Unless they cast them using magic, which they could do from the ground. They are precise, and magic would allow for that, although Fitz may be able to suggest other options. I would think that would take time to do manually."

Vik lifted the scope again, puzzling over the yantras. "These do suggest there is a human behind this. A creature would not leave a yantra."

"Which confirms our suspicions. Some progress, at least."

But before Ed could even begin to puzzle it out, Fitz shouted, drawing their attention to the jetty again. A flash of light bloomed around him, temporarily hiding him from view, and there was an enormous splash.

Vik yelled, "Stay here and keep watch! I'll go!"

***

Fitz flailed in the water, the icy coldness wrapping around his limbs. He kicked upwards, but his boots and clothes were heavy.

He cast a spell, using elemental water to propel him to the surface with so much force that the plume of water threw him onto the jetty where he landed with a thud, further knocking the wind from him. He inhaled, greedy for air, water streaming over his face and into his eyes, and when he finally focussed, he wished he'd remained submerged.

A strange, claw-footed creature was advancing towards him, limbs—far more than four—outstretched as it tried to reach Fitz. Fitz prided himself on his composure, but panic-stricken, he scrambled backwards, glad the water had thrown him so far down the jetty. The creature had murderous intent, and desperate to save himself, he sent out a blast of pure energy, designed to knock the creature backwards.

Unfortunately, it seemed to absorb it instead.

It picked up its pace, its pounding feet shaking the jetty so violently Fitz thought it might crack, or even throw him into the water again. He changed tack, blasting instead with jets of water that he sucked up around him. He thrust the water forward in an enormous wave, momentarily halting it.

Fitz scrambled to his feet, running through spells as he looked around for his staff, but Vikram ran past him on silent feet, sword gripped in his hand. The blade swallowed all light, adept at soaking up supernatural energy like a sponge. A spell that Fitz was immensely pleased with. Vikram struck the creature with vicious accuracy, almost severing one limb, before he rolled to avoid another, and rose up behind him. The creature, bellowing with pain, was caught between Fitz and Vikram, and separated from the rift at the end of the jetty.

Fitz was about to cast a spell to freeze it in place when a volley of gunfire from behind threw his concentration, and seeing Vik dive for cover, so did he. The creature thrashed wildly, turned, and vanished into a new rift that sealed instantly.

Damn it.

Turning around, still on all fours, Fitz saw half a dozen *sepoys* approaching, Townsend right behind them, red-faced, furious, and also shocked. They halted a short distance away, rifles aimed ahead, and Townsend shouldered through them to glower at Fitz and Vikram.

"What are you doing? How did that happen?"

"If I knew that," Fitz said, rising to his feet, soaking wet and equally furious, "we wouldn't be in this mess. Your soldiers could have killed us!"

"They were saving you from that...that *thing*."

"I can assure you it didn't feel like that." Fitz had felt the whizz of bullets passing him, and he sought out Vikram, relieved to see that he was back on his feet. "Are you all right, Vik?"

"Annoyed, but uninjured." He rolled his shoulders, then grinned, never down for long. "I injured it, and I have its blood on my sword."

"Good. Wrap it up and keep it safe. It will be useful later." Fitz studied the far rift, invisible from here, but he felt the energy still. The other rift that the creature had stepped into had utterly vanished. *Another conundrum.* The creature had summoned its own doorway. *But to where?*

Townsend's anger was clearly building, fuelled by fear, Fitz thought, although he tried to hide it well. "Keep watch," he barked at his men. "Don't hesitate to shoot if it appears again." He glared at Fitz and Vikram. "How did that thing disappear?"

"The same way it arrived. Through a type of doorway it seems to summon at will. But Vikram has injured it, which is excellent news for us. Your bullets might have injured it, too."

"*Might?*"

"Yes. It's supernatural, and therefore not all weapons are effective. Vikram's sword has various enhancements."

"Enhancements or not, I suggest you leave before it returns. The shots will have attracted attention."

Fitz had no intention of leaving now, and he turned to Vikram. "Are you injured?"

"No. I am perfectly able to continue, and so is Ed." He gestured to the deck of a large vessel, and following his pointing finger, saw Ed waving enthusiastically. "Plus, we have discovered more interesting information. We need to continue our search."

"I agree." Fitz turned back to Townsend, intending to use magic to dry his clothes as soon as he could get rid of the man. "We stay. We have a lot more searching to do before this night is out, and I for one will welcome its return."

Townsend stepped closer, fists clenched. "Did you summon it?"

"If I did, it would only be to kill it. But no, I did not. It appeared of its own volition. Step aside, Townsend. I have a job to do. And by the way, I will not inform the Resident that your men nearly killed us, but if it happens again, I might."

"They were aiming high."

"Not high enough. Now, step aside please, or you can answer to Henry for impeding our investigation, too."

Townsend retreated grudgingly, and Fitz knew they had made an enemy, but for what reason, he wasn't sure. Which meant he now had to investigate Townsend, too.

Eleven

Moonfell 2025

Morgana had just placed the extravagant chocolate cake batter in the oven when the reverberating gong of the doorbell vibrated through the house.

She licked the cake batter off her fingers and walked to the door, shocked to find not only Olivia on the doorstep, but also Harlan Beckett and an elderly gentleman. The man had white hair and a trim build in a dapper suit, completely in contrast with Harlan, who was wearing jeans and a leather jacket. Olivia, as usual, looked elegant in heels and a slim-fitting dress that moulded to her growing baby bump.

"Sorry, Morgana," Olivia said, looking apologetic, "but we were all at the office when I took your call, and someone couldn't resist inviting himself along!" She stared pointedly at Harlan, the American occult collector.

"As if Morgana cares," Harlan said breezily.

"*I* didn't!" The white-haired man said, clearly affronted, but looked Morgana over with interest before his attention drifted to the hallway behind her. "Harlan invited me." He stuck his hand out. "JD Mortlake, their boss. A pleasure to meet you. Harlan and Olivia speak most highly of you and your family. Please, call me JD."

"Morgana Cornelius," she answered, shaking his cool, dry hand that had an unexpectedly firm grip. "Call me Morgana."

Harlan rolled his eyes as he followed her inside. "I had to invite him. He sulks if he's left out. Besides, it's the first time he's left his house in weeks, so he needs the exercise."

"I'm not a dog, Harlan."

"But you know exactly what I mean. Plus, he was very interested in what you've found."

"Please don't get too excited," she warned them as she led them to the kitchen. "It might not interest you at all, but we thought that considering your line of work, you might know of other things like this."

"I can't wait to see them," Olivia said, eyes darting around as she walked. "This place looks and smells wonderful as always, Morgana. It always feels so safe to me."

"Excellent structure," JD observed. "I gather it's been in your family for years."

"Five hundred, actually."

"And steeped in magic, too. Wonderful. I remember this place from..." And then he trailed off, fussing with his lapel.

"From when?" Morgana asked, curious.

"Oh, a few years ago. That's all. Nothing really."

Morgana could detect a lie a mile off, but she kept silent for now.

Harlan leapt into the silence. "Maverick is here?"

"Yes, with Arlo and Monroe. They're in the garden. They needed to run." She had no idea what JD knew about Storm Moon, but he clearly knew she was a witch. She was not about to reveal the true nature of Maverick's pack, though.

Olivia waved it off. "JD is fully up to speed with the wolf-shifters, although he hasn't met them yet. At least, I don't think so?"

"No, I have not, so I'm looking forward to that, too." JD grinned, his earlier reticence vanished. "This is proving to be an interesting day."

"Are they helping you?" Olivia asked.

"Not yet, but I'm sure they will if we need them." Morgana entered the kitchen and pointed to Ed's equipment that was still on the table. "That's what we have found so far. Some of the journals are there, while others are in the library with Horty and Birdie. Coffee, tea, anyone?"

She took their requests as they gathered around the equipment, JD placing a pair of reading glasses on his nose. While they were occupied, she studied him. There was something about him that wasn't quite right. His energy felt odd. Old, and powerful, too, but not with magic. Not her type of magic, at least.

"Actually," Morgana added, "I'd love to know if you're acquainted with anyone at the Royal Society. A personal contact could help us a lot."

"I used to, but not anymore," JD murmured.

"I'll check my contacts," Olivia offered, her hand resting protectively on her small baby bump. "I knew someone there, but it was a while ago, and I haven't needed to speak to them since. What do you need to know?"

"Information about Edmund Swift, who it seems was a good friend of our ancestor, Fitzroy Westerly, in 1792. From what little we have gleaned so far, we understand he was a member of the society. We don't understand why *we* have his journals, though, and not his own family.

I mean, he was Fitz's friend, so maybe he wanted him to have them. After all, they travelled extensively together."

"Edmund Swift?" JD spun quickly to face her. "That's who made these?"

"It seems so. His journals are filled with the most amazing drawings, and not just of these tools, but paranormal creatures, too." JD's face had paled, and it was pale already when he arrived. Morgana doubted he saw much sunlight at all. *Was that what she sensed? Was he some kind of paranormal night creature?* "Have you heard of him?"

JD fumbled for a chair and sat down. "Sort of. Slightly. I've heard of his uncle."

"Benjamin Swift?"

"JD?" Harlan glared at him. "If you know something, you better spit it out."

"Well, I wasn't always around, you know, and it was hearsay..."

"Hearsay?" Morgana's witchy instincts were well and truly aroused now. "That's a word generally reserved for contemporary stories."

This time it was Olivia's turn to tut at JD. "I told you that you can trust them, so can we please drop the subterfuge? Besides, Morgana, I mentioned his name the other week. Remember? I sort of dropped it out."

"I guard my privacy..." JD said grumpily.

"And so do Morgana and her coven, and yet you know all about them, and you know that she is looking after me and my baby." She crossed her arms over her chest, eyes narrowing as he fell silent. "Besides, I was trying to help!"

Morgana suddenly felt a complete fool. Olivia had mentioned a man named JD only weeks ago, and she had been so caught up in the issues with the missing shifters, she hadn't picked up on it properly while they discussed the tokens. She'd said something about him being advisor to Queen Elizabeth I. *Her magician.*

Morgana's breath caught and she stepped back as the implications became clear. *That's why his energy felt so different.* "By the Goddess. You're immortal."

Harlan shrugged, uncomfortable. "Sorry, I should have said, but it's his story to tell really."

"Of course." She floundered, her usual composure gone.

"JD," Harlan remonstrated. "We talked about this, and you agreed that if the need arose, then you would explain! You really are annoying sometimes."

Morgana needed to sit down. She placed their drinks on a tray with a plate of shortbread biscuits that were so buttery they would loosen anyone's tongue, and sat at the table. JD was clearly a man who liked his ego to be stroked. "JD, far from being one to pry, as I also value my privacy, the truth is out. I can vouch for my entire family that we will keep your secret. Besides, who the hell would believe us? My brother arrives today, so he will know, but obviously we won't tell my nieces—they are far too young." She passed him his coffee in one of her most attractive earthenware mugs, and pushed the plate of biscuits towards him. "John Dee, I presume? A contemporary of my ancestor who was first given this estate." She felt dizzy with the thought of it.

He fixed her with a forthright stare, and she realised how sharp his hazel brown eyes were. How penetrating his gaze. He had seen things she could never hope to understand, but she knew her history, especially about witches and magicians, and she knew he was a brilliant man. And flawed. Very flawed.

An expectant silence had descended on the kitchen. *Her kitchen. Her domain.* All of it filled with Moonfell magic. And she was equal to anyone, immortal or not. It was as if they were the only two people in the room. "I think, Mr Dee, that you are far too old and wise to dissemble now. It's a great honour to have you at Moonfell, but please don't play me for a fool. What do you know of Edmund and Benjamin

Swift? Perhaps you knew Peregrine Westerly, too? The head of our coven at the time. Master of Moonfell."

He sipped his coffee, suddenly circumspect. "Just call me JD. It was a very long time ago, and as you can imagine, I have met many people in my exceedingly long life."

"And yet, you were like a startled rabbit at the mention of Edmund's name." She pushed the plate in front of him. "Have a cookie. Olivia, Harlan. Please sit."

The pair complied mutely, both sipping their drinks.

JD looked as if he would decline a biscuit, but then he reached forward and took a bite, and Morgana saw his demeanour soften. "It was a tricky time, and I didn't like Benjamin Swift at all."

"Why?"

"He was ambitious. I generally have no problem with that. I am—*was*—ambitious, too."

"Still are," Harlan grumbled.

"There is nothing wrong with ambition. I thirst for knowledge still, but back then I wanted influence, as well. Benjamin Swift was ambitious in the worst way. He wanted power, influence, money, and status, and thought that introducing his clever nephew, Edmund, to the Royal Society would aid his cause. But Ed was different. A true pioneer, but in a very unusual way. That put him at odds with everyone."

Odette loved the hushed space of the attic, with its many portraits, collections of clothes, and furniture that didn't belong elsewhere for now.

Moonfell wasn't inhabited by ghosts, but she often felt the presence of their ancestors up here, echoes more than spirits. Their numerous protection spells certainly kept them away, but the witches also ensured that their dead passed on peacefully to the spirit realm. If they didn't manage the dead properly, Moonfell would heave with ghosts. As it was, the house found ways to share their insights, secrets, and past lives, especially through the moon gates.

The attic was enormous, spread across most of the house, and broken into rooms by stone walls and wooden partitions. Light gleamed inside through the many small windows set under the gables, leaving portions of it swathed in shadows, and it was always warm up here, too. A contemplative space. Many portraits were in the largest room, but because of the number of them, they spread everywhere like the branches of their vast family tree, should it ever be fully mapped out. The image struck Odette so forcibly, that she stopped dead for a moment, her mind's eye seeing the truth of it.

That's exactly what the attic was. An enormous family tree in portrait form, but lacking characters, and jumbled with missing connections she could imagine on paper would be filled with question marks and blank spaces. Unfortunately, they weren't always hung up in order, for some odd reason, and there were many other paintings and drawings, too, such as images of the gardens, the orchard, and the bees, turning the attic into the heart of the house. The place that held its secrets.

Taking a deep breath and filled with new insights, Odette set off again, the creaking of floorboards marking her pace as she crossed centuries and wandered deeper into the past, before she finally stopped in front of an imposing man with a shock of salt and pepper hair framing an angular face and a strong nose.

So that was Peregrine Westerly. He really did look like a peregrine falcon as he stared down at her as if she were prey. But his eyes weren't unkind, just intense. It was an enormous oil painting portraying him full-length, rather than just head and shoulders, like some portraits. He was dressed typically for the time with tight breeches and stockings, buckled shoes, a fine waistcoat over a white shirt, and a frockcoat. His clothes were smart but not ostentatious; however, he also wore a black cloak over them that spread voluminously behind him, as if keen to impart his Master of Moonfell status.

He wasn't alone, though. His wife, Perdita, was next to him, also dressed very elegantly with a tight bodice over a full skirt, with a sort of striped coat over it that matched the bodice. She had a mass of red hair and lively eyes, and they made a handsome couple.

Interesting, Odette mused as she studied them. Not many of the heads of Moonfell were painted with their spouses. Neither were they painted standing in front of what looked like a shop rather than somewhere at Moonfell. The double-fronted shop had small-paned windows and a sturdy wooden door with a sickle moon glass pane in it. The sign above it read *Westerly's Botanical Remedies*, next to a painted image of a pestle and mortar surrounded by green leaves.

They owned a business?

She had never considered that her ancestors would be business owners, but why shouldn't they be? They needed to earn money, and even now they all had businesses or employment of some kind. For some reason, she had presumed everything ran from Moonfell, but why not have an apothecary? That was the perfect place to use their knowledge of herbal remedies legitimately, and draw in new customers who might need more specialised magic. Odette leaned in, studying the painting closely, and was able to discern items in the window. A selection of jars of various sizes, especially large ones filled with coloured liquids. Hopefully, she would find more information about where this apothecary was, but now she needed to look into Melusine.

Glancing around her, she noted that this section of the attic also contained a few items of damaged antique furniture that could well have been from that era. An armoire with a missing door, a writing desk with rickety drawers, a broken easel, and a chair with stuffing bursting out of the faded silk brocade upholstery, chipped gilding on its carved woodwork. Other much smaller portraits were hung between the wooden struts and old, rustic plasterwork, tricky to see well even with the electric lights on. A witch-light revealed several paintings of a cluster of children of various ages: on a garden bench in front of a pond, posed by the Waxing Moon Gate set within the yew hedge, sprawled in dappled sunlight in the orchard, and other idyllic spots. Names she didn't recognise were next to them, but she suspected these were Peregrine and Perdita's children, and from their relaxed composition, suspected a family member had painted them. *Perhaps that was why the easel was there?* Something else she would look into another time. But there was no indication of Melusine.

Odette decided on another strategy. She had the old tarot card pack they had found in the glass cabinet—the *broken* glass cabinet—and it was now with Meli's book, as it probably always should have been. It was clear she had been an early practitioner of tarot reading, and maybe other types of divination, too. When she had first picked up the deck, she experienced a frisson of magic, but that could have been the spell that helped preserve the cards, or from any witch that had used the cards since. Or a combination of all of them, of course.

Deciding it would be fitting to read them under Peri's portrait—a very informal name for such an imposing man, which already made her feel much fonder of him—she sat cross-legged on the rug on the floor and started shuffling the pack. For a while she emptied her thoughts as much as possible, letting the smooth cards slide beneath her fingers as she decided what to ask them, but in the end only one question presented itself.

Who was Melusine Westerly?

A card sprang from the pack and landed face up in front of her. The High Priestess. *Interesting. Had she become Mistress of Moonfell after Peri? Or was this card telling her about her personality?* The High Priestess denoted intuition, mystery, the duality of light and dark, and the divine feminine.

Rising to her feet, High Priestess card in her hand, Odette studied the paintings on either side of Peregrine and Perdita, dismissing many as she didn't recognise the names, but then laughed out loud when her eye caught a painting further along the wall in the next section of the attic where there were double and triple rows of portraits mounted irregularly. An image of a woman seated at a table in candlelight was arresting. She was dressed in occult regalia, wearing a cloak with arcane symbols over a rich, rose-red gown that complimented the woman's creamy skin tone and dark hair. On the table in front of her was a spread of cards.

The plaque next to it announced *Melusine Westerly. High Priestess of Moonfell*. But the years marked were short, only 1804 to 1807.

What had happened to Melusine?

Twelve

Rajgarh 1792

It was going to be one of those conversations, Fitz thought to himself, his annoyance building.

"Townsend tells me there was an incident last night," Cavendish said to Fitz, nostrils flaring with disapproval. "The creature appeared, and they fired at it. Why didn't you catch it?"

"Because," Fitz said waspishly, too tired to be diplomatic, "it's supernatural, we don't know what it is, and it vanished in the blink of an eye after attacking and nearly killing me!"

"Lucky Townsend and his men were there, then."

It was mid-morning, and they were in Henry's spacious office. Fitz and Ed had risen late and had consequently missed breakfast, except for a cup of strong coffee. Ed had immediately returned to his room to process their findings from the night before, while Fitz dealt with Cavendish after being summoned to his rooms by a servant.

"Actually," Fitz said, patience running out, "we had it in hand, and Vikram injured it. The shots scared it off when I was trying to capture it."

Cavendish frowned. "Townsend said there was a dreadful noise that could have woken everyone around the docks."

"The gunfire certainly added to that. Hunting paranormal creatures is not always done with stealth."

Henry paused as if considering his next words, and then nodded. "Of course. I suppose I should be pleased that it showed itself. Are you all right?"

"Surprised by its speed, but I'm fine, thank you. I fell in the river, but we have some of its blood, thanks to Vikram, and also other evidence to process. Ed is starting that now, so I need to join him. Any objections if we have a light meal sent up to our rooms?"

"No, not at all. " Eager for information, he leaned forward over his mahogany desk covered in stacks of paperwork.

"Data that we collected. I won't bore you with the details, but I will summarise our findings and report to you later." As much as Fitz hated this part of the process—the necessity of explaining things that most people would never understand—he knew that he had to with someone such as the Resident of Rajgarh. "The good thing is that we've investigated the dock thoroughly. We will go back tonight to set up traps."

Cavendish stood abruptly and paced to the doors that opened onto the terrace at the side of the house. They stood open to let in the fresh air, except that it wasn't really fresh. It was turgid and hot, even in the deep shade offered by the veranda. The view beyond was of a lush lawn with a formal rose garden and a couple of shade trees, including a large banyan tree beneath which the Resident's children were playing, looked after by their *ayah*. Alicia was close by, painting a large canvas set up on an easel, and her sister was writing at a small table. It was a charming scene. Fitz hoped they had checked for snakes in the area.

"Do you think," Cavendish asked, "that it will travel farther along the river?"

"It's possible, but I think it would have done so already. And there might be more than one. Just because there wasn't last night, I'm not ruling it out."

"But if it's—they—are threatened?"

"It's possible. If you like, I can set up protection around the Residency—invisible to the naked eye, but effective. Having seen this creature only once, I can't tell you exactly what it is, but there are still measures I can take."

He nodded and cleared his throat. "Yes, please. Obviously, we have soldiers here, but…"

"They will be of limited use against the supernatural. The creature was quick. It seemed to unfold out of the air itself, through what I can only call rifts."

"Could it appear in a building?" Cavendish asked, whirling around, alarmed.

"Of course, but it hasn't yet. At least as far as we know." Fitz hesitated, wondering if he should mention their other concern, and then decided he needed to be honest. "We are considering the possibility that someone human is behind this. That he is directing its movements."

"Someone could actually do that? How?"

"Using occult means. It strikes us as odd that only the port is affected. Obviously, it could be a creature that prefers to be close to water, but why just the docks? Or it could be attached to some trade goods, but that seems unlikely. It's just a thought, of course, and we might be wrong."

Henry had become very still. "You're suggesting sabotage."

"Perhaps."

"Then this is worse than we thought." Henry staggered back to his chair and sat down. "Who would do such a thing?"

"Someone who resents the Company, I would imagine. But I must stress," he said, fearful that Henry would do something that would only exacerbate the matter, "that this is the early stage of our investigation. Let us see what happens tonight."

"Of course. Could you protect the dock as you are the Residency?"

"Not if we want to catch it. If you'll excuse me, I'll join Ed now, and then I'll start the protection on the Residency. You may see me pacing the perimeter looking...odd. Just ignore me."

Henry composed himself. "Odd?"

"I'll be painting occult symbols known to be effective." *Along with lots of other things, such as spells.* "It will take me some time."

Henry gave him a long, considered gaze, and then nodded. "Of course. Please join us for lunch, however. The doctor will be there, and I would like you to meet him."

"I'm afraid that will be impossible. We have much to do today if you want us to catch this creature quickly."

"Dinner, then."

"It will be our pleasure."

Fitz was huffing with annoyance by the time he arrived in his and Ed's shared sitting room that had been put aside solely for their use, and that was kept locked when they weren't in there. Ed's equipment was spread across all surfaces, and the room was dark as the shutters and curtains were closed. Fitz's frustration with the circumstances immediately vanished as he saw an image on the bare white wall, projected from the Lumina Lantern.

"What is that?"

Ed grinned as he turned. "I captured the rift by the *ghats*. Not well, but even so."

"It's astonishing! Is that on your glass plate?"

"Yes. It was an experiment that I wasn't sure would work. I used my Temperometer with the Lumina. Tricky, but effective."

Fitz had left Ed on high ground while he and Vikram investigated the dock, and was glad he had. "It's bigger and narrower than I thought. Barely a seam of light. Why didn't the creature use it?"

"I don't know. Perhaps it is fixed and the creature needed flexibility. That is the one at the far side of the port, but this," he said, changing the slide, "is the one at the end of the jetty."

Fitz recognised the inky waters of the Ganga behind the seam of light. It was a silver-grey, like starlight; far less luminous than it appeared the night before. "It either opens into a place that has those colours, or it is an Otherworldly light. It didn't feel Otherworldly, but it did have magical energy." He heaved a sigh. "Of course, this could be an illusion meant to confuse us. The more I think on this, Ed, the more I believe there is a clever mind behind all this. It is no random attack."

"I agree. Have you told Henry?"

"Yes, and he was horrified."

"I'm not surprised, but you will be pleased to see," Ed said, changing the slide, "that I also managed to get this image, but it isn't clear. Everything happened so quickly."

Fitz gasped in shock as another image flickered on to the wall. "You caught the creature!"

"A bit of it. It moved too quickly, as you know, to get a clear shot. But it also has a silvery-edged quality. I think it is more apparent because it is blurred. Again, I used the Temperometer with the Lumina."

But Fitz was too sidetracked by the image, which had thrown him right back to the attack. To the leering, sharp-toothed creature of many limbs that had stepped out of something far smaller. Its energy had been huge, but focussed. His gaze fell on the bloodied cloth on a side table. "I need to set up protection around the Residency, but after that I will use its blood that Vik gave us to make a spell to try out tonight. In fact, we'll ask Vikram to come this afternoon. Unfortunately, we need to have dinner with everyone, as the doctor will be here."

"We need to fortify ourselves for this evening anyway, and I do want to meet him. Hopefully Townsend will be there, too."

"You want to see *him* again?"

"Yes, don't you?" Ed smirked. "I want to see the dynamic here. To witness how he is with the Resident. And then Anthony needs to give me his lists of staff at the docks, so he better have them ready."

Fitz felt overwhelmed by the amount of ground they needed to cover, and the speed in which they should do it. Already, he was considering spells he could cast that night. "And the sigils you saw on the buildings?"

"Go cast the protection spells. I'll have them ready when you return."

Fitz knew exactly the type of protection spells to use at the boundary of the Residency, and he made a simple potion to take with him. He always travelled with a variety of dried herbs, and harvested many on his travels, varying traditional English ingredients with local Indian varieties. Of particular value in India was the number of spices he could procure.

He ground cinnamon, cloves, and neem leaves and infused them into warm water inside a stoppered jar, along with a portion of cloth with the creature's blood on it, and placed it in his bag, as well as a chunk of charcoal and cinnamon for burning, and then left the house for the main gate. Not wishing to attract attention, he cast a simple spell that ensured anyone observing him would be disinterested, and started his incantations, progressing clockwise around the garden.

He set the cinnamon to burn in a bronze incense burner on a chain, wafting the smoke around him as he painted sigils of protection into the air with the infused water, spellcasting as he did so. He watched with satisfaction as the tell-tale shimmer of the spelled sigils took hold. Essentially, they would stop the creature from accessing the grounds, specifically targeting it alone.

It was hot work, and the boundary long, and by the time he reached the river, he was sweating. But it had also enabled him to see the full extent of the buildings in the grounds. The place was far bigger than he realised. Pausing at the riverbank, he relaxed in the shade of a banyan tree, wishing he could sleep for a few hours, lulled by both the heat and lapping of the river, but he couldn't stop. Momentum was building as his spell grew in power. Readying himself once more, he jumped when a voice called out to him close by.

"Mr Westerly, what are you doing?" Alicia crossed the short space between them with a determined stride, skirts swishing.

"Surveying the grounds, Miss Markham, to assess our risk of attack."

"Then why are you carrying incense and making strange gestures?"

Her sharp eyes clearly missed nothing, and he mentally berated himself for letting his own personal protection spell drop. He had been so caught up in the greater spell, and his surroundings were so quiet, he had assumed a false sense of security.

Deciding it was pointless to deny it, he said, "I am protecting the grounds from attack using protection symbols and incantations." She blinked in shock, and he pushed his advantage. "How much do you really know of the supernatural and of what my team does? You claim to know what is happening in the port, but how much do you really know of that, either?"

She gathered herself, straightening her shoulders. "I know there is a creature with many limbs and claws that seems to step out of thin air, and that you hunt such things. I wasn't lying the other day, and I resent the implication that I was. I gather you saw it last night?"

He ignored her outrage. "How do you know that?"

"Gunshots were heard, and I know you went to study the docks last night. Anthony said so."

He nodded. "Yes, that would be Townsend and the *sepoys*. We saw it, and we injured it, too."

"You mean Captain Townsend did?"

"No. *We* did. Captain Townsend provided support." *And interfered unnecessarily*, but he wouldn't say that. "Creatures like that can't be killed with bullets alone. The Resident summoned us here for our skills in battling such adversaries. If Captain Townsend could deal with it all on his own, why bother?"

"I've offended you."

"Not at all. But I think you have severely misjudged what we're up against. Whispers and rumours are often inaccurate. You offered to help us, though I still don't see how."

Alicia pursed her lips, eyes narrowed with annoyance. "My contacts—the women—can get news you can't."

"We have our own methods of gathering information, and already have made headway. I appreciate that you are clever, and probably bored, but this is not a job for—"

"A *woman*?" Alicia was furious, her fists clenched, he noted with surprise. He was glad there was no one close to see them.

"Not at all. I suggest you calm down, Miss Markham. Women are quite capable of dealing with such things, but the ones I would trust to help me have skills you do not."

"Such as?"

How much should he say? How much did she want to know? She was a curious woman, and if she was a witch at Moonfell, she would enjoy much greater freedom. *In private, at least.* He positioned himself with his back to the house, and ensuring no one else was around, conjured a ball of fire in his palm. "My family, women included, can all do this."

Alicia's eyes widened with surprise, but rather than step back, she leaned in to watch the flames. "Magic."

"The simplest form." *Not entirely true, but close.* He closed his fist so that it vanished.

"You're a witch."

"It runs in my blood. We are healers, protectors, and when necessary, we fight the unnatural elements that would do us harm. Today, I am casting a protection spell around the house in case the creature decides to leave the port. I need to finish it. Alone."

She nodded and stepped back, but her eyes didn't leave his. "What you do sounds exciting."

"It's dangerous. Ed and Vikram have great skills that compliment my own. You need to let us work."

"I still think I can help."

Fitz weighed his options. Someone was behind this, he was sure of it. *But how much could he trust Alicia?* And then he remembered their discussion the previous night, and how they had wished to meet lots of people from the area who might be involved. "Can you arrange a dinner party? Or something bigger? Persuade your sister to ask the Resident. I should have asked him earlier, but I became sidetracked. We need to meet the local merchants and other important people. There is more to this than just the creature, Miss Markham. You could be my guide. Point out who everyone is. If you know, that is?"

"I know them all." She smiled mischievously. "Yes, we can arrange a party, but it is very short notice."

"I know, but it's important."

"Tonight is impossible, but tomorrow, if we act now, it could probably work. However, we would need to make it attractive to them. Perhaps you and your friends would be that lure."

"How?"

"Rather than all this subterfuge, we announce you for what you are. *Monster hunters.* That will ensure a very good turnout indeed."

Thirteen

Moonfell 2025

"I need a breather," Horty declared, overwhelmed by the grimoires in front of them and Odette's news. "But at least we know why Peri has a wealth of spells on herbal magic and potions."

While Odette had been in the attic, Horty and Birdie had categorised what they had pulled off the shelves earlier, and it was intriguing. Peregrine's grimoire was decidedly that belonging to a green witch, and they had discovered not only spells, but pressed flowers and herbs in spectacular books, with carefully annotated notes. Horty was appalled that she didn't even know it existed, and decided it needed to be displayed somewhere it could be appreciated.

"An apothecary, though?" Birdie shook her head. "I wouldn't have considered that. Most intriguing."

"Ingenious, really. Would it have been frowned upon, though? I mean, how rich was our family then? Obviously, we had Moonfell, and had the patronage of King Charles II a century earlier, but appearances were everything in those days. Would running a shop have been bad?"

"We were never titled," Birdie said, shrugging. "Surely, running a well-respected business put us in the merchant class. We just happened to have a large house and land. It counts for a lot. We could have been eccentric, and they wouldn't have cared, either."

"Much like now," Horty pointed out.

"Exactly. Wealth allows you that, as long as you aren't politically ambitious, and we weren't."

"We think."

"We would know," Birdie said, very sure of herself, and Horty had learned to trust her.

"I've found it!" Odette called down from the mezzanine where she had gone to search through the tarot display.

"Found what?" Horty stepped back and looked up, but the mezzanine level was so deep it was hard to see to the back of it from such an acute angle.

Odette appeared at the rail holding a large square of black cloth covered in occult symbols. "Meli's tarot cloth. Be down in a minute."

Birdie tutted. "It's not helping us with Fitz, is it?"

"It will. Meli was obviously close to him. And of course, Morgana needs to read those letters. If she doesn't pull her finger out, I'll read them myself."

"We have enough to do."

"It's just reading."

"But we need to organise Beltane."

Odette joined them before they could bicker any longer, flourishing the black velvet cloth, her hair wild and untethered as if she'd been wrestling with the display. "I saw this in the painting. It was spread on Meli's table, under the cards. The candlelight glinted off it. We keep so many things that I hoped we'd have this, too."

"What will you do with it?" Horty asked, taking it from her and stroking the soft cloth. "She must have hand painted these symbols herself."

"Place it under Meli's cards and do a tarot spread, of course."

"I've never got to grips with the tarot," she admitted, handing the cloth back to Odette. "I can never seem to let go enough for them to impart any wisdom. I'm too uptight." Even confessing it made her feel the formality of her clothes that she'd adopted over the years of country living. "I can't access Moonfell's eccentricity like you all can who live here."

"Bollocks!" Birdie said forcefully. "You are very eccentric. You wanted to dance skyclad around the fire, remember?"

Odette laughed. "Horty, you're so funny. Of course you're eccentric. You just don't see it. Anyway, I have cards to read. I'm going back to the attic."

Birdie frowned at her. "Not yet. We still have visitors—including Arlo. Surely you want to say hello?"

"I'm in my headspace, Birdie. You know how it gets me."

"Then you need to ground," Horty added decisively, worried about her great-niece. "Cake and coffee are in order. Besides, that very loud doorbell gong went off, so other visitors are here, too. They might inspire you. I certainly need food and fresh air."

Plus, Horty thought as they left the library, *she was very curious about who was here, and she certainly needed to meet the shifters.* Even a few years before the witches and the Storm Moon Pack had fallen out, partly down to Odette and Arlo, she had still never met them. They had seemed to have more of a business relationship with the pack then, especially as Maverick hated witches. However, recent events had changed all that, and Horty could feel change sweeping through Moonfell.

Was it because Birdie had received a new lease on life? Could it be because of their renewed and much closer association with the shifters? Or was it the bees? She paused at the bottom of the curving stairway while the others progressed to the kitchen and peered at the underside of the treads where they had discovered the clue to finding Sibilla's gift. *Or was finding the wooden replica of the original house to blame, and the birthday of five hundred years of Moonfell?* They had cast the biggest protection over the house at Yule than they had done in years. The past was knocking, demanding to be seen—as if the whole place was waking up and stretching after a long, languorous sleep. *Was she feeling it more strongly than the residents because she didn't live there all the time?*

Interesting. And here she was, talking about Beltane fires to bring in new energy, and that was already happening. *In which case, what would Beltane do?* She put those jumbled thoughts aside and hurried to the kitchen to meet the newest guests.

"Oh good! You're here," Morgana said, as her relatives piled into the kitchen. "Harlan and Olivia have brought JD with them. He's the owner of The Orphic Guild, and he has very interesting news."

A flurry of greetings and introductions followed, but she took very little notice of Birdie and Horty, instead watching Odette, curious if her magic would see JD's age. It seemed that it did.

Odette stopped at the kitchen table, eyes on JD. "You carry more years than would seem possible. I feel the weight of them. I see them in your eyes." Her gaze travelled around him before finally focussing on his face again. "The years are like a great cloak of knowledge shimmering with arcane symbols."

JD, previously self-assured, stuttered. "I-I, what?"

Harlan laughed. "Odette sees to the truth of things, JD. There's no fooling her."

Morgana intervened. "JD is immortal. He's John Dee, magician to Queen Elizabeth I, and alchemist extraordinaire. I have assured him that his secret is safe with us. He has news about Edmund Swift."

"Immortal!" Horty huffed. "Not another one who's dodged time's cruelty."

"Oh, give it up," Birdie said, rushing forward to welcome JD.

Five minutes later, after everyone had settled down and a fresh pot of tea was on the table, Morgana brought her coven up to speed. She had been shaken by JD's news, though. Having first-hand knowledge of Edmund's past was unnerving.

"JD was a Fellow of the Royal Society," she told them. "He remembers Ed, but knew his uncle more."

"I wasn't known as JD then, obviously," JD said with a shrug. "I have had to change my name many times over the years, and have actually been a Fellow of the Royal Society several times, but have generally skipped a generation or more. I lived abroad for a time, too. Anyway, the late 1700s was a fascinating time. So many great men, and such wonderful discoveries. James Watt was a fellow, and he obviously pioneered the steam engine. Sir Joseph Banks was president of the society at the time." He sighed as he was met with blank looks. "He accompanied Captain Cook aboard The Endeavour. Completely transformed the Royal Society in some respects. Obviously, he was a fan of exploration, but there was a big focus on astronomy at that time, something I have always been interested in. I have an observation room in my home, even now. I kept a low profile, you understand, even though I was a fellow. I valued being around other great intellects, but had to be careful not to show interest in the occult. That's why I remember Ed. He presented his Temperometer in the 1780s, I think. It caused great interest, but also consternation, because he talked about seeing energies that weren't of this world." He tapped an instrument on the table. "This very one, I believe. It had been enhanced by magic, I knew that much, but he couldn't say that."

"They wouldn't have accepted it?" Birdie asked.

"No. It was science all the way. He did come up with an interesting formula to explain it, but I know magic. Plus, we knew he was investigating the supernatural in India, and several fellows were not impressed. It seemed like quackery. Benjamin, his uncle, was there for that presentation. He had sponsored his fellowship, after all, but his face was like thunder. Ed went abroad again after that."

"I asked JD if he knew Fitz," Morgana said, "but he says no."

"Only as Ed's companion, who I never met. I knew of Moonfell, though." JD smiled broadly. "But I never visited here. I was too tied up with other things. It had a certain reputation even then. As I said, I had learnt not to draw attention to myself, so kept my distance."

"What kind of reputation?" Horty asked.

"Perhaps *reputation* is the wrong word. There were times when there were lots of parties here, but for the most part, the residents kept to themselves, only opening their doors for those who needed help. Discreet help. It had an air of mystery, and still does." He shrugged. "I travelled, moved out of London, went to Europe for years, and reinvented myself constantly. When I came back, sometimes I forgot this place even existed at all. Magic, perhaps."

"But what about Ed?" Birdie asked. "And all these things? Why are they here and not with his family?"

"I honestly don't know, but I suspect from what I saw of Benjamin that he would not have wanted the family to have Ed's inventions and paperwork. I believe he thought Ed had squandered his talents.

I didn't—and don't—agree. But Ben had a reputation to uphold and was a big investor in the East India Company. I think he disowned him—well, almost."

Olivia looked horrified. "What about his mother and father?"

"Edmund was an embarrassment, and the second son. I think they wanted him to return to India and disappear, which is a great shame, because he was clearly very clever."

"Do you know what happened to him?" Birdie asked.

"I'm afraid not." He turned to Morgana. "You might not find out much more at the Royal Society, either."

"I have to try." Morgana was fired up now, and incensed that his family seemed to have disowned him. "Plus, I will read more letters tonight. Fitz will tell me what's happening." Fitz seemed so close now, she felt she knew him, and that made her even more invested.

Fourteen

Rajgarh 1792

Vikram loved the marketplace. The scents, sounds, and noise energised him as he strolled past the vendors hawking their wares. He paused to buy a bag of dates and then pushed deeper, heading to the warren of buildings at the rear of the open market.

No one gave him a second glance. There were no white-skinned foreigners there, but plenty of others, including Bengali, Kashmiri, Pathan, and Punjabi traders, as well as tribal people from the surrounding area, the babble of their raised voices almost deafening in places. Vikram ignored all of them. He was seeking out an acquaintance of Harishchandra's, a man who was known to have many contacts and information that might help their investigation. Hand on his hidden dagger, he entered a narrow alleyway that was dark despite the midday sun, the heat stifling.

The area was far worse than he expected, the alleyways narrower, dirtier, and more threatening. He quickly found the wooden door Harishchandra had described with a curious sigil marked on it, battered and distressed as if it had been kicked in, but it stood firm when he rapped on it using the code he had been given. The door opened quickly, and Vikram stepped into the gloom beyond, the door thumping shut behind him. Light flared in a lantern, and a wizened man stood in front of him. He studied Vikram, then turned silently and led him down a dingy passageway that reeked of sweat and rotten food.

Gripping his dagger even more tightly, Vikram followed, aware of every dark doorway they passed, and the chance that someone could step out behind him. Within a few turns, however, they pushed through another sturdy door into a small, dusty courtyard with a lemon tree in the centre, surrounded by high walls. A square of blue sky looked down on a man who sat beneath the tree on an old carpet. He was dressed in *dhoti* and a tunic, and was much younger than Vikram expected, but his eyes were as dark as his skin, and they fixed him with an assessing stare. He may look young, but he was far from inexperienced.

He gestured to the rug, speaking in the local dialect. "Sit, friend. Sharma Sahib says you are a hunter."

"Of sorts." Vikram warily checked his surroundings, noting one other door in the far wall that was shut, but not one single window, leaving them unobserved. And he was trapped. "Makkar, I presume." A nickname that meant tricksy in Hindi. He would need to keep his wits about him.

"That is one of my names."

Vikram sat cross-legged as the young man sent the servant scurrying to get mint tea. Even when associating with the criminal underworld, there was a veneer of civility. "I gather you know many things in Rajgarh. I need to know about the creature that stalks the docks."

"First, tell me about you."

Vikram expected this. Information sharing came at a price. "I am the son of a court scholar who is an old friend of Harishchandra Sharma. For many years they studied together at an old Mughal court in Rajputana, collecting and analysing mystical texts. My father passed on that interest to me, and for a while I also followed that path, delving deep into ancient lore. But then fate intervened." He paused, unwilling to say more, but Makkar just waited. "Some family members, cousins, were killed in a supernatural attack. I went to avenge them. I was also provided with military and weapon training as a youth, so I know how to fight. I never returned to court. I found my calling."

"But you hunt with the *Angrezi*." He meant the English.

"They have skills that compliment mine, and helped me defeat the monster that killed my family. We have worked together for many years now. And what of you and your position in Rajgarh?" Vikram did not expect an answer but asked anyway, genuinely curious.

"I grew up on the streets. It made me inventive. I made it my business to know many things and have many contacts."

"Even wealthy merchants, such as Harishchandra Sharma?"

"Especially so." Makkar smiled broadly. "You keep secrets, so you understand."

"Not as many as you, I'm sure." Knowing he would tell him no more, but deeply curious about his friend's relationship with this man, Vikram moved on. "Please tell me about the creature in the dock."

Makkar spread his hands wide. "What is there to say? It stalks the docks."

"It kills and must be stopped. We suspect someone directs it."

"How is that possible? It is a creature of myth."

Vikram smiled. "You are testing me. I saw it last night, and it is no creature that I know, and I have seen many. It is a mix of things, and moves in strange ways. I think you know this. You are wise, with many ears. Tell me what you hear."

"What will you do with this creature?"

"It depends on its true nature. If necessary, we'll kill it, or we will banish it back to where it came from. If someone is behind it, then we shall deal with him, too. I cannot say for sure until we know. But one thing for certain is that it must be stopped. We can do this without you, but if you know anything at all…"

The servant returned with their mint tea, and once he'd poured it and left again, Makkar said, "The Company makes enemies."

"Because of their trade?"

"The limits they impose on the docks, trade, power—all of it." He clenched his fist. "They squeeze until all choke. Perhaps it is good that they suffer."

Vikram suddenly wondered if Makkar was behind it all, but he didn't think so. He would use other means to intimidate, not paranormal creatures, and he sensed no magic about the young man. However, the fact was that the Company also employed lots of locals, too. There were benefits to their presence. "The English are not the only ones to suffer. Indians are dying, not white men. If this escalates, it will get worse, and more may die. If the English die, or trade is affected more than it is already, more soldiers will come. Help us catch this creature." He leaned forward to emphasise his words. "You know this is true."

Makkar sipped his tea and then nodded. "The Indian merchants have the most to lose. Even your friend. Some of them plot and scheme. Deepak Verma of the House of Verma leads them. He has wealth and a vast library of mystical texts. It is whispered that he has powers that he hones under moonlight. I suggest you start there. But tread warily. They have almost as many eyes as me."

"But my friend is not involved." It was not a question, but he had a sudden moment of panic. *Harish couldn't be, or why send him to Makkar?*

"Not as far as I know." But Makkar's expression was sly, and Vikram couldn't help but feel there was more to this situation.

Vikram hoped that Harishchandra would know Deepak Verma and could introduce them, but he did not wish to endanger his friend. Suddenly eager to leave, and feeling the walls of the courtyard closing in, he pressed Makkar for more information, but either he didn't know more, or wasn't prepared to tell him. However, Makkar continued to ask him questions about his companions and their hunts, and Vikram tried to answer honestly without compromising them all.

When he finally emerged into the winding, filth-ridden alleys behind the market, it was darker and the heat more stifling. Suddenly wary, he wrapped his thin cotton scarf about his face to hide his appearance, and hand on his dagger hilt, hurried away. However, he had gone only a short distance when he heard footsteps behind him, and turning swiftly, saw a tall man, face covered in dark cloth, behind him, a gleaming blade in his hand. And then another thump in the other direction revealed another man blocking his exit. He was trapped, and both men advanced quickly.

Vikram threw his blade at the closest target with lightning reflexes, but the man retaliated quickly, a flash of metal armguards glinting as he swept his hand up to deflect the blade. Fortunately, Vikram always travelled with more than one weapon, and he accessed the throwing knives strapped to his forearms, spinning to attack both combatants. One sank deep into the chest of one man and he fell, but another man appeared behind him, and then another, and Vikram realised they would keep coming until he was dead, the doorways in both directions no doubt hiding more. Back to the wall, he watched men close in on either side.

Vikram quickly weighed his options. The chances of him escaping unscathed, even if he killed more, were low. If he spread his arms, he could easily touch the walls on either side, the stones rough and unfinished, and he suddenly made up his mind. He kicked out at one man, landing his foot square in his chest with enough force to propel him backwards into the men behind him, sending them all sprawling into a heap. He stepped onto them and leaped upwards, fingers gripping the uneven stonework, legs bunching, feet against the wall. Twisting, he jumped to the opposite wall, and finding firmer footing, scrambled upwards to the blue sky and the roof above.

Stone crumbled beneath his fingers, but he was moving so quickly now that it didn't matter, and in moments, had dragged himself onto the roof. Peering below he saw a few men following, others racing to the alley's end to try to cut him off. Fortunately, he had walked the market the night before and knew the lanes and roads around his friend's house. He made a point of learning the layout of anywhere new as quickly as he could. He set off immediately in a crouching run, leaping across precarious roofs and alleyways, zigzagging and changing direction often to put off his pursuers.

Taller buildings approached, and he jumped onto a balcony and ran through cramped rooms, emerging into narrow corridors, before finding steps leading upwards. Bursting through a door, he arrived on another roof and kept running.

All the time he was wondering who had known where he was and whether he had been followed or set up by Makkar. Whoever was behind the attack was desperate enough to kill him, and that meant they might attack Ed and Fitz, too.

Ed watched Vikram clean his wounds, wondering how many enemies were allied against them. "Do you think Makkar was behind the attack?"

Vikram shrugged. "Perhaps, but to my mind, it is too obvious to attack so close to where I met him."

"Would it matter, though, if you were dead? That was clearly the intent."

"Yes, it was, which makes me fear for you, too. Both of you." He finished cleaning one set of scratches on his arms and moved to the grazes on his knees and legs, caused by scrambling over roofs and down walls. "If I had been killed, they might have left my body there, or dumped it in the river. You would have been none the wiser. After all, I didn't tell you where I was going. Harish-ji had organised it and told me over breakfast."

"So he organised it while we were in the port," Ed said.

Fitz was silently mulling over the attack, subdued ever since he had completed the protection spell around the house. Alicia seemed to have bothered him, but Ed hadn't questioned him, deciding to give him space. Instead, they had spent hours working on spells involving the creature's blood, ready for the night ahead, only stopping when a servant announced Vikram's arrival.

Fitz finally stirred. "In theory, then, only your friend and Makkar knew of your visit."

"Plus the servant on the door," Vik added, "and his people, perhaps. I doubt he was the only one in that building. But Makkar could have killed me there if he'd wanted to. I was enclosed in a courtyard.

Strangely, he did not take my weapons upon entering the building. He must have felt very sure of himself." He shook his head. "No, the more I think about it, the less I think Makkar did it. But I don't like the other option."

"That Harishchandra betrayed you," Ed said.

"He's an old family friend. I don't see it."

"Then someone else either learned where you would be, or you were followed," Ed reasoned. "Perhaps there are servants in your friend's household that informed on your whereabouts. Plus, we were all seen in the port yesterday, and word will get around about what we are here to do. Everyone will know where we are staying. You could have been followed from the second you left the house."

"Unfortunately," Fitz said, "we cannot discount your friend...not if what Makkar said is true. One or all of the merchants could be behind this. You reached out to him for a place to stay, correct? Perhaps he saw his chance. Have you seen him since the attack?"

"No. I came straight here after I escaped to warn you. His place was much closer, but part of me didn't want to risk it, either. However, I must go back. I have to see his response to my attack."

Ed considered the evening before, and how Harishchandra had been with them. "I can't see that he's behind it, Vikram. He seemed genuinely concerned, but who knows what pressure he may be under, or how his business might be suffering. Perhaps one of us, or both, should go with you," Ed suggested. "For safety."

Vikram shook his head. "I would rather face him alone. I can gauge his response. It may be that he suspects some of the merchants, too, and wants me to look into them where he cannot. Perhaps sending me to Makkar was a way of doing that."

Fitz huffed. "He has plenty of privacy in his own house. He could have talked to all of us last night."

"But Makkar gave me a name that we did not have before." Now that the aftereffects of Vikram's fight had worn off, he seemed tired. "I will not second guess his actions. I'm going back, but I will be very careful to stick to the main streets. You say you are meeting more of the Residency at dinner?"

"Yes, the doctor and Townsend will be there," Ed informed him. "But we will meet in the port again after that. Can you stay a while longer so that we can run through our plans for tonight?"

"Of course." Vikram straightened up, injuries now clean, and brushed the dust off his clothes. "I presume we are using the creature's blood?"

Fitz took the lead. "Yes. I have prepared a series of potions with the creature's blood at the heart of them. We can craft sigil traps for it that, in theory, should mean it cannot move once within them. A form of demon trap." He showed Vikram a sheet of paper with a few designs on it. "Can you suggest anything extra? And what do you think is the significance of the yantras Ed saw on the buildings last night?"

"They are perhaps a beacon, or a way of amplifying the rifts."

Ed nodded in agreement. "They were spaced out regularly around the port, so amplification is an interesting idea. What do you mean by beacon?"

"We are presuming the creature is directed, like a puppet. Maybe the sigils draw it in." He ran his hands through his thick hair. "Hopefully, we will know more tonight. There are so many variables to consider. What really puzzles me is why this creature's appearances are so spaced out. Why haven't the attacks magnified quickly? That's what normally happens."

Ed shook his head. "That's not true, Vik. Some, yes, when the bloodlust takes them, but some paranormal creatures are clever. They pace themselves, striking when needed and no more, depending on what drives them. Or they move and keep moving, so we end up following their trail of destruction for weeks."

"Agreed, but this one has stayed put."

"Has it?" Fitz asked. "It might be attacking in more remote places that we haven't heard about yet. Perhaps that is where it goes. Of course, there is another horrible option."

He hesitated and Ed pushed him, a knot forming in his stomach as he suspected what Fitz was about to say. "Go on."

"The cynic in me thinks—considering that you were attacked, Vik—that the whole event is bait for us."

Vikram sat heavily into a chair, as if punched. "That is a disturbing thought. Why would anyone want to kill us when what we do is necessary?"

"Maybe we have upset someone on our travels. Or perhaps the fact that we are English banishing Indian creatures is problematic."

"But I am Indian, and I was attacked," Vikram pointed out.

"But you are closely associated with us. I think we must be extra careful now. Alicia was again pressing to help us earlier. I told her I am a witch after she saw me casting the protection spells around the grounds and it didn't seem to upset her. I asked her to push Henry for a party, as we discussed, Ed. I said we needed Indian merchants to be there, too. Anyway," he shrugged, "for now, we must concentrate on tonight, so let's plan."

Fifteen

Moonfell 2025

Birdie wasn't sure if she was intrigued or unnerved by the fact that JD was an immortal human. He was disconcerting to be around because his energy was so unusual, but maybe that's because they were witches and could feel it more than most.

At least Harlan and Olivia trusted him, so that was a good thing. He also had excellent information on Edmund and his slippery uncle, and understood how Ed's instruments worked far better than they did, as he ably demonstrated.

"This," JD said, holding up the lantern with the glass slides, "is an adaptation of a magic lantern that was all the rage at the time, so you're quite right in thinking it as a projector. He's obviously tweaked it." JD held one of the slides up to the light. "I don't think these are painted. I think he's actually captured the image of what he was looking at."

"Like a camera?" Odette asked, surprised.

"Exactly. But clearly with magical properties." He rummaged through the books. "You say he has technical drawings?"

Horty picked it out for him. "Yes, in this book."

JD thoughtfully leafed through the pages. "Fascinating. I would love to study these. Any objections?"

"None at all," Birdie said, "but they must stay here, for now. If you like, you can study them in the library. You'll have more peace in there."

"Sounds wonderful. I can never resist a library. I have a modest one of my own."

"Modest my ass," Harlan drawled.

"JD," Olivia said, rolling her eyes, "we cannot wait here all afternoon for you."

"I can make my own way home. Both of you can leave me here." He made a shooing motion with his hands that made Birdie want to strangle him, even though it wasn't aimed at her.

They both, however, seemed to take it in their stride, and Harlan asked, "Is that okay with you, Birdie?"

"Perfectly fine. The more we know, the better." But before any of them could say anything more, a howl ruptured their conversation. "Bloody hell! What now?"

Within seconds, everyone was running out of the house and into the garden, following the noise to the west. Odette and Harlan sprinted ahead, and JD, Birdie, and a heavily puffing Horty arrived last. The three wolves were waiting for them at the edge of the pond that had been transformed by a proliferation of lotus flowers blooming a glorious pink.

"Wow!" Morgana's eyes were shining with excitement. "Lotus flowers. It must be the projection that caused it." An enormous black wolf rubbed his head against her legs, and she smiled down at him, her fingers burying in his thick fur. *Monroe.* "Hey you," she said affectionately.

"I take it," JD said, "that the flowers do not normally exist here?"

Odette shook her head. "No, not at all."

Harlan gave out a low whistle. "That's seriously impressive."

"Especially," Birdie said, "because they weren't here a few hours ago."

Horty, breathless from the chase, gripped Birdie's arm as if to stop herself keeling over. "This is amazing."

"And very worrying!" Birdie stood with her hands on her hips, lips pursing with annoyance. "I will not have anything else brought to life in this garden that shouldn't be here. We had a bloody Earth elemental last time! I do not want some weird, Indian paranormal monster rampaging through the house."

Maverick shifted to human. "If it's any reassurance at all, we can't sense anything threatening here. Just a strange, buzzy energy."

Horty gripped Birdie's arm even tighter as she muttered in Birdie's ear, "Good Goddess. What a sight! And I don't mean the flowers."

"Shush, Horty."

Maverick waded into the water and picked up one of the flowers. "Look! It's real. It has roots."

"So does he," Horty said, transfixed.

"For God's sake, Horty, anyone would think you hadn't seen a naked man before."

"Not like *that* I haven't. Not in years."

Fortunately, no one was taking the slightest bit of notice of Horty, because Arlo and Monroe had also changed to human and waded into the water, the splashing and laughing covering up all conversation. Harlan stripped off his shoes and socks and rolled up his jeans, as did Odette, and they waded in, too. And then, unexpectedly, so did Morgana.

"Something is wrong," Birdie said. "Morgana does not wade."

"Maybe that spectacular shifter next to her has something to do with it," Horty pointed out. "If that's Monroe, she is a very lucky lady indeed. I think I'll move back in if they're coming around often."

"You will look like a leering old lady and will do nothing of the sort," Birdie clucked. "Horty, focus. Something really is wrong." Only Olivia now remained on the bank, but Horty, Birdie, and JD were all much farther from the water's edge, and Birdie stepped forward tentatively. Within a few paces, she felt a strong pull towards the water. She stepped back, throwing a protection field in front of them. "Magic. Do you feel it? Either of you?"

JD shook his head, but his eyes gleamed with intrigue. "Not a thing."

"I do," Horty said.

"Olivia, step back here, please," Birdie called to her. "Why aren't you affected?"

She shrugged, clearly puzzled, as she joined them. "I have no idea, but I have no wish to jump in there, no matter how pretty it is."

"Nephilim baby," JD said. "Obviously, it gives you protection in some way. However, this is an excellent time to experiment with Edmund Swift's equipment."

"But what if they drown?" Olivia asked, watching them splash each other with water. "Or freeze. It's not exactly a warm day." She raised her voice. "Harlan! Aren't you cold?"

"It's refreshing," he shouted back, and ducked under the surface before emerging, soaked through.

Birdie was at a loss. "I honestly don't know what to do. There's clearly some kind of enchantment on the pond, but it doesn't seem malevolent. Bloody hell, Horty. Those slides have a hidden spell. Fitz must have intended that they give Melusine a real experience of India."

"Why is the kitchen fine, then?" she argued.

"You're right. It's the moon gate."

JD stepped between them. "Excuse me, but what moon gate?"

Birdie shifted position and pointed across the pond. "The bronze gate. We shone the images through that last night." She explained about Odette's painting being framed by the western moon gate and how they thought Fitz had sent the images back for Melusine. Then she remembered his suggestion. "You think Ed's equipment will help us?"

"We can but try."

"Go ahead, then. Set up wherever you like."

"I'll help," Olivia said, escorting JD back to the house.

"And we," Birdie said to her sister, "need to decide on a spell to extricate them if all else fails."

And then a loud screech made them spin around as a peacock stepped onto the gravelled path and spread its magnificent tail feathers. Birdie groaned.

Horty sniggered. "Oh no. What else have the slides manifested?"

Despite the intense cold of the pond, a strange, languorous feeling was stealing over Odette, just as if she'd had a full lunch on a hot day.

Heat seemed to shimmer on the pond's surface, and she watched the far bank warp through it, the moon gate and the summerhouse fading in and out like a mirage. But the sky was getting cloudier by the minute, and as the sunlight faded, another image began to reveal itself on the water. A pavilion in the Mughal style, just as they had seen last night.

"Arlo! Can you see that?"

He turned toward her, laughing as he swooped an armful of water in her direction. "This is great! I feel like a kid again."

"Listen to me, idiot. Can you see the pavilion? The one on the lake?"

He turned around, frowning, following her pointed finger. "I can see something. Is that a mirage?"

But with every passing second, it became more visible, as did a couple of narrow marble bridges that led to it from the east and west sides of the pond. However, both fell short of the bank, instead sloping directly into the pond. She hurried towards one, mud squelching beneath her bare feet, and tentatively touching it, she almost recoiled in shock.

"It's real! I can feel it." She clambered onto it, aware that the others had seen the bridges and shimmering pavilion, too.

"Wait!" Arlo grabbed her arm, his touch giving her an unexpected jolt of pleasure. "This shouldn't be here, Odette. Is it safe?"

"You're the voice of reason now?" She laughed. "That's unexpected."

He looked hurt, eyes clouding. "Lotus flowers are one thing, but this is something else."

"I have to see it. It's here for a reason." She gently removed his hand and ran towards the pavilion, scared it might vanish before she got there. With every step, however, it became more solid, and when she reached it, she stepped onto it with relief.

Whatever his doubts had been, Arlo had cast them aside, because in seconds he was next to her, and the others weren't far behind. The pavilion felt as real as Moonfell, made of smooth, creamy-pink marble with beautifully carved arches and delicate fretwork that offered tantalising vistas of the garden that surrounded them. In the centre were deep divans laden with cushions.

Monroe threw himself down on one. "This is fantastic! What magic is this?"

"It's not ours," Morgana informed him, her long hair swinging wet, the grey streak pale against her darker tresses. "It's our ancestors' magic. We think."

"Good ones, I hope?" he asked.

"They better be." Morgana turned to Odette, a mixture of worry and excitement in her eyes. "We shouldn't be able to be here. It shouldn't be this solid."

"And yet it is." Odette fixed her gaze on the bank, half wondering if a view of long-ago India would soon replace the grounds of Moonfell. "It must be a message."

"Why?" Harlan asked. "Why can't it just be a beautiful gift?"

Now that the initial excitement had worn off, a wary silence fell as they all considered where they were, but the pull of the place, the need to just be there was so strong, that Odette's worry was fleeting.

"Perhaps," Maverick suggested, "more is still to come. I mean, maybe more will be revealed," he added when they all looked at him. "In which case," he said, settling himself on a cushion like some reclining Greek God, "we'll wait and watch."

Sixteen

Rajgarh 1792

Fitz couldn't wait for dinner to be over. It was a tense affair, and getting worse by the moment.

"I intend," Captain Townsend said, face flushed with annoyance, "to be at the docks again with my regiment. I don't like this way of working at all."

He was dressed in regimental uniform, and the rest of the gathering were in formal dinner clothes. Henry was seated at the head of the table and his wife, Elizabeth, sat at the other end. Anthony, Roger, Captain Townsend, and Dr Montague Robinson were seated opposite Fitz, Ed, and Alicia, as if they had aligned themselves for battle.

"You really don't need to be inside the area," Fitz said, trying to remain reasonable. "Guarding the main gate and the streets outside is a good idea, but hopefully unnecessary. We are confident in our ability to contain the *issue* tonight." He looked uncertainly towards the women, not sure how much he should say at dinner. He had expected the subject to be brought up later over port.

Captain Townsend checked himself, but was clearly furious about the whole thing. "I have the safety of Rajgarh to consider."

"Of course," Henry interjected. "You will be present, but I think we must respect Mr Westerly and Mr Swift's request that they work better alone. This is a sensitive and unusual situation, which is why they are here in the first place."

Fitz inclined his head towards the Resident. "Thank you. Our methods are unusual, so it's best to be safe. Especially after last night." He stared pointedly at Townsend.

The doctor, a robust man in his forties with thinning blond hair and a pale complexion, who they had met only briefly before dinner, looked around the table uncertainly, as if unsure how much to say. "So, this is your regular type of employment?"

Ed sipped his wine and nodded. "Yes, but this case is more unusual than most for reasons we won't go into now. We will know more tonight."

"I think I should remain awake to hear your news," Henry said, assuming the mantle of control. "If you are not successful, we need another strategy."

"Sometimes," Ed warned him, "we require several attempts. Nothing can be presumed. We investigate, adjust our tactics, and innovate."

Fitz tried not to laugh at his calm explanation of the mayhem that could ensue when monster hunting. He instead looked towards Alicia, and catching her eye, raised his eyebrows. He had gathered in their talk before dinner that she hadn't yet raised the idea of a party the next evening, and that was leaving things very late.

Alicia nodded towards her sister as if to involve her, and then twisted to address Henry. "Henry, I know it's short notice, but with the uncertainty of what's happening at the dock, perhaps we should display a show of strength and unity and invite the merchants and other interested parties—English and Indian—to a party tomorrow evening. It might even be a celebration of success." She smiled broadly.

"Splendid idea," her sister said, clapping her hands together. "It's been so long since we had a party, Henry. It's just what we need. I'm sure the staff could organise the food quickly. A formal dinner would be far too much work, but light food with drinks on the terrace would be wonderful."

"After all," Alicia added, "the Company does such good work in Rajgarh, and Mr Westerly and Mr Swift should meet everyone."

Henry shifted uneasily in his seat as if he might object, but Fitz leapt in. "Thank you, Ms Markham and Mrs Cavendish. That is an excellent idea. Should we not be successful tonight, it will not impede us, as we can go to the docks after the party. In fact, having quite a few people here will ensure no one is tempted to go to the docks tomorrow. Sometimes, curiosity means even people with the best intentions sometimes stray where they shouldn't. I also think getting a real feel for everyone in the community will be interesting."

Ed nodded enthusiastically. "I completely agree. Excellent suggestion, Miss Markham."

"But hopefully," Anthony, the Assistant Resident said, glancing uneasily around the table, "it will be a celebration. This issue must be resolved swiftly."

"Of course." Fitz shrugged. "We aim to have the docks running smoothly again as quickly as possible."

"Actually," Roger, said, leaning forward to catch the Resident's eye, "Benjamin Swift has been in touch today. I didn't have the chance to mention it earlier. He arrives in Rajgarh tomorrow, and wishes to see his nephew." He smiled at Ed. "I'm sure you will appreciate seeing him. A party would serve us well. It goes without saying that we wish to impress on Mr Benjamin Swift just how much everything is under control."

Fitz felt Ed's demeanour shift and his body stiffen, but it would be hopefully imperceptible to everyone else. "My uncle is coming here? Well, of course, it will be wonderful to see him."

Which was a complete lie as Fitz knew well. Benjamin disapproved of their lifestyle, and the longer it continued, the angrier he became with Ed. Benjamin had invested a lot of money in the East India Company, and having Ed 'charge around India,' as he put it, was not befitting of Ben's status. He considered that Fitz and Vikram were equally to blame for this, and consequently held Fitz in low regard. He had met Vikram only once, and was rude and dismissive. Neither Fitz nor Vikram cared for his attitude, but both felt bad on Ed's behalf. However, as much as they all wished to ignore him, it was hard, because he now held influence and had the power, should he wish, to make life hard for all three in India, especially in the English community. Fortunately, it was just posturing at present, and they were at a stalemate. That was partly because Ben didn't like to draw attention to their business. However, now that they were in Rajgarh, assisting the Company at supposedly his suggestion, would that change?

"I take it that Benjamin Swift suggested we help you?" Fitz asked, just to clarify the situation. "You mentioned that he knew where we were and that's how you were able to contact us."

"Ah, actually," Roger said, "the suggestion came from our staff. We approached your uncle afterward."

"Your staff? Who?"

"Akash, of course. The *khidmatgar*," Henry explained. "Didn't I say? He always can be relied upon in moments of need."

"I see," Fitz said, surprised, but that in many ways made more sense than Ben recommending them. He must ask him how he had heard of them.

"Will my uncle stay here?" Ed asked, directing his question at Roger and Henry.

"No, he's staying at The Residency Grand Hotel in the town," Roger confirmed. "Of course, I offered a bed here, but he declined."

That was something at least, and Fitz felt Ed's tension ease. Fitz wondered if he should cast a spell on Benjamin. Something to diffuse the situation, or even to make him forget them. A spell to cast them in shadow in his mind. He would think on it, and possibly even use it the following evening, depending on his attitude.

Alicia, however, redirected the conversation. "So, it's agreed? We shall have a party? I'm sure Mr Swift will come with other East India Company staff. It will be perfect."

Everyone looked expectantly at Henry, who finally nodded at his wife. "If you think it can be achieved quickly, my dear? No expense spared, of course."

"I shall speak to Akash following dinner. In fact, if we are finished here, Alicia and I will organise it now." Elizabeth smiled brightly, leaving Fitz to wonder exactly how much she knew of what was happening. Alicia must have prepared her, or maybe she just enjoyed parties. He was paranoid. At least the grounds were well protected now, so everyone would be safe here.

Henry stood. "Port then, gentlemen?"

"Not for us, thank you," Ed said, as everyone rose to their feet. "We have work to do. I'm sure you understand."

Vikram was unsure of his reception at Harishchandra's house, but when he finally arrived after a long, careful walk home, he found Harishchandra anxiously awaiting him in the grand salon.

The house was hushed and the light low, so that his friend was almost invisible in the shadows that reached inside the room, caused by the setting sun behind the trees and the pillars that lined the covered walkway.

"There you are! You have been gone for hours." Harishchandra rose from the depths of the divan and stared deep into Vikram's eyes, as if already detecting his wariness. "Is everything all right?"

"Sorry. I explored the town and then spent a few hours with the team preparing for tonight. In fact, I should freshen up. I'm very dusty."

He studied Vikram, eyes narrowed. "That can wait, if you don't mind. Perhaps we should sit, and you can tell me how everything went. This morning included. Let us head to the pavilion."

Vikram wasn't sure if he was imagining things, but the house felt too quiet. Usually, there was a bustle of servants, the shouts of Harish's grandchildren, and the strident tones of his sons who also lived in the spacious building. "Where is everyone?"

"My sons are busy organising a shipment in the office, and the servants are preparing dinner."

Vikram glanced around as they walked, trying to relax, but neither spoke again until they reached the pavilion in the centre of the pool.

When they were settled on the large floor cushions, Harishchandra asked, "Did Makkar give you worrying news?"

Harish looked tired, his eyes puffy, and he wasn't as composed as usual. Perhaps it was worry for Vik's safety. Or maybe it was the fact he was still alive. Vikram had enough questions of his own, and wished he'd have asked many more that morning before he set out to meet Makkar. Harish had made it sound so casual, and yet it had been secretive and dangerous.

"How do you know him?" Vikram asked. "He seems an unlikely contact for a man such as you, Harish."

"You know that it is necessary to cultivate contacts that span many levels of society."

"Even one such as Makkar? You arranged that we met in the deepest, darkest part of the backstreets surrounding the market. Not exactly a safe area, and not what I was expecting."

"It was better there. It's easier to slip in unseen."

"If your relationship with him is so good, then why did you not meet him? Why send me?"

"I could not risk it." He regarded him with impatience. "I am well known here. I cannot go running off behind the *bazaar*."

"So you've never met?" This was not what Vikram had been led to believe, earlier.

"Once, years ago. Since then our communications are occasional, and always through trusted servants."

"And yet you thought it was fine to send me? How did you even arrange it in the first place? Or even become acquainted?"

"Vikram, there are ways, you know this. I am influential, and so is he, but in a different way. It suits us to keep each other apprised of things. He contacted me first, years ago, but that is all you need to know."

"Do you trust him?"

"Yes, as much as I trust anyone." He frowned. "What happened? Did he tell you something?"

"He told me many things, but it was what happened when I left that is the issue. I was attacked by a group of men who were intent on killing me."

Harish drew back looking suitably shocked. "Where?"

"In the narrow alleys. Men in front and behind, all armed. It is lucky I am so skilled at climbing and fighting or I would be dead now."

"You think that I am responsible, or Makkar?"

"If I really thought it was you, I wouldn't be here." *Not entirely true.* "But Makkar? Maybe. Unless, of course, I was followed, but I didn't see anyone behind me when I entered the alleyways."

"Please, Vikram, believe me. I am not to blame, and I don't think Makkar is, either. But it means your presence is enough to scare someone."

"Could anyone have heard that I was going there?"

"It's possible, but unlikely. I use my most trusted servant to meet one of his men."

Vikram hated to ask, but... "What about your sons?"

"They do not know of my arrangements. This I swear. The youngest, as you know, is travelling on business. The older two run my company now and are far too busy to know what I am up to." He paused, then nodded to himself. "I will make enquiries. You were my eyes and ears today. To hurt you hurts me. Did he know anything of this creature?"

"He suggested a merchant could be behind it. Deepak Verma of the House of Verma. Do you know him?"

Harish's eyes widened with surprise. "No! Surely not. He's one of the most respected merchants in Rajgarh, and has one of the largest and oldest businesses."

"But does that mean he pays lots of money to the Company in duties and fees?"

"That he can afford." He leaned in, as if to emphasise his point.

"You sent me to Makkar for information, so surely we have to consider it is correct."

Harish fell silent, clearly perturbed at the suggestion, and tiredness swept over Vikram. "Promise me you will think on it. In the meantime, I need to wash and rest. If you'll excuse me."

He didn't wait for permission and left the pavilion quickly, desperate for the cool of his room, and the privacy and time to think. Everything felt wrong, and he considered the earlier conversation with his team.

Was the creature at Rajgarh an elaborate trap for he and his friends? If so, why? What had they done to merit such a thing? Was this even about the East India Company and their expanding trade, or was it a front for something completely different?

Seventeen

Moonfell 2025

The scent of chocolate cake filling the kitchen was enough warning to alert Horty, and she whisked it out of the oven before it burned, thanking the gods she hadn't been upstairs with Birdie, but instead rummaging in the still room for spell ingredients.

Olivia and JD were in the garden experimenting with Ed's equipment, while the shifters and her great-nieces were in the middle of an enchanted pond with a bloody great Mughal pavilion in the middle of it. Since they had returned to the house, all she could hear was the screeches of peacocks wandering the grounds. *This was a fine fettle.* She checked the spell ingredients' list against the assembled dried herbs, plant cuttings, and waxing moon water, nodding in satisfaction. She was so distracted that Birdie's arrival made her jump.

"We'll need more moon water than that if we're to counter the effects of the gate!"

Flustered, Horty swung to face her. "There's already a litre of it. Are you planning to bathe in it?"

"The gate is rather large, in case you've forgotten."

"You're dowsing the whole thing?"

"We clearly need to negate whatever the Lumina Projector has done to it."

They had decided to cast a spell on the moon gate rather than tackle the whole pond. "Do we dare do it while they're in the pavilion?"

"The non-existent pavilion?"

"They're all sitting in it. Of course it exists." *Honestly, Birdie was such a twit sometimes.*

"Not in this reality."

"Tell that to them!" Horty bundled the ingredients in a large basket and hurried out the door. "Have you got the spell?"

"No. I left it in the library. Of course I have it!"

"Well," Horty said, marching up the kitchen garden path and manoeuvring around a peacock, "we need to get them out of the pavilion first. Otherwise, they might go with it."

"Go where?" Birdie asked scathingly.

"Back to bloody India, of course! We have no idea what's going on here. Is it a time thing, or just a wonderful snapshot of the past? They might just end up in the pond, which of course would be the best solution rather than 1792 Bihar. I rather like the lotus flowers, though. Can we keep them?"

"I doubt we can pick and choose." Birdie cracked her staff onto the ground as she walked, intent rattling through her every step. She was on the warpath. Every part of her small frame vibrated with it. She felt guilty, too, Horty could tell.

"You know, this is not our fault."

"Of course it is! We got carried away last night, and look what's happened. Things are manifesting."

"We weren't to know that this would happen."

"But we knew *something* would."

"Maybe it's Beltane? The veils are thinning, so perhaps that has enhanced Fitz's spells—and Moonfell's magic, of course. There is a lot of it here. At the time, it might just have been a simple illusion."

"Perhaps." Birdie didn't sound convinced, but Horty wasn't either, and when they reached the edge of the pond, Birdie muttered, "Bloody hell."

The pavilion was even more apparent now, situated majestically in the middle of the lotus-filled pond, magnificently lit by sunshine that did not belong in their time or place, but to another sun-drenched afternoon over three hundred years earlier. Figures lounged in the centre of it, seemingly unconcerned about their situation. Birdie didn't speak, but instead set off at a trot around the pond towards the moon gate and JD and Olivia, who had set up next to it. Horty drew her cardigan around her to fend off the stiffening breeze, wishing she'd have borrowed one of Birdie's cloaks instead.

JD was barking orders at Olivia who was jotting down notes in a notebook, but she looked up as the witches approached. "JD can see energy fields," she said, excitedly. "Through the scope."

"He called it," JD said, eye still fixed to the scope which was mounted on a tripod, "a Temperometer. Designed to detect changes in energy fields. Maybe temporal distortion, too. I believe there is some kind of magic used on the lens. I wonder if Edmund ever dabbled in alchemy." He straightened up, hands on his lower back as he stretched, his lips twitching with amusement. Despite his age—his *considerable* age—he hummed with a vibrant energy that Horty wished she could bottle. "Your entire garden is a vast magical field. Did you know that?"

"Of course!" Birdie drew herself up to her full, although diminutive, height. "I'm the High Priestess of Moonfell. Of course I know. We all know. We all feel it and tune in to it and draw on it when necessary.

I happen to feel it more than most. The entire place is imbued with our magic. Centuries of it. The boundary in particular has strong protection spells."

"I know. I can see the power of them." He paused briefly, considering the sisters. "Interesting. I have a few theories I would like to explore."

"What?" Horty asked, suspicious.

"I'm interested in trying to identify the type of magic present. Whether it comes from the place or the people or both."

"Another time, perhaps," Olivia said, looking apologetically at the witches. "He questions everything, so feel free to tell him to keep his nose out of your business. Any suggestions about the pavilion, JD?"

"There is most definitely a vortex of energy that is concentrated on the pavilion itself, although of course the lotus flowers are included. It has a different weight to the rest of the garden. Denser and darker in appearance. As for the gate..." He studied it, lips pursed. "It's a conduit. It was the first thing I checked. The metals are an interesting combination."

"I know. I considered them this morning." Birdie said. "What do you mean by conduit, exactly? It's an interesting word choice, because I think this gate feels charged with energy right now, and it doesn't normally. Almost as if it collected the energy from the projected image."

"Exactly that!" JD said, finger wagging enthusiastically. "You illuminated the image with your witch-light—more magic. It hit the metal gate—more magic, again. And then hit the pond. Hence, conduit. It all combined to have the desired effect. You stood where exactly last night?"

Horty walked over to the spot. "Here. Far enough away to frame the image, just like in Odette's painting. Or so we imagined and she told us. *We* haven't actually yet seen it."

"No?"

Anxious to head off further tangents, Horty hurriedly said, "No, but you can see it later if you want. But that pavilion isn't in her painting. Odette painted what she believed to be the Residency. That's what we started with, then we changed the slides and that was on one of them—and it seems to have taken root."

"Images?" he asked. "As in, more than one?"

"Yes, we tried a few. It was wonderful to see them magnified. I can only conclude that this one is fixed because it is over water. It has symmetry with our pond."

"Another interesting suggestion."

Olivia said, "I see what you mean now. Yes, the image must have resonated. You have several moon gates, right? Perhaps the slides were all designed to be shown through moon gates?"

"Excellent reasoning," JD praised her. "A gift that incorporates the whole garden. Maybe a gift for Fitz himself. A way to remember his adventures."

Horty realised they should probably have read the journals and letters completely before they started messing around with the slides. "Birdie, if Fitz sent them to Meli—or any of his family—he must have provided instructions. We really need to finish the letters."

"It's possible, but he might just have brought them home with him. Let's focus on getting this resolved now before we go charging off to do anything else. We have a spell to try, and if we fail, then we'll read the letters next. Well, we'll read them anyway, but you know what I mean."

JD ran his elegant fingers through his groomed beard. "Would you mind going over your spell with me?"

While Birdie discussed their plans with JD, Horty lowered her eye to the scope and looked through it, and realised JD was not exaggerating. Moonfell magic appeared as shimmering auras of different colours across the garden, almost as if the Northern Lights had settled over the grounds in a varied display of colours. Perhaps spirit-walking would show the same thing, but unfortunately it was a skill she didn't have. The magical aura over the pond, though, was in darker tones of purple, like a bruise.

"Beautiful, isn't it?" Olivia said dreamily. "Your ancestor must have used the scope to detect creatures' auras in monster hunting."

"I guess he must have. I wonder what spell he used. It's quite ingenious. What a team he and Ed must have been to combine their skills. And Vikram, of course." Her eye was still pressed to the scope, and as she watched the swirling energy, an idea struck her, and she quickly stood. "It's like a fairy ring, or a hag stone. It allows you to see what can't be seen by the eye alone."

Olivia smiled. "I love that idea. A fairy ring caught in a scope, and then captured on a slide. Ingenious."

Birdie interrupted them. "Come on, Horty. We have a spell to do. You two need to step back, and take all the equipment, please."

Morgana felt carefree and giggly, as if she'd drunk a bottle of champagne.

Lounging on the plump divans in the centre of the pavilion felt decadent and Otherworldly, which was a ridiculous thing to be thinking, considering they lived at Moonfell. But it felt timeless, as if she had all the time in the world to do whatever she wanted. The sunshine bathed them in glorious heat, and the edges of the lake shimmered like a mirage.

The shifters were naked except for lightweight cotton blankets they had found on the divans that they had wrapped around their waist. They reclined as they chatted, and she was enjoying talking to Monroe, who as usual looked magnificent. *If only they were alone...*

Harlan had stripped off his shirt, but rather than relaxing, he prowled around the pavilion, hand shielding his eyes from the sun, while studying their surroundings. "I swear that it keeps changing. First it looks like Moonfell, then I can see what looks like a *haveli*."

"A what?" Arlo asked, twisting on the divan to look at him.

"A *haveli*. An Indian house. Aren't you the slightest bit interested in this?"

"No. As long as I'm not being attacked."

Odette joined Harlan, squinting at the far bank. "I'm interested, but I'm finding it hard to summon the energy to stay that way. I can see Horty and Birdie, though. They're at the moon gate with JD and Olivia. He's interesting."

"JD?" Harlan laughed. "Yes, he is. And he's also one of the most infuriating men I know, and probably the most brilliant. If anyone can help you with this, he can."

"Do you need help?" Monroe asked Morgana, amused. "I mean, you could shake this off, right, if you wanted?"

"Possibly. If I wanted. I'm a little spellbound I think, and yet I can't muster enough energy to worry about it."

Harlan waved his arms around. "This place is probably drawing on you. It's sort of symbiotic."

Morgana dragged herself upright, feeling like her bones had turned to mush. "Bloody hell, Harlan. You might be right. No wonder I feel weird. Odette, what about you?"

Odette's attention was transfixed on the bank by the moon gate. "Yes, maybe. My thoughts feel a bit muddy. You seem okay, Harlan."

"I'm not my normal self, but I'm just too fascinated by the whole thing to care."

What about you shifters?" Morgana asked the group.

Arlo shrugged. "I feel a bit drugged, like I'm slightly stoned, but nothing horrible."

"Me, too," Monroe nodded. "I wish I had a pint. That would be great."

"Trust you to think of beer," Morgana said, laughing.

"Rum and Coke for me," Maverick added, rolling on to his side to gaze out at the water. "I guess I should be feeling more worried. The club will be opening soon, and everyone will wonder what's happening. Maybe I should swim to the shore."

"I wouldn't," Morgana warned him. "We're still not sure what's happening."

And then Odette almost squealed with excitement, the sound enough to bring all of them to their feet. Morgana ran to her side, realising that outside the pocket of light they were suspended in, the garden beyond had gone very dark. "What's wrong?"

"Over there." She pointed to a figure strolling along the edge of the pond wearing a long dress. "I think it's Meli."

"*Meli*? Fitz's sister?" Morgana watched the swing of the woman's skirts, almost hearing the swish of them in the grass before she vanished. "That's nuts. We must be seeing flashes of India and Moonfell in the past. That will be the moon gate's doing."

"I can't see her," Harlan complained. "Damn it."

Odette looked bereft. "It was fleeting. I can't see her now."

"Are you sure it was her?" Morgana asked, studying her cousin's pensive profile. "I couldn't see details."

"No, but I know it was her. I *felt* it." Odette looked at her and smiled. "You know how it is."

A flash of light drew Morgana's attention, and she turned back to the moon gate that was now bathed in silvery starlight again, hearing Birdie and Horty's voices across the water. The path between the pavilion and the gate lit up like the Milky Way before turning an inky black. In moments, the pavilion shimmered and vanished, and they all plunged into the very cold waters of the pond.

Eighteen

Rajgarh 1792

Fitz finished the second trap that he had set under the rift at the end of the jetty, the place where he was attacked, and stepped back to survey his work.

Both rifts now had traps beneath them, and because it had taken a while to complete them well, it was now dark. As requested, Townsend's men were outside the dock area, but Townsend was not happy about it. Fitz didn't care. They needed the docks to themselves.

"It looks good," Vikram said, checking the trap. "Now we just need to hope the creature uses the rift." His lips twisted into a wry grin as he withdrew his sword. "Something tells me it won't."

"I wish you didn't look so happy about it."

"Someone is playing games with us. I think we're equal to the challenge."

Fitz loved Vik's confidence, but couldn't share it. "We're really not. We have no idea what we're dealing with."

"Isn't that part of the fun?"

"What has got into you? Earlier this afternoon you were despondent, thinking your friend had ambushed you, and now you are like a bull!"

"There is nothing like a brush with death to make you appreciate life. Besides, after questioning Harish, I do not think it is him. However, I suggest we are careful leaving here tonight. Another ambush could well be possible."

"I think this place is ambush enough."

Ed joined them from the end of the jetty where he'd been surveying the docks again. The whole place was much more crowded with goods than the previous night, and clearly not everything had been stacked into warehouses. "Those sigils on the buildings seem to be glowing even brighter tonight. I've realised something else, too." His teeth worried at his lower lip. "From this angle, I see that they intersect."

"Where?" Vikram asked.

"Out on the main part of the dock, in front of the Customs House. They emit faint lines of energy overhead." He pointed upwards.

"They intersect in the air?" Fitz asked, confused.

"Yes. Odd, I know. I think we need more traps on the ground so that we can stop the creature if it strays where we don't expect, and one under that specific point."

Fitz reached out with his magic, trying to detect energy fields or manifesting power, but felt nothing. "You see it with the scope?"

"Yes, faint lines overhead," he repeated. "I couldn't see them last night. I don't know what they do, though. Focus power? Provide an overhead rift? Both are possible."

"Plague on't!" Fitz didn't normally swear, but he was exasperated. "After all of our talk today, especially your meeting with Makkar,

Vikram, and our exploits last night, too many people know we're here. I feel we're sitting in a gigantic spider's web." He grabbed his bag and strode to the end of the jetty, intending to set up a trap under the conjunction of lines as Ed had suggested. The need to act quickly was pressing on him now.

"You still think this creature's attack was meant to draw us here all along?" Ed said, racing after him.

"I think it's a possibility we cannot ignore." He slowed down, marshalling his thoughts. "Let's summon the damn thing. We have its blood."

"Summon it? We shouldn't deviate from our plan yet."

"That's *exactly* what we should do! We need to catch whoever is behind this unawares."

"Too late!" Vik said, and Fitz heard the whisper of Vikram's sword being withdrawn. "Over there."

A flash of light was all that proceeded the creature's manifestation in front of the Company's office building. It was even bigger than the previous night, with no sign of the injury that Vikram's sword had caused, and it was facing towards the sprawl of warehouses belonging to the independent merchants, in the opposite direction to them.

Fitz pulled them all backwards, cloaking them in a shadow spell, and in a low voice said, "Wait. I don't think it has seen us yet. Let's keep it that way. This is our opportunity to study it."

The creature was enormous, well over twice the height of a human, with eight limbs, three grotesque heads, and half a dozen eyes on each one. Its skin was mottled brown and green, and as it turned, an enormous tail swished into view. One gaping mouth revealed a blood-red interior that appeared to be partly a beak.

"What manner of creature is that?" Ed hissed. "Is it a hybrid?"

"A Rakshasa, I believe," Vikram answered. "They come in many forms, but you might be right. Each head is different. One like a bird, one like an elephant—see, it has a trunk, and one..."

He trailed off, and Fitz knew why. It was hard to categorise the third head. However, as it lumbered around on enormous, clawed feet, it lifted the unidentified head and sniffed, revealing more of its shape.

"It's a snake," Fitz said confidently. "I think it's a Chimera."

"A Chimera Rakshasa, or something else?" Ed asked.

"Hard to say. It certainly wasn't what attacked me yesterday. For a start, all of its limbs are intact, and it had only one head."

"But if it's a Chimera, that makes sense," Vikram pointed out. "Let me draw it towards the trap. You circle around and attack from behind. Force it in the direction we want. I'll upend a crate or something when I'm ready."

"Which trap?"

"The *ghats*. It will offer us more space to fight it. I can use the crates and boxes to give me cover."

Fitz surveyed the area, assessing his plan. They were currently in the central part of the dock, but the *ghats* were reasonably easy to access.

"Sounds good to me," Ed said.

"Agreed, but be careful," Fitz warned.

Vik slipped out from the shadow spell and ducked behind the huge crates and lifting equipment that crowded the area, making his way silently across the dock. The creature continued to lumber around, lifting its head in an effort to sniff them out.

Fitz and Ed meanwhile headed in the other direction, Fitz pulling Ed next to him. They had barely manoeuvred into position when a huge crate crashed to the ground towards the *ghats*, and the creature charged towards it far quicker than Fitz was expecting. They raced after it, Fitz readying his staff, just as Vikram emerged on a stack of wooden crates brandishing his sword. The creature roared, flinging away boxes, stacks of lumber, and anything else in its way as it tried to get to him.

Fitz was desperate to attack, but knew it would only draw the creature away from Vikram. He had to trust his friend's speed. The creature was single-minded in its advance, but the destruction it was causing was making it hard for Fitz and Ed to advance, and Fitz abandoned the shadow spell as he leapt over splintered wood and fallen crates. He clambered onto the prow of a docked boat and raced from boat to jetty and boat again in an effort to keep up. Finally, he saw Vikram behind the trap, and although he couldn't see the rift, he knew it was there. Unfortunately, that's when the creature stopped and bellowed with fury.

Fitz hurled a ball of swirling elemental fire and air energy at the creature, designed to knock it forward into the trap. It worked—for a short distance. It staggered forward, stopped, and then whipped around. Fitz threw another and used his staff to enhance it. The blast struck the creature fully on its chest, and it staggered back again. Vik darted around the trap, putting himself right under the creature's feet, and hacked at its legs with his sword, clearly trying to make it fall. Fitz kept advancing, but where was Ed?

Then he heard the creaking of an enormous wooden beam swinging overhead, and the whip of a chain. Shocked, he saw that Ed had somehow set the crane moving towards the creature, and was hanging from the chain. He propelled himself through the air, using the crane's momentum to swing into the bellowing monster. Fitz could scarce believe his eyes. But just as the chain was about to strike, Ed dropped onto the deck of the closest boat, and the chain whipped across the creature's chest, the weight of it too great to counter. The creature plummeted backwards, dropping into the trap, and with an audible snap, the trap activated. A muddy red light shot up forming a net around the creature, and Fitz took a brief moment to congratulate themselves on making such a large trap.

Unfortunately, his happiness didn't last long.

A flash of white light to his right had him spinning around, and with horror he saw another creature appear, and it looked like the one he had fought the night before. There weren't any traps close to it, and spotting Fitz, it charged.

Vikram yelled to Ed, "Stay here and ensure that thing remains trapped. I'll help Fitz!"

Vik raced across the dock, leaping over broken equipment and splintered wood, closing the distance quickly. The creature was intent on Fitz, its eyes glowing a hideous red as it advanced. It had obviously manifested out of its own rift again, and was far closer to Fitz than Vik. Sheathing his sword, he shifted his spear to his right hand and aimed it at the creature, adjusting for its speed.

Unfortunately, Fitz hadn't seen Vik and was already hurling spell after spell at the creature. It adopted counter measures, weaving erratically towards him, and Fitz bounded away, boats rocking beneath him. As the creature lumbered after him, it exposed its back to Vik, and he released his spear. The spelled tip embedded into its spine, and the blade released its magic. The creature staggered a few steps further, and then collapsed.

Seizing his advantage, Vik charged towards it, and saw Fitz do the same. Breathless, they arrived on either side of it, but Vik continued running in, bounded onto the creature's back, and pulled his spear out with an almighty heave. Not waiting to see if it was already dead, he placed the spear over its neck and stabbed down again. The creature trembled once and then stopped moving; almost instantaneously, a sizzling white light flashed over the body. Vik leapt away just in time, landing on the dock with a thump as the creature evaporated into grey dust.

Winded, he looked over at Fitz. "What on Earth was that?"

Fitz walked to his side and pulled him to his feet. "Either its master called it back, or that was part of its death cycle. Are you all right?"

"Well enough." He grinned. "One down. One to go."

Ed paced around the trapped Chimera Rakshasa and it paced inside the trap, watching him just as intently.

Every now and again the creature tested the trap's boundary, hissing with fury when it sparked beneath its clawed fingers. It was obviously intelligent, because it tested different parts of the trap every time, looking for weakness. One set of eyes was permanently trained on Ed, and despite knowing that the trap was sound, Ed kept a healthy distance, and a wary eye on where he knew the rift to be. If anything came out of it now, he'd be in big trouble.

Fortunately, Vik and Fitz had vanquished the other Rakshasa, and he waited for them to join him. They had wreaked havoc on the dock. Some of the lifting equipment was broken, and crates—empty, by the look of them—had been smashed. They were going to be in big trouble with the port staff, and probably the Residency, too. At least Townsend and his soldiers hadn't entered the dock yet, and he wasn't sure whether that was good or bad.

"Here you go," Vik said, hurrying into view and handing him his leather bag with his equipment. "You're lucky it survived. He's ugly. Or maybe she?"

"Possibly both," Fitz quipped, eyes on the creature.

"Are you two all right?" Ed asked, noting that both men looked winded but unharmed.

"Better for having killed one. Did this react to the other's death?" Vik asked.

"Not as far as I could tell," Ed said as he extracted his scope. He trained it on where he suspected the rift to be, easily spotting the slender, dull-silver shimmer now he knew what to look for. "The rift is still there, which must be good news."

"Is it?" Vik frowned. "Then why isn't anything else coming through it?"

"I wonder if whatever is on the other side can see us?" Ed said thoughtfully. "Or hear us, perhaps? Maybe these attacks were to test us. See our response?"

"If they can, then they know we are good at this. Any thoughts as to what we do now?" Fitz asked as he paced around the trap.

The creature's head swivelled to watch him, the other two heads with their multiple eyes watching Ed and Vik.

"I was wondering," Ed suggested, "if we could send it back and track it from here?"

"I'd love to do that, but how?" Fitz asked.

"I actually have no idea."

Fitz rolled his eyes. "Thanks, Ed."

"Blood, you fools," Vik said. "You can do one of your tracking spells, Fitz."

"We haven't got this creature's blood, only the one we killed. And why didn't you think of that before we killed it?"

"Well," Ed pointed out, "this trap was made for the other creature, not this one, but it still works. That suggests the blood is effective for both."

"Perhaps. The trap itself is designed for all manner of creature. The blood was a back-up," Fitz said. "I just adjusted a trap that we designed for other demonesque monsters. Thank the gods it worked."

The longer they lingered, the more likely the creature would find a way to escape, or more would arrive. They needed to make a decision. Training his scope on the sigils on the buildings, Ed noticed that the shimmering lines that emanated from them were growing in intensity, and he summoned his team's attention. "I think we have more problems. The lines from the yantras are more intense than earlier. Whether they are drawing on your magic, Fitz, or something else, we may have more trouble. We need to destroy them."

"The yantras?" He looked sceptical.

"Yes. Will the spells you have woven into my staff do that?"

"Perhaps. Let me see." Fitz bent his head to the scope. "They have been applied magically, so in theory, yes."

Ed studied the cranes he had used so effectively earlier, and reasoned he could utilise them again to get close. It meant working high above the ground, but what other choice did he have? "Okay, leave it with me. You tackle this. Do you have a spell you can use to kill it?"

"I have many. Go ahead, we'll join you when I'm done."

Nineteen

Moonfell 2025

"Well," Birdie said with a note of satisfaction, "we at least know how to diffuse the spell on the moon gate. Plus, none of you ended up in India in 1792. Another win."

Her granddaughters and Harlan were wrapped in towels in front of the fire in Moonfell's kitchen, sipping hot chocolate laced with brandy, but the shifters had shaken the events off easily and looked completely unconcerned by it all.

"I saw Meli," Odette said, "so we were seeing flashes of Moonfell's past, too."

"Ed was a bloody genius," JD said from where he sat at the kitchen table, still studying Ed's inventions. "To truly capture a place, and then transfer it to another. Marvellous."

"Aided by Fitz," Horty reminded him archly. "Our ancestor's magic is what resonated with the gate."

"No offence intended, madam," JD said, barely looking up.

"We must check the other gates," Birdie said, to no one in particular. "Test the slides and see what happens."

"Are you sure that's wise?" Maverick asked, cocking his head.

"Well, nothing bad happened, and if there's a message in these, I want to find it."

"You still have peacocks," he reminded her. "From 1792 India. Do you really want to potentially add to that?"

"They might be from 1792 Moonfell," Morgana suggested. "We have displaced energy, and the peacocks are part of that."

"Which means," Odette said, "that whatever we have set in motion isn't over yet. Maverick might have a point."

"Whatever it is," Maverick said, standing reluctantly and nodding to Monroe and Arlo, "we have to go. We'll be opening in a few hours, and Saturday night is always busy. If you need us, though, just call."

"I'll be back after the shift, anyway," Monroe said to Morgana. "Save me some of those letters."

She smiled. "Of course. I'll see you all out."

"We should go, too," Harlan said, shrugging off his towel. "I only intended to be in the office for an hour or so today, although I have to say, this was fun."

"You can leave me here," JD said, burying his head further in his book.

Birdie laughed as she caught Olivia's exasperated expression. "Sorry, JD. We have family arriving and Beltane to organise, but you are welcome to study Ed's book another time."

Olivia hustled him out of the chair. "Come on, JD."

He groaned and shut the book. "If I must. Ladies, it has been a pleasure." He studied the kitchen once more, and then the four witches. "It's good to finally see the inside of this place—and meet its exalted occupants, of course. I will definitely return."

Birdie would welcome learning more about the enigmatic JD, too. "Olivia and Harlan can give you our numbers. I mean it. You are welcome to come back."

Harlan snorted. "You may regret that."

"Maybe I'll see you tomorrow," Arlo said, bending to kiss Birdie's cheek.

"Of course, sweetie."

She watched him give Odette a shooting glance, and in minutes their visitors had gone. She sank into the sofa. "Well, that was something I didn't expect today. Meeting an immortal man, that is."

"You expected magical mayhem, then?" Horty asked, plonking herself down in a vacated armchair. "I suppose anything is possible here. Did you mean it about testing the other gates?"

"Of course. The Waning Moon Gate is charged with an unusual amount of energy, and I wonder if Fitz designed the slides to affect it that way."

"I agree with you," Morgana said unexpectedly as she returned to the kitchen. Birdie was lately expecting her to challenge everything, but she looked energised, excited even, as she sat on the sofa. "We should look at all of them. The magic in the projection was stronger than it felt around the gate itself. It really did feel bewitched. I said as much to Harlan." Her gaze became distant. "As if we were caught betwixt."

"Betwixt?" Horty asked.

"What a great word for it," Odette said, nodding. "Betwixt is perfect. We were caught within something timeless. I sensed that, too. We saw the past and present at the same time, as if through a prism. No. A *kaleidoscope*." Suddenly radiant as a broad smile erupted, it reminded Birdie forcefully of how very pretty Odette was. "I wish we could have fixed it in place, but I think we would have lost something if that happened."

Morgana adjusted her position to look at her cousin. "Yes, we would have. Part of the spell's charm was its ability to reveal just snatches of the past, in layers. And I felt so relaxed. I mean, anything could have happened, and yet I didn't worry at all, and I think we all know how unusual that is." She gave Birdie a wry smile, and Birdie immediately felt terrible for feeling so mean.

"Because we were safe, and we knew it," Odette said, a trace of wistfulness in her tone. "The shifters weren't worried, either, and they sense danger very quickly."

"I'm envious," Birdie confessed, now wishing she had experienced it, too. "We sensed the spell pulling us in and deliberately drew back."

"And a bloody good job we did, too!" Horty was clearly exasperated with them. "What the hell is the matter with you all? You know you were bloody bewitched! I think you still are. I'm all for experiencing something magical, but how long would that have continued for? Hours? Days? *Months*? You might have wasted away in there and died from starvation."

"Good grief." Birdie rolled her eyes. "They could have left at any point."

"But they didn't. They were there for nearly two hours before we nailed that spell. And," she added, jabbing her finger at Birdie, "we were starting to get in a right bloody pither with it. It wasn't as straightforward as we thought. JD and Olivia were so caught up in their investigations that they didn't even question how long it took."

"Two hours!" Morgana sat up in shock, all trace of relaxation vanished. "That long?"

"Look at the time." Horty gestured to the clock on the wall. "You must feel it, too. We haven't had lunch because we were so engrossed with the whole thing. I'm starving." Her stomach grumbled to accentuate the fact. "Plus, the weather is turning. What if it had rained?"

"It was beautifully sunny and warm in the pavilion," Odette said, but even she now looked doubtful.

"Be honest." Horty was well and truly fired up now. "Could you have left? Really? It was strong magic. Strong enough to make the pavilion real!"

"We considered it," Morgana admitted, "but were worried whether we would cross to our Moonfell or find India on the bank. Or even Moonfell in 1792. Especially after Odette saw Meli."

"Exactly!" she said, harrumphing in vindication, a most peculiar sound. "It was a gloriously pretty cage, but you were all in a spell, shifters and Harlan included."

"It's not like our brains had turned to mush. We admitted we felt drugged," Odette said, "but we were thinking rationally."

"No, I don't think I was," Morgana confessed. "I was actually loving the lack of responsibility. I felt so carefree, and that's not me at all. You all know that."

"Morgana, you aren't that bad," Birdie reassured her. "You consider things calmly before jumping in normally, and that's a very good character trait to have as High Priestess. Plus, you were with Monroe, and no doubt that was having an effect, too. However, Horty is right, as much as I hate to admit it. It could have gone on for hours. I mean, perhaps it would have worn itself out, but how long would that have taken?"

"If Fitz was behind it, he would not have endangered anyone," Morgana insisted.

"You've only read two letters," Horty said. "You can't know that yet. He might have been a maniac. Or Ed might be. He's involved, too, remember. Maybe Fitz crossed him, and he did something to the slides."

By now, Birdie was starting to feel very uncomfortable about the whole thing. And then something else struck her. "Lotus flowers!

That myth about the lotus-eaters from Homer's *Odyssey*. If I remember correctly, they ate lotus flowers, got all drugged up, and lived on an island in a perpetual state of bliss. They cared about nothing!"

"Well, we may have been surrounded by lotus flowers, but I certainly didn't consume any," Morgana said. "I know that much."

"But lotus is used for spiritual insight and meditation," Odette pointed out. "Maybe the scent was potent. It's all so confusing. Damn it. We really should have harvested some. Every part of it is useful."

Birdie hated missing the chance to collect fresh plants. "True, but we were worried that if we got any closer to the bank, we would have been spelled, too. You clearly didn't think to do it. Besides, they might have vanished anyway. A beautiful illusion."

"We can't forget that it's Beltane tomorrow." Horty stood up. "The veils are thinning, and we need to fortify ourselves—mentally and physically. We need food, restorative tea, and a plan. I'm scrambling eggs for everyone, so don't argue."

"I wouldn't dream of it," Birdie said darkly. "You're so bossy sometimes."

"Pot, kettle. I don't care. How long have we got before Merlin gets here?"

Morgana checked the time. "Another hour or so, I think. Why?"

"He can help with the gates, of course, while the girls can help with Beltane preparations. That should keep them out of trouble."

"I suspect," Birdie said, mentally reviewing her list of what they still needed to do, "that once they know of this mystery, they will want to be involved."

"All the more reason to get the Beltane prep finished."

While Horty bustled about, Birdie studied her granddaughters. Both looked subdued, as if they were still under a magical influence. *Betwixt.* She capitalised the word in her mind, feeling how right it was. "After we've eaten, you should go to the attic," she said to Odette.

"Use this lingering mental state for investigating Meli's tarot cards. Morgana, you should read some more letters."

Odette just nodded, but Morgana hesitated. "There are other things to do."

"No, there aren't. While you are still caught up in the magic, use it."

As she said it, the tinkling of silver bells sounded again, as if to emphasise her point.

Moonfell agreed.

Odette entered the attic with a renewed sense of purpose.

She certainly saw the attic differently after her earlier insight. In her mind's eye now, she was in the upper branches of an enormous tree, along with hundreds of High Priests and Priestesses and their many relatives. She could almost feel them around her like birds perched among the leaves, their many eyes in the portraits watching her pass.

She headed directly to Melusine's portrait and studied the space it was in again, and this time saw what she had missed earlier because she was so intent on her discovery. Both sides of the area were covered in old paintings, and there were also old items of furniture, much as there were everywhere, but there was no doubt that the section by Melusine's portrait looked more arranged than others. An imposing, wing-backed chair in black velvet was placed behind a round table inlaid with different woods in an intriguing design, and to the right of it was a glass cabinet filled with different types of candle holders, and a few bowls and vases of varying designs.

Looking from the chair to the portrait and back again, it was obvious that this was Melusine's chair depicted in the painting, and Odette was pretty sure that this was the same table that was in the painting too, as was a three-branched candelabra in the glass case. Withdrawing it to replicate the arrangement, Odette sat on the chair, spread the tarot cloth on the table, and lit the yellowed stumps of the candles with a word of magic. Eye to eye with Melusine, Odette shuffled what they believed were her cards and talked to the portrait as if she were there.

"I want to know about the gates and magical slides, Meli, if I can call you that. And I want to know why you were only High Priestess for such a short time. We are caught up in something now, and it feels momentous, but maybe that's just us getting carried away." Meli stared back. "I haven't found your grimoire, but you must have had one, and so must Fitz, so where is his? Perhaps his was in India and got lost there. Or," she studied the long rooms stretching away to either side, "they are here for some reason, in the attic. Did he get into trouble? Did he shame the family?" And then another horrible thought struck her. "Did he die in India? No! I'm jumping ahead."

As if the tarot would answer so directly, anyway. She was muddled, and perhaps being with Arlo had added to that. As always, his potent shifter energy mixed with hers, until sometimes she didn't know where he ended and she began.

Wait? What?

"I'm not thinking about Arlo! I am Betwixt. Caught between Moonfell and India, just as I suspect you were for a while. Morgana said you were too young to travel with Fitz, and yet his letter made her think that you were independent. What happened in 1807 that you should not be High Priestess of Moonfell? I refuse to believe that you died so young." *Please no.*

Yes, that was key. Or one of them, at least. *Thirteen years after the events at the Rajgarh docks would have made her how old?* She needed to check with Morgana. *Mid-thirties, perhaps. So, did that mean Peri died in 1803?* Annoyed with herself, Odette put aside all thoughts of anyone else. This was about Meli and her cards.

Odette closed her eyes as she continued to shuffle the deck, deciding not to pull a card, but let the sensation of shuffling do its work, a hypnotic enough motion in itself. The thick silence of the attic seemed to lift, and just as it had done a few weeks before, she felt a fluttering sensation around her face and her hair lifted slightly, as if a window had opened in the attic.

And then she heard a thump, and her eyes flew open.

Twenty

Rajgarh 1792

Fitz was covered in blood and guts and stank like a cesspit. "By the gods, that was worse than I expected."

"Then get in the river and wash it off!" Vik had sheltered behind the corner of the closest building just in case he was needed, but now emerged, laughing at the state Fitz was in.

Fitz had used one of his most effective spells to kill the trapped creature as humanely and swiftly as possible. It was a well-aimed and targeted spell designed to blast through the trap's boundaries and pierce the creature's armour-like skin in seconds. He had enhanced the spell with his staff, and the effect had magnified, virtually shredding the creature into chunks. Fitz hated killing things, even Chimera Rakshasas. He only did it to keep people safe, and he accepted what he had to do to achieve that.

Siphoning water from the river, he blasted the dockside, scouring the remains of the creature into the river, and washing most of the trap away, too.

"What about the rift?" Vik asked, stepping in front of where it was, identified by a symbol Fitz had scored into the ground below it. "Can we close it? I still don't understand its purpose. The creature didn't use it at all. Neither of them did."

"Perhaps. Let me wash first. I can't think straight."

The spell had drained Fitz, as had the fight before it, and he walked to the *ghats* and into the river, sluicing water over his head, but careful not to drink any. The river's strong current tugged at his waist, but he resisted it, and turned to face the dock, pleased to catch his breath, but then nearly choked as he inhaled sharply.

Ed had swung onto one of the cranes close to a building with the yantra-mixed sigil on it, and had clambered to the top. Now, he blasted at it, using his magic-loaded staff like a gun, and the blast ricocheted around the docks as plaster went flying. He had the scope with him, so Fitz presumed he knew where to aim.

"Have you seen that madman?" Vik came running. "The Company will be furious with us for this damage."

"We have killed two creatures and are hopefully stopping more, so they should be grateful." Fitz emerged from the river dripping wet, and only smelling marginally better than when he went in. "He's got the right idea, though."

"We've closed portals before. This rift could be the same."

"Could be. I'm reluctant to do anything until we know exactly what it is." He dried his clothing with a spell so he was damp rather than soaking, and paced around the rift. Now that he had time to think, he had another idea that he wished he'd have considered before. He conjured a revealing spell and cast it over the area, uncovering the slender, oval rift that shimmered in the air above them with a dull, metallic gleam. "That's better."

Vik folded his arms across his chest. "That is not a portal."

"I agree." Portals to other dimensions were generally much bigger. "Unless it can expand, the creature could not manifest through that."

"It gives off little energy that I can feel." Vik stepped closer to it. "People must walk under it all day long. I daresay, some of the equipment they use here would even move through it."

"Then perhaps it is as we think. An observation point." As Fitz paced around it, he discovered that it looked the same from all angles. "I'm going to test it."

"How?" Vik withdrew his sword again.

"Something simple." Fitz conjured a witch-light and threw it at the rift. The first one missed and floated above Vik's head. The next one was more accurate, and the rift swallowed it whole.

Vik caught his eye. "Interesting. Where has it gone?"

"Perhaps it was destroyed or was absorbed into the rift itself, but the size hasn't changed." He sniggered as another thought struck him. "Or it's landed in someone's lap and the creator is debating what to do with it."

They stood for several moments waiting for a response of some kind, but when nothing happened, Fitz said, "I'm heading to the jetty to investigate the other one."

By the time Fitz arrived at the next rift, Ed had reached another sigil—or so he assumed. He was precariously balancing on the broad wooden beam of the crane, and curious to see the magical lines that Ed had described discovering with his scope, Fitz decided to use the same spell he had cast to expose the rift. He aimed his spell high, rewarded immediately when the lines illuminated overhead. Following their paths, he saw one leading towards one of the largest warehouses, and another to the Customs House.

Before Fitz could even fathom what they meant, Ed fired again, but this time, the yantra retaliated. The spell that blasted from Ed's staff rebounded back at him, missing Ed by mere inches. He flattened himself on the wooden beam, and the blast cracked the beam behind him. With a hideous splintering and groaning, the beam cracked in two and shuddered towards the ground, crunching into the roof of a lower building. Ed desperately tried to hang on but was quickly bounced off, and Fitz lost sight of him.

Simultaneously, the exposed energy lines fizzed and exploded overhead, sending bolts of magical power everywhere. Fitz sprinted through them, risking getting hit, but desperate to reach Ed. He couldn't even see Vik.

"Ed! Where are you?"

Fitz upended crates and pulled splintered wood aside, heading towards the damaged building that the crane's beam had fallen on, finally finding Ed crumpled but alive on a collapsed roof of palm leaves that made temporary shelter for the fruit sellers. Gripping him under the shoulders, he hauled him away, fearful more masonry would soon collapse on their heads.

"Ed! Can you hear me?"

"Yes. I'm half dead, not half deaf." He struggled upright as another chunk of the crane collapsed a short distance away.

Vik came to a skidding halt next to them. "We've got trouble."

"Please, not more creatures." Fitz was shattered.

"Worse. Captain Townsend is here."

Actually, Ed reflected, as he winced in pain from his probably broken ribs, *Captain Townsend was the least of their worries*. He had sent for Anthony, the Assistant Resident, who descended on the docks like a plague within ten minutes of Townsend storming into the port.

Captain Townsend had taken one look at the damage and rounded them up like convicts, making them sit on a row of crates surrounded by soldiers, as if they might escape. All three were far too tired to complain.

Anthony clattered into the compound on his horse, dismounted with far more grace than Ed expected, and after one sweeping glance at the port, looked so red in the face that Ed was worried he might explode.

"You have destroyed the docks! What were you thinking? Look at the broken crates. And the crane!" he said, voice raising an octave. "Oh dear God in Heaven. You have blasted the buildings, too. This is insufferable and absolutely inexcusable. I shall have you all sacked!"

"Actually," Ed said, before anyone else could answer, "the Chimera Rakshasa destroyed the docks. Two of them, in fact. Fortunately, we killed them, but we barely escaped with our lives. You're welcome, by the way."

Anthony stopped his tirade dead, finally looking at all three of them properly. They were a sorry state. Ed's clothes were torn and blackened from the blast and the fall, and plaster dust had settled into his sweat, making him look even worse. Plus, he was grimacing horribly because of the pain that he was having difficulty hiding. Vikram was covered in blood spatter, and Fitz was damp and stank of the river and something deeply revolting. *Dead supernatural creature.*

Anthony visibly swallowed. "You killed it? *Them?*"

"Yes," Fitz answered, "but there may be more. It's doubtful that this is over."

"You must be joking!"

"No." Fitz pointed at the rift that was fortunately still illuminated at the end of the jetty—or maybe *fortunately* was the wrong word. "We cannot explain *that.*"

Anthony's nostrils flared with disdain, and then a trace of fear. "What is it?"

"A rift in this world, we think, but why it's there eludes us for now. We will find out."

"And cause more damage?"

"As we said, that was the creatures' actions, not ours."

"So you say," Townsend spat with a snarl.

Fortunately, no one had seen Ed clamber up on the crane, so no one could blame him for that disaster, he hoped. Its breakage had damaged the Port Office building and the storage facilities close by.

Anthony now rounded on Townsend. "Why weren't *you* in here supervising?"

"I was forbidden to interfere, so I followed orders." He stood to attention in full captain-mode.

"You must have heard something!"

"Of course I did, but it wasn't until I heard the unmistakable sound of a building collapsing that I entered."

Anthony's hands were on his hips. "Did you hear the creature?"

For one horrible moment, Ed thought Townsend would lie as he hesitated, shooting the three men venomous looks, but finally he nodded. "I did. I heard unholy bellows."

"So, it's true?" Anthony looked around again. "Where are their bodies?"

"One of them dissolved into dust," Vikram said, pointing at the spot, "and I am covered in its blood. Chunks of the other are in the river. I can show you."

"I really don't think that's necessary," Anthony said, stepping backwards as if Vik were infected.

"I think it is, actually," Fitz said, standing abruptly. "You want evidence, we'll show it to you. Then we'll go home. Ed is injured, and we are all exhausted from our battle. I doubt anything else will happen here tonight. Our enemy has suffered losses, and will no doubt need to regroup. However, I suggest you seal off the docks. We have more work to do here tomorrow."

"Keep it sealed tomorrow?" Anthony's eyes widened in horror. "But goods are expected!"

"Do you really want anyone to see this mess?" Fitz asked, incredulous. "Or risk them being attacked? I fear the creatures will grow bolder now. The goods can wait in the boats."

Anthony looked as if he might complain, but in the end added another order, his chin jutting out belligerently. "You will see the Resident immediately, of course."

"Of course. I will personally give him an explanation of our activities. I'm sure he'll find it enlightening. Oh, and Ed needs to see the doctor, so make sure he's awake and ready when we get back."

He shot Ed a sympathetic look, and Ed nodded in gratitude. No doubt there would be many more questions for them all before bed that night.

Twenty-One

Moonfell 2025

The bright blue skies of earlier that day had vanished under a thick bank of grey clouds, and rain was threatening to fall when Morgana settled in her armchair next to the fire, Fitz's letters at her side.

She still felt odd after her experience in the pavilion, and carried a wistfulness she couldn't quite explain. It was as if she'd lost something, and she hoped the letters would bring it back. She checked the date, making sure that she was reading sequentially, and plunged in.

Dear Meli,

I have had the most awful sleep, despite the fact that I was exhausted when I retired to bed last night, so here I am at dawn, wide awake, and full of a mix of excitement and dread at what the day might bring.

I am currently sitting on the covered veranda that stretches along the length of the first floor, mirroring the one below it. It is broad, and like the rest of the Residency, beautifully appointed with painted balustrades, decorative latticework, and cane chairs and tables spread along its expanse. It is quiet except for the raucous cries of the birds as they awaken, and the faint sound of the muezzin calling the faithful to prayer. The calmness of it is a balm to my soul after last night, but I shall come to that shortly. I am trying to focus on the beauty of the river and the garden.

You would love it here. The Ganga is wide and flat, but I know there are strong currents beneath that placid surface. At the moment, mist rises off the water and travels across the lawns of the Residency. It won't last. Already, heat is rising, and I sit in my linen shirt with my sleeves rolled up and the faintest breeze in my hair. Soon, the sun will burn the mist away and bake the earth again. The peacocks are already strutting and displaying their magnificent feathers to the peahens, and they make such a noise. Can you imagine if we had them at Moonfell? I think they would drive us all to madness.

I don't think I have even mentioned the monkeys yet, which is a dreadful oversight. They are called "macaques" and are a reddish-brown in colour, but their teeth are perilously sharp and pointed! They are quite ferocious, so we keep our distance, but they love to raid the fruit trees. I can see them now, chattering and bickering as they chase after each other. Can you imagine those at Moonfell, either? I think we have enough activity in our garden without adding to it. The Residency staff are forever chasing them away.

You know, I would love to be able to show you what it's like here. I fear my descriptions are inadequate. It's not just how it looks, but how it feels, too. I will ask Ed if we can capture images of Rajgarh for you, and other places, too. There is a timelessness about India. The way that the villages and towns have maintained their way of life for hundreds, if not thousands of years. I feel suspended in time here sometimes, especially now, on the cusp of a new day. It doesn't escape me that May Day is approaching, either, and while they may not celebrate that here, I feel it in my blood. A liminal time. Perhaps that is why we battle with such odd creatures now.

So, to our matter at hand. As I told you in my last letter (which I am aware is still sitting in my cupboard waiting to be sent to you, and that potentially you are reading all these together, so this is a diary of sorts for me) we visited the port properly two days ago to assess what we needed to do, and then that evening we were invited to dinner at Harishchandra Sharma's house, Vikram's friend. He lives in a stunning haveli with his wife, children, and extended family, and it seems he is semi-retired, as his sons run his business now. I gather he trades in indigo, primarily. It was a refreshingly informal meal. Again, how much you would have loved it. We ate spiced meats and vegetables, all seated around a low table. After that we visited the port at night, where I'm afraid to say I was attacked. Fortunately, the creature took itself off swiftly, vanishing into some kind of portal we cannot discern the nature of.

Fitz went on to describe the events of the night, and then how he had protected the Residency grounds and their subsequent plans, but Morgana was fixated on the creature he and his companions had fought, struggling to imagine how it looked because it was so outside the realm of her experience. It sounded awful. Fitz, however, seemed to take it all in his stride, which made her realise how often these encounters were part of his life. She hadn't questioned his job before—although she found it intriguing, of course—but reading about it made her realise what an insane occupation it was. And how deadly it could have been. But as she read on, it became even worse as he described the two creatures that appeared the next evening. Chimera Rakshasas.

This is a strange business, Meli. These creatures do not act alone, and there are odd rifts in the port that I cannot explain, as well as magical energy lines that also seem to have no function that appear to be emitted by a type of sigil called a yantra. These are sacred, geometrical designs traditionally used for meditation, but can also channel occult powers. They appear to have been mixed with other sigils, but as I mentioned, their purpose is unclear, and they were positioned high up on several buildings.

Ed tried to destroy them, but they reacted strongly and attacked him in some kind of self-defensive measure. He has broken several ribs after a terrible fall. The doctor examined him and said there is no other damage, but he winces with every breath. I hope he is still sleeping now to conserve his strength for later. I would rather not risk his health by taking him back to the docks, but we need his insight. Besides, I know he will not stay back here unless completely incapacitated.

All most peculiar as you can see. I apologise. I think I'm rambling.

As for the two rifts, they are even stranger. They are slender, oval shapes that emit a dull metallic glow, and I wonder if they are observation points, because there is no doubt in my mind that these creatures are being guided. Perhaps they are merely meant to perplex and confuse and lead us astray. We will return to the docks today to see what else we can learn.

The Resident is not pleased, because the port must remain closed. He did not rage as Anthony, the Assistant Resident, had. Instead, he fixed his steely, disapproving gaze upon us. Fortunately, Vikram was not present, having been escorted to his friend's house instead, so he escaped that censure. I wondered if Henry might want to dismiss us, but to be honest, how could he? Despite the damage caused in the port, he still needs us. I managed to persuade him that it is not over yet and that we think more attacks will occur, but it is so hard to explain these things to people who do not understand the supernatural.

I forget how deeply our lives are entwined in it—mine and yours. Moonfell is a magical place, full of the uncanny, and we residents accept that as part of our normal life. Magic runs thick in our grounds and in our blood. Even so far from home I can feel it, especially now at dawn, as I write to you. I feel an almost unbroken connection across the distance. I don't miss it as such, because I am enjoying my life here, but neither can I forget it.

Morgana paused, lifting her head for a moment as she absorbed Fitz's words. Her family all understood that Moonfell was special, and that each visitor reacted differently to it—as did family, for that matter—but to read Fitz referring to it in the same way made her feel even more connected to them. To him. To know that they felt the same. Her hand stroked the paper, and she felt that she could almost touch him. Especially now that they had found Ed's sketch.

Shaking off her thoughts, she continued to read as he described the attack on Vikram behind the market, Alicia and Elizabeth's plans for the party that evening, as well as learning of Benjamin Swift's arrival.

To return to our issue, Captain Townsend's regiment continue to guard the docks, and no ships will be allowed there. It would be unusual for the creatures to appear in the day, but we will take all precautions. Besides, the damage caused by our fight was substantial, so I gather the regiment will also be required to clear it today.

Now you know why I cannot sleep. I feel we have stepped into a trap that is slowly tightening. Wish us luck, sister. As for you, I hope you are having fun at Moonfell and expanding your magic and interests. If life feels a little boring right now, at least you are safe.

*I will write with updates later. I know I sound para-
noid, but I can't help it. By the way, Alicia knows I am
a witch, but seems to accept it easily. I think I can trust
her.*

Your beloved brother,

Fitz

Morgana rested the letter on her lap, staring instead into the flames
in the fireplace, pondering over the odd magical lines, yantras, and oval
rifts. *No wonder Fitz was perplexed.* It all sounded very confusing. She
was suddenly worried for him. It sounded as if they had enemies, and
perhaps Edmund's uncle was one, too. Plus, the Resident must have
been worried if he asked Fitz to cast a protection spell on the house.
As for Rakshasas, she needed to look those up, and hopefully Ed had
drawn them in his journals.

She looked back over the second letter, clarifying the timeline.
What struck her was that Fitz had commented that it was close to
Beltane, although he had called it May Day. Rather than read any
longer, she put the letters aside and headed to the shower. Merlin and
her nieces would be here soon. She could read more that night with
Monroe.

Birdie smiled as Merlin and his daughters arrived with a flurry of bags and teenage excitement, their energy adding to the already potent mix of Moonfell magic. As usual, they gathered in the great Gothic kitchen first as the coven updated Merlin with their latest news. A peacock's screech in the background served to confirm the truth of it.

"I expected some magical shenanigans," Merlin said, amused as he studied Ed's Lumina Lantern, "but not this! Never a dull moment, eh, girls?"

Marion, at fourteen the younger of his two daughters and as dark-haired as her father, was already staring through the kitchen window, hoping to catch a glimpse of it. "The peacocks are magical ones?"

"I wouldn't say that exactly," Horty said, as she placed the pot of tea and mugs on the table. "They are here by magical means."

"And," Morgana warned her, "they might not last long. The rest of the spell has already vanished." She side-eyed Birdie. "They seem real enough, though."

"But can we see them? Before it rains?" Marion asked, clearly itching to be outside.

"They're just peacocks," Ellen said, rolling her eyes.

"Are they boring you?" Birdie asked, watching the sixteen-year-old wind her long, honey-coloured hair around her fingers, black nail polish glinting in the lamplight. She was a very pretty girl, and *very* sixteen. Birdie had trouble keeping the sarcasm from her voice. "Would you rather go home and miss Beltane? Miss the chance to see and make real magic? Then by all means. We'll organise it somehow."

Ellen's eyes widened in shock, a challenge in her stare as she looked at Birdie. "No, that's not what I meant."

"Good, because we have plenty for you to do. The Beltane fire needs building, so you can do it with your sister." She turned to Marion, softening her tone. "Of course you can see the peacocks, but don't go too close, or wander off too far. It might rain heavily."

"Ellen," Merlin said, staring meaningfully at her, "go out with your sister. It's been a long drive, and you should stretch your legs."

"I don't need to stretch my legs."

"Ellen, please don't argue."

She stood with another dramatic eye roll. "Fine."

Merlin laughed as they left. "Don't worry, Ellen is not like this all the time. She only has pouty moments. It's her age. Fortunately, it hasn't hit Marion. Yet."

"Good, because I might strangle them."

"Birdie!" Horty said, hands on her hips, "that's terrible."

"I know, but she doesn't know how lucky she is. Look at this place!" Birdie scowled and threw her hands out.

"Which is why we're here," Merlin said, trying to appease her. "A little magical grounding. They've been caught up in school and exams. And boys." He took a breath. "That's been trying. Ellen is actually very excited to be here. They both are. It's just uncool to show it too much."

Horty snorted. "Wait 'til they see the magical projections. That will shock her out of being cool!"

"Personally, *I* can't wait!" Merlin took his offered tea and smiled. He was dark-haired like Morgana, but already a little grey was seeping in at the temples. Unlike Morgana, though, he didn't have a grey streak, although he wore his hair slightly long, so it brushed his collar. He certainly didn't emulate his namesake with long hair and a beard.

"Good," Horty said, settling next to him. "We have another gate to test, and we were waiting for you."

"Excellent. I look forward to it. You look miles away, Morgana," he said, turning to his sister.

She shrugged. "I'm having trouble shaking off the spell from earlier, and the letters—well, letter, I only read one this afternoon—have just enhanced that. I feel like I know Fitz now. His voice—his tone, rather—is in my head."

Her statement made Birdie more worried. Morgana was pragmatic, not dreamy. That was Odette, and yet she'd certainly been caught up in all this. Now she regretted asking her to indulge the mood. "Let's drink our tea quickly and get in the garden. I'd love to test one more gate before it's dark." *And with any luck, banish this odd mood that had settled.* "Do you think Odette is okay?"

"Where is she?" Merlin asked.

"In the attic, trying to connect with Meli," Morgana explained. "That's who Fitz is writing to. She was younger by about fifteen years, I think. We still need to sort out the family tree properly. Meli was an early experimenter of the tarot, and for a short while was High Priestess of Moonfell. We don't know why it was so short, though." She turned to Birdie. "Odette will be fine, I'm sure. She'll join us when she's ready."

Birdie hoped so. Both her granddaughters seemed connected to this whole business far more closely than Birdie and Horty. She shrugged it off. As usual, she was probably worrying about nothing. But Horty caught her eye, and from her expression alone, Birdie could see she was worried, too.

Damn it.

Twenty-Two

Rajgarh 1792

With the port illuminated by bright sunshine, Fitz had to admit that the place looked even worse than it had done at night. In fact, it *was* worse than the night before.

"Something returned after we left," Fitz said to Ed, pointing to the jetty with the rift at the end that was now broken into pieces. "The jetty is destroyed, and it wasn't last night. And one of the boats has been sunk." The spars poked out of the river's mud, and despite the *sepoys'* best efforts, a group of Indians gathered on the *ghats* to stare.

Captain Townsend glowered at them. "I don't think you have the slightest idea what you are doing. This thing is making a mockery of you."

"There are several creatures," Fitz shot back, "and as I said before, they are being directed. They are vindictive."

"And creatures aren't normally?"

"No. While sometimes they hunt for sport, mostly they hunt for food, and sometimes they strike out because they have been disturbed or hurt, but in general, they have no interest in the world of men. They have no need for trade!"

"Then do something!" Townsend was red-faced again, no doubt aggravated by the heat as well as the situation. "This has got worse since you arrived, not better."

"Just supervise your men and leave us to our job," Fitz said, the truth of Townsend's statement jarring him. "If they find anything odd while they're cleaning up, I want to know."

"What kind of odd?"

"Anything that shouldn't be here." Fitz stalked off, eyes darting everywhere, as Ed tried to keep up. Feeling guilty, he slowed down well away from everyone. "Sorry. Are you all right?"

"I'm sore, but I'll be fine. You mustn't let him get to you."

"But he's right. This has worsened since we arrived."

"Which suggests that we're right, and this is aimed at us. Someone wants us dead, or at least out of business. News of the East India Company travels far and wide. No one will want us after this."

"We have solved many of these cases before, and will do again."

"No one was working against us then," Ed pointed out. "You know, I hate to say this, but I feel my uncle's hand in this."

Fitz stared at his friend, but he wasn't joking. "You think he would go this far?"

"He hates what I do, we know this. What if he's tired of waiting for me to stop and has decided to force the issue?"

"By trying to kill us? I know he's a difficult man, but even so... Surely, this has to do with trade."

Ed studied the dock. "If someone really wanted to hamper trade, they would make the creature damage buildings, burn down warehouses, and destroy goods and ships, but none of that has happened."

"They killed men."

"Who are replaceable. Sad, but true. Meanwhile, trade continues, albeit restricted, except for today, at our insistence."

"Because of the destruction."

"Yes, but only of empty crates mainly, and of course the crane that hit the building, which was initiated by me, and was an act of retaliation. Just look at how many crates there are around the place. I noticed that as soon as I arrived last night, and yet didn't question it. I just thought they had run out of time to store everything. Now, I'm wondering if they were left out deliberately."

An uneasy feeling crept through Fitz. The smashed crates were empty, that was true enough. "But that happens. Docks are always messy, crowded places."

"You're trying to talk me out of it, but you can't. There weren't just a few crates, there were lots of them. The main damage was done by me on the crane. I bet they didn't expect that. I destroyed a yantra, and it—whoever or whatever it is—didn't like it. It struck back. How is that possible?"

Fitz shook his head. He hadn't expected that argument, but there was no denying that Ed had seen something he hadn't. "I don't know, and that is a good point, but that means there are collaborators in this."

"More than likely."

Fitz sighed, not liking the way this was going, and instead considered the odd yantra attack. "It looked like lightning shooting out of those overhead lines. Are they still there?" He gestured to the scope over Ed's shoulder in its case. "Can I borrow it?" Ed passed it to him, wincing as he did. "Are you still aching?"

"Unfortunately yes." He touched his left side. "All down here where I fell."

"I can't believe your uncle would try to kill you, or me."

"Or Vik? He was attacked in the street yesterday, in case you've forgotten."

Fitz trained the scope on the walls of the Customs House, not sure whether to be relieved or not when he saw the yantra sigil was still there. But then he saw something different. "It's singed or burnt, perhaps." He fell silent as he studied the others, noting the same thing. They had shimmered before, but now they were a blackened orange. "I think that when you destroyed one, it set up a chain reaction. They were linked by those magical power lines, so in theory they would have transmitted the attack. After all, you used magic. Maybe there was a spell to prime them, like a magical bomb." He moved the scope and refocussed. "The rifts are still there. Maybe," he said, becoming excited as an idea struck him, "their purpose is to detect magic. We said it felt like a web. The spider is elsewhere, monitoring our actions."

"How?"

"Scrying, perhaps? A crystal ball. And maybe..." he hesitated as he thought it through. "Maybe they enhance the creatures, too. After last night, those magical lines were overloaded. Perhaps," he said, cocking an eyebrow at Ed, "that means their detection system is no longer working."

"If that's even what it is."

"True, but I think I'm close. They knew to attack when we were here, not before. Last night after we left was retaliation, or they didn't know we had left."

"My uncle can't do magic, but he could be working with someone who can."

"Even though he hates you using it?"

"He has to *because* we do. Or rather, you do."

Fitz started pacing as the patterns began to emerge. "Very well, I will accept your assertion. After all, it does feel personal. Is he working with Deepak Verma, or was that name suggested just to put us off?

Vik did visit Trickster, after all, and tricksters will trick by their very nature. Or is it some other Indian or Englishman? Or in fact, any other European? There are enough here."

"It would need to be a local contact," Ed agreed. "Vik should be at Deepak's house now, so we shall see what he finds. As for us," Ed gestured to the docks. "Let's see if they have left a clue."

"Plus, we still have the party to look forward to tonight," Fitz reminded him. "If all else fails today, we still have that."

Vik had slipped over the high walls of Deepak Verma's grounds like a snake, and hunkered down beneath the broad leaves of a peepul tree to study the grounds.

He had watched the place for an hour before he acted, clothed in the garments of a street hawker to disguise his appearance. Like Harishchandra's house, Deepak lived in the wealthy merchant area around the marketplace, the walls that surrounded his home high and imposing. He hadn't even told Harishchandra where he was going, instead saying he was joining his friends at the port.

Once in the right area, he had made discreet inquiries on the streets as to the whereabouts of Deepak's house, and once he found the family's symbol above the door, had searched the area thoroughly, ensuring that no one had followed him. Getting inside had been tricky, but he had found an area of the wall that was more uneven than the rest and scaled it quickly. Now, he caught his breath.

Like many Indian gardens, this one had lemon and orange trees, pools and fountains, and pavilions to shelter from the sun. The house was magnificent, even more so than his friend's home. Arched windows and doors with decorative reliefs scored every part of the house, and he could hear music and laughter. Deepak had an office in the town, so in theory, although the dock was closed, he and his sons would be there. *But how to get inside?* He reached into his tunic to check that he still had the glass bottle that Fitz had provided. It contained a shadow spell should he need it, but Vik was planning on saving it for absolute emergencies. Fortunately, many doors and windows were open, and the main building wasn't too far away.

Ensuring there were no snakes underfoot, he progressed silently along the border under the wall, and then slipped inside the dark interior. A magnificent room stretched before him, darkened from the closed shutters that kept the heat out, and after waiting once more to listen for any footsteps, he progressed to the door.

On the other side was a corridor with richly-decorated tiles underfoot. He surmised that if Deepak was involved with, or at least interested in the occult, he would have a room dedicated to it. There was no other way but to be methodical and search everywhere.

Ed dug through the rubble beneath the building where he had blasted the first *yantra*, hoping to find a piece of plaster. He had a theory that if he could find a chunk with the *yantra* on, it would still contain a portion of the magic used to create it.

Unfortunately, because of the crane's destruction and cataclysmic collapse, plaster, rubble, and wood were strewn everywhere, and look-ing up at the destroyed portion of the next building, it was hard to believe that he had been so high up the previous night. He had been so determined to do something that he hadn't stopped to consider the danger.

The regiment was working doggedly in the heat and sun, but there was so much rubble to clear that it was hard going. The main issue was the broken crane. The wooden beam and the thick chain and ropes were tangled and half wedged under the damaged roof that had collapsed on it. Fortunately, the soldiers were too caught up with their own work to notice his business. Fitz was engaged in an altogether more unpleasant task of securing a piece of the creature he had blasted into the river for spell purposes. Together they had an idea for something they could fashion.

Finally, after using his scope, he found a few chunks of plaster with a portion of the *yantra* on it, and he quickly secured them in his leather bag, just as a shadow stretched over him. Wincing with the effort of pushing to his feet, he presumed it was Townsend or Anthony come to nose at his business, until he heard his uncle's voice.

"I was told I'd find you here, but I didn't expect to see you scrabbling in the dust like a common rat." Benjamin Swift was as big and imposing as his voice, and he was making no effort to hide his disdain.

"I'm looking for evidence, but unfortunately," Ed said, lying smoothly, "have found none."

"Why doesn't that surprise me?"

Ed stepped into the shade in an attempt to see his uncle better. The glare of the sun was behind him, and he seemed to enjoy his position. When Ed's eyes adjusted to the light, he saw that his uncle was dressed in smart clothing that was far too heavy for such weather, and sweat beaded his brow. *Good.* Ed hoped he'd sweat to death. His greying hair was swept back and oiled into place, and his enormous moustache quivered with anger that Benjamin was not trying to hide. He was odious.

"What are you doing here, Uncle?"

"Assessing the damage you have done. It was with the greatest reluctance that I told Henry of your location, but he insisted that he needed you to resolve this issue. I hoped you would redeem yourself. Alas, not."

"Why do I need to redeem myself? Our team is good at what we do."

"Because this is an unseemly business, as you well know."

"I don't cause these problems, I resolve them. Someone needs to do it."

"But not *you*!"

Ed took a breath, not wanting to argue, but he also couldn't forget that he now suspected his uncle was behind this mess, or at least involved somehow. Forcing a calm he didn't feel, he said, "I know that you don't like what I do, but I enjoy it. Furthermore, we're good at it, and nor does it interfere with what you do in the slightest! You make it bigger than it is because it suits you to do so. However, this case is more unusual than most. We suspect," he watched his uncle's expression carefully, "that someone is behind this, and is purposefully manipulating these creatures."

"That's your excuse for this wilful destruction of Company property?"

That was not the response he expected. "*Wilful*? I didn't cause this! Neither did Fitz, nor Vik. The creatures did. Very large, destructive, vicious creatures. That, incidentally, we killed before they killed us. I would say that's progress, wouldn't you?"

Benjamin clearly wanted to retaliate but then stopped himself, eyes narrowing as he took in Ed's appearance. "Yes, it is. You killed two, you say? So it's over?"

"We doubt that. Our experience tells us that much." Puzzled, he asked, "Why did you say wilful? That's an odd word to choose."

"Because of the scale of damage, obviously." Benjamin blustered, arms gesturing at the rubble around them. "When will this be over?"

"I don't know, but soon, we hope. We are working on options right now."

"What options?"

"You wouldn't understand them, and I will not take up your valuable time any longer. I have much to do."

He made to push past his uncle, but Benjamin stood his ground, blocking him into a pile of masonry. "Will you be at the party later?"

"Of course. The Resident has been most generous in arranging it."

"Surely, you'll be too busy here to attend?"

"Don't worry, I won't be an embarrassment to you. I'll save your precious Company, and once this is over, we'll be out of here. I have no wish to linger in Rajgarh."

This time, he pushed past Benjamin forcibly, sick of being near him, but Ben called after him. "It's not enough. If you don't stop this, I will speak to your father about disinheriting you."

Ed spun around to face him, thinking he was hearing things. "You'll do *what*?"

"The money that funds this little operation. I'll see that it stops. I suggest you go home now and find a proper occupation."

Ed's blood thundered in his ears, and he stepped up to Benjamin, no longer caring who saw them, or whether he was being disrespectful. "I will not be dictated to by you or my father, and for you to think I would be only shows how little you know of me."

"I have other options, you know," Ben said, his hot breath on Ed's face carrying a trace of cigar smoke.

"So do I, so don't threaten me."

Certain now that his uncle was involved here in some way, Ed walked away. Whatever happened now, there was no going back.

Twenty-Three

Moonfell 2025

"Come on, girls, this way," Horty said, determined to keep the teenagers busy and progress their Beltane plans. "I don't think it will rain, which will be a blessing."

The two girls followed her, the youngest looking enthusiastic, and the eldest as if she were going to the dentist for an extraction. Both wore jeans and t-shirts, Wellington boots, and jackets over the top to keep out the chill wind, and both had long hair that was tangling in the wind. For all that Ellen was cultivating a sulky profile, Merlin had assured Horty that she loved magic, but had a hard time showing it. *Teenagers.*

"Where are we going?" Marion asked, trudging behind her and carrying a basket.

"We're going to the hedgerow to collect hawthorn branches." Horty's eyes widened as if with a question. "Please tell me that you know your Beltane lore."

"Of course." Ellen answered, flicking her hair like a weapon. "It's when the Goddess makes out with the Green Man."

"Makes out?"

Ellen giggled. "Yes, Auntie Horty. You do know what that is?"

Fine. If that's how it was going to be... "You mean they have mad, raging sex? Absolutely. I've had plenty of that myself, especially in these gardens. I should hope they do, too. A few snogs won't cut it for Beltane. It's a fertility festival, girls! The rites of spring are upon us! Life is burgeoning everywhere. That's what this is about."

Marion blushed at Horty's confession, shooting a furtive gaze at her sister, but Ellen was made of stronger stuff, and she looked Horty full in the eye and said, "You've had sex in this garden?"

"Many times, but don't tell your father I said so. And I'm not suggesting you do, either, before you go thinking that. However, to be more specific, Beltane is the sacred union of the God and Goddess. It's not just sex! In addition, the Goddess is transforming from maiden to mother, out of her first flush of youth. She is supporting life itself!"

Horty marched onwards towards the broad, mixed hedges that lined the walls of Moonfell, currently full of chattering bird life, smirking as the girls whispered behind her. *Ellen was a little smart arse. Was she so cheeky when she was their age? Probably.* And then there was Henry, her youthful lover, of course. She wasn't lying about their trysts. He was her first foray into sex, and it was bloody marvellous. She should probably change the subject, though.

"All right, tell me more about Beltane."

"It's a fire festival," Marion said, seeming to have recovered from her embarrassment. "It represents purification and passion."

Not passion again. "Yes, and a love of life. Historically, huge bonfires would be lit and cattle would be led around it to stave off diseases."

"And there are maypoles. A phallic symbol," Ellen added with a twinkle in her eyes, likely just to provoke Horty.

"Indeed." Horty was more than ready for this madam. "They represent a union of the opposites. What other symbols are there?"

While the girls rattled them off, they reached the hawthorn hedge that was on the verge of being wild. Already, leggy branches were thrusting out, and fresh blossoms was emerging.

"Excellent, and here is our beautiful hawthorn," Horty said. "Another symbol of protection and fertility, but what else?"

Marion dipped her head into the blossoms and inhaled deeply. "It's a fairy tree."

"Exactly. It is believed that it marks the entrance to the fairy realm. A threshold between worlds. It's easy to believe, isn't it? It's cloudy now, but these still dance with light, as if we could crawl right inside and find a way to the Otherworld." Horty dug out a small bottle of mead from her bag, and some ribbons. "I have brought a little offering for the fey, so here you go, Marion. Find a spot for the mead—made from our own honey, too." The bees were already buzzing in the blossoms. She handed the colourful ribbons to Ellen. "Let's tie a few of these in, too. Gently, mind." Horty was pleased to see that the girls were already more enthusiastic. "Beautiful hawthorn, we have brought gifts, and now ask your permission to cut some of your branches to honour the Goddess and the Green Man at Beltane. We come with light and love. And bees," she eyed them nervously as their buzzing stilled and the wind that was rustling the branches died down, "we ask for your blessing in this act, please."

Horty wasn't sure what would happen, especially now that the bees were involved, but the profound silence that fell was intense, as if they had stepped into a void, and she felt Ellen and Marion stop shuffling beside her.

Horty suddenly realised what she should do. "Bees, I must apologise. This is Ellen, oldest daughter of Merlin, brother to Morgana, and this is Marion," she gestured to the youngest, "who is Morgana's youngest niece and Ellen's sister. We shall of course visit the hive later, but they have only just arrived, and are so very excited to celebrate Beltane, aren't you?" She nudged them. "Say hello."

Horty had not expected to have to do this, but that was her error, not theirs. *Idiot.* They would have to rectify this later. Meanwhile, the girls murmured their hellos. Suddenly, the spell was broken, the silence vanished as the bees buzzed again, and the hedge shivered in the wind.

"There we go. Permission given, but be gentle."

Horty had been intending to leave them to it, but decided to spend a few more moments, just to make sure nothing untoward was about to happen.

"Can I make a flower crown?" Marion asked. "Will the bees mind?"

"I think they'll be quite happy about it." She handed out secateurs, showing them how to cut the branches. "We'll need to spread out, so we don't take too much from one spot. We're not going to be greedy."

"What else do we need this for?" Ellen asked, as she joined in.

"We need to decorate the outside fire area, and the altar that we'll make in the morning. We'll also plant some seeds in the glasshouse, make some oatcakes, and we need to build the fire. We already have lots of wood for that, so plenty to keep us busy. Have you set some intentions?"

Marion shrugged. "Not really."

"They don't need to be big. Just something positive."

"Isn't Beltane when the veils thin, too?" Ellen asked, looking over her shoulder as if a ghost might step out.

"Yes, it is. We think that may be why our ancestors' magic is so strong right now."

Ellen nodded and seemed to focus properly. "So, what is happening, Auntie Horty? I don't understand." No one ever used the 'great' in their titles. It was far too wordy, and like Birdie, Horty hated being reminded of her age too forcefully.

"If I'm honest," Horty admitted, "we don't understand it all, but essentially we have found magical items that are linking us to our past and our ancestors. You know that the whole place is magical, right? The garden and the house?"

"Dad says so, but he's exaggerating, isn't he?" Marion asked, looking both worried and excited.

"No, he's not, but it's good magic." *Most of the time.* "How long has it been since you have been here?"

"A couple of years, I think," Ellen said with a careless shrug. "School keeps us busy."

"I'm sure it does." Horty also knew that Merlin didn't want to overexpose his daughters to Moonfell. It could become a little addictive and overwhelming, as Como and Lam were finding out. "I guess it's easy to forget what it's really like when you're not around something all the time, but yes, it's very magical, and that's because of the centuries of our family's magic and all the spells we practice here. And the bees, of course, who are very magical themselves. There are times when the place lets us see our ancestors more clearly. Sometimes it just happens, and at other times, we instigate it, often unknowingly. Magic can be tricky, but hopefully you already know that. It must always be respected, no matter how much you think you know."

"So not even Birdie knows everything?" Ellen asked, cocking her head.

"No one does, although she knows a lot. Same goes for your aunt, Morgana, who will be High Priestess next. The time you think you know it all, you're dead," she said forcefully. "There is always something to learn, as our current predicament tells us only too well."

"But we're here to celebrate Beltane," Marion said.

"Yes, which is a good time for divination, too. Tarot, scrying, runes, pendulum—whatever takes your fancy, really." Horty stopped, suddenly having an idea. *Divination. Maybe they should try to connect to Fitz or Meli in other ways.*

The sound of voices carried across the garden, and she needed to discuss her idea with the coven. "Okay, I'll leave you to it. Join us by the north moon gate when you're done."

"Where is that?" Ellen asked.

Horty pointed. "Over that way. Look for the large moon gate made of stone and covered in ferns." As she said it, Hades emerged from the undergrowth, his silvery grey Savannah cat markings helping him blend seamlessly with the shadows. He fixed his amber gaze on her and then the girls, and although she couldn't communicate with him like Birdie, she knew exactly what that meant, and she smiled. "Hades will show you the way."

Odette's heart was still racing when she joined the others in the garden, a painting clutched to her chest under her jumper.

Morgana, Birdie, and Merlin were at the north moon gate, officially called the New Moon Gate, and had already set up the Lumina Lantern on the path of stone chippings that ran underneath it. The gate loomed large in the cloudy afternoon, the dark, layered stonework nestling all manner of ferns and mosses and insects, and the air smelled damp and earthy.

Merlin, tall and rangy, was dressed in corduroy and wool, with a big, waterproof jacket that made him look twice as big as he was, and she realised that Lamorak looked a little like him. "Hey, Merlin! They've roped you into this already?"

"Odette!" He embraced her in a hug. "I'm happy to be involved. I always forget how crazy Moonfell can be when I haven't been for a while." He held her at arm's length as he studied her. "Are you okay? You look a little pale."

"I had an experience in the attic."

"A ghost?" Birdie asked, eyes wide.

"Sort of. I was using the tarot to commune with Meli, and a painting fell off the wall further along the attic. I've found Fitz and Ed."

Horty paled. "Not their bones, I hope."

"Good grief, Horty! What are you thinking? I said a *painting*."

She pulled it out from under her jumper, sheltering beneath the stone arch to keep out of the wind, and the others crowded around. "I think that Meli painted it. It has the same style as her tarot book's illustrations."

The painting was about A4 size, and was of Ed and Fitz standing in front of the south moon gate, arms crossed in front of them and broad smiles on their faces. It was hard to discern their features with any great detail, but Odette knew it was them because their names were scribbled on the back of the mount. The gate was covered in greenery and sprigs of white and yellow flowers that Odette thought were honeysuckle. Dominating everything, though, was Moonfell's huge, Gothic house behind it.

"Look," Odette pointed out, in case they had missed it, "the Lumina Lantern is set up on a table, just through the gate. See it?"

"It's set up to point to the south," Merlin said, nodding.

"Exactly. It looks as if there's a formal garden there. You can just see the start of the clipped hedge."

"I wonder if it has significance," Birdie said, "or if it's just a painting. You know, whether it has a message."

"I'll study it later," Odette vowed, tucking it away again. "I'll set it up in my studio."

"Well done," Morgana said, smiling at her. "That is a find. You say it fell off the wall?"

"I felt a presence, and then a thud."

"They are entwined, all three of them. That's how it seems to me, anyway. What do you think?"

Odette nodded, feeling the truth of it. "Yes, they are, more than just with the letters. It will all unfold, I'm sure. Anyway," she squared her shoulders, trying to stay focussed, "let's do this instead. What slides are we trying?"

"Land-based ones," Horty said. "And we're directing it southwards, towards the house. Although, after seeing that painting, maybe we're directing it the wrong way."

"We can try both," Birdie reasoned, "and besides, last night we faced into the garden, not out, and that worked perfectly well."

As they had the previous night, they all lined up behind the gate, the projector in front of them.

"This isn't metallic, though," Merlin said, rubbing his chin thoughtfully. "Surely, it won't have the same effect."

"Stone holds memories," Odette said, sure of herself. "It is of the earth, after all." *But would it hold Moonfell memories and magic, or something even older?*

Horty placed the first slide in. "Here we go. Now, this should be a tree, but we're not sure where it is."

As the witch-light flickered and bloomed, so did the projection. It hit the stone gate and expanded onto the broad path behind it, the shrubs acting as a natural border. Immediately, a large tree appeared, huge branches and multiple roots erupting from its trunk.

The faintest breath of heat wafted across Odette's face, and she heard unusual birdsong, as well as the full-throated chatter of something she couldn't identify.

"That's exotic looking," Morgana said. "A banyan, if I'm not mistaken. Oh, no! Shit! Stop!"

"Why?" Horty had already stepped back, but she fumbled forward again. "What? It's just a tree!"

Already, memories were assailing Odette of the night that the Earth elemental appeared in the garden in the shape of a wizened tree, and for one horrible moment, she thought it was back. But this tree was quite different to that one. It was broad and full of leaves and life. Sunshine filtered through it, casting dappled shade onto a lawn below that wasn't theirs.

Then she saw what had worried Morgana, just as she cried out, "Bloody monkeys! Fitz said they were everywhere in the Residency garden. Stop it! They'll be everywhere here, just like the peacocks!"

But it was already too late. A cacophony of monkey calls echoed out from the tree, just as half a dozen scampered from the branches, out of the projected image, and into Moonfell's garden. One raced to the moon gate and scrambled over it, chattering at the group and exposing huge, sharp teeth before it darted away.

"Bollocks!" Birdie said, blasting a spell after it that missed the animal. "They'll wreak havoc. Catch them!"

"Catch them how?" Horty asked, exasperated. "With a butterfly net and a banana?"

"I was thinking of spells, you imbecile. Why the hell did you pick that slide? Didn't you see the monkeys?"

Odette, however, was already giggling, and Merlin joined in with a full-throated laugh. "Good grief. You lot never do things by halves."

Birdie ignored them and scowled at Horty, still complaining. "I said to pick an innocuous slide!"

"It was a *tree*. How the hell was I to know bloody macaques were in it?"

Even Morgana, so panic-stricken before, was now laughing. "They're just monkeys. How much damage can they do?"

"When they get in the orchard?" Birdie's hands landed on her hips in tiny fists. "Lots."

"Let's hope the bees take care of them," Odette said, thinking that they actually would. "And perhaps we should warn the girls to steer clear of them. In the meantime, where do you think this is?"

"The Residency," Morgana said confidently, stepping forward until she was on the edge of the image again. "I can feel its pull again, but it's not as powerful as last time."

The witches spread out along the edge of the projection, the sunshine of an Indian summer shimmering through the branches. "Why," Odette mused, tempted to step into the image again, "would they include monkeys in the image?"

Merlin laughed. "Because they didn't know they were there, I presume. Does it tell us anything about Fitz and Ed, though?"

"Not really," Birdie said with a sigh. "Let's try another."

"Do we want to see the port?" Merlin asked.

"No!" Morgana said immediately. "Absolutely not. In the last letter I read, Fitz described some truly horrible creatures." She described their fight. "It really brought home to me exactly what Fitz, Ed, and Vikram did. They were mad."

"It's only what Nahum and Harlan do with Nahum's brothers," Odette pointed out.

"They are treasure hunting, not monster hunting. Any monsters they encountered were an unfortunate side line."

"But the root of this is that they faced an unusual case," Merlin reasoned. "By the sound of it, anyway. Isn't that why you are all caught up in what happened?"

"Not entirely," Odette said. "We were more curious to find who the explorer was in the family, or at least the man behind the Wayfinder and the India room. We might have had a few explorers," she qualified. "It seemed a great shame that all of this stuff was in there—beautiful, amazing things—and yet we knew next to nothing about how they came to be here. Once we started searching, literally days ago, we became obsessed, especially when we found the journals and letters. I would love to know more about *all* the objects in that room, and their travels, not just this case. Can you imagine what a great book it would make?"

"Or a great series of paintings," Morgana suggested. "A visual travelogue."

As soon as she said it, Odette could see them unfolding, and she nodded enthusiastically. "Of course. That would be a wonderful project."

Merlin nodded. "It would, but you were compelled to paint the Residency."

"Yes, the Rajgarh Residency. Well," Odette said, looking to Morgana for confirmation, "we're pretty sure it is, from what Morgana has read. In fact," she banished her doubts, "I know it is."

"Despite the fact that this Fitz travelled all over India with these men, you have focussed on that place. Why? Why are you so sure that the slides relate to Rajgarh? They could have been taken in any part of India."

"That is a reasonable question," Birdie said, looking between Odette and Morgana.

"Because of Alicia, who Fitz met at Rajgarh," Morgana explained. "She reminded Fitz of Meli, and that's why he started writing again. That's why they sent slides to her—or brought them here, after it was all over. And I think the letters were his way of talking through an unusual case. He himself describes them as a diary."

"So it was an unusual situation," he pressed.

"Yes. Fitz said they couldn't understand certain aspects of it. Plus, he felt like he'd walked into a trap."

"I sensed that, too, in the painting I drew," Odette said. "A shadow."

"Plus, their friend Vikram was attacked," Morgana continued, "and wasn't sure if he could trust who he was staying with."

Odette gasped. "You didn't mention that!"

"I've only just read it. It's as if with every step, they find something weirder."

"Ah, so that's it." Merlin looked at the banyan tree that still baked in an Indian summer because Horty hadn't changed it yet. "It's the urgency of it. There was a danger to this that surpassed all others. A sense of betrayal. It leaves a mark, doesn't it? It scarred Fitz in some way, and Ed. Maybe Vik, too. It has resonated, all these years later."

"We're Betwixt," Birdie said, repeating what they had said earlier. "Caught between past and present, as ensnared as the lotus-eaters."

"You need to finish the letters, then," Merlin said to his sister. "Why delay?"

"Well, I have been busy, but I'm also strangely reluctant to rush. It would be wrong. I want to savour it. Besides, I only found them yesterday! It's not like we've been sitting on them for weeks. And even if I finish them tonight, it won't tell me why the images are so real. Plus, there are still the journals to unpick, including Ed's."

"It will unfold as it must," Odette repeated, knowing it to be true.

"Is love involved in all this somehow?" Merlin asked. "I mean, it is Beltane, after all. Maybe that's why it's resonating, too?"

"Let's hope it wasn't doomed," Horty said, briskly whipping out the slide. "Maybe that's why we're all feeling it."

Twenty-Four

Rajgarh 1792

There was something uncanny about Deepak Verma's house, despite its beautiful furnishings and luxurious décor. The more that Vikram explored, the more he felt it press in upon him.

He had successfully evaded the staff after a few close calls, and explored the ground floor and first floor, all except for the women's quarters, of course, but he couldn't imagine that if Deepak did have a room dedicated to the occult that it would be in there. Although, it would be a good place to hide it from everyone else.

He considered his options and headed to a window to look out on to the grounds, considering what he would do in such a situation. *Where would he put his occult studies? Behind a locked door, where everyone else was forbidden?* Surely, that would raise too many questions. Plus, it wasn't necessarily an unusual hobby. His own father had researched several esoteric texts, as did many others. Vikram had found an office of sorts, and all it contained was trading business. However, he had not explored the grounds, which he realised was an oversight, too eager to enter the house instead. He was currently in one of the highest rooms in the house that offered a good view of the grounds, and he looked across them now. Beyond the tiled and cool courtyards was a section of the garden that was denser in vegetation than most. Tucked into a far corner, close to the high walls.

Just as he was about to exit the room to make his way down there, he heard voices in the corridor outside. Scanning the bedroom that had a small, adjoining sitting room, he saw there was another door, but if it led to the main corridor, he would be no better off. He needed to leave quickly. Outside the window was a small balcony, and standing on it and looking down, he could see a series of staggered roofs from lower levels. Without hesitation, he swung over the balustrade and worked his way quickly down, just as voices sounded in the room above him. Landing as nimbly as a monkey, he raced across the roofs, hugging the walls, before finally dropping down into the shady gardens. Pausing only to study his surroundings and get his bearings, he quickly crossed the grounds, trying to slow his rapidly beating heart.

In moments, he reached the far corner where the dense planting hid everything, even the high walls that he knew were behind them. His keen eyes picked up a narrow path into the undergrowth, and he edged his way through, keeping a wary eye out for snakes, but found nothing except a door in the wall. He paused, confused. *Was this just an external door to the street?* It was robust, of dark, thick wood, and had a large keyhole. On closer examination, he found that the hinges were well-oiled, and depressing the handle, discovered it was locked. The walls here were covered with climbers, so he ascended quickly and peered over the edge, careful to keep his head low as he suspected buildings would be easily visible.

However, the wall was far thicker than he anticipated, certainly thicker than the wall he had used to enter the garden. Thick enough, in fact, to hide a passageway. Across the narrow alley that bordered the external wall was another building that was very old, but nowhere near as ornate and impressive as Deepak's house, and many of the windows were shuttered. Ensuring no one was around to see him, he shimmied to the wall's edge and looked down, and discovered there was no corresponding doorway in the wall to the street.

Could this be it? Had he found Deepak's private space? Or was there more at play here?

Descending to the garden again, he withdrew his lockpicks, and when the also well-oiled lock opened, he slipped inside. As he'd expected, he found he was inside the thick wall, the air clogged with the scent of decaying vegetation. However, it was still relatively clean, as if it were used regularly. The space ran out to several paces on either side, but came to a dead end. On his left, however, was a set of stairs leading down. Not knowing what to expect, he had come equipped with all manner of things, and now he withdrew a tiny oil lantern from his pack and lit it, pulled the door shut behind him, and descended the stairs.

At the bottom they turned right and ran under the street, before another set of steps ascended within narrow walls on either side to what he presumed was the opposite house. He pressed his ear to the door at the top and listened closely. When he heard nothing untoward, he cautiously opened the unlocked door, one hand cupped around his lamp to dim the light, and stepped into a grand room that was well past its days of glory, and mostly empty except for a few items of furniture. The scents of incense and decay were thick here too, but there was a chink of light visible through the opposite door, and light filtered through the badly-shuttered windows. Turning off his oil lamp and placing it carefully in his pack, he crossed the floor soundlessly and peered into the next room.

For a moment, he could barely take it in. The space ahead was long—a series of interconnected rooms with arches, pillars, grand frescoes, and marble floors. However, nearly every wall and surface were covered in sigils, yantras, and strange symbols that he had never seen before. Candles and oil lamps flickered in small nooks, many grotesque statues were placed around the space, and a series of traps were marked out on the floor.

Vikram withdrew his dagger and edged inside, suspecting someone must be there to tend the candles and lamps. He noted the acrid scent of something unpleasant, which he eventually tracked down to a small salver where charred remains were smoking over a tiny brazier in the fireplace. Prodding it gently with the tip of his dagger, he decided it was some kind of meat. *A sacrifice, perhaps, but to who or what?* Power swelled in this place. The air resonated with it, and he wished he had Ed's scope to discern magical energy. Perhaps the yantras here connected, as they had at the dock.

In fact, he realised, as he stepped closer to examine them, some looked burned into the wall. *Had these actually connected to the ones in the dock?* As his eyes adjusted to the light, he spotted something he had missed earlier. A large, dark disc in the centre of the floor that he realised was inky black water. *A scrying bowl that would allow a way to see the port and other places, perhaps.* He stared into it, but only saw his reflection. *Could it be deep enough to be a well?*

He must have found the source of their issue, and it had to be Deepak or one of his family members who was behind it all. Maybe all of them. After all, it was accessed from his grounds, and the door was well maintained. *Was this all about the Company, after all? And what now?* Exploring the rest of the house might be dangerous without support. *Did he try to destroy everything here, or would that only make it worse?* The silence of the house settled thickly around him, and he suddenly felt as if a thousand eyes were on him. He should leave before he was discovered, and then he could warn the others and they could tackle it together.

But then the inky water at his feet rippled, and looking down again he saw a shape take form, and he realised he was looking into an enormous eye. Horrified, he stumbled back, and without waiting to see what would happen, fled to the door.

"You did well to find these," Fitz said to Ed as he studied the portions of plaster with the yantra on them. "Did Benjamin see you find them?"

"No. It happened just before he arrived, and I'd tucked them into my bag."

"Did he really threaten you?" His friend was certainly more serious in mood than normal.

"I'm afraid so. I have never seen him so openly aggressive towards me. Usually, he hedges and complains, but he was furious. I can't believe he'd sink so low with such a threat. Not that I care, of course. I don't need the money or my family's approval." But Ed looked regretful.

"You don't want to be disowned, Ed. That would be terrible. You love your sisters and your brother, even though you are nothing alike."

It was late afternoon, and they were in their private room in the Residency, surrounded by the detritus of their investigation. The shutters and windows were thrown open to catch a breath of wind, but the afternoon was hot and still. The room at least was cooler, as

Fitz had set the cloth fan swinging using a spell, rather than have a *punkah-wallah* sit outside their room, listening.

Periodically they checked the veranda to make sure no one was loitering, but the business of the Residency carried on around them, and fortunately the staff were far too busy preparing for the party to want to cater to them.

Ed stood at the doors to the veranda, looking out vacantly, shoulders tense, before turning back to Fitz with a sigh. "I won't be dictated to. This is my life, and I am harming no one. We're here helping the Company at the Resident's request. My uncle is unbelievable! No," he shook his head, "that's stupid of me. He is all too believable. I should have seen this coming. Unfortunately, I didn't think he would resort to this."

"No, neither did I." Fitz had no concerns that Ed would back out of their lifestyle, or in fact starve. They made enough money without the need for outside funds, and he knew Ed had money tucked away, but he would help him if necessary. "You know I will always support you, no matter what. Your uncle's opinion means nothing to me, and he has no power over me, either. There is always a place for you at Moonfell if you need it."

Ed smiled. "Thank you, but I won't need it. Besides, I have no intention of running back to England yet, despite my uncle's threats. In fact, if I am cut off, there is no place for me there anyway."

"You still have many friends there, and family who I am sure won't agree with Benjamin's dictatorial attitude. Your mother surely wouldn't want you treated this way."

"Perhaps not."

"Plus," Fitz added, hating to bring something up he had long mulled over, "there will come a time when we won't want to do this. We will be too old, and will have new plans. Perhaps we should consider what happens then."

Ed rolled his eyes. "We are too young to consider that yet."

"Why don't I put a spell on him? I've suggested it before and you said no, but if you've changed your mind…" The words hung between them, and Fitz saw him consider it. "Just a small spell to make him care a little less about what we do. Nothing major, of course. Just enough to send him on his way, so we can get on with our business." He joined him in the doorway and leaned against the frame, watching the gardeners busily tending the grounds and setting up lanterns for the night ahead. "I hate that he treats you like this."

"And I hate that you would break your magical code for me. You don't put spells on people."

"I do if they are acting in an underhand manner. I swear, it would not bother me at all."

Ed smiled, but he didn't lose the tension behind his eyes. "Let us see what happens tonight. I thought we would have heard from Vik by now. Should we search for him?"

"Let's give it half an hour, and if he doesn't appear, then we will. I can cast a finding spell with the amount of his things that are here. In the meantime, let's look at this yantra."

"Fitz, if we're talking finding spells, can you cast one on the yantra?"

"Perhaps." Fitz headed back to the few plaster remnants that Ed had found. Close up, he could see a faint scarring on the surface that showed a portion of the yantra's geometrical shape. "I thought it would be invisible to the naked eye, but I can see it now. Is that because you damaged it?"

"Possibly. Or perhaps we just couldn't see it at a distance before. We certainly needed my scope to detect the magical lines."

"True." Fitz passed his hand over it. "I can feel an echo of the power it once had, but maybe that is enough to discern who designed it. All magical workings and spells carry something of their maker."

"Even yours?"

"Of course. Every practitioner and witch have their own combination of magic, even if we cast old spells with our own magic, we add our power to another's. That's sometimes why old spells don't always work quite as you expect them to. Actually, I have an idea." He cleared a section of the floor, drew a circle in salt, placed a candle, a bowl of water, a feather, and a small bowl of salt at the relevant cardinal points inside the circle, and then finally placed the sections of plaster in the centre. Then he positioned a large floor cushion next to it and sat down. "I'm going to try a spell, but it is experimental."

"To do what?"

"Draw out a clue about the spellcaster. You're welcome to watch, even take notes if you want. Can you close the shutters first, though, please?"

Ed nodded, swiftly shuttering the room into darkness, gathered his notebook and pencil, and sat opposite Fitz. "Far enough away?"

"I think so."

Fitz always carried his grimoire, but it was much smaller than many his family owned, and that's because he needed it to be light for travel. He kept only the most salient spells in there related to their business, so the one he was about to try would be cast from memory and instinct. He was essentially looking for a magical signature.

He closed his eyes and took several deep breaths, letting his awareness expand. When he opened them again, he focussed only on the circle in front of him.

"With breath of air and candle bright, salt of earth, and water's might, show the magic that in this dwells, that I might find the source of the spell."

The flame flickered and the feather lifted slightly off the floor, but the water reacted the strongest, the surface shimmering before the water overflowed onto the plaster pieces. Fitz's first instinct was to pull them out, fearing they would be damaged and unusable, but as the water bubbled and frothed, turning some of the plaster to a muddy mess, portions of the sigils floated free to hang in the air before them. They were incomplete but at least visible, and seemingly made of tiny droplets of water. It seemed that someone who wielded water elemental magic was behind this. That made a certain sort of sense, considering that the attacks were by the river.

"Water that flows strong and free, show me the face of who commands thee."

The geometrical signs shimmered in the air like a tiny rain shower, as if resisting his instruction, but Fitz asked again, voice rising with power as he made his intention clear.

This time, the water droplets rearranged themselves into a face so craggy that at first Fitz thought it was some kind of monstrous creature. But then as it refined itself, it became clear that it was an old face, lined with wrinkles and with deep-set eyes. It certainly wasn't Harishchandra.

"Show me where!" Fitz shouted. "Where in Rajgarh will I find this man?"

But instead of rearranging into a map or a building, the face changed into an inky, circular form as slick as spilled blood, and for the briefest moment, Fitz saw a shadowy room lit only by the flicker of candles, and the shape of something monstrous before the water scattered in a mist and vanished.

Twenty-Five

Moonfell 2025

Birdie was ruminating in the potting shed by the yew hedge with a large glass of gin and tonic in her hand, and the beginnings of a headache growing when her familiar, Hades, found her in a deck chair looking out across the dark garden.

He rubbed his head against her knee. "Problems, old friend?"

"Less of the old, thank you." She stroked his silky ears. "I can't decide what to do about the monkeys and peacocks. I can hear them now, squawking and chattering. They shouldn't be here."

"You're worrying too much," he said as he jumped on the chair next to her and kneaded the cushion. "They are here because of Moonfell magic."

"So was the damn earth elemental, and we know what a disaster that was. You vanished to some weird Never-Neverland."

"Not exactly," he said, patiently. "For a wise woman, you say some very odd things."

"You know what I mean. Bloody bee magic caused a disaster. What if this does the same?"

"This is different. These animals are a gift of love."

"*Love*? The monkeys are running around everywhere! And have you seen the size of their teeth?"

Hades blinked slowly, his large amber eyes fixed on hers. "They won't hurt you or anyone else here. They just carry a bit of old magic with them, and you love magic."

She huffed. "I do. Most of the time."

"All of the time! You can't lie to me. And you know more than anyone that you can't control it all the time, either. The slides were a gift so that Meli could see where Fitz had been."

She narrowed her eyes. "Did you know them?"

"No, but I've been listening and watching. There is nothing sinister about this. You have triggered," he paused, his whiskers twitching, "a time capsule."

"I suppose that's one way to think about this."

"I think it's quite a lovely gift."

"Yes, it is. I'm worried about Odette and Morgana, though. They both seem very caught up in this. Odette's response is not so surprising, but Morgana doesn't get all dreamy. She's pragmatic. Sensible."

"That's not strictly true. Morgana is a romantic soul who had to adjust her expectations after her marriage collapsed. She married a musician, Birdie! No one marries a musician unless she, or he, is prepared to embrace a little chaos. Unless they have a creative soul themselves! Plus, Morgana favours velvet and old lace. More than anyone else in this house, she loves to raid the old clothes in the attic wardrobes. Stevie Nicks resides within her."

Birdie almost choked on her gin. "What the hell do you know about Stevie Nicks?"

"I'm not deaf or blind, but I'm beginning to think *you* are."

Birdie sat upright, glaring at him. "That's a very mean thing to say."

"But still true. You have a blinkered approach to Morgana in some ways. You appreciate her magical knowledge, yet you miss other things about her. Don't you remember how she was in her youth? The clubs she would visit in London. The crazy jazz she listens to, even now. She retreated here once her marriage ended, and you let her."

"What was I supposed to do? Throw her out on the street? This is her home. It was her home during her marriage. You're making no sense." Birdie had come here for peace and quiet, away from the house where they were swimming in flower garlands and plotting Beltane. She wanted to work her way through this situation, and now that Hades was here, she also wanted to be reassured, not lectured.

"I don't mean that she retreated to the house, exactly. I'm well aware she lived here with her family for a good while. I mean she retreated like a snail into its shell in this house. Her husband, Lewis, buggered off, and Lam went with him. She wrapped herself up in her work and little else. You must have seen it."

Birdie groaned. *Was this another failure as High Priestess?*

"I can hear that," he chided. "No, it isn't. She gets on with things, just like you. You are startlingly similar in some ways. Just not in a Stevie Nicks way."

"I could be Stevie Nicks!"

"You really couldn't."

"So, who am I? Doris Day?"

"Don't be ridiculous."

"Who, then?"

"I'm not sure it would be a musical icon. I'll think on it." He cleaned his paws, leaving her speechless, and then said, "To get back to

Morgana, I think that her retreat happened so gradually that I doubt she even saw it herself."

"Unfortunately, you're right," Birdie said, recalling a young, slightly hippie Morgana. "I think Lam deciding to come back here has made a difference."

"And now she's seeing a wolf-shifter." Hades licked his lips and grinned. "Winds of change are sweeping through here."

"Have you been chatting to Horty?"

"You know I do not chat to anyone else."

"Well, she said that very same thing this afternoon."

"She's perceptive within that bombastic exterior."

"I know. She's being very good with the girls—who, by the way, I must reintroduce to the bees. I'll keep it simple this time."

"Very wise. And then I suggest that you go to Storm Moon tonight."

"Why?" She studied him for any sign of subterfuge.

"Because you need a break, that's all. Merlin and the girls will love it."

"Teenage girls and attractive wolf-shifters? It's a recipe for disaster."

"But you're inviting them tomorrow night, anyway."

"True." She rose to her feet, knowing the wisdom of his words. "Yes, I need to regain my equilibrium. Thank you."

"That's what I'm here for."

Birdie left him cleaning himself vigorously and weaved her way across the garden to the house, the sound of music and laughter drawing her on. The glasshouse was glowing with a warm yellow light in the dusk, and when she entered, she found the entire family gathered by the long work bench set against the wall of the house. The scent of hawthorn filled the entire space, and arrangements of the blossom-filled branches were in large vases ready for the house.

"You've been busy," she observed. "And have done a beautiful job."

Marion was already wearing her flower crown, and she grinned at Birdie. "I'm going to make a willow fairy ring next."

"Are you?" She looked to the others for explanation. Looking through rings of woven willow was supposed to offer a view of the fairy realm.

Horty fished a bundle of the narrow shoots out from under the bench. "I put some to soak this morning. As it's one of the nine sacred woods of Beltane, I thought it might be fun."

Birdie laughed. "I think we're seeing enough odd things here today already, but fair enough. However, it's bee introduction time, so that will have to wait. And then we're going to Storm Moon."

Startled, Morgana asked, "How come?"

"Because we need a break and a fresh perspective, so get your glad rags on. We're going dancing!"

Horty had no wish to be involved in the bee introductions. She had a feeling that the more people who were involved, the bigger and more dramatic it would become. The bees loved an audience, that much was clear.

Merlin and Morgana would accompany Birdie, Marion, and Ellen, and that was more than enough, which meant that she had time for a quick look at the rest of the paperwork they had discovered before she changed for the evening.

She called after Odette as she headed up the back stairs, "What should I wear later? I'm going to look an old fuddy duddy!"

"Honestly, Horty, it's very laidback. You don't have to worry. Lots of different people of all ages go there. Just wear something comfortable. A nice dress, perhaps?"

"What will you wear?"

Odette looked down at her old jeans and long, baggy jumper and gave Horty an impish grin as she tucked her hair behind her ear, effortlessly chic. "Probably not this. Cleaner jeans and a top, perhaps."

"Let's face it, Odette, you could wear a bin bag and still look fabulous. What does Birdie wear when she goes there?"

"A dress, but nothing too flash. Just wear something you're comfortable in. There's a bar on the ground floor, and the club is in the basement where they have bands playing, but most of the time we're just in the bar. I'll ask Arlo to reserve us a table. Honestly," she said, noting Horty's hesitation, "you'll love it."

Horty considered the clothes she always kept in her room at Moonfell. "I can find something, I'm sure. Are you getting ready now?"

"No. I'm heading to the studio first."

"I haven't been in there in ages. Any objection if I pop in later?"

"Of course not." She waved the small painting at her as she walked backwards up the stairs. "I'm going to look at this. Laters."

Casting aside her absurd fears of going to a club at her age, Horty sat on the sofa in front of the fire and searched through Ed's journals and sketches. Although intrigued by his clever inventions, she was more interested in who he was, so that's what she focussed on. They already knew his surname was Swift and that he was a member of the Royal Society, but if he was a friend of Fitz's, he must have lived locally. Morgana had already set up a visit with the Royal Society, but that was on Monday, and she wanted to know more now. Plus, she had a wealth of information here at her fingertips.

She skimmed through the books, sorting them into small piles. One for inventions, one for sketches, and the other of what looked to be conventional journals. The dates ranged from the 1779 up to 1792. That brought her up short. *Nothing after 1792? That was ominous.* In fact, there was nothing recorded of Rajgarh at all, except for a couple of sketches of the Rajgarh Port *ghats*, the layout of the port, and the markings on it that he had labelled "rifts." *Interesting.* These must be the same rifts that Morgana had read about in Fitz's letters. He had also drawn a few interesting geometrical designs, but they were patchy, as if unfinished, and had lots of question marks and squiggles next to them.

"Too busy to write, perhaps," she murmured to herself as she turned to the earliest date in the journal. "By the gods, his writing is shocking."

Fixing her glasses firmly on her nose, she scanned the earliest entries, and realised they picked up from earlier journals that must be stored elsewhere. They described finishing at Oxford University, where he gained a First, and then setting out to see Europe with Fitz. There were huge gaps between dates, and some of the entries were just lists of places mixed in with reflections. It was clear that however well-educated Ed was, he was not a writer. Sketches were interspersed with his notes, too. He had even sketched the famed Notre Dame.

However, he clearly loved to travel. Over months and years, he and Fitz had travelled across Europe, occasionally mentioning the names of people they had met and stayed with—old Oxford contacts, by the sound of it—and only occasional visits home. What was exasperating was that he never mentioned where home was for him, other than London. And then, finally, Horty found the reference she needed. They had been traveling through Austria and Bohemia when he said they had decided to return home for a much needed break, especially as winter was rolling in.

Winter is likely to be severe this year, already rivers are icing up, so Mayfair calls. I confess I am actually looking forward to spending

Christmas at home and catching up with my sisters, and seeing per-haps what new interior designs my mother has wrought upon Swift House. It changes every time I return. Heaven knows what she will have done to our estate in Surrey. I must make sure to buy presents en route, or I shall never hear the end of it. Perhaps while there, Uncle B. can use his influence with the R.S.. Fitz of course will return to Moonfell, and I will spend a little time there too, I hope. Peri has always been welcoming, and I am keen to see how well their new enterprise is doing.

Horty whooped and punched the air. "Yes! Swift House, and an estate in Surrey."

Checking her watch, she decided she had just enough time to speak to Odette before changing, and after navigating endless passages, found her thoughtfully looking at a painting of a garden. Horty had been deliberately loud as she approached the room, not wanting to startle her, and Odette greeted her as she entered.

"You look pleased, Horty, and you have a decidedly jaunty bounce to your walk."

"That's because I have found where Ed lived." Horty, however, had other things on her mind now. Odette didn't paint convention-ally . She used broad, sweeping brushstrokes and was almost im-pressionistic in her style, but this painting was detailed and precise. "That's stunning. I want to walk into it."

"I think I have on several occasions."

"How did it feel?"

"Hot, muggy, and tense."

"It's such a skill you have. I'm envious. And that is Fitz and Alicia?"

"Yes. She's forthright. I can feel her energy as I paint her. She's significant. I'm sure she did more than just facilitate a party."

"Did you discover anything interesting about the painting of Fitz and Ed?"

"I found a note on the back of it." She pointed to where the painting was lying on a table, out of its frame. "It says, 'The summer that everything changed.' And a tarot card was tucked in the back, too. The Fool."

"The Fool?" Horty picked up the old tarot card with its primitive image. She wasn't a tarot expert, but she knew a little. "Doesn't this indicate the start of a journey?"

"Usually a spiritual one. The first card in the Major Arcana. Along with her note—at least I presume it's her note—it's quite indicative, isn't it?"

Horty studied the looping writing. "That's intriguing. Any idea what changed, or what the journey was? Or even a date?"

Odette shrugged. "No. Just another mystery to add to the pile. And Ed's house?"

"It was in Mayfair, so tomorrow we need a trip out because I'd love to see it. I'm sure it still exists. You know how these old houses in Mayfair are now. They're either posh clubs or hotels or something. If it's still private, we should break in. You might detect something." She wiggled her fingers. "With your witchy woo-woo."

"Horty!" Odette's mouth dropped open in shock.

"I know. I'm going to a club tonight *and* planning a break-in. Life is so exciting sometimes!"

Twenty-Six

Rajgarh 1792

Vikram was still agitated when he arrived at the Residency to see Fitz and Ed, and even being with his friends was not calming his mood.

"I swear I saw an eye in that pool. Monsters I was expecting, but not that. I escaped as quickly as I could."

"And saw no one?" Ed asked.

"No. A few close calls in the main house, but I'm confident no one saw me. As soon as I went back out to Deepak's garden, I escaped over the wall. I checked several times to make sure I wasn't being followed." He took a few deep breaths, the cool, darkened room with their equipment and magic finally soothing his rattled composure. "That room was full of unusual statues and packed with sigils and yantras. The power was palpable, and I felt as if I was being watched, too. I put it down to nerves, but that eye…" He tapped his forehead. "I can see it still. When I close my eyes, it's worse."

Fitz patted his shoulder. "You did well to discover it, and it supports what my spell uncovered. Explain the room to me in detail again."

Vikram steadied his thoughts as he took a seat, and then described what he'd found. "There could have been much more in the rest of the house, but I dared not risk being found."

"You did the right thing." Fitz started pacing. "Now we need to decide what to do. Deepak Verma must be involved, and maybe his family, too. We saw a face, though, very old and wrinkled. Did you see anyone at all who that could be?"

"No. An elderly servant, or Deepak's father, perhaps? I gather Deepak is not that old. Perhaps he even employs a guru of sorts." Vikram shrugged and ran his hand through his hair, feeling dust in it. "He could have been in the upper floors of the house. As for the eye, it didn't seem human, but maybe that's just my nerves talking. The thing is, it saw me, so it doesn't matter that I wasn't followed. *Something* will know I was there."

"It might have even seen us, too," Fitz said to Ed before turning back to Vik. "We saw the pool of water before it became something monstrous. All right, let us be logical. We know that whoever is behind this is powerful, and that his magic is strong with the water element. The same yantras that were in the port were also in the room you discovered. In the port they connected like a web. Did they do so in the room?"

Vikram tried to recall the arrangement. "I couldn't see if any magical lines connected them, obviously, but there were many symbols all around the room. It's very possible they do. I could feel the magic in there, and the pool was dead centre of it all. Potentially, they could intersect over it. Of course, I should say that I could not see how deep that water was. It could be a shallow bowl, or it could be a well."

"Interesting," Fitz mused as he picked up a portion of the remaining plaster that had been salvaged from the port. "A well of power. Even if it isn't a deep well, it could connect across the void. The water is a portal, perhaps. What if Deepak has trapped something in there that lends its power to him?"

Ed gave a dry laugh. "That is a most intriguing suggestion. I was convinced that my uncle was involved, but now I am not so sure. This sounds too bizarre. Why would he get willingly mixed up in the very thing he hates me doing?"

Unperturbed, Fitz said, "Let us continue reasoning this through. The supernatural creatures that we have encountered are more than capable of destroying the dock in hours, and yet they have waited almost three weeks before inflicting any real damage. Yes, men were killed, but that was only to demonstrate how dangerous they were and to create panic. It was also to demonstrate the nature of the issue. An unnatural threat. At which time, after several attacks occurred to drive home the threat, we were summoned. We know that the butler, Akash, a calm and knowledgeable man, knew of us and our activities, and suggested that we could help. That is believable, yes?" He cocked his head at his companions. "We have a reputation of sorts, and deliver on our promises. Not all do. There are plenty of charlatans in this business. I would imagine that whoever is behind this, possibly still Benjamin, would rely on that, and trust that we would be summoned and no one else. Furthermore, we are English, which means the Resident will trust us, and additionally, Ed is known to be the nephew of Benjamin Swift, a senior officer in the East India Company. But Akash does not know where we are, and so they contact Benjamin, who does. We are contacted and make our way here. And once we enter the docks, the attacks escalate to the point where we might have been killed if not for our exceptional skill. In fact, we strike back."

"Are you saying," Ed asked, confused, "that Akash is involved?"

"No. Anyone could have recommended us. We have worked with many Indians who regard us highly, so if Akash hadn't, someone else would have. Your old friend, Harish," he said, turning to Vikram, "knows of what we do. It might have been that he could have recommended us if no one else had. So, the attacks were to lure us here, to either kill us or discredit us. You were attacked, Vikram, after visiting Makkar—a visit we cannot forget was arranged by Harish. I, meanwhile, have magically protected the Residency, and we travel regularly with the regiment, which gives us protection. But the big question remains, *why* attack us? I can think of only one good reason, and that is because not only does Ed's uncle find us an embarrassment, but perhaps the Company itself does. Not this Resident, necessarily, but the senior officials. They are growing in power and gaining land, and they demand respect."

Vik shook his head, utterly perplexed. "Are you seriously saying that because of the work we do, we undermine the Company's authority? That's utterly ridiculous! We are three men, not an army. But say you are right, why would an Indian merchant work with the Company? A well-established Indian merchant, who is, according to Harish, very angry about rising costs to access the p ort."

Fitz had been pacing, but now he stopped suddenly, staring at the wall before whirling around to face his companions. "Because they have offered him a deal! What if he was secretly offered better rates at the dock for helping them destroy us? If Makkar knows of his occult activities, perhaps someone else does, too."

Ed looked at Vik, doubt in his eyes. "It sounds unlikely, and yet it has logic. My uncle was furious this morning. All restraint had gone. He made out that he was angry about the damage to the docks, but what if he was cross because we were still alive and had killed two creatures?"

"But," Vik said, still needing to iron out inconsistencies, "I was attacked, and only Makkar and Harish knew where I was."

"You cannot presume that," Fitz said. "This giant eye in the pool could have been watching us all. We have no idea of what or who it is, or what it can see. It could well have watched the docks and directed the creatures' attack by means of the yantras. Just because we don't understand it, doesn't mean that couldn't be the case."

"Can it see us now?" Vikram asked, alarmed, looking warily at the ceiling as if it might be hovering there.

"I have cast a protection spell around the Residency, so in theory, no."

"But it saw me at that old house, in the room full of occult objects. It knew I was there. It blinked." Vikram thumped his chest. "I was *seen*."

"As were we, through my spell, potentially," Fitz said. "So they might be expecting us. How do we make this work to our advantage?"

"More importantly, how do we unveil a conspiracy?" Vik asked. "Is there a spy in this house?"

Ed shrugged and moved closer, lowering his voice. "Possibly. There are lots of staff here, but we haven't discussed anything with the servants. Unless one of the Residency team is a spy? When we arrived here, Roger had a limp. He said he'd fallen off his horse, but maybe he was dealing with monsters? Townsend is aggressive, and Anthony has been officious. Henry has been the most supportive."

"What about Alicia?" Vik suggested. "She has been very keen on being involved in this. Subterfuge perhaps?"

Fitz scratched his chin, a dark shadow of beard visible, ingrained with dust from that morning's work. "It's possible she's involved, but I doubt it. Anyone could come in this room and see our work. They might not understand any of it, though. Plus, I have been writing to Meli. It has served as a type of diary of our last few days. I'm trying to remember what I've written, but if someone was going through our belongings, they will see that I am considering that this is a trap."

"Then how to turn this on its head?" Vikram asked. "They think they have us. We are, after all, planning to go to the port again. What if it's when, having assessed our first response, they strike again? Or just destroy the port, anyway."

"And that was something else," Fitz said, jabbing his finger at Vikram. "The crates were empty, so the destruction looked dramatic, but nothing of value was actually lost. No. They will not destroy the port. Too much stock and too many ships are there. This is not about the port or the Company. It's how they get to us!"

"Bandits on the road would have done that just as easily," Ed said.

Fitz snorted. "No they wouldn't. Vik's skills and my magic would have ended something like that quickly. No. If I was going to end a group of monster hunters, I would lure them in this way. But do you think my theory is right?"

"That someone from the Company, maybe Ben, has colluded with Deepak?" Vik asked. "I agree that it's possible. It still leaves us with how to deal with it all. That's twofold. Destroy any other creatures that might exist, and save our skins and business."

"And stop my uncle from threatening me," Ed added.

"Well, we have a party tonight," Fitz said, a twist of mischief to his smile. "I suggest we use it to our advantage. Everyone of note will be here, and we are the centre of attention. We must concoct a plan, and I think we will need Alicia's help."

Ed sighed. "Fitz, we don't even know if we can trust her."

"Then that's the first order of business. I'll use a truth spell. Ed, can you call her here please, for something frivolous? Our dress for tonight, for example."

"Now?"

"Right now."

"What about the room I discovered?" Vik asked before Ed could leave. "We have to destroy that."

"We are short of time, and I cannot be everywhere at once."

"Then perhaps Ed and I can do something. I have gunpowder that we can place strategically..."

"No!" Ed shook his head. "If we do something destructive now, then our enemies will flee and could even regroup later. We have to pretend we know nothing of its existence."

"But the eye—" Vik protested.

"We take our chances, and deal with it later."

"Maybe from here," Fitz said thoughtfully.

"My friends," Vik held his hand out towards them in their time-honoured gesture when they knew the odds were stacked against them, "by blade, by book, by bond, by all three are we made strong."

As they repeated it together, Vik felt his strength and resolve renew. *Tonight, whatever happened, they would end this.*

Fitz began preparing his spell as soon as Ed departed to fetch Alicia.

"Are you sure you should be doing this?" Vik asked. He stood at the door to the veranda, ensuring no one was listening to them. "It seems unethical."

"I will tell her what I'm doing."

"Doesn't that defeat the point?"

"You cannot lie under a truth spell. Even being forewarned will not stop it."

"Are they complex?"

"They can be, but I have a simpler solution. I will use a combination of runes, a spell, and glamour. Plus, I will only ask specific questions. No unethical behaviour, I promise." He flashed a grin at Vikram.

"You like her."

"I admire her fortitude. Her wish to be independent. Plus, she is very intelligent. That's why she reminds me of Meli."

"And attractive too, I note."

"I am too busy to notice such things."

"You are a man. Don't be ridiculous. You could truth-spell the Resident, but you choose Alicia."

Fitz laughed. He couldn't deny that he found her attractive, but he had buried it beneath business. *Besides, what good would it do?* He would move on after they were done here, and she would not. "I like a pretty face, and she offered to help, so why not?"

"I can think of many reasons."

Fortunately, Ed returned with Alicia to save Fitz from arguing further.

"Alicia, thank you for coming so quickly," Fitz said, turning towards her.

She narrowed her eyes at him. "I sense subterfuge. From all of you." She studied Vikram at the door to the veranda, and then where Ed waited at the door from the corridor. "I can definitely say you need to bathe before tonight, if that's the advice you need. You all look dreadfully filthy."

Fitz decided she would appreciate bluntness. "I promise we will, but we need your help in other matters. First, I need to know if I can trust you."

"Of course you can!"

"In everything? For example, will you betray us? Are you already betraying us?"

She jerked back, alarmed. "How dare you? I offered you my help!"

"Of which I am deeply appreciative." He had to admit that she looked magnificent. Her eyes were full of fire, and her hair was caught up, revealing her long, slender neck. "We would like your help very much. However, I cannot explain how until I first ascertain your trustworthiness. I would like to perform a truth spell on you."

"A *what*?" She stared him directly in the eyes, a mix of uncertainty and outrage showing in her own. "You doubt me?"

He stepped forward, closing the space between them. "I doubt *everyone* except the two men in this room right now. My gut tells me that I can trust you, but I need to be sure, because much is at stake." Her eyes softened at that, and he pressed his advantage. "You are brave and resourceful, but I need to know without a doubt. Will you let me perform a simple truth spell? All I will ask is a couple of questions. Nothing except what concerns our current business. If you don't want to, then leave right now, and we shall continue our business without y ou."

Amusement sparked in her eyes. "You know very well that I wish to be involved. This is the first interesting thing that has happened here for months."

"Then you consent?"

"Yes, I consent. What will you have me do?"

A weight lifted off him that he didn't know he carried. "Thank you. Take a seat, please." He gestured to the chair by the table, and once she had sat down, said, "I will make a sign in front of your face, but do not be alarmed. This will not hurt you."

She nodded. "I trust you."

He smiled. "Do you?"

"Just get on with it."

He laughed, almost forgetting that Vik and Ed were in the room. *Focus.* He drew a sigil in the air in front of her, a mix of runes imbued with his magic, and they ignited briefly before turning into smoke and wafting over her. Her pupils grew larger as she inhaled. He exerted glamour next, letting it wash from him as he uttered a simple spell to ensure the truth. "Clever tongue that could tell lies, now be bound beneath these skies. Let no falsehood pass your lips, truth alone from tongue now slips." Her breathing slowed, and she blinked as if her lids were heavy, and he decided on a couple of simple tests. "Alicia, I want you to tell me a lie. Tell me that the sky is red today."

"The sky isn't red. It's blue."

"But tell me that's it's red." He watched her wrestle to speak, lips working but struggling to form the words.

"It's…it's—it's blue! Blue."

He smiled. "It's a simple thing. Tell me a fish barks like a dog."

Fury built in her eyes as she tried to do as he asked. Finally, she shouted, "I cannot!"

"Is Edmund Swift my friend?"

"Yes, of course." Her relief from being able to answer correctly was palpable.

"Good. Alicia, are you working with someone to kill us?"

"No, absolutely not."

"Are you giving information about us to anyone in this house or grounds?"

"No."

"Even your sister?"

She swallowed. "I have told her that you're here to stop the attacks in the port."

"Did you tell her that I am a witch?"

"No." She shook her head. "I said you had hunting skills."

"Are you betraying us to serve the needs of the Company?"

"No."

"Will you keep our secrets, no matter what they are?"

She sighed, eyes heavy again. "Yes."

"Do you want to help us stop this?"

"Of course."

"Why?"

"Because men are dying, and the Company is losing money. Plus, Henry might lose his job. It would be a terrible failure, and my sister likes it here, for all that she complains of the insects and the snakes. They might be sent somewhere else in India. A small town, perhaps. A backwater. Neither could bear it." She looked horrified at how much she had shared, and she glared at Fitz, clasping her hand over her mo uth.

"I didn't ask for all of that."

She whipped her hand away. "You asked for the truth."

He held his hands up, apologetic, and quickly dispelled the en-chantment. "It is done. Gone. Thank you, but I had to be sure. Shall we be more civilised now? If you'll forgive me."

"I understand, and yes, I forgive you. But please, never do that again. It was horrible. Tell me what is so terrible that you had to do this?"

"We think that someone in the Company, possibly in this very house, is behind the attacks on the port."

She looked at Ed and Vikram before facing Fitz again. "You seri-ously think that?"

"Yes. And we believe they are working with someone local." He ran through the big list of events and their reasoning. "Do you see why?"

She sank back into her chair. "I must admit, I wondered why the attacks were so sporadic."

"Tell me, is there anyone in the household, Indian staff or other-wise, who you think are behaving suspiciously?"

"I hate to say this, but Anthony is not himself. He has always been officious from what my sister says, and works very hard. He is dedicated to this place, obsessively so. But he is shorter tempered than usual. Even I have noticed, and I have only been here for six months. Henry has actually remarked on it to my sister. I presumed it was the attacks, but I think it started before that." She looked vacantly at the wall as she considered her statement. "Yes, possibly two months ago I noticed it. I put it down to being busy, but if he was planning anything, that might tie in."

"What about Benjamin Swift, Ed's uncle?" Fitz asked, nodding to where his friend watched them by the door. "Does he visit here?"

"On occasions. The last time was about two months ago, too. Yes, mid-February, I think. But he didn't stay long. A day or two at most, at the hotel again, and had a dinner here with us. I learned Anthony met with him about port operations, but that's all I know. Oh, and I know of Deepak Verma, too."

Vik had been staring out the door to the veranda, but now he turned to face her. "Do you know him well?"

"No, but I understand he is annoyed by the Company's presence here, because Henry complains of his attitude on the odd occasions when he forgets himself in front of us, the women. We are too delicate to know of such things." She gave a weary laugh, but her amusement quickly vanished. "To think he is involved in the occult is concerning."

"He is coming tonight, I hope?" Vik asked.

"Yes, along with Sharma Sahib and other merchants, including several Europeans. It was short notice, but everyone has responded quickly. As I suspected, when we mentioned we were celebrating your success at the port, everyone wanted to come."

"Good." Fitz nodded, already running through ideas. "Now we must think of a plan to unveil the conspiracy. Are you still happy to help?"

Alicia smiled. "More than ever. But I think you should involve Akash, the *khidmatgar*."

"Is that wise?"

"Yes. You need the servants on your side, and he will know exactly who is reliable."

"All right." Fitz had to admit that made sense. "I'll speak to him with you."

"Good. What do you want me to do?"

"I think I need to cast spell traps across the house, the nature of which I haven't completely decided."

"You are running out of time," Ed told him.

"I know." Which meant he had to act fast.

"Then let us," Alicia suggested, "speak to Akash now. I'm sure he'll have excellent suggestions."

Twenty-Seven

Moonfell 2025

Morgana's plans to read Fitz's letters in bed that night while nestled with Monroe in a post-coital glow were suddenly put aside when they all heard Horty's news over the table in Storm Moon.

She looked at Horty, incredulous. "You can't break into Ed's old house! And besides, what could it possibly tell you now? If it's even still there!"

Horty's lips puckered with frustration. "We don't know what it will tell us until we try to listen. At least we can look at it, if we do nothing else."

"I must admit," Merlin said, "it will be good to see the house that Ed grew up in, if it's there."

Morgana pulled her phone out of her bag. "Have you tried to search for it?"

"No. I thought I'd leave that to you young people. Phones should be for calling people, not all of that searching malarkey."

She rolled her eyes at her brother and Odette. That *malarkey* presumably being using the internet. "Did you say Swift House in Mayfair?"

"Yes." Horty fished the book out of her capacious bag and laid it on the table. "I came prepared."

Birdie looked excited. "If we're going to break in, we should do it tonight. We can't very well break in during the day."

Ellen and Marion had so far said nothing, their attention fully on the staff at Storm Moon—human and shifter. They had only met the tall, athletic Vlad, and both had been unusually quiet as they stared at him, a little starry-eyed. *Or maybe lustfully, on Ellen's part.* Now, however, Ellen suddenly paid attention. "Did you say we are going to break in somewhere?"

Merlin intervened. "Absolutely not. Well, you certainly aren't." He glared at Birdie and Horty. "What is wrong with you two?"

"Oh, come on," Birdie said, pouting. "Who would suspect two glamourous old ladies?"

Odette almost choked on her drink. "Are you serious? You're going alone?"

"Not alone," Birdie said, frowning. "With Horty."

"You cannot possibly think that this a good idea," Morgana said, trying to rein in her negativity, as she knew it riled Birdie. "You're Moonfell's head witch."

"I know, which means I am the perfect person to go. We can use cloaking spells, disarm alarms, and unlock doors." She wafted her hands about breezily. "All of that."

"Ah, yes," Odette said dryly. "I forgot you were an experienced thief."

"And if you need to make a speedy escape?" Morgana asked. Birdie and Horty were not exactly fast on their feet.

"We won't. We have magic."

"What if the house still belongs to Ed's family," Odette asked, "and they use magic, too?"

"Then we'll reevaluate."

Morgana couldn't contain herself. "That is reckless!"

"If it all turns to custard, then you can come and help. But it won't." Birdie folded her arms across her chest and stared at Morgana. "You were the one who wanted to know more about Ed."

"Not like this."

Merlin shrugged. "Birdie is right, Morgana." He gave her the look that told her to shut up. "They are more than capable of investigating this. We can enjoy a nice evening here, go home to Moonfell, and continue whatever we need to do—which is probably bed for me, and especially these two," he gestured to his daughters, "while these two gad about London."

"Absolutely," Odette said, demurely sipping her drink. "I intend to do a little midnight moon gate gazing, anyway. You can still read Fitz's letters, Morgana." She nodded at Morgana's phone that was forgotten in her slack hands. "Have you found Swift House?"

Clearly, she was to let Birdie and Horty just get on with it. "Give me a few moments."

Ably assisted by Ellen, who was now thoroughly intrigued by the whole thing, they searched for Ed's house on the internet, using all manner of search terms. Morgana tried to block out the others' discussions of spells to use, figuring that Merlin and Odette were right. They were old enough to look out for themselves.

"Here," Ellen said, leaning in to show Morgana her own phone. "This is Swift House Heritage Hotel Group. Do you think this is the same place? It looks amazing."

A large, Georgian house loomed on the screen, with a symmetrical façade, cream-painted stone trim, and sash windows on the upper floors—four stories, by the look of it. The ground floor had smoked glass windows with gilt lettering on them, set on either side of an impressively grand doorway with dramatic columns. The website was impressively grand, too, and Morgana scanned the description, heart pounding as she did. "Oh, great Goddess! Listen to this, everyone. 'Discover the world as Edmund Swift intended. Our founder's 18 [th]-century expeditions laid the foundation for today's most authentic travel experiences. Swift Heritage Travel offers bespoke journeys to historic destinations, luxury base camps, and the finest travel accessories—because every great adventure begins with proper preparation.'"

Horty clutched her arm with a surprisingly strong hand. "No! Have you made that up?"

"Of course not. Why would I do that?"

"They founded their business because of him?"

Morgana wasn't sure what to think. It was so unexpected. She turned to her niece. "Ellen, thank you. This is fantastic."

"It was an easy search," she said, shrugging it off with the insouciance of youth. "What does it mean?"

Merlin grinned. "Well, for a start, it means Horty and Birdie don't need to break in anywhere."

"Oh, yes we do," Horty said. "I have my heart set on it. Especially now!"

"It's a hotel," Odette pointed out. "We can look at it tomorrow."

Morgana, however, wasn't paying attention. It just didn't feel right.

Merlin nudged her. "What's wrong?"

"Everything I've read so far suggests that Ed was at odds with his uncle and his family, so why celebrate him with a flashy boutique hotel group and what seems to be a travel company?"

"Because sometimes you need a good hook to land your marketing on."

"But why not Benjamin, the rich uncle who invested in the East India Company?"

"Maybe they discovered he was dastardly after all? Sometimes history does right wrongs. Maybe their descendants discovered the truth. Are Birdy and Horty persuading you to break in after all?"

She rolled her eyes. "Good grief, no. However, I would like to go tomorrow. Monroe is coming round tonight. You'll meet him soon." She leaned closer to her brother and lowered her voice, although with Marion and Ellen giggling with Birdie and Horty as they planned their break in, gently guided by Odette trying to modify their actions, no one was listening to her. "Are we really letting that pair do this?"

"Yes. I've had it with wrangling older relatives. I'm sure they'll have fun, or just chicken out. Just let it roll, Moonbeam."

"Moonbeam! You haven't called me that in a while."

"That's because you haven't been her for a while. You're different now. Lighter. The sister I remember as a teenager and in your twenties, before that wanker musician." He lowered his voice so that it was almost a whisper. "Morgana Moonbeam, gentle and wise, with stardust dreams in her deep brown eyes."

Unexpectedly, the old rhyme hit her hard as memories of another Morgana flooded back. "Stardust dreams. Yes, I had those." *Stupid happily-ever-after dreams that didn't pan out.*

"And still do, I hope." Merlin studied her. "You're still very young."

Morgana felt this was all becoming dangerously insightful, and she tried to remember her old rhyme for Merlin. "Little Merlin with his wand so bright, casting backward spells all through the night."

"So funny. I do not cast backward spells. But don't think you're wriggling out of this discussion. It's this bloke who's made a difference. It must be."

"Monroe?" She tried to contain her impatience, because she was actually very pleased to be spending time with her brother. He looked so well and happy, and was clearly a good father. "You know it's not all about men for us women, right?"

He smiled, teasing her. "I know, but I can't help but wonder..."

"He's lovely, but it's not just him. It's a few things. I'm really excited about Lam coming to stay at Moonfell. We had such a good time at Ostara, despite the unexpected dramas. And these guys, actually." She nodded around her at the various Storm Moon Pack members. "They're fun."

"You're their healer now?"

"Yes, and we're all good friends. Even with Arlo."

Merlin knew exactly who Arlo was. "Good. I'm glad things are working out. You've moved rooms, too, I hear. You must show me tomorrow." And then his eyes widened as he looked behind her. "There is a very big man heading this way, and he looks dangerous."

She looked over her shoulder and smiled as Monroe leaned in and kissed her cheek. "Hey, you. Monroe, I'd like you to meet my brother, Merlin, and my two nieces, Ellen and Marion."

Merlin leapt to his feet and stuck his hand out. "Nice to meet you, Monroe."

"You too, and your daughters." He shook their hands in turn. "Anyone need drinks? I have a few minutes to spend with you before I have to head downstairs again."

"Let me," Merlin said. "Sit down and relax."

Monroe shook his head. "It will take me only seconds. Perks of the job."

He took their requests and headed to the bar, leaving the girls looking after him in stunned silence.

"You really should have warned me that he was so large," Merlin said, sitting again.

"And miss seeing that expression?" She laughed. "I don't think so."

"Smug."

"I know." And she immediately put all thoughts of Ed aside until later.

Twenty-Eight

Rajgarh 1792

E d adjusted his collar as he checked his appearance in the mirror, and satisfied with his clothes, swept the comb through his hair. Benjamin might moan all he wanted, but at least Ed looked smart and well-groomed, far better than he had earlier that day.

Hearing a knock at the door, he turned and called, "Come in!"

"Only me," Fitz said as he entered, similarly dressed and looking distracted. "Are you ready?"

"I think so. Are you? You have had far more to do than I."

"I cannot deny that it's been a rush, but Alicia was right. Akash is a wonder." Fitz headed to the doors and stepped out onto the broad veranda. "The guests are already arriving. I wonder what they must make of all this."

"You mean the port attacks? Clearly it isn't interrupting their social life." A dozen guests were already mingling on the lawn, and a young couple were practising lawn bowls. "Someone must be organising a game," Ed said, pointing them out.

"Akash's suggestion. Most likely, it will keep guests who have nothing to do with this out of the way."

Ed had a last-minute moment of panic. "Have we invited too many people?"

"I trust that Alicia and Elizabeth have done the right thing. They know who would normally come to such an event and who wouldn't. Besides, I also gather that events at the Residency don't occur all that often for the larger group of Europeans, English Company members and staff, and the Indian merchants." He gave Ed a wry smile. "It gives them an opportunity to feel grand for the night, and to indulge in gossip. I am confident that my protection spell will keep everyone safe from attack. Part of my preparations was to hide protective sigils around the house, too. There is only one space that I have left unguarded, and that is deliberate."

"The pool with the fountain. I still think that's risky."

Now they knew that the man behind the occult activity was strong with water magic, and that there was an eye within the dark pool in the house next to Deepak Verma's, they wanted to give him an opportunity to attack them, but in a controlled manner. The boundary was protected from external forces, but someone with enough power could circumvent it and attack internally. The small pool with a central fountain could be that spot. However, they had set up a protective magical force around that, too. Far enough away to lure out whatever creature may appear, but not let it escape. Plus, a small number of the regiment would be on the grounds.

"If it appears here, are you sure you can control it? Consider how many people could die."

"I would not do it otherwise," Fitz insisted. "I have crafted an excellent counter-measure, too."

Ed trusted his friend and knew how powerful he was, but even so. However, he turned his attention elsewhere. "You think our conspirators will huddle together?"

"Probably. Akash has briefed several servants that he trusts to listen and watch carefully for any suspicious behaviour." Fitz's gaze shifted to the boundary and then back to the guests. "Perhaps we should have talked to Akash before now. He might have been able to help us."

"We have been here for a few days only and have been very busy. We cannot do everything. Besides, I think Akash would have approached us if he had anything helpful to share. I get the feeling there are lots of rumours and very few facts." Ed straightened his collar again, preparing himself for the night ahead. "I have a spelled dagger tucked inside my boot, and my scope is set up here, ready to inspect the gardens. I shall try to get away regularly."

"The spell I have cast on all four of us should help with that."

"The early warning system."

"Yes, the bells. Nothing too loud, just enough to alert you that magic is moving against us."

"And that no one else will hear?"

Fitz grinned. "No. Tinkling bells like the *nautch* dancers wear that are for our ears only." He referred to the Indian dancing girls. "Hopefully, I will feel the magic, but I don't want to presume. And if it's across the grounds..."

Fitz's inventiveness with spells never ceased to surprise Ed. They both hoped and feared the men moving against them would be at the party, but potentially their team would be spread throughout the guests, making communication difficult. The spell itself had been simple enough to cast, or at least Fitz made it seem that way. He always did, though.

"And the loudness of the bells will indicate how close we are?" Ed asked, making sure he had understood correctly.

"Yes. The louder they are, the closer you are to the magic. We will converge on it. I just wish there was another witch who could help."

"We should get down there. There is nothing more we can do from here now." Ed headed to the door, but then turned back to Fitz who was still studying the garden. "We should tell Captain Townsend what we're planning, if only so he can put a watch on the house Vikram found. He has done nothing to make us suspect him." Fitz just nodded wearily. "Good. I'll do it the first chance I get."

As soon as they reached the ground floor, Alicia, who had obviously been watching out for them, gathered them up like errant children. "Excellent, you're here."

"Has Vik arrived yet?" Ed asked, looking across the crowded drawing room.

"He's outside with Sharma Sahib." She nodded towards the veranda. "First, however, let me introduce you to everyone."

The next ten minutes seemed endless as Ed and Fitz were introduced to people that he knew he would never remember, including minor Indian nobility who glittered in gemstones and fine jewellery, senior members of the Company, and several merchants. Everyone was wearing their most fashionable clothes, and the room was vibrant with colourful silks and fine linen. He realised that Fitz and he were unfashionably late, and all heads were turning as they worked their way around the room. Servants silently moved among the guests, carrying drinks on silver platters, and a small group of Indian court musicians must have been positioned outside, because music drifted in through the doors.

"Good grief, Alicia," Ed said, surprised. "I can't believe how many are here, and how magnificent the house looks."

"Akash and his staff have worked relentlessly," she said, lowering her voice. "I told you everyone would come."

The Harbour Master was also present, and he looked grim as he approached them, his only terse comment by way of greeting being that the port needed immediate repair.

"But the creatures were destroyed," Ed said to him firmly. "Of course, we will do one final sweep in the morning before we leave."

Moustache bristling, he huffed. "Another day? I thought this evening's event was to celebrate your success."

"It is," Alicia said forcefully. "Dear Mr Swift, Westerly, and Singh are most diligent. Have the regiment cleared the area well?"

"Yes, and the dockhands, of course."

"Excellent news." She moved them swiftly on until they stood before Henry Cavendish, Elizabeth, and his Uncle Benjamin, who held himself as stiffly as if he had a gun to his head. *Pompous idiot.* Ed steeled himself for what might come.

Henry greeted them enthusiastically as he shook their hands. "Here they are! Our heroes."

"And yet the destruction in the port is quite extreme," Benjamin said. He was flushed from either the heat or the alcohol, but his clothes were immaculate.

"Not exactly," Fitz said easily. "We noted the crates stacked in the dock were empty, and that not one single warehouse was damaged. Fortunate, don't you think? Especially considering what we had to face. Ed here," he slapped Ed's shoulder, "was a marvel. I never realised he had such a head for heights. And of course, the creatures we faced..."

Henry cut in with a nervous glance towards Elizabeth, Alicia, and the guests nearby. "Probably best not to elaborate on that."

"Of course not. My apologies." Fitz dipped his head towards Elizabeth, who quickly smothered a smile. "Our difficulties were numerous. But I must admit, Henry, that all is not as it seems, as I suggested to you only yesterday."

"Then your assumption is correct?" Henry looked alarmed. "Someone wanted to attack the port deliberately. Sabotage?"

"Not exactly." Fitz leaned in, his tone conspiratorial, "Although, that is what we were supposed to believe."

Henry's eyes hardened. "You mean there is other subterfuge at play?"

Benjamin puffed, nostrils flaring, in a clear attempt to undermine them. "I think you have taken leave of your senses. Of course the port was the subject of the attacks!"

"Oh? You know something about them, Uncle?" Ed asked, feigning innocence as he watched his response.

"I meant that the port was targeted, that's all. Nothing else in Rajgarh has been attacked."

"And yet," Fitz continued, looking Benjamin squarely in the eye, "deaths aside, we must consider that no goods were destroyed, and only one boat and one jetty were damaged."

"You consider the damage to the buildings inconsequential?"

"Of course not, but the offices can be repaired. No warehouses or their contents were damaged. Curious, don't you think?" Fitz glanced between Henry and Benjamin.

Benjamin was about to object, but Henry frowned. "You're quite right. But surely in time..."

Fitz pressed his point. "Three weeks. Nearly four. Plenty of time to have completely destroyed the port, and maybe Rajgarh, too."

"Then what are you suggesting?" Henry asked, too curious now to consider his wife's sensibilities. "And does it even matter, if it is over now?"

"We're not entirely sure it is, unfortunately," Ed said. "But we are close to ending it. Hopefully tonight."

"How?" Henry asked, eyes narrowing. "Are you returning to the port?"

"I'd rather not say," Fitz said, giving an easy smile of reassurance, "but I don't wish you to worry. You hired us to solve it, and we will. I think it's fair to say that Ed, Vikram, and I are confident the end is near. All being well, we will leave tomorrow, and the business of the Company can continue unhindered."

"Really?" Henry turned to his wife and Anthony, the Assistant Resident, who had just joined them. "Excellent news, Anthony. Did you hear that? Mr Swift and Mr Westerly will be on their way tomorrow, if their final plans work out tonight. Isn't that wonderful?"

"Excellent news," Elizabeth said demurely. "You three are worthy of your reputation—of which, of course, I know very little, other than what dear Henry has told me."

Anthony was less gracious. "It's done, then?"

"Other than a few loose ends," Ed told him. Hopefully, this talk of them leaving unscathed would rattle the conspirators into action. "Now, we will leave you to enjoy the party and find Vikram and Sharma Sahib. Please excuse us."

"First, let me introduce you to just a couple more guests," Alicia said, pointing to an Indian gentleman a short distance away. "I would love for you to meet Mr Deepak Verma, one of the most illustrious residents of Rajgarh."

"Excellent," Fitz said. "I have heard great things of him."

Ed, however, had barely made two steps before Benjamin cornered him, alone. "What game are you playing?"

"There is no game. I haven't forgotten that men have died here. However, it's important that we share our observations. Surely you must think it odd that despite everything, the port continued to function in the day, and that no one lost goods? Isn't that incredibly convenient?"

"I think no such thing."

Ed wondered if that was a trace of fear he saw behind his bluster. "Clearly that is why you do your job and I do mine. After many years of researching and fighting dangerous supernatural creatures, these act like no others we've seen. It's as if..." he paused, wondering whether to say their real suspicions, and then threw caution to the wind. "It's as if this was all done to draw us here and attack us. But who would do that, when our actions are always to save others?"

"I do not like your tone."

"I do not know why. I am not blaming *you*."

"I think you're paranoid."

Ed smiled. "Let's hope so, and then this really is over. As we said, we will depart tomorrow if we can find nothing to substantiate our claims. We will know tonight, one way or another."

Ed turned away, knowing he had given his uncle plenty to think about. If he was behind this, he now knew he would need to act quickly. Deepak Verma was only a few steps away, and under the guise of refreshing his drink, Ed took a moment to study him. He looked to be in his mid-fifties, with thinning grey hair and a neat beard. His eyes were dark and deep-set, and they were fixed on Fitz intently. Ed was used to the feel of magic and power, but he couldn't detect anything from him. Unless, of course, he was masking it. He decided to let Fitz deal with him, knowing he would discern far more than he could, and instead walked outside to find Captain Townsend.

The veranda was lined with tables and chairs, although most were empty as the guests milled about talking to each other, some spreading out onto the grass, and others playing lawn bowls. Servants circulated endlessly, and the *punkah-wallahs* positioned along the floor ensured the guests were kept cool as large fans flapped overhead. Captain Townsend was talking to the doctor at the far end of the veranda, and Ed hurried to join them.

"Captain Townsend, Doctor Robinson, I apologise for interrupting, but may I speak to you, Captain? It's quite urgent. Privately, sorry," he said apologetically to Montague.

Montague shrugged. "No matter. I need to speak to Roger, anyway. Is everything all right?"

"Just a few loose ends to tie up," he said, intending to spread the word far and wide. "We're hoping to leave tomorrow."

"So soon?" he asked. "Have you really stopped this horror?"

"Almost."

Unexpectedly, the doctor floundered at this news. "I thought you'd be here for days yet."

"Well, last night we killed two of the creatures and destroyed the method of their attack—we hope. As I said, just a few loose ends. Good news, surely?"

"Of course!" Montague adjusted his collar nervously. "I'll leave you to it."

"I must confess," Townsend said coldly when they were alone, "that is not the impression you gave me today."

"Things have advanced this afternoon." Ed took a breath, hoping he was right in his assumption. "We have discovered what we believe to be the source of the issue. We are working on resolving it tonight, but need assistance."

"From me?" Captain Townsend smirked, the first *almost* smile Ed had seen from him. "I thought I was in the way."

"Do you want to help or not?"

"Of course I do. Anything that will end this."

"Good. Then listen carefully."

Twenty-Nine

Moonfell 2025

"A re we insane?" Horty asked as she exited the taxi a short distance from Swift House Heritage Hotel in Mayfair. "I think the gin must have addled my thinking."

"Well, that's been going on a dreadfully long time, then," Birdie replied acerbically. "And no, we are not. This is exactly where we need to be. Gosh. This place never ceases to amaze."

"Mayfair, you mean?" Horty studied the expensive shops, hotels, restaurants, and private clubs that surrounded them. "It's been years since I've been here. It makes me want to spend money."

"Buy me a cocktail, then."

Horty loved a frivolous spend. Something pretty, hopefully useful, and utterly decadent. Mayfair was full of it. "If the hotel has a bar, I certainly will. Well, shall we?" she asked, strolling down the road towards the hotel.

They had driven past it, having asked the taxi driver to drop them off a short distance away. Even at this late hour, well beyond her normal bedtime, the streets were busy with people leaving or entering pubs and clubs. They had left the rest of the family enjoying Storm Moon before anyone had talked them out of their plan.

They kept to the opposite side of the busy road, mingling with the Saturday night crowds, until they stopped directly opposite the hotel where they halted to study it. It looked far more impressive now than it did on the website.

Horty admired the red brick and stone trim, tipping her head back to see the roof high above. "Blimey. How much do you think this place is worth now?"

"Oodles. They must have had a lot of money at the time, too."

"And an estate in Surrey, *daaarling*," Horty said, drawing the word out. "I'd love to know if the family still owns this place, or whether it's just marketing."

The ground floor had large, modern windows overlooking the road, although they had been designed to fit in perfectly with the style of the house, revealing soft lighting inside and tables to the right of the door. The sign announced the Swift House Heritage Hotel, and there was a smaller sign by the glass and brass double front doors that said Residency Bar. On the left, however, above the other large window, was an equally intriguing sign. Swift Heritage Travel Company, also in gilt lettering and matching font, making it clear that these businesses were linked.

Horty's heart was pounding. "They've called it the Residency Bar? Does that mean they know things?"

"What things? Get a grip, Horty. Benjamin was high up in the East India Company. They had Residencies spread all over the damn country, especially by the time Queen Vic got dragged in." Her cheeks dimpled as she grinned. "This is so exciting. Come on."

They hustled across the road, and Horty, desperate to get in first, elbowed her sister out of the way to reach the steps before her. A very nice man in a suit stood on the other side of the doors, and he opened it for them, revealing an elegant hallway with several doors and an open, arched entrance to the bar. "Welcome, ladies. Residents, or just drinks?"

"Just drinks, please," Horty said, eyeing the impressive room beyond.

"In that case, I recommend the Wayfarer cocktail."

The bar area was all polished wood, mirrors, leather seats, and leafy green plants, but the designers had kept all the architectural features of the original house. Once the drinks were ordered, they settled at a table, fully able to absorb the atmosphere.

"I absolutely love this place." Horty soaked it all in. "This is where Ed lived! I can't believe it."

"And was persecuted," Birdie added with a huff.

"Was he? They specifically mention him by name. See!" She pointed to the drinks menu that had regurgitated the description Morgana had read out. "Edmund, not Benjamin. They don't mention his monster hunting, but honestly, what sane person would?"

"Through there," Birdie said, nodding towards another grand doorway across the spacious reception hallway, "is the travel company. They are obviously aiming for high-end clientele."

"They must have more information on Ed in here somewhere." Spotting a few glossy brochures at the end of the bar, Horty picked two up and returned to her seat. "One for you, too. This says they have hotels in India and Europe. Swift Villas in Florence and Umbria, and also in Nice. I adore Nice."

"Swift Lodge in Rajgarh!" Birdie jabbed the page. She rarely swore, but she did now. "What the absolute fuck is going on? Are we in some parallel universe?"

"The F-word? Really? Honestly, Birdie."

"Horty! Rajgarh. Focus!"

But Horty was already ignoring Birdie, not really giving two hoots about swearing, but liking to antagonise her older sister. Instead, she was already reading the blurb on the back of the glossy brochure. "By the Goddess. He died!"

"Of course he did, unless he discovered immortality, like JD."

"In Rajgarh." Unexpected grief swept through Horty, and for a second, she couldn't see the room, but only the painting of Ed and Fitz looking so happy by the south moon gate. "I feel quite sick."

Birdie scanned the information, too. "Okay, so he isn't their founder as such, but in 1807 a man called Jeremy Swift set up the enterprise based on his uncle's adventures. He wanted a way to mark his great achievements in travel, and his unique scientific mind." Birdie's eyebrows shot up. "*Unique?* Is that another word for supernatural?"

"Does it say how he died?" Horty couldn't bear to look. She had imagined Ed sauntering into old age with a family, or continuing to explore continents. "All that promise. He was so young."

"No details of his death at all. Just an unfortunate accident, apparently."

"Accident my arse!"

"Language." Birdie smirked.

"Call someone over! Somebody here must know something."

"The bar staff? Don't be ridiculous."

"This is our chance to break into Swift Heritage Travel." From her seat, Horty could see the shadowy interior of the shop beyond the doors across the hall.

"Or we could ask the hotel staff? The lobby is through that door." Birdie pointed to another door at the rear of the reception area. "Surely the Duty Manager would know something of the history of this place. Heritage is in the bloody title, after all."

Horty lingered over her drink. "I'm not sure I'm ready for this. Just give me a moment."

Birdie nodded. "I know. Me neither. I wonder what changed in the summer."

"Meli's note? Maybe Vik and Fitz split up. Although," Horty hesitated, "something doesn't feel right."

"That's just wishful thinking."

"But it doesn't explain why we have Ed's books. Why weren't they returned to his family?"

Birdie tapped her nose. "More secrets. Come on. Drink up. I think we should book a room."

Odette could feel the veils between worlds thinning as she settled on a garden bench to watch the Full Moon Gate in the south of the garden.

Storm Moon had been fun, and she'd even danced to the band's music, keeping an eye on her young cousins while they revelled in the party atmosphere. Merlin had been only too glad to hand over their supervision, and Arlo had helped. He stayed close, but not too close. Observant, solicitous, magnetic. Even when she couldn't see him, she could feel his presence. Now she needed quiet to marshal her thoughts.

Moonfell's house sprawled behind the gate, mostly in darkness, but the occasional light gleamed in windows scattered across the different levels. A house full of history, dramas, laughter, hopes, and dreams. A refuge from the world. A place of magic. And secrets.

Beltane was a fire festival, so not only was this the right gate for the time of year, but it was also where Meli had drawn her painting. Odette eased back into the rose arbour cloaked in shadows, Meli's painting on her lap, and drew the blanket she'd brought with her around her shoulders.

"Come on, Meli," she murmured under her breath. "Show me what happened here. It was important to you."

It was late now, and Odette could feel sleep pulling her, her eyelids growing heavier and heavier, but she forced herself to stay awake, taking in big breaths of the sharp April night. A low ground mist was rising, and a peacock strutted through it, tail feathers spread to catch the glint of starlight. *Do they never sleep?* Perhaps, she considered, they strolled in Indian sunshine, and they had no idea they were in an English garden right now. *And why hadn't they got a peacock topiary?* Surely that would be a stunning addition to their collection. *Something to suggest to their gardener, perhaps.* A little tweak of magic, and it wouldn't take long. *A monkey too, maybe,* she thought as three ran in front of her, chasing each other like toddlers in a playground.

She was just a step away from India and the Residency garden. She could feel it close by, as if she could walk right into it. The moon gate beckoned, the breeze lifting the honeysuckle that still rambled over the stonework, and something shimmered within its dark depths. She blinked to clear her vision, but it was still there. No shapes emerged, though, no view of people beyond. Like a sleepwalker, she stood up, the blanket and painting falling to the ground, and crossed the lawn to the gate, the monkeys chittering around her.

Odette laid her hands on the stone, and it thrummed beneath her like it was alive. The scent of sandalwood and jasmine mingled with the honeysuckle, and the hot breath of a still evening pulled her forward. Trance-like, she stepped beneath the gate's arched roof, and within a few steps was through and in another world, like Alice through the looking glass.

The Residency sprawled ahead of her, as white and grand as a wedding cake, and glittering with lights under a star-filled sky. She was under the spreading branches of a tree, and a river gurgled against the banks behind her, while lush lawns separated her from the house and a huge number of people in all manner of dress. Uniforms, long dresses in silks and chiffons, Indian gentlemen in glorious clothing, frockcoats and boots, and a myriad of servants between them. Indian music travelled along the lawn to meet her, and she wanted nothing more than to cross the grass to join the party. *But a party to celebrate what?*

Odette had never had a more realistic vision before, and her eyes welled with tears as the breath caught in her chest. The sense of ennui was so strong she could taste it. Her hand was still on the warm stone of the Full Moon Gate. *If she let go, would it vanish? Would she have travelled through time? Would she be able to travel back? And would they see her, or would she move amongst them like a ghost from another time? Which of course was exactly what she was.*

Frozen with a mixture of indecision and a dreamlike inability to move, she could discern the tinkling of bells they had heard in the garden for the last few days. The sound of the bells that graced the Indian dancers, she now realised. But they sounded urgent and close by now.

Two men ran across the lawn in front of her, heading to the left of the house, and her breath caught again. An Indian man with a thick head of lustrous dark hair, athletic and handsome, and a man with reddish-blond hair that glowed in the lights. Something was happening. Something terrible. She could feel the weight of it carrying through the years, and such was her alarm that her somnolent, hypnotic state vanished, and she took her hand off the stone gate as if to run in to help.

But the spell was broken by her movement and the Residency at Rajgarh vanished, leaving an ache in her chest and sorrow breaking like a burst dam, and when Merlin found her only seconds later, standing bereft and heartbroken, she fell against him and cried, wishing it was Arlo comforting her instead.

Thirty

Rajgarh 1792

F itz was tense all evening, alert for any suggestion of magic, or an attempt to get past his magical protection on the house.

He circulated the party, keeping a careful eye on the guests, particularly Deepak Verma. The man had been very polite when they were introduced, his voice low and even, and he was clearly intelligent; frustratingly, Fitz could detect nothing from his person that suggested magic of any kind. He also seemed to have no interest in talking to Benjamin Swift at all. Neither man moved near each other all night, keeping to separate conversations. *Perhaps that was a clue in itself.*

Several men, mostly clerks who worked at the dock, asked him many questions about the nature of his business, and Fitz, used to keeping a low profile, found the attention unnerving. He successfully kept the conversation away from magic and focussed purely on the physical side of their exploration and travel, citing their interactions with the occult as something they had stumbled into. When pressed for details, he talked tactics and weapons. If they had hoped for a blow-by-blow account of their exploits, then they were very disappointed. As soon as he could politely move away, he headed to the lawn for a brief respite, but in moments Alicia hurried to join him.

Darkness had fallen, and the lawn and trees were lit with lanterns. Laughter and music filled the grounds, and the dancing had spilled onto the lawns. Seeing Alicia dressed in her finery, he wished he could forget their troubles and dance with her—even though he had two left feet. It would be nice for just one evening to pretend that his life was ordinary. But it was impossible. The person responsible for the monstrous creatures was still at large, the conspiracy was yet to be uncovered, and time was running out. They had set their trap and hoped someone stepped into it. But their enemies were clever and skilful. Thanks to regular updates from the regiment at the docks and around the house containing the occult room, he knew that both areas remained quiet. *Had he made a mistake earlier by not examining the room that Vikram had found?* But they were so short on time. *What if someone was dismantling it and moving it already via the underground passage?*

"I think I've made a mistake," he admitted to Alicia, and told her his concerns.

"Surely if the place Vikram found was so complex, it would be impossible to move."

"In theory, yes, but our opponents are so devious."

"And so are you." She smiled, but it didn't reach her eyes. "I say that in the nicest way, of course. But I have news."

"Is there a problem?" he asked.

"Hard to say. that none of the staff have overheard anything of significance, but Monty hasn't been seen for a while."

"The doctor? Is he in his room?"

"He has his own small place in the Residency grounds. One of the single-story villas."

"Oh? I don't know why, but I presumed he lived in the Residency."

"No, he likes his privacy. I have asked Akash to check, and he has sent one of the servants to investigate. Of course, it could be nothing..."

"Ed said the doctor was very surprised to hear we would be leaving tomorrow. Disappointed, even."

"You suspect he's involved?" Alicia looked surprised.

"I have to keep an open mind. How do you find him?"

"He is always polite, and extremely efficient at his job."

"Has he been absent more than usual lately? He wasn't around when we first arrived."

"He was still in Rajgarh, as far as I know. Sometimes he just chooses to dine alone. He's been busy recently. The stress of the dead men at the docks, injuries, worries about the attacks, and the occasional absentees, I gather."

"That's understandable. I must admit, I didn't consider that." He studied the house and the parade of lit windows, their own included. "Perhaps we should have questioned him more. He might well be a source of information. He could have heard rumours we would not."

"Do you want to find him now?"

Fitz shook his head. "If he is resting, then I don't want to bother him. What about you? Are you all right?"

"I'm perfectly fine. All this intrigue is invigorating! I have been circulating and listening to as many conversations as possible. You three have attracted a lot of attention, but there's all the usual gossip, too. Overall, however, everyone is relieved that this is over."

"Except that we lied."

"Well, it will be. Perhaps we need to prompt some action, somehow. Force someone to make a mistake."

"I thought our talk of leaving tomorrow would do that."

Alicia looked at the house, and then turned to the river so that her face was in shadow. "Are you really leaving so soon? I thought you might stay for a while and rest. Henry is happy to accommodate you."

"If we can solve this tonight, I would like to stay." He turned so that he faced the river too, enjoying the cool breeze that drifted off it, and tried to explain the nature of his life that he knew would be so different to Alicia's. "We travel, explore, make notes on villages, cities, towns, people, and religions, as well as the creatures we face. Ed is always developing new ideas and trialling instruments. Vikram hones his fighting skills, and I practice magic. We all, however, study the occult and the many mysteries of this world. We are lucky to be able to indulge our passions at our leisure. We stay where we want for as long as we want, and sometimes we don't fight monsters for months." He looked at her, and found she was watching him closely. "We are lucky to be so independent. We stay in grand hotels or tiny settlements, depending on where we are. Life is always varied. And the wildlife! Such wonders. I sometimes think that I will never grow weary of our life. However, we need to settle somewhere over the summer when it becomes too hot to travel, so we must decide on where that will be soon."

"Perhaps here, then?" She said it casually, but watched him intently. "It will be good for all of us to have new faces for our summer parties."

"As long as we survive the night, then perhaps we will." He would like to spend more time with Alicia, but their lives were so different. "You remind me of my sister, Melusine. She is independent-minded, but constrained by her age, at present. Fortunately, Moonfell provides her with plenty of distractions."

"Moonfell?"

"My family home in London."

"What an intriguing name."

He smiled. "And an even more intriguing place. Should we ever be in England at the same time, you must visit."

"Which means we must keep in touch."

"Indeed." The party faded into the background, a peculiar intimacy falling between them that Fitz thought he should probably break. And then he noticed one of the servants hurrying across the lawn, and something about his posture caught Fitz's attention. "Alicia, let's find out what's worrying that man. Do you know him?"

"Of course. That's Mohan, one of the messengers."

They intercepted him close to the veranda, and Fitz drew him aside. "Is there a problem?"

"It's the doctor." His eyes darted towards Alicia. "I shouldn't..."

"I am perfectly able to hear any news," she assured him.

He stepped closer, drawing them away from the guests. "The doctor is dead. He is in his room. I must inform Akash and the Resident immediately."

Alcia gasped. "Oh, no."

"How did he die?" Fitz asked. "Is there any sign of attack?"

"No, but he looked terrible. His face..." he trailed off, clearly unwilling to say more.

"I must examine him," Fitz said. "Now. Is anyone with him?"

"Another servant, Sahib. Very trustworthy."

"Good, thank you. Go and tell Akash." He watched him hurry away, thoughts churning. "Tell me how to get there, Alicia, then find Ed or Vik. And make sure you keep to well-lit areas."

Vikram located Ed as soon as Alicia informed him of the doctor's death, leaving her to find her sister. "We have done something terribly wrong. This was not meant to happen."

"The doctor's death has nothing to do with us," Ed said forcefully.

"It has *everything* to do with us. We set a trap!"

"If the doctor is dead, it is because he was either involved up to his neck, or knew something that he should have told us. This is not our fault."

They stood at the end of the veranda, and fortunately it seemed that so far, the guests had no idea of what had happened. That would not last long. "Nothing supernatural could have got in here without us knowing, so his murderer is present."

"Let Fitz examine him first before we leap to conclusions. Plus," Ed added, "Akash's intelligence network might have heard something."

And then Vik heard tinkling bells, and he lifted his head. "Do you hear them?"

"Yes! Faintly."

Trying to stay calm, Vik looked around and attempted to discern the direction of the sound. "Logically, it must be the fountain."

He set off towards it and Ed followed, and as Fitz had promised, the bells grew louder. The fountain was to the side of the house, and at their instructions it had been left in darkness so as not to attract the partygoers, but as they rounded the corner, he saw there were two men and two women, illuminated by a bluish light that emanated from the fountain. Vik estimated they were probably within the protection boundary that Fitz had set.

"Get away from the fountain!" Ed shouted, attracting their attention. "Move!"

Vik put on a burst of speed, reaching their side just as something rose out of the water. He bodily pushed them all away. "Get back to the house. Now!"

A woman was transfixed on something behind him, and Vik whirled around, daggers in hand, just as Ed grabbed the woman and yanked her backwards, shouting, "Are you deaf? Move!"

She started to scream, until Ed muffled her and addressed the two men. "Keep her calm and leave now. Tell Captain Townsend, but no other guests!"

But Vik's attention was now solely on the gigantic snake with one eye that had risen out of the water, sinuously weaving its head as it looked around.

"Have they gone?" Vik asked, exchanging one dagger for his sword.

"Yes, though I suspect that we'll have an audience soon."

"Then we need to stop this. Have you got the spells Fitz prepared?"

"In my pocket."

"Then get ready!"

The snake heaved its body over the lip of the fountain, and Vik ran at it, slashing its body before it could fully leave the water. Despite its size, it was agile and swift, and as he leapt onto the fountain's stone edge, he noted that the normally clear water had been replaced by the inky blackness he had seen in the occult room. His momentum almost took him right into it, but he balanced on the edge and then leapt onto the grass as the snake darted at him. He fell backwards, the snake's head whipping over him, but his sword remained extended in an attempt to wound it. Unfortunately, the snake remained beyond his reach, and it slid past him to try and get to Ed. Vik bounded upright and lunged, managing to inflict a long but shallow cut.

Ed launched one of Fitz's spells, sealed by wax in a bottle. His aim was good as it struck the fountain and shattered, the spell blooming around the snake, and Ed quickly followed it up with the required incantation. The spell was designed to damage whoever controlled the creature, rather than the snake.

However, the snake advanced, and just as Vik was panicking that Fitz had set the protective boundary too far back, the protection spell ignited with a fiery light that encompassed the entire fountain. Still, the snake's tail remained in the water. *How long was this hideous creature?* Vik leapt on to it, his blades a blur of speed, but there was no doubt now that the snake was only interested in Ed.

"Ed! Run!"

All three were now within the protective spell, and as Ed dived out of the way, the snake hit the fiery wall, rebounded backwards with a hiss, and fixed its huge eye on Vik. He knew that intense stare. It was the one he had seen in the occult room.

The next few seconds were a blur of running, attacking, slashing, and diving out of the way. He and Ed could have broken through the protective circle and left the snake inside, but Vik was now possessed with the desperate urge to end the creature, and it seemed so was Ed, who dexterously avoided the snake and threw another spelled bottle at the monster.

But then the snake darted so quickly, neither of them could react fast enough. Its tail clattered into Ed, sweeping him into the pool. Horrified, Vik leapt onto the fountain's edge, but Ed had already disappeared into the frothing water.

The snake immediately retreated, submerging itself within the inky depths, and feeling he had no other choice than to help his friend, Vik leapt in after it.

Thirty-One
Moonfell 2025

"**T**his really is a beautiful hotel," Birdie said as she and Horty finished checking in. "It must have so much history."

The concierge, a pretty, young French woman who spoke excellent English, nodded as she organised their electronic keycards. "Yes, we have been open since 1807. Of course, it's been modernised since then, but the owners have made every effort to keep the authenticity of the building."

"Is anything private now?" Horty asked. "I mean, are there rooms that belong solely to the founding family?"

"You mean in the building? Oh, no. The family doesn't live here anymore."

Horty brandished the brochure she had picked up in the bar like a weapon. "The Swifts, I believe?"

"Yes." The woman looked puzzled. "Do you know them?"

"No," Birdie said, interrupting. "We are just curious about these grand houses and what they were like before they were businesses. We're amateur historians. When we had a drink in the bar, we knew we had to stay here."

"You are lucky we have a room. We are often fully booked." She peered over the counter. "You have no luggage?"

"No, this is impromptu. A Saturday night bit of fun between sisters."

The woman smiled indulgently. "It sounds lovely. Our rooms are fully equipped with toiletries, but if you need anything, please ask." She handed them the cards. "Third floor. The lift is in the corner if you'd rather use that than the staircase."

With the booking complete, Birdie relaxed a little. She had no idea why she should feel so nervous, as if Benjamin Swift's ghost might leap out at her at any moment. "Can you tell us about Edmund Swift, who the hotel honours?"

"I'm afraid I don't know the details. Just that he extensively explored Europe and India. His nephew, Jeremy, decided to capitalise on the development of Mayfair in the early 1800s and turned this into a hotel. Travel, of course, was very popular at the time, especially luxury travel. He was an entrepreneur."

"Ah, yes. The Grand Tour," Horty said, referring to the aristocrats and the wealthy class who toured Europe in the 18th and 19th centuries.

"Exactly. That is when the travel company began, as well. Of course, it wasn't called Swift Heritage Travel then, but it was luxurious. They used all the latest modes of transport. There is more information in the building next door. They liked to cater to women travellers, too."

"Really! Why?" Birdie asked. "Wasn't that unusual?"

"A business opportunity, perhaps?" The woman shrugged. "Women had few chances to be independent then, so tours specifically for women were a way for that to happen." She rolled her eyes. "Can you believe what women had to put up with? The staff next door could tell you more. It will be open for a few hours tomorrow. There is a small sitting room on the first floor with shelves of books, should you need anything to entertain yourselves tonight, including a few books about the family. Nothing elaborate, but you might find them interesting. Breakfast is served in the dining hall to the rear." She pointed to the door. "Do you need help finding your room?"

It was a polite dismissal, but Birdie couldn't wait to explore. "No, thank you." As soon as they were alone in the lift, she said, "Did you hear that? Independent travel for women. That can't be a coincidence."

"You're thinking of Meli."

"I am. She was desperate to travel. Fitz said as much."

"But Ed was dead, and that would have been, what, fifteen years after he died? And what would Jeremy Swift have known about Meli? That was Fitz's sister, not Ed's."

"It means something, I just know it," Birdie said. "I feel it in my bones."

"Maybe Fitz kept in touch."

"Perhaps."

The lift opened onto a broad landing that had corridors on either side. The same rich, wooden floors were on this level, and the walls were a mix of wood panelling and wallpaper. They followed the signs and found their room that had a similar style of décor to the hall, with an enormous bed, a desk, wardrobe, two comfortable chairs next to the fireplace, and a chest of drawers.

"No expense spared here," Horty said, heading to the window. "We're overlooking the road."

Birdie spelled the lamps on as Horty shut the curtains. "Now we just have to decide what to do, other than soak in the atmosphere."

"A séance, perhaps?"

Birdie shuddered. "Not likely, after the last time."

"Then let's drape ourselves in shadow spells and wander around. There'll be storerooms as well as the other rooms the concierge mentioned. Plus, we might dream something later."

Birdie's energy was waning, but they could definitely snoop around more at night than the day. "I'm far too excited to sleep. Let's investigate Swift Heritage Travel first."

"I thought tonight would never end," Morgana said, as she entered her bedroom with Monroe.

He threw his jacket across the back of the chair. "You didn't have fun?"

"I had plenty of fun, but I'm side-tracked by letters and journals...and you."

His huge smile erupted as he teased her. "Me? How nice."

"Better than nice." She stepped into his arms, enjoying the feel of them circling her waist, and his broad chest pressed against hers. "I love Storm Moon, but at times the night felt interminable."

"Your brother looked at me like I was the devil at first."

"He likes you, though. It's your natural wolfishly threatening demeanour that initially put him off. I quite like it."

"My wolfishly threatening demeanour? Wow. And good. Is this Beltane passion getting under your skin?"

"No. Just you."

She thought she might behave a bit skittishly around Monroe, like being a teenager again, but actually he was very grounding. He demanded nothing of her, accepting her for exactly who she was. He found her interesting and funny and clever, and it was incredibly liberating, as if she'd been given permission to be herself again. A completely ridiculous idea, of course, because she was always herself, and if she hadn't been it was no one's fault except her own. As she'd said to her brother earlier, her current mindset was down to several things, and Monroe was just one of them. Experiences or events or whatever she should call them were aligning.

"What are you thinking?" he asked, his dark eyes glowing like a banked fire again.

"That I'm awake for the first time in years."

"Good, because I have no intention of letting you sleep yet," he said, before giving her a long, slow kiss.

"That's not exactly what I meant," she said, catching her breath afterwards.

"I know. I heard Horty wittering earlier about the winds of change. Why have we still got our clothes on?"

But Monroe had only pulled his t-shirt over his head when Morgana's phone started ringing. "It's Merlin." Worried about her nieces, she answered quickly. "Is everything all right?"

"It's Odette. She's had an experience by the south moon gate. I'm sorry, I know you're with Monroe, but will you come down? She's okay, just upset. Very upset. I think I'm pretty useless in these situations. We're in the rose arbour."

"You're not at all, but of course I will. Be there in a moment."

She ended the call and grabbed a large wrap she kept by the bed. "I'm sorry, but I need to go. I think Odette has seen something through the moon gate at the front of the house."

"I'll come, too."

He didn't bother putting his shirt back on, and she knew he'd shift once they reached the garden. Within a few minutes, during which she imagined all sorts of disturbing things, they reached the garden and saw Merlin wave from the bench under the roses, Odette tucked under his arm as she leaned against him.

"I'm going to have a sniff around," Monroe said, stripping off. "I'll join you soon."

Morgana left Monroe to investigate and sat next to Odette, horrified at how upset she was. "What's happened? Did you see Ed?"

She was still crying and sniffing. "I saw Ed and Vikram running around the Residency, and something bad was happening. I just know it."

"The Residency?" Morgana looked around, as if she'd run straight past it in her haste. "Where?"

Merlin answered for her. "Through the moon gate. She stepped through it and found herself at a party at the Rajgarh Residency. That's about as much as I've got." He spoke over Odette's head that was still on his shoulder, mouthing almost silently, "She won't stop crying."

"I'll be fine, honestly," Odette mumbled, trying to sit up. "I was just overcome with emotion, and I feel so drained. I know I saw the night that everything changed."

Morgana wrapped her arm around her and her brother, pulling them all into a hug. "Do you think you can explain how it happened? I'm trying to get some context."

"I was just sitting here, waiting. I came with the painting because it was painted here, and just hoped to see *something*." She thrust the painting that had been wrapped under the blanket at Morgana. "I was so tired, and I fell into a sort of trance. The gate pulled me to it, and I thought I'd see something through it—you know, like I do—but it was not like I expected." She clutched Morgana's free hand, looking up at her with a mascara-streaked face. "The gate was warm, and it hummed like it was alive, and suddenly I was there. Right there. The music, the dancing, the house... It was beautiful. And I saw Ed and Vik. Ed's hair was red in the light, and Vikram was so handsome. Like a Bollywood star. And I heard bells. The tinkling bells we've been hearing around the house. Everything changed then. I know it." She trailed off again, eyes vacant as she stared at the moon gate.

"Stay here with Merlin. I'm going to look." Morgana sought permission from Merlin with a questioning tip of her head, and he just shooed her away with a reassuring nod. Odette stayed silent.

Morgana never worried about Odette. She might be uncanny, but she was strong. However, after the events with the Storm Moon Pack only weeks earlier, and now this, she wondered if she was feeling things too strongly. *But what could they do about that?* She wished Birdie and Horty were there to seek their advice, but had no intention of disturbing them. If Odette had honestly seen so much, then that was one of her strongest visions yet.

When Morgana reached the gate, she put her hands on the stone carefully. The surface was cold and inert, with no sign of the thrumming lifeforce that her cousin had described.

Monroe was close by in his wolf, sniffing around and tracking as he paced back and forth, but seeing her, he shifted to human. "I can feel magic, and smell the usual Moonfell animals, and the peacocks and monkeys. What did she see?"

Morgana explained everything she knew. "I'll ask her more tomorrow. She's too tired and upset now. I don't know what to do, though. I don't want to leave her alone tonight, for many reasons. I mean, it might happen again, and I don't want her wandering the grounds in this state, or even just in bed alone, crying. She won't want Merlin, so I think I'll have to stay with her."

"If that's what you need to do, that's fine, but I have a better suggestion."

"What?"

"Call Arlo."

"Arlo? Are you mad?"

"No. She trusts him, and he'll look after her."

"I think that's a really bad idea. They've only recently started talking again."

"And can barely take their eyes off each other. They gravitate together. You must see that."

She knew that Monroe was right. "Of course I do, but them circling in each other's orbit is not the same as us calling him to comfort her. All night."

"He'll keep her safe. He'd follow her to Rajgarh if he had to." Monroe locked eyes with her. "I'll call him, and will happily take the blame if Odette is not happy about it. He'll arrive while we're still fannying around out here. I presume there is more nosing around to do?"

She sighed and smiled. *How was she this lucky to have a piece of Monroe? Would he follow her to Rajgarh, too?* Then she chided herself for thinking such things. *Too soon.* "Just a little. I'd like to talk to Merlin, and then cast a few small spells."

"Good. I'll call him now, then."

Thirty-Two

Rajgarh 1792

Fitz stepped away from the doctor's body, knowing he had died by occult means. The expression of horror on his face certainly suggested he had experienced something terrible before he died.

Although the living room in the doctor's villa looked normal enough on a cursory examination, there was the whiff of something dank that he couldn't identify. However, within minutes of Fitz's arrival, Henry swept into the room, eyes landing on the doctor's body before darting around the simply decorated living area.

Henry was blunt. They were alone, the servant outside the room. "How did he die? There's not a mark on him."

"Magic. A curse, perhaps." Fitz checked around the body again, wondering if there was a cursed object he had missed. Usually, it would be something familiar that the victim would use regularly.

"But why?"

"I suspect he was involved with the deception."

Henry just stared at him, assessing the truth of his statement, probably. Fitz had always known how powerful the man was; after all, he was the Resident of Rajgarh. A political appointment given to those who knew how to deal with foreigners and employees alike. Henry was no fool.

Finally, Henry said, "I think you are withholding more information. I need to know what it is. Right now." When Fitz hesitated, he said, "This business is not putting you in a good light. You may have a good reputation amongst the Indian community, but not ours, and at this rate, despite the fact that you and Edmund have good backgrounds, you will be seen with distrust and superstition everywhere you go. What is going on?"

"You won't like what I have to tell you."

"I don't care."

"Edmund is under extreme pressure to give up this lifestyle. Benjamin Swift hates it, and has actually threatened today that his family will disinherit and disown him if he does not give it up. We think that he is behind this attack, working with someone to undermine us. To undermine Edmund, specifically."

Henry whipped his handkerchief from his pocket and wiped his sweat-beaded brow. "You're accusing Benjamin Swift?" His voice was low, almost a hiss. "Are you *mad*?"

"No, and trust me, we don't want to believe this, either. He is Ed's uncle, after all, and frankly his threats today were bad enough. To think he would risk killing us and especially Edmund just to destroy our lifestyle and reputation is horrific!" He stepped closer to Henry, keeping his voice low, but keen to impress the seriousness of the accusation. "This is why I have not told you. I am well aware what position this places you in, as well as us. Benjamin is powerful and influential. However, *everything* else is true. Can you not see it? The port is still running! No one has lost goods! Are you blind?"

"You are really saying that these attacks—these monstrous beings—were designed to lure you here?"

"Yes."

Henry passed his handkerchief over his brow again, and then his eyes hardened as he put it in his pocket. "Unfortunately, I must admit that you make sense, although I hate it. If Benjamin is involved, who is he working with?"

"Deepak Verma." Fitz relayed what Vikram had found out that day. "If it's not him, then it's someone in his family or household. Captain Townsend has sent men to monitor the house right now."

"You told him and not me?"

"He does not know our suspicions about Benjamin. As for the doctor, I don't know if he was always involved, or perhaps learned too much and was killed because of it. I do believe that someone in the Residency is guilty, however. Maybe Anthony or Roger? Benjamin could have bribed them with money or the promise of better positions. But we are running out of time to uncover this. We have said we are leaving tomorrow to goad them into action. After all, so far we have succeeded in killing two creatures, we are uninjured, and our reputation is only enhanced."

"The dock sustained a lot of damage!"

"It was all superficial damage. But it is being repaired now, and will be operational tomorrow. If Benjamin wants us out of business, then something major has to happen tonight." Despite his reservations, Fitz knew he had to tell Henry everything, so he outlined the plans they had set up for the party.

"Good grief. This is worse than I imagined. You involved *Alicia*?"

"Yes. She has been most helpful." He thought he'd better not mention that Henry's wife knew of their plotting, as well.

"There are a lot of *ifs* in your argument, but," Henry rubbed his jaw, clearly perplexed, "if someone in the Residency is involved, then I need to know. I will not have untrustworthy employees here, especially as my wife and children are put at risk. You should have trusted me with this information sooner!"

"Well, you know now, so what do you suggest?" Fitz could hear raised voices outside the bungalow, and knew they had only a few more moments alone.

Henry turned and barked out an order. "Everyone stays out until I say so!"

"Of course, I could use truth spells on the staff," Fitz suggested. "It would take time, but we could uncover them that way."

"No. There has to be a quicker option. I know my staff well, and if I were to suspect anyone here, it would be Anthony. He is very ambitious and has a devious streak that I do not like. Roger is weak-willed, despite his confident appearance. Unfortunately, it is all too easy to be paranoid about someone in these circumstances. What are you doing?" he asked, as Fitz started examining the room again.

"I told you that the doctor has most probably been cursed, and if that is true, the object will be here somewhere. I have to find it." The doctor had died in the middle of the room, his body crumpled next to a low table covered in books. *If he had picked something up...* "Henry, help me turn him, but be careful. Touch only his clothes."

Together they gently rolled the doctor onto his side so that he was propped against the table, and Fitz spotted a silver-handled lancet on the rug beneath him.

"That's the cursed object," he said, pointing at it. "I can feel the dark magic on it. The fact that it is used to draw blood adds an extra potency."

"His lancet was a gift from his father when he qualified," Henry told him. "He carried it with him always. I remember him saying earlier today that he'd misplaced it. He was very worried."

"Which is possibly why he left the party early. It must have been bothering him, and if it had sentimental value, then he would have wanted to find it quickly." Fitz used his handkerchief to pick it up and wrapped it carefully. "I will keep it safe until I can examine it later. Obviously, this was stolen and cursed today, or late yesterday."

"Anyone who knew him well would know about its significance to him, especially as his father died a few months ago." Henry sighed. "Poor man. It was the perfect object to use."

Fitz stood once they had laid him back down again. "So, he comes here, probably finds it positioned on the table in easy view of the door, rushes over to pick it up, and dies immediately. But we are no closer to finding out who stole it. Has anyone left the house for a significant time today?"

"Anthony has been at the port for much of the day, but I have been with Roger. We have had a lot of work to do."

"But Anthony could have gone anywhere, really. Something to think on. In the meantime, we should allow the servants in to prepare the body. I suggest we keep this quiet for now. Let the party progress as normal."

And then Fitz heard the tinkling of bells, as his alarm system activated. "I must go. There is an incident."

"What incident? Something else?"

"I suggest you head to the house."

"No, I'm coming with you."

"Then you better start running."

Fitz burst out of the bungalow, hearing Henry shout some hurried orders before following him. Fitz rounded the row of villas and outbuildings, raced onto the lawn, and accelerated his pace as the ringing bells exacerbated.

He could feel the ripple of unease spreading in the crowd, and heard the occasional shout as he flew by. Ed and Vik were nowhere in sight, and with increasing panic, he rounded the side of the house and saw the fountain and the fiery protection spell that surrounded it. But Ed and Vikram still weren't there. Instead, half a dozen English soldiers were gathered around it, weapons drawn, Captain Townsend in their midst.

Alicia had been in the shadows by the house, and she ran towards him. "I saw it end, Fitz," she said, voice tight with panic. "There was an enormous snake. Ed was swept into the fountain, and Vikram jumped in after him. It happened mere seconds ago."

"Alicia, you should not be—" Henry tried to complain.

She cut him off abruptly. "Henry, I am not a child."

"She's right," Townsend said, cutting through the rising tension. "I saw it, too. There was nothing we could do to stop it, and I wasn't sure about that circle of light."

Fitz commanded, "Stay back, all of you. The light is not dangerous for us—as long as you mean no harm."

"No," all three said forcefully, following him as Fitz stepped through his protective circle and peered into the fountain.

The water was almost clear, but a black stain was swiftly vanishing in the centre of the pool. His friends had been transported somewhere by magic, and he was pretty sure he knew where.

Fitz considered his options. "I have to get to the house next to Deepak Verma's. Or better still..."

He whirled around, ended the protection spell, and marched towards the house. The music was still playing, but it was obvious that more than a few guests were now aware there had been a disturbance. Murmurs rippled around him like an incoming tide, but he ignored them as he searched for Deepak Verma, with Alicia, Townsend, and Henry on his heels.

Akash intercepted them as they entered the house, and ushered them all into an empty room. "Verma Sahib has left already. He sends his apologies and thanks you, Cavendish Sahib, for an excellent evening. I could not make him stay. I'm sorry."

"And Benjamin Swift?" Fitz asked, hands clenched. His magic was rising, and he wanted to strike out.

"He is most agitated. He is looking for you, Sahib." Akash directed this at Henry.

Henry nodded, tight-lipped. "Thanks, Akash. I will speak to him. But Fitz, what will you do now?"

Fitz tried to keep a calm head, but he had no time to waste if he was to help his friends. "I have to get to the house Vik found earlier. It is behind Deepak Verma's home."

Townsend said, "I can guide you there. We have horses ready to go. My men are still there, and as yet, all is still quiet."

"I have a feeling that will change presently. As for Benjamin—"

But Fitz couldn't complete his sentence, because the door flew open and Benjamin entered, saying, "Get out of my way!" to a servant who looked stricken with nerves. "There you are!" He pointed at Fitz. "What have you done now? I hear there was a disturbance at the fountain. A monstrous snake with one eye that *you* let in here!"

Fitz was about to rant and rage, but then hesitated. "What do you mean, that I let in?"

"I mean that you have overlooked an area of the garden to protect, you imbecile." His voice was deliberately loud, designed to attract attention, but Akash shut the door.

Fitz, however, was now icy with controlled anger and thinking very clearly. "How do you know what I did to protect this house? I haven't said anything to you, and I know Ed hasn't."

Benjamin stumbled over his words. "Well, it's obvious. Of course that's what you would do. It's your job. But you failed again. It was incomplete. You allowed something in. Some of the guests are absolutely terrified."

"No. I ask again, how do you know that I allowed something in? We told no one of our plan, and the only people who would know of a breach in our defences are those who would breach them."

"I do not like your tone."

"And I do not like how you have come to know my strategies. That you do suggests duplicitous behaviour. But I will deal with this later. You will not delay me from saving my friends by arguing with me now. I suggest, Henry, that you keep a close eye on Mr Swift until I return."

Fitz pushed past him with Townsend, knowing there was no time to waste.

Ed held his breath as soon he was swept into the cold, black water of the fountain with the enormous snake.

He floundered, desperate to reach the surface, but it had unfathomable depths, and it was as if an enormous whirlpool was sucking him down, down, down into the darkness. The snake's muscular body wrapped around him, cradling him like prey, and he quickly stopped kicking in a desperate attempt to save himself against another threat.

But the water ceased to be just water, and was instead something quite different. A churning void of something barely substantial. Like oil and water and air, all at once. It was quickly over, and the next thing he knew, he seemed to have been pulled through some topsy-turvy portal and was spat out onto a cold, marble floor. Drawing in a deep breath of air, he almost choked on the thick incense and scent of musk. Wiping the water from his eyes, he saw the room Vikram had described.

The snake was nowhere to be seen, but a wizened old man was seated on the other side of the pool, eyes open but unfocussed, as if he were seeing something very far away. He knew the face. It was the one they had seen using Fitz's spell earlier. The yantras drawn upon the walls glowed with a silvery light, connected by visible filaments, and they reached towards Ed like ghostly fingers. He had lost one dagger in the fall, but he withdrew the other from the sheath by his boot, and leaping to his feet, slashed at them.

A man laughed behind him, and Ed spun around.

Deepak Verma was seated on an elaborately carved chair, watching calmly. "Your knife is of no use here, Edmund." He was dressed in a midnight blue cloak that was covered in all manner of esoteric symbols embroidered in silver and gold thread, and an aura of power pulsed around him that he had hidden earlier.

Edmund was tempted to throw it at him, but kept it close just in case. "*You*! We knew you were involved."

"You merely suspected. Do not exaggerate."

Ed needed to buy time if he was to figure a way out of this. "What is this place?"

"My soul's delight. The place I can plunge into the world's darkest mysteries."

"And the man seated behind the pool?"

"A mystic who controls the one-eyed serpent."

"And what does that do?"

"I don't think this is the time to share all my secrets."

"I think this is exactly the time." Ed looked around again and saw that the surface of the water was beginning to ripple. "The water. It's a portal?"

"Let's talk about what we are going to do with you. I think that's far more interesting."

He stood and snapped his fingers, and the tendrils of light that had hovered over Ed's head now tangled around him, and although he slashed at them, there were far too many to deal with. A wave of despair washed over Ed as they lifted him into the air.

"Those filaments of power," Deepak explained, "can draw strength from anything—organic or not. They use blood, auras, magic...anything, in fact, that they can store and that I may use at a later time. Clever, aren't they?"

The tingling tendrils were like ice as they gripped Ed's limbs, and on his bare flesh he could see welts of blood start to rise. "What are they doing?"

"I told you. They will absorb you, little by little, until there is nothing left. You understand that I have nothing against you personally. This is just business."

Horror raced through Ed at the prospect of being eaten alive by the gigantic web. He kicked out and shook his limbs, but the tendrils only tightened their grip. "This is my uncle's doing."

"Yes. I'm afraid you have upset him greatly. I would not move against my family in such a manner, unless they had betrayed me. Mr Swift clearly has a lower threshold of anger than I. We have come to a satisfactory arrangement."

The wizened man's eyes were still vacant, but his entire body was tense, as if he were fighting something unseen, and as the pool rippled again, Ed wondered if Vikram was struggling to follow him.

"Please let me go! You can pretend I am dead, and I will run far from here. No one need know. You can still say you have completed your deal."

"I'm afraid not." Deepak smiled up at him, his eyes as dark as the inky pool. "The magical filaments will absorb your knowledge to add to mine. All your hunting of the supernatural will not go to waste."

The black water was churning even more now, and a coil of the snake broke the surface, as did a kicking human limb. *Vikram.* Ed didn't have too much freedom of movement, but he had enough. His dagger with the spelled blade was still in his hands, and although it might not help him, it could help his friend. He twisted his arm and wrist and flicked the knife at the old man. It struck his thigh with enough force to embed in his leg, and the man screamed with pain and lost his concentration.

Vikram's blade slashed out of the water and plunged into the snake, dragging deep along its body, and as the snake writhed, Vikram used its momentum to break free of the water and out of the pool.

Deepak rushed towards the old man, shouting "No!"

Ed felt the filaments that gripped him weaken slightly, and shouted, too. "Vik! You're under attack. Kill the old man!"

He wasn't sure of Deepak's relationship with the elderly mystic, but it was obvious that he was a source of great power. But just as Ed thought he was breaking free, the filaments dragged him upwards and pinned him against the ceiling.

Thirty-Three

Moonfell 2025

I t took a complicated set of spells to enter Swift Heritage Travel, but Horty was determined to do it, and after combining a selection of shadow spells, glamour, unlocking doors, frying cameras systems and alarms, spells to distract staff, and other numerous tools of subterfuge, they entered the travel office.

"Good grief, Horty," Birdie said, as they slipped inside and shut the door softly behind them. "I could never be a burglar."

"I think we'd be excellent, although honestly, what a kerfuffle." The shop doors contained smoked glass panels, just like the windows, so Horty darkened them completely with a spell, giving them absolute privacy.

Swift Heritage Travel had a large world map spread across the opposite wall in coffee tones with bronze lines marking borders, and gilt lettering showing the places where travellers could stay. It was like a scattering of constellations.

"We could have waited 'til tomorrow," Birdie pointed out.

"But they wouldn't have let us poke about and go in back rooms. Now we can do both." Horty followed the lines across the map, using a spell to give them a faint glow. "Ed and Fitz's travels. Look, there's an information sign."

"There's more than that," Birdie said from behind her. "It's like a little museum here."

Horty turned. On the wall next to the door was another series of large plaques that outlined Ed's travels across Europe and into India. There was no mention of Fitz or Vikram, but they did talk about his journals and observations, and his enquiring, scientific mind. Underneath them, against the wall, was a long, glass display cabinet.

"Fancy not mentioning Fitz," Horty said, disappointed. "They make it sound as if he travelled alone."

"Perhaps because it better suits their marketing. Have you seen these maps, Horty?" She pointed them out in the cabinet, next to old compasses and mapmaking equipment. "I wonder if they're genuine, when we have so much ourselves."

"He must have left some things at home. In fact, this place is part of the original house, too. If only walls could tell stories. Or rather, specific ones."

"Exactly," Birdie said, moving to the rear of the room, past the three large desks with computers that took up most of the floor space. "We'd be overwhelmed if you tried to pull memories without parameters."

Horty released the lock on the cabinet with a spell, opened it, and picked up an antique compass, hoping to feel residual magic. It was possible, if it was something he'd used with Fitz. However, the metal was cool to the touch and told her nothing at all.

She huffed with disappointment. "I don't think these are really his. They're just to set the scene."

"We're thinking about this all wrong," Birdie said, exiting the door at the rear of the room. "We're focussing on Ed, but according to their brochure, he died in an accident in India and never came home again. Years later, his nephew starts this hotel and travel business. Why then? Why not sooner?"

"Maybe no one wanted to. Plus, the family still lived here." She looked behind Birdie. "What was in there?"

"A very uninteresting staffroom. But that is Jeremy," she said, marching over to a large copy of an oil painting on the wall, "and Ed is next to him. His hair is redder than I imagined. Why is there no mention of Benjamin? He was a bigwig in the East India Company. Surely they'd splash his name all over this place."

Horty remembered what the receptionist had said. "There are books on the family upstairs. I think we're done in here, so we should look there instead."

Ten minutes later, after further subterfuge, they were in the lounge on the first floor, and Horty was very glad they didn't have to resort to sneaky behaviour there. It was an easy matter to find the small print editions of the *History of the Swift Family*, and most of it looked to be very dry indeed, but Horty was searching only for Edmund and Benjamin Swift.

"Here we are," she said, summoning Birdie's attention. "There's a section on Ed's travels, but again no mention of Fitz or Vikram at all!" She felt quite annoyed on their ancestor's behalf. "It's really very rude."

"Look for Benjamin," Birdie instructed, leaning over her shoulder.

Flicking to the next page, Horty found Benjamin's name, his list of achievements, and the date he died. "He died in 1803. That's interesting!" She continued to scan dates and names.

"Four years before the hotel opened. It might mean something."

"And," Horty said, with a note of triumph, "in 1805, Rupert Swift died, Ed's father. The eldest son, Ed's older brother Framlington—dear Goddess, what a name—inherited the estate, and it's his son, Jeremy, who started this business."

"It's almost," Birdie said, a gleam in her eye, "as if their deaths precipitated change."

They were on to something.

It didn't matter how hard Odette tried, she just couldn't shake off the strong sensory impressions that seeing the Rajgarh Residency had left on her.

Part of her wanted to make it happen again, while the other part wanted to go to bed and forget it ever happened at all. She was mentally all over the place, unable to move beyond that pivotal moment at the Residency. She was alone on the bench now after urging Merlin to join his sister at the moon gate. They were casting all sorts of revealing spells, and if they were having any sort of success, she couldn't tell. Monroe was in his wolf investigating, too, but she knew deep down they wouldn't conjure the vision again. She should go to bed, but the thought of lying there alone with this playing on her mind was horrible.

Vaguely aware of headlights cutting along the drive, she wondered if Birdie and Horty had decided to come home, but then she saw Arlo walk across the lawn with that long, loping stride that she would recognise anywhere, and after speaking briefly to Morgana, he crossed to Odette's side.

His expression was almost invisible in the dark, but her heart eased as he sat beside her, careful not to touch her. "I came as quickly as I could. Are you all right?" He looked down at her, his pupils ringed with a golden glow that meant worry, anger, or passion.

For a moment, she couldn't speak. *Had he heard her thoughts somehow, earlier? Her wish that it was Arlo rather than Merlin who comforted her? No. That was madness.* When she did find her voice, all she could say was, "What are you doing here?"

"Monroe called me. He told me what happened." His thumb stroked her cheek, brushing away the dampness left from her tears. "Bloody hell, Odette. He scared me. Are you all right?" he repeated.

She wanted to say yes, but found she couldn't, and cried again. "No. I feel terrible. Like there's a weight on my heart. A sense of doom. I can't shake it."

He pulled her to him, his strong, familiar arms wrapping tightly around her, and she wrapped her own arms around his waist and buried her face against his shoulder and sobbed. "I don't know what's wrong."

"Yes, you do," he said softly. "You have connected with Fitz and Meli, and Beltane is bringing it all a little closer. That's twice today that you've stepped into India. No wonder you're feeling it."

"But I can normally step back and gain perspective."

"And you will again. It's just a little raw right now. In fact, you've stepped inside the painting you've been making, too. I don't cast spells, Odette, but I feel magic, and normally yours is bright and cheerful, like birdsong at dawn. Unfortunately, right now, it's tangled and muddy. You need to sleep. It's all a bit too real right now."

"I can't bear the thought of it going round and round in my head, in my room, alone. I've even considered sleeping on the sofa, but that sounds worse." She could sleep here, though, within the curve of his arm, her head on his chest. The thought was delicious. She could smell his wolf, and also the peppery, musky scent that was all Arlo. She thought she'd broken her addiction to him, but she clearly hadn't, and she knew that now.

"I'll stay with you."

"You don't want to do that. Just because Monroe—"

"I *do*. I want you to be safe, and no one wants you to be alone. Merlin can't. It wouldn't be right, and he wants to check on his daughters, but Morgana has also offered, if you prefer."

"No, I want her to be with Monroe." Odette watched her cousin talking animatedly to Monroe, and didn't want to deprive her of his company for even a second.

"Then that leaves me. I'll sleep in my wolf in your room. How does that sound?"

"It's an imposition."

"Nothing you ask me is an imposition. I'm here now, aren't I?"

His voice was a deep rumble against her ear, and already her mood was easing. She was too tired to work out if that meant anything, and she was scared to look at his expression. "That would be great, as long as you don't mind."

"Never." He stood, keeping her close to his side. "Time to go before you collapse."

"Is this just Beltane?" Morgana asked Merlin and Monroe, as they watched Arlo and Odette leave.

"It's many things," Merlin said, inspecting the gate again. "Beltane, the magical slides, the painting...all of it. It's like I said earlier. The weight of betrayal has left a mark. Whatever Benjamin did to Ed and

Fitz, and Vikram too, I guess, has scarred them. Until we find out what happened, I don't think this will stop, either." He gave a rueful smile. "History is knocking and wants to be heard. How are your energy levels, Moonbeam?"

She scowled at him. "Funny! You'll start Monroe off on that now."

Monroe laughed. "Moonbeam? You must tell me all about that. For now, though, I think it's time for bed. Are you going to find anything else out here?"

"No, I'm sure of that," Morgana said, and Merlin nodded in agreement. "I think it's time we finally read those letters."

"Now?" Merlin asked, amused. "I'm beyond shattered."

"I can't sleep until I've read some more. You go to bed, though. We'll tell you what we learn in the morning."

"And I," Monroe said, pulling his jeans on, "am wide wake and ready to listen, so let's do this."

Morgana was agitated by the time they returned to her room, and certainly wasn't in the calm, considered frame of mind she wanted to be in, but she was desperate to know more. Rather than changing into her night clothes, she slipped her shoes off and sat in the chair by the fire, igniting the logs she had set ready, and Monroe sat opposite her.

"Here," he said, thrusting a glass of brandy at her. "Fortify yourself."

"Thank you." She took a large gulp and placed it on the table, eager to read the next letter. "Shall I read it out loud?"

"Yes, please. I'm invested after all this."

"My dearest Meli, the last few hours have been the worst of my entire life. There has been a terrible fight, and I'm afraid everything has changed. Brace yourself, for what I have to tell you is not good..."

Thirty-Four

Rajgarh 1792

Rolling on the floor, bruised and battered from his battle with the snake, Vik knew he had to act quickly.

"Behind you!" Ed yelled from above. "Kill the old man!"

Vik rolled over, just quick enough to avoid the slashing stroke of magic from Deepak Verma who raced to the old man's side. Deepak threw his hand out again, and Vikram felt the strike of power as it propelled him across the floor. The light filaments that had trapped Ed now rushed towards him, but his sword was spelled with much stronger magic than Ed's. He slashed at them and they skittered away, and withdrawing another blade, he threw it at the old man before Deepak could block him. It embedded deep into his chest, and Deepak howled with a mixture of grief and fury.

A crack of thunder resounded, the room shook, and water bubbled from the black pool.

Desperate to free Ed, Vik slashed at the filaments, but they had withdrawn higher, and the yantras they connected to were hard to reach. Deepak had retreated to the far side of the room, placing himself between two marble columns, hands planted on either side against sigils that appeared to be feeding him power. Light flooded into the man, and the monstrous statues that had been so still moments before erupted into life.

Just as Vik was preparing himself for battle, the door to the room burst open, and Fitz rushed in, followed by Townsend and half a dozen guards. Gunfire erupted, and Fitz blasted a spell at Deepak. The fight was on.

The next few minutes were a horrifying mixture of gunfire, sword fighting, and spells, but Vikram knew how to undermine Deepak now. While he fought Fitz, Vik swiftly killed the old man, who was still clinging to life, and threw him into the black water. It swallowed him with barely a ripple, and then he focussed on destroying as many sigils and yantras as he could reach, while the soldiers fired at the creatures.

All of them were connected. A whole mess of power and magic, but with the mystic gone, the creatures were losing their potency. As he struck another sigil, the silvery tendrils that gripped Ed receded even more, and before Vikram could intervene, Ed landed heavily on the floor with his leg twisted beneath him, horribly still.

Fitz had never fought with such blistering intensity, especially against a man who had so successfully disguised his own power earlier. But seeing Ed crash to the ground incentivised him even more.

Whatever Vik and Ed had done before he arrived had already made a difference. The old man's death had struck Deepak like a punch to the gut, and Fitz launched spell after spell at him, varying balls of power and fire with more subtle spells. He tangled Deepak's feet so that he fell, used ice to freeze his skin, and slashing spells that cut deeply across his chest and limbs. But Deepak had deep resources of power, and he blocked attacks and cast counter-spells, forcing Fitz to dodge and weave and block too, performing a macabre dance across the room. Deepak tried to force Fitz into the raging creatures that fought the soldiers, tore up the room, and crashed into the marble pillars, causing the ceiling to crack. Dust billowed as plaster fell, and gunshots thundered around them. But Fitz resisted, moving farther into the recesses of the room, even as Deepak drew on the silvery web around them.

While Vikram protected Ed, Townsend and the soldiers alternated shooting at the creatures and the sigils, and with every bullet that found its mark, Deepak weakened even more. The flood of light and power pouring into him slowed to a trickle, and stumbling to his knees, he appealed to Fitz.

"Let's call a truce." Deepak held his arms up, hands extended outwards in surrender.

Blood stained his clothes and dripped into his eye from a cut on his forehead, and Fitz feared he looked no better. Every part of him ached from the blows and spells that had struck him. But Deepak had a feverish gleam to his eye that suggested he wasn't done yet.

"It's too late for a truce. You tried to kill us." He called over his shoulder as the room quietened, not taking his eyes off Deepak. "Vik, how is Ed?"

"Not good. He landed badly."

"But he lives?"

"Yes." But Vik's voice caught in his throat, and Fitz shifted to look at him, fearing the worst. Deepak lunged at him, and gunfire erupted again as Vik yelled, "The snake is back, Fitz. Keep clear!"

Deepak struck quickly, pushing Fitz to the floor so he was unable to keep track of the fight behind them. He landed on top of him and wrapped his hands around Fitz's throat, eyes wild with the need for revenge, knees trapping Fitz's arms close to his sides. Fitz struggled to break his hold, but finally tipped Deepak over so that he lost his grip.

Fitz drew in a ragged lungful of air as they wrestled back and forth, no longer using magic, both desperate to kill the other with brute force. The handkerchief fell from Fitz's pocket in the fight and landed on the floor, the cursed lancet tumbling out of it, and Fitz seized his chance before Deepak spotted it. He gripped Deepak's head and slammed it onto the lancet, and then sprang backwards. Deepak started convulsing, face turning a horrible purple as his fingers scrabbled at his own throat. The curse was effective, and within seconds, Deepak was dead.

Fitz was aware the room had fallen silent again, and looking to the far side, saw Vik, Townsend, and a couple of soldiers sheathing swords, the snake's dead body at their feet. The rest of the place was a broken, chaotic mess of destroyed furnishings, bloodshed, dead creatures, and injured men. The room reeked of curses and blood.

And Ed lay unmoving on the ground.

Thirty-Five

Moonfell 2025 and Rajgarh 1792

The Beltane sun was bright and promised a beautiful day when Birdie arrived at Moonfell with Horty.

They had taken full advantage of the large breakfast laid out by the Swift House Heritage Hotel, keen to get their ducks in a row before they headed back to Moonfell. Plus, it gave them a chance to question the staff in the travel company. Consequently, Moonfell bustled with activity as the taxi dropped them off on the broad sweep of drive by the front door.

Blankets were piled by the Full Moon Gate as if ready for a picnic, firewood had been stacked, ready for that night's bonfire, and two wolves were in the garden—not just one. *Interesting. Something has happened here.* Birdie could feel the shift in the magical energy of the grounds.

"Arlo's here," Birdie said, smiling mischievously at Horty. "What does that mean?"

"Beltane passion?"

"More than that, I think. Time for a change of clothes, and then I think a cuppa and a coven meeting. And by the way, let's not tell them of Ed's death yet. The letters might give us more context."

The house was filled with hawthorn blossoms and fresh flowers in a variety of colourful vases, and as they progressed to their rooms, they were accompanied by the tinkling of bells again. Knowing that it would take a while for everyone to assemble, Birdie magically rang an enormous bell to summon everyone to the large, Gothic kitchen, and by the time she and Horty arrived, Moonfell's residents and guests were waiting at the kitchen table. Morgana sat by Monroe and Ellen was next to him, looking thrilled to be near the huge shifter. Merlin was next to Marion, and Odette was beside Arlo, who Birdie always loved to see at Moonfell. He was part of the fabric now.

"Arlo!" Birdie beamed at him. "What an unexpected pleasure to see you."

"Morning, Birdie," he said easily, his expression giving nothing away. "Did you two have fun last night?"

"We did. Did you?" she asked, a glint in her eye.

"It was interesting."

"I had an experience," Odette said, cutting in quickly with a warning glare at Birdie. "It was very unnerving."

"Oh?" Birdie thumped down in her seat as Horty made tea. "What happened?"

As they all relayed the events at the moon gate, Merlin and Morgana butting in with Monroe and Arlo helping as needed, it became clear that she and Horty had missed something significant.

"This house," Birdie said, drumming her fingers on the table, "has a way of making its intentions known a little too forcefully sometimes."

Ellen pouted. "Which means what?"

"It needs us to uncover this Machiavellian tale. Do not underestimate this place, Ellen. Are you all right now, Odette?"

"Yes, thank you. A good sleep has helped. I'm still sad, though. Something terrible happened." She sat very near Arlo, not touching him, but close enough. *What has happened there?*

"Your aura," Horty said loudly, "is telling me that you are out of whack, my dear. Beltane should recharge you. A little fire magic is exactly what we need. A cleansing of energies and a mental reset."

"Exactly," Birdie agreed. "When we have dealt with this India conundrum, we shall throw ourselves into Beltane preparations, although I am pleased to see you've already done so much. Fortunately, Horty and I had our own little adventure last night, and we have uncovered something interesting." She outlined their investigations and impressions, and then said, "We discovered that Swift House became a hotel in 1807. Benjamin Swift died in 1803. Rupert Swift was Ed's father, Ben's younger brother. He died in 1805."

"How did you find out all this?" Merlin asked.

"Courtesy of this book," Horty said, throwing the slender volume on the table with a flourish. "We stole it."

Merlin sighed and looked at his daughters. "Not to be repeated. You two," he said, glaring at Horty and Birdie, "are terrible role models."

"We'll take it back eventually," Birdie said, unconcerned. "It's a temporary loan. Anyway, we thought the dates were interesting. Jeremy is Ed's nephew—his older brother's eldest child."

"Framlington," Horty said, placing the teapot down with a thump. "What a bloody name."

"It seems," Birdie continued, "that Framlington preferred country living, so Jeremy started the hotel."

Monroe shrugged. "It appears straightforward enough. With Ben and Rupert out of the way, the younger family members could do what they wanted."

"But why not mention Benjamin?" Birdie asked. "His name is kept out of the hotel's history, which is clearly meant to honour Ed and his legacy. Why? After all of Ben's threats and him saying Ed ruined the family name, what changed? I'm hoping, Morgana," she said turning to her, "that you have read more of the letters. Did you have time last night?"

"We made time to read one, and I've brought another with me now. But," Morgana slid a couple of letters on to the table, "there is a hidden message in them."

"How do you know?" Odette asked, wide-eyed.

"I can feel the magic. Plus, the wording is odd. I thought I would save it so we could uncover it together."

"But what does the letter say, Auntie Morgana?" Marion asked, brushing toast crumbs off her chin.

"Shall I read it aloud?"

"Yes, please." Birdie said, gripping her mug of tea and hoping it would fortify her for what was to come. The tension in the room deepened as everyone settled in to listen. Even Ellen had stopped fidgeting with her hair.

"Wait!" Horty said. "Not here."

"Herne's Horns, Horty," Birdie huffed, enjoying using Harlan's unusual cursing. "What now?"

"I want to hear it in the Residency garden." She paused for a moment, looking around the table. "What? Don't you? Either there, or the grounds of the lovely Indian house. It seems appropriate."

Merlin shuffled uneasily in his seat, looking at Odette. "Isn't that rather risky, considering it's now Beltane, and what happened last night?"

"Agreed," Arlo said, protectively moving closer to Odette.

But Odette smiled at Horty. "No, Horty is quite right. We must listen in Rajgarh. We won't go there, I know that now after last night. The slides are beautiful, magical illusions for Meli, and last night the moon gate gave me a little more. I can deal with this. I promise. Let's sit under the banyan tree by the south moon gate. If I'm there with everyone, it will be fine. And it's too lovely out there to just stay in here."

Horty leapt to her feet with startling speed, grabbed the Lumina Lantern, and lightly kissed the top of Odette's head. "Thank you."

Horty decided she had never loved anything more than these slides—except for her husband and children, of course.

Once the image hit the gate, it became even bigger than it had the previous day, ballooning until it was gloriously large on the front lawn. The banyan tree spread its branches above thick grass that was quite different to an English lawn, and when they all stepped within the illusion, the heat hit them as if they had just entered a tropical glasshouse. The two young girls had grabbed the blankets and arranged them on the grass for the group to sit on, along with a pile of cushions. The monkeys raced across the lawn and leapt into the branches above them, the peacocks strutted, and for a moment, they were in Rajgarh and Horty could swear she saw the Residency in a sort of heat haze. *Betwixt,* she thought with a frisson of excitement.

But now they would hear of Ed's death, so she steeled herself, glad they hadn't told the others what they'd learned.

"*My dearest Meli,*" Morgana began. "*The last few hours have been the worst of my entire life. There has been a terrible fight, and I'm afraid everything has changed. Brace yourself, for what I have to tell you is not good.*

"*Last night we set out to uncover the conspiracy that is behind the attack of the monstrous creatures on Rajgarh's port. As I mentioned, we feared we had been sent into a trap, and that Benjamin was behind it all. Unfortunately, we were right, although I'll say right now that there is nothing we can do to prove that it was him. He is far too powerful, and even Henry Cavendish, the Resident, fears he cannot move against him.*

"*Anyway, to the events of the evening. The Residency threw a party, and everyone was invited, including our chief suspects. Alicia has become invaluable, as has Akash, the khidmatgar. Even Captain Townsend proved his worth and trustworthiness. But let me start with what Vikram discovered, at much risk to his own safety.*"

Morgana read the letter in her clear voice, describing the room that Vikram stumbled upon, the spells and traps they had set for the party, the doctor's death, Ed and Vikram's fight at the fountain, Fitz's pursuit to help them at the house, and the final battle with Deepak Verma. Horty was transfixed, seeing it all in her mind's eye, and the vision of the Residency, so hazy to start with, grew more visible with every word Morgana read, and every rustle of the pages turned.

"*My hands are shaking as I write this, so you must forgive my handwriting, Meli. Vikram and the soldiers slayed the terrible snake and the creatures that manifested, and I defeated Deepak Verma who in the end died at the hands of his own curse. But I couldn't save Ed. He died on the floor in that accursed room, and we are burying him later today, along with the doctor. He will never leave India, and he will never see his family again. Our brotherhood is over.*

"I have decided to stay on in Rajgarh to recover, as has Vikram, who will continue to stay with Harishchandra Sharma. We will remain here for the summer, as it is too hot to travel now, and to be honest, I haven't got the heart for it. I'd like to be where my good friend is buried for a few months. I will return to Moonfell in September and bring Ed's journals and belongings with me. I'm sure my grief sits heavily in these lines. Forgive me for breaking the news to you this way. I will write more in the coming days, but I must now write to his family and tell them the terrible news, too. Forgive me, and I hope that you are well. Yours always, Fitz."

Silence had fallen at the news of Ed's death that at least Horty and Birdie had been partly prepared for, but it was still terrible hearing that it wasn't an accident, but cold-blooded murder.

Horty broke the silence first, asking, "What makes you think there is a spell?"

"His handwriting," Birdie said, sounding very sure as she stared at Morgana.

"Yes. His handwriting is slightly different, an underlying unsteadiness to it as if written quickly, and the words about his grief being heavy in his lines. But as I said, there is magic in this letter, too. Only faint, but enough for me to tell, and therefore Meli would have detected it, too. I think he's hiding something, and I think it will be a simple enough spell to uncover it. For witches, at least," she said as she spread the pages across the blanket and cast her spell. "Sunlight, sun bright, words that are hidden in full sight, unfurl your lies and reveal to me, the truth concealed within these leaves."

The words lifted off the pages and floated in the air, swirling like blossoms on the breeze, but rather than settling on the page again, a voice spoke instead. Clipped and cultured and very English. *Fitz.*

> *"Forgive my subterfuge, but I dearly hope that you can hear this. I will now relay the truth of it all. But I cannot risk the wrong eyes seeing this, or all our planning will be lost."*

Rajgarh 1792

Fitz scrambled to his friend's side. His leg was twisted beneath him, and his head was bleeding where he had struck the column's base, but he was breathing shallowly. Fitz's thoughts were scattered after the fight, but he tried to summon his energy and focus, passing his hand over his friend's head injury to find out how bad it was.

Vikram dropped to his knees next to him. "Will he live?"

"It's a nasty head wound, and as you know, I am not a skilled healer." He considered his options. "If I can get him to the house, I have potions and balms that can help."

"If his leg is broken, I can help set that," Vikram added, assisting Fitz to move Ed into a more comfortable position. "But these welts on his skin are from those things!" He pointed at the damaged sigils and the tiny tendrils of light on the ceiling. "The source of Deepak's power."

"They have drained Ed's energy, but he will recover. He just needs time."

"And that," Townsend said, interrupting them, "you don't have. You need a strategy."

Henry entered with a couple of soldiers, and leaving them to guard the door, hurried to their side. "I came as quickly as I could. Benjamin is in a foul mood, and was desperate to know where you had gone, so I did my best to keep him out of your way. I managed to get Roger and Anthony to distract him while I came here, but I wasn't sure whether we could trust Anthony as you know. I certainly think you are right about Swift."

Fitz struggled to his feet so he could face them both. "You believe me that he's involved?"

"I'm afraid I do," Henry said. "This puts us in a difficult position. Have you proof?"

Vik shook his head. "Deepak confessed his involvement, but he is now dead. I have no proof otherwise."

"Nor I," Fitz said, looking around the room, as if evidence of Benjamin's involvement would be obvious. "But what can he do now? We have survived his attack, and Ed will get stronger with rest and treatment."

Townsend sighed. "It's not that easy. I know men like Benjamin. They are used to having their own way, and he will not stop."

"I don't understand." Fitz thought the fight must have addled his thinking.

Henry nodded in agreement. "Townsend is right. Benjamin wants his nephew dead. You know that. If his threats to disinherit him don't stop your work, he won't stop trying. He might well want to kill all of you next. From his conversation earlier, it is certainly clear to me that he knew some of your plans."

"Which could only have come from Deepak and his dead mystic," Vik said. "It is as we suspected. That pool allowed them to scry, and must be connected somehow to the unusual rifts at the port. But Ed will not care about being disinherited. He has said as much already."

"Plus, I doubt his mother would allow him to be disowned," Fitz added.

"She may not," Townsend added darkly, "have any say in the matter."

"But if Ed stays in India, he will always be at risk," Henry reiterated. "You all will be, if you stay together. Benjamin will try again, and he may not be so subtle next time."

"Then what are we supposed to do?" Fitz could see the life they loved vanishing, and all because of Benjamin. "Ed is injured and needs time to recover, but what then?"

"I have an idea," Henry said, lowering his voice, "but you might not like it. In fact, I know you won't. Ed is already badly injured, yes?"

"Yes, look at him!" Vik said, voice filled with anger and despair.

"Then pretend he has died."

Fitz thought Henry had gone mad. "But then what happens?"

"I have power, Fitz, although I might not wield it as forcefully as some. I also want to impress upon you that you *do* have friends here. I do not like what Benjamin has done, but neither can I move against him. But I can help smuggle Ed out of India. Give him a false name. Akash is loyal to a fault and admires what you have accomplished here. He has many contacts who will help."

Fitz exchanged a puzzled glance with Vik, who looked as shocked as he felt. "But you would put yourself at risk."

"I really wouldn't." Henry smiled. "I am above suspicion. I have saved the port with your help. Whilst Ed is believed to be dead, Benjamin has no need to do anything else. His family name is safe. Let us capitalise on that. You have magic, I can supply papers, and you can adjust his appearance—I hope?"

Fitz nodded. "A glamour spell. It will hold for a while, especially if I am with him."

"And I'm sure that Harish will allow him to stay at his house while he recovers," Vik added. "I will be there, too. I have resolved to stay and help him in all ways. Plus, Harish has resources, as we know. I hate the idea, but it will work."

Henry nodded. "Good. Fitz, you can stay at the Residency over the summer. It will be natural to visit Vikram and recover from the fight. You can have the doctor's villa, or another, in fact. I think you need time to plan what you do next." Henry patted his shoulder. "You think this life is over, but it isn't. It will just be different."

"But Ed's family..." Fitz stuttered, thinking of the implications. "They must believe he is dead, too. I cannot make a decision like that for him."

"We must, and he will understand. Plus, he could stay at Moonfell when he returns to England," Vik suggested. "We will find a way to make it work."

"Then we must act now," Townsend said, voice quickening with urgency as more horses were heard outside. "I have seen your magic, and you have more skill than I knew was possible. I confess I think it is ungodly, but clearly you do God's work. Cast a spell or whatever you call it to make him appear dead. He will have died in the fight. The soldiers will attest to it. They are too absorbed with their own fights and injuries to see what we are conspiring about now."

"And then," Henry added, "when the dust settles, we will find the truth of all of it. I promise."

As Benjamin's booming voice announced his arrival, Fitz looked at Ed's stricken body at his feet, and knew he had no choice.

Moonfell 2025

"And so," Morgana said, as she finished scanning the other letter she had brought with her, heart pounding with excitement, "he continues the subterfuge in this letter, too. Fitz talks about what he gets up to in Rajgarh—visiting Vikram, their unmasking of the co-conspirator, and his summer with Alicia, but I think there is also a hidden message in this one."

"Don't rush it," Odette said, leaning over to gently push the letter down. "Enjoy it later. I'm just happy to know that Ed doesn't die so young. Benjamin is still a bastard, though." She looked over at the moon gate that basked under the midday sun, and she seemed lighter, as if a weight had lifted off her shoulders. "I saw the night they decided on the lie. How terrible."

"But he survived," Arlo reminded her, "and came back here. Meli painted Fitz by the gate with Ed, and he looked happy enough. I think things worked out."

Horty slapped the blanket, eyes gleaming. "Odette, what date did Meli stop being High Priestess?"

"1805, I think."

"The year that Ed's father died! That is a coincidence. Too much of one."

"I agree," Merlin said. "Maybe when Ed's father died, Ed decided to inform his family that he was alive, tell them the truth about Benjamin, and travelled properly again under his own name with Meli and Fitz?

You can't be High Priestess of Moonfell *and* travel extensively. And of course, it means that Fitz's older brother must have died if Meli became High Priestess. We still have so much to learn, but it will be in the library." He winked at his daughters. "I think we can find time to help uncover it all while we're here. Getting involved in our family history will be fun."

"Especially," Morgana said, smiling at Horty and wiggling her fingers, "when Horty uses her spells to find books."

Monroe nudged Morgana. "There's a lot more to find out in those letters. How many more are there?"

"Quite a few, actually, which suggests he continued to travel." She squeezed his hand, her emotions at war. "It's exciting, but you're right, Odette. I need to read these properly, not in a rush, but I really want to know what happened during that summer in Rajgarh *today*. If I could squeeze out just another hour here..." She looked at Birdie, hoping she'd agree.

Birdie checked her watch and smiled. "I think there's time for all of us to listen. You've already done a lot of Beltane preparation, and," she looked around with satisfaction, "it will be lovely to linger here a little longer. In fact, we should leave this little piece of Rajgarh here all day. I want to come in and out of it as we prepare for Beltane. Perhaps, when we know everything, we should contact Ed's descendants. I think they would like to know what we have found."

"I agree," Horty said, her expression dreamy. "Moonfell should be full of Fitz and Ed and Vik today. The house has been nudging us here for days, so let's do it!"

"Over the coming weeks I'll continue to paint," Odette added. "The letters will help inform me."

"We can finally put the India room in context," Morgana said, bubbling with excitement.

Arlo stretched out on his back, looking up into the branches of the trees where a monkey hung upside down. "Mentally, I'm already in India, so go for it, Morgana."

Morgana smoothed the letter out on her lap. "It's dated August 1792. Let's hear the real version," she said, casting the spell again, and Fitz's voice swelled around them as if he sat on the blankets with them.

"Dear Meli, despite all of our woes, it has been a wonderful summer in Rajgarh so far. I trust you are now reading—or should I say, hearing—the true version of events, rather than the lies I am forced to commit to paper in case my letters are intercepted. I designed it so that a Moonfell witch could unlock it easily. A rather clever spell, I think you'll agree.

"First let us speak of Ed. Despite his terrible injuries, he has made a good recovery and has forgiven Vik and I for the rather large decision made on his behalf. We were right to do so. Benjamin, despite our hope that he would leave for Calcutta quickly, stayed in Rajgarh for several weeks after Ed's 'death,' an unwelcome blight on everything. Only Alicia, Elizabeth, Captain Townsend—who despite all my previous complaints has been most supportive—and Henry, know of the deception we have promulgated.

"*Poor Henry was obliged to invite Benjamin to the Residency for dinners and parties, where he watched me suspiciously the whole time, questioning me as to my plans, which I have deliberately kept very vague. Vikram and I suspected he had spies that followed us around Rajgarh, and Vikram, always clever in such matters, spotted one of them. I used spells to unveil them. He still engages two young English Company men to follow us, even though he has now left, and it makes me wonder if he suspects our secret. Either that, or he wants to make sure we are not stirring up any more occult activity in Rajgarh.*

"*However, we keep to ourselves here, enjoying the East India Company and the Indian communities' parties, and the summer activities are extensive. Ed is, of course, housebound, but seeing as Harish's house is large, it has been no great hardship; plus, for weeks he was unwell, anyway. He has occupied himself making some wonderful slides for you so that you can appreciate our adventures here. Now, however, we have made plans to return to England in September. Ed will travel under a new name. We still have to fine tune the details, but all will work out. I am looking forward to seeing the family and Moonfell once more.*

"*As for our future plans, they are still to be decided, because my dear Meli, I have news. My decidedly bach-*

elor days are over, as I have fallen in love with Alicia and was brave enough the other day to ask for her hand in marriage. Despite thinking I knew her feelings, I was still ridiculously worried, so you can imagine my relief when she said yes. We are to be married next week by the English chaplain who resides in Calcutta, but who has come to attend to the needs of Rajgarh after our exploits. Of course, the wedding will take place on the Residency grounds. By the way, the chaplain sees me as a soldier of God who successfully works against the devil, so I have no fear of censure from him!

"Alicia will travel to Moonfell with Ed and I, and I cannot be more thrilled that she will meet you, Meli. I know that you will get on well. Please tell everyone, and prepare us a suite of rooms. I think my old one will not suffice. Also, Ed will need one too, as Moonfell is to become his home now. My only regret is that my family will not be present at our wedding, but of course for us to travel together we must be wed quickly. As you can imagine, the Residency gardens are being transformed for the wedding as we speak.

"It is our intention to explore Europe together eventually, but we will winter in England first and decide if our occult adventures shall continue. Surprisingly, Alicia is hoping that they will. She has developed a keen fascination for all of it. As for our good friend, Vikram,

he will stay in Rajgarh for the time being. I hate to leave him, but he does not wish to travel to England. For now, our monster hunting days are over.

"By the way, Benjamin will not be at my wedding. I plan that Ed will attend in disguise!

"You must be wondering about the doctor's death, and his involvement in the duplicitous tale. It seems, after extensive questioning and investigations, that Monty was Benjamin's contact the entire time. Monty had come here from Patna, and after Henry talked to the Resident there, found that Monty and Ben had met in Patna years ago. It seems Monty had a secret gambling vice that not many knew about—except for Benjamin, and the Resident at Patna. An addiction that we discovered continued in Rajgarh. We believe—of course, we will never know for sure—that Ben exploited Monty's secret and Rajgarh connections and made him work with Deepak to create the web of magic and subterfuge at the port. I think, however, he was having second thoughts about his involvement, and that is why Deepak killed him. Or perhaps Deepak just wished to eliminate him to reduce the chance of his occult secrets escaping. There is no doubt that Deepak cursed that lancet. I recognise his magic now.

"It is hard to know for sure, of course, as Deepak is also dead. That was far more complicated to explain to the community, but as everyone in Rajgarh knew that the port was attacked by supernatural means, we have made Deepak out to be the hero. We have put forth the rumour that he found the base that the mystic was using and was killed trying to stop him. Alerted to the fight, we arrived too late to save him. The house that the occult room was in burned down two days later. How convenient!

"So, neither Anthony nor Roger were involved, and once more trade and the Company business flourishes at Rajgarh. I am living in Monty's bungalow in the Residency grounds and enjoy my privacy greatly.

"We have booked passage on an East Indiaman leaving in early September. If we are lucky, we will be in London for January, but if not, I will see you in spring. I will leave it here, dear sister, and post this quickly in the hope that it will arrive before we do. Take care, and I will see you at Moonfell. Your dearest Fitz."

Fitz's voice faded, leaving the listeners waking as if from a spell.

"I feel even more *Betwixt* now," Morgana said, languid in the Indian summer heat. "If only the moon gate would show us the wedding."

Monroe laughed. "The way it's going, we will see it."

"I love a wedding," Horty declared, "so I am very happy that dear Fitz found love! And at Beltane, too."

"And you," Arlo said, nudging Odette, "knew Alicia was important."

"I could feel it. See it, even, from the way they were together in my painting." Odette smiled at Morgana, her equilibrium seemingly restored after the events of the night before. She looked so comfortable with Arlo that Morgana knew Monroe had been right to suggest calling him. "I'm glad we found time to hear that. I can throw myself into Beltane now."

"We all can," Birdie said, stretching as if waking from a long sleep. "There's still much to learn, but the rest can unfold gently."

Her nieces, Morgana noted, looked a little overwhelmed, and she caught Merlin's attention. "I think some Beltane fun is in order. Let's put some music on while we prepare. And perhaps a little dress up?" She winked at Marion and Ellen. "Shall we visit the attic for clothes?"

He nodded as he tousled Marion's hair. "Excellent idea."

"What kind of clothes?" Ellen asked, perking up.

"Any kind you want. Something befitting a celebration."

And perhaps Morgana would find something new, too. Something made of Indian cotton with a bright print from the seventies, perhaps.

Birdie rose to her feet with a wince, as if her knees were aching again, but her eyes were full of fire. "Our party tonight will be wonderful. I can feel it. A celebration of past and present, which in Moonfell is exactly as it should be."

Epilogue

Moonfell 1805

"I think," Ed said, lowering the magnifying glass as he straightened up after examining the mechanism, "that if you try that spell again, we should find this is a much more effective compass now."

Fitz rubbed his beard that had a smattering of grey in it now. "Excellent. If we can really differentiate between the various types of shifters, it will revolutionise our hunts. Especially our latest one."

"We should send one to Vikram. Even if he hunts less now, he would love to have it."

Ed sighed with exasperation. "It has taken months to perfect! I can't just produce another one so quickly. Honestly, Fitz. You are so unrealistic sometimes."

"I know it will take time. I just mean when it's ready. Perhaps we could take it ourselves next year. It's been over seven years since we last went to India." Fitz leaned back against the workbench that was covered in Ed's tools. "Vik's children will be much bigger, and I would like to see him again. And ours will now be old enough to travel so far."

"According to you. Alicia might well have a different opinion."

Fitz huffed as if she were tiresome, but Ed knew he didn't mean it. He adored Alicia and their three young children, all under the age of seven. They had waited to start their family, as Alicia had wanted to travel instead. Now, they were all at Moonfell, which was Ed's home as well as Fitz's.

It had been thirteen years since their fateful stay at Rajgarh when Ed had ceased to be Edmund Swift, and had instead become Ambrose Manners, the affable man of science from Oxford who Fitz had met on the ship back to London in September 1792. The year he had lost his family, but had found a new one.

Fitz's family had been generous, and he would be forever grateful to them. He had been given his own suite of rooms at Moonfell, and the use of this large stone workshop in the garden that was perfect for his experiments and projects. Meli had insisted on it, saying he needed space to continue his work or else he would lose himself completely. Meli, who against all expectations, was now his wife, as well as the High Priestess of Moonfell.

Unlike Fitz and Alicia, though, they had not had children. Meli had never wanted them, and her magic enabled that to happen. Ed was indifferent. If she had wanted children, he would have been content, but he was secretly pleased she hadn't. Both were obsessed with their inventions, magic, Moonfell, and travel. Travel that revolved as it always had around the occult, their passion for new places, and their love of exploring. Their interests had taken them through England and Europe, and even back to India with Fitz and Alicia. And then Peregrine, Fitz's older brother, had died and Meli had become High Priestess. But the role chafed her, despite the fact that the house had chosen her, and she was already preparing Peri's oldest child for the role. He was approaching twenty-one, and was more than ready for it, and that left them with choices.

Fitz lifted his head and looked at the entrance that led to the garden in that uncanny, knowing way he had always had. "We have visitors."

There was a tapping at the door and Meli and Alicia entered, both in their casual Moonfell dresses of loose linen, their hair flowing down their backs. Meli's was full of chestnut hues and was glorious against her pale skin, and her dark eyes that saw so much settled on his. Alicia, her honey-coloured hair in sharp contrast to Meli's, had curls too, and they cascaded freely as she sought Fitz's side.

They had an air of gravity that immediately unsettled Ed, and he asked, "What's happened?"

"I have news, my love," Meli said, stretching to kiss his cheek with her soft lips. "There is no easy way to tell you this, but your mother sent word that your father died this morning at your Surrey estate. I'm so sorry."

Ed sagged into the closest chair, emotions whirling. "You know, despite everything, I thought perhaps that one day I should speak to him again, but now..."

Meli gripped his hands as she knelt in front of him. "I hoped so too, but he would have never welcomed it. Your mother would have told you immediately if she thought he'd changed his mind."

Fitz broke in. "I am so sorry, Ed. We'll leave you in peace."

"No. Stay. Both of you." He held his hand up to stop his closest friends from leaving. He needed their strength and wisdom now more than any other time.

Three years earlier, when Benjamin had died of Malaria in India, Ed had decided to contact his mother with Meli's help, and had revealed that he was still alive. They met at Moonfell, and she had been overjoyed, but also furious at his deception. She had been even angrier to find out that Benjamin had been responsible for Ed needing the subterfuge. But she also confirmed what Ed had feared was true. His father would rather he be dead. His creative science experiments and occult interests were an embarrassment, and his father would never want to hear criticism of his older brother, Benjamin.

And so, despite his wish to walk away from Ambrose Manners and reclaim his family name, he could not. Until now.

He stood up. "I need to see my mother."

"She asks that you wait for a few days," Meli said, standing with him and pulling a letter from her pocket. "She explains in here, but essentially, she will break the news of your new life to your family first. Your brothers and sister, your cousins. Everyone. Then you can visit them all."

His hands closed around the letter, his throat so thick with emotion that he could barely get the words out. "She'll tell the entire family?"

"*Everyone*. She wants to redress the grave wrongs that you have suffered. And she wants you to go to the funeral—if you wish to, that is. She has had enough of subterfuge and secrets."

Ed sat down again as his legs gave way beneath him. "I don't know if I want to go. Should I?" He looked over at his friends, hoping to see a clear answer.

Alicia, always so calm, just said, "Think on it. It may be a chance to lay old hurts to rest, but only you will know that. If you prefer, considering how he treated you—or the memory of you—we can have a memorial here instead."

"No." He shook his head vigorously. "He does not deserve Moonfell. I know that much." And in the space of seconds, he had decided. "I cannot go to his funeral, even for my mother, but I welcome the chance to be reunited with my family. But you know what else?" He looked at his wife and friends' expectant faces. "Edmund Swift is dead. I am Ambrose Manners now. It is as Ambrose that I found true happiness with my beautiful Meli," he kissed her fingers, "and had—and will have—many more adventures. I am a lucky man. Ed can be remembered for what he was. A monster hunter with his great friends, Fitz and Vikram."

"Are you sure?" Fitz asked, gripping the top of his arms and studying him. "It is soon to say such things."

"I have learned things from my wise witch friends," Ed said, smiling. "Always trust your gut."

"In that case," Meli said, "I have made my decision. This summer I will step back from being High Priestess of Moonfell. My nephew is able to take on the role very well."

"Are you sure?" Ed asked her, searching her expression for doubt or worry. "If we don't travel as extensively again in the future, I will be fine with that. Do not give up being High Priestess for me."

"You know how I feel about this. Moonfell chose me, but it also knows I need freedom. It's happy that Tobias will be High Priest, just like his father. He is old enough now. The wheel is turning, my love," she said, eyes burning with excitement, "and I am ready for it." She turned to her brother. "You feel Moonfell's approval, yes?"

Fitz nodded. "Yes. It feels settled. Hopeful."

"In that case, so am I," Ed said as he kissed his wife's cheek. Feeling lighter than he had done in years, he turned back to his workbench. "Now, where were we?"

"Is there a rush with this object?" Alicia asked as she wandered over to the bench. "You two have been locked in here for hours!"

Fitz looked guilty. "Have we not told you? We suspect there is a werewolf in London. Several of the king's deer have been attacked and killed in Richmond Park. We are planning our strategy, and this will help us."

Both women glared at him, and Alicia said, "I sincerely hope you were not planning to leave us out of this?"

"As if we would dare," Ed said, amused. "This is a family affair now. Step closer while I show you how this works. Tonight, we hunt."

Thank you for reading *Amber Moon: Secrets, Ink, and Firelight*. I love writing the Moonfell Witches, and I hope you have enjoyed reading it. There will be another book in this series out next year.

The next book I'm writing will be White Haven Witches Book 14, and it will be released in December 2025.

Newsletter

If you enjoyed this book and would like to read more of my stories, please subscribe to my newsletter at https://www.subscribepage.com /tjgreensnewsletter. You will get two free short stories, Excalibur Rises and Jack's Encounter, and will also receive free character sheets for all of the main White Haven witches.

By staying on my mailing list you'll receive free excerpts of my new books, as well as short stories, news of giveaways, and a chance to join my launch team. I'll also be sharing information about other books in this genre you might enjoy.

Ream

I have started my own subscription service called Happenstance Book Club. I know what you're thinking! What is Ream? It's a bit like Patreon, which you may be more familiar with, and it allows you to support me and read my books before anyone else.

There is a monthly fee for this, and a few different tiers, so you can choose what tier suits you. All tiers come with plenty of other bonuses, including merchandise, but the one thing common to all is that you can read my latest books while I'm writing them – so they're a rough draft. I will post a few chapters each week, and you can read them at your leisure, as well as comment in them. You can also choose to be a follower for free.

You can comment on my books, chat about spoilers, and be part of a community. I will also post polls, character art, share rituals and spells, share the background to the myths and legends in my books, and some of my earlier books are available to read for free.

Interested? Head to Happenstance Book Club.

https://reamstories.com/happenstancebookclub

Happenstance Book Shop

I also now have a fabulous online shop called Happenstance Books where you can buy eBooks, audiobooks, and paperbacks, many bundled up at great prices, as well as fabulous merchandise. I know that you'll love it! Check it out here: https://happenstancebookshop.com/

Substack

I now write over on Substack, and my page is called Where the Witches Gather. I'd love to see you there. Substack has a wonderful community of witchy writing and seasonal celebrations. You can find me here: https://substack.com/@wherethewitchesgather

YouTube

If you love audiobooks, you can listen for free on YouTube, as I have uploaded all of my audiobooks there. Please subscribe if you do. Thank you. https://www.youtube.com/@tjgreenauthor

Please read on for a list of my other books.

Author's Note

Thank you for reading *Amber Moon: Secrets, Ink, and Firelight,* book two in the Moonfell Witches series.

I've really enjoyed exploring more of Moonfell's past and seeing the witches' ancestors out of Moonfell and somewhere new. I love India and have read lots of stories set there, in addition to visiting it about ten years ago. We explored Rajasthan and absolutely loved it.

The history of the East India Company is fascinating. It started as a trading company in 1600, focussing on the spice trade and expanding through Asia, until it evolved into a powerful political and military force, particularly in India, where it began acquiring territory and administrative control through a combination of diplomacy, warfare, and strategic alliances with local rulers. It is a vast topic, but after the Indian Rebellion in 1857, India came under control of the British Crown, starting the period of colonial rule and what became known as the Raj. I am obviously condensing hundreds of years of history into this small paragraph. If you are interested in reading more, I'll be posting a blog on my site with some references, but a simple internet search will provide you with lots of information as well.

Delving into Moonfell's past characters is a lot of fun, and I can't wait to do it again. Of course, growing and developing the main, present-day characters is absorbing, too. They continue to show me new sides to themselves, as does Moonfell, so I am looking forward to writing many books in this series and exploring their relationship with the Storm Moon Shifters.

If you'd like to read a bit more background on the stories, please head to Where the Witches Gather on Substack. I have moved many of my blogs there from my website, www.tjgreenauthor.com.

Thanks again to Fiona Jayde Media who keeps producing such fabulous covers, and thanks to Kyla Stein at Missed Period Editing for sorting out my knotty—or perhaps naughty—sentences.

I must also thank my wonderful Happenstance Book Club members, who read an unedited version of this book before anyone else. I loved hearing their feedback as I was writing it. Please join one of the tiers if you want to read early versions of my work, as well as receive other goodies!

Thanks also to my beta readers—Terri and my mother. Their reassurance as they read each new book always soothes my nerves. Also, thank you to my launch team, who give valuable feedback on typos and are happy to review upon release. It's lovely to hear from them—you know who you are! I also love hearing from all of my readers, so I welcome you to get in touch.

I encourage you to follow my Facebook page, T J Green Author, Magic, Myths, and Mystery. I post there reasonably frequently. In addition, I have a Facebook group called TJ's Inner Circle. It's a fab little group where I run giveaways and post teasers, so come and join u s.

About the Author

I am a writer, a pagan, and a witch. I was born in England, in the Black Country, but moved to New Zealand in 2006. I lived near Wellington with my partner, Jase, and my cats, Sacha and Leia. However, in April 2022 we moved again! Yes, I like making my life complicated... I'm now living in the Algarve in Portugal, and loving the fabulous weather and people. When I'm not busy writing I read lots, indulge in gardening and shopping, and I love y oga.

Confession time! I'm a Star Trek geek—old and new—and love urban fantasy and detective shows. Secret passion—Columbo! My favourite Star Trek film is the *Wrath of Khan*, the original! Other top films—*Predator*, the original, and *Aliens*.

In a previous life I was a singer in a band, and used to do some acting with a theatre company. For more on me, check out a couple of my blog posts. I'm an old grunge queen, so you can also read about my love of that on my blog: https://tjgreenauthor.com/about-a-girl-and-what-chris-cornell-means-to-me/. For more random news, read: . To read about my journey as a witch, check out: https://tjgreenauthor.com/leaning-into-my-witch/.

Why magic and mystery?

I've always loved the weird, the wonderful, and the inexplicable. My favourite stories are those of magic and mystery, set on the edges of the known, particularly tales of folklore, faerie, and legend—all the narratives that try to explain our reality.

The King Arthur stories are fascinating because they sit between reality and myth. They encompass real life concerns, but also cross boundaries with the world of faerie—or the Other, as I call it. There are green knights, witches, wizards, and dragons, and that's what I find particularly fascinating. They are stories that have intrigued people for generations, and like many others, I have added my own interpretation.

I love witches and magic, hence my second series set in beautiful Cornwall. There are witches, missing grimoires, supernatural threats, and ghosts, and as the series progresses, even weirder stuff happens. The spin-off, White Haven Hunters, allows me to indulge my love of alchemy, as well as other myths and legends. Think Indiana Jones meets Supernatural!

Have a poke around in my blog and you'll find all sorts of posts about my series and my characters, and quite a few book reviews.

If you'd like to follow me on social media, you'll find me here:

f   facebook.com/tjgreenauthor/

P   pinterest.pt/tjgreenauthor/

♪   tiktok.com/@tjgreenauthor

▶   youtube.com/@tjgreenauthor

g   goodreads.com/author/show/15099365.T_J_Green

◉   instagram.com/tjgreenauthor/

BB   bookbub.com/authors/tj-green

|●   https://reamstories.com/happenstancebookclub

Other Books by T J Green

Rise of the King Series

A Young Adult series about a teen called Tom who is summoned to wake King Arthur. It's a fun adventure about King Arthur in the Otherworld!

Call of the King #1

The Silver Tower #2

The Cursed Sword #3

White Haven Witches

Witches, secrets, myth, and folklore, set on the Cornish coast!

Buried Magic #1

Magic Unbound #2

Magic Unleashed #3

All Hallows' Magic #4

Undying Magic #5

Crossroads Magic #6

Crown of Magic #7

Vengeful Magic #8

Chaos Magic #9
Stormcrossed Magic #10
Wyrd Magic #11
Midwinter Magic #12
Sacred Magic #13

White Haven Hunters

The fun-filled spin-off to the White Haven Witches series! Featuring Fey, Nephilim, and the hunt for the occult.

Spirit of the Fallen #1
Shadow's Edge #2
Dark Star #3
Hunter's Dawn #4
Midnight Fire #5
Immortal Dusk #6
Brotherhood of the Fallen #7

Storm Moon Shifters

Storm Moon Rising #1
Dark Heart #2
Wolfshot #3

Moonfell Witches

The First Yule (Novella)

Triple Moon: Honey Gold and Wild #1

Amber Moon: Secrets, Ink and Firelight #2